DIE LONELY, DIE HARD . . .

"Hello the cabin!" called Red. "Anybody here?"

Only silence greeted him. His Colt in his hand, he kicked the dead leaves away from the door and swung it inward. The cabin was larger than it appeared from the outside. Red could see an entrance—without a door—into another room. He made his way to the curtainless, doorless opening that led to the next room. Suddenly he halted, the macabre thing on the dirt floor drawing from him an involuntary gasp of surprise.

Lying on its back, arms outflung, lay the skeleton of a man. The bony fingers of the right hand still gripped a Colt, and just above the eyeless sockets of the skull, there was what could only be a bullet hole . . .

THE
WINCHESTER
RUN

Ralph Compton

St. Martin's Paperbacks

THE WINCHESTER RUN

Trail map design by L. A. Hensley.

ISBN: 0-312-96320-3

Printed in the United States of America

St. Martin's Paperbacks edition/September 1997

St. Martin's Paperbacks are published by St. Martin's Press, 175 Fifth Avenue, New York, NY 10010.

10 9 8 7 6 5 4 3 2 1

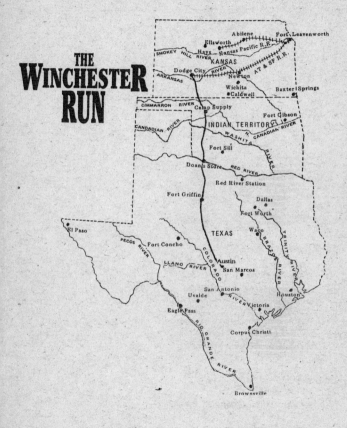

THE WINCHESTER RUN

AUTHOR'S FOREWORD

The Atchison, Topeka, & Santa Fe railroad reached Dodge City, Kansas, in 1872. While such progress helped to advance the westward movement, there was still a need for the big freight wagon which had long been essential to the commerce of the Plains.

The military outposts—forts—south of Dodge City were still dependent on the slow-but-sure wagons. Most prominent were the forts in north Texas—Fort Elliott, Fort Worth, and Fort Griffin, but there were others to the south, as well as in Indian Territory.

Until 1874, when Quanah Parker and the last of the Comanches surrendered, there was almost constant danger from Indian attack. But when the Indian menace eventually came to an end, the looting and killing did not. While the Civil War had ended in 1865, the conflict had spawned renegades who had learned to kill. These men—dregs from both the blue and the gray—gathered in the wilds of Indian Territory. (It wouldn't become the State of Oklahoma until 1907.)

While the Chisholm Trail had come into use in 1868, and Texas herds were driven to the railroad in Wichita, little was done to civilize Indian Territory insofar as the numerous outlaws were concerned. They still galloped into southern Kansas and northern Texas, and after killing and looting, returned to their sanctuary in Indian Territory.

The freight wagons, unlike those belonging to settlers on the Oregon Trail, relied on mules instead of oxen. While oxen could survive on grass, mules could not, requiring daily rations of grain. Caravans of wagons drawn by mules became known as "corn freight," and those rare ones depending on the slower oxen were referred to as "grass freight."

While the hazards of freighting south were great, there was no shortage of teamsters. There were cowboys who had driven herds north and had gone broke in cattle towns, and ex-buffalo hunters, skinners, and bone pickers who suddenly had nothing else to do. Until railroads spider-webbed the West with track, the big wagons rumbled on, creating a place for themselves and their hell-for-leather teamsters in the pages of American history.

PROLOGUE

Kansas City, Missouri. September 10, 1873.

"*N*othin' but a damn fool drinks whiskey while he's playin' poker," said Mac Tunstall in disgust.

He stood on the boardwalk outside the Star Saloon, with his three companions, Buck Prinz, Haze Sanderson, and Red McLean.

"Now you tell us," Red McLean said. "Why couldn't you of come to that conclusion before we was dead broke?"

"No use blamin' it on the whiskey," Haze Sanderson said. "We was cold sober when we decided to come here. If any of us had the sense God gave a goose, we'd of rode out of Wichita and went home when we was paid off at the end of the drive."

"Maybe we can find some kind of work," said Mac. "We got our bedrolls, so we can skip the hotels. All we need is money for grub."

"Yeah," Buck agreed. "Our horses can make it on grass, if we don't push 'em."

"Well, I'm damned if I'll swamp a saloon, even for grub," Haze said. "Let's look for something that's half-way respectable, for God's sake. We're Texans."

"Broke and hungry Texans," said Mac, "a hell of a long ways from Texas."

"I reckon we can all agree that we need work," Buck said. "There's bound to be some freight outfits in this town. Hell, we can hitch and unhitch teams, if nothin' else."

They rode through the industrial part of town, stopping at the various warehouses in which a freight line was located. Not until they reached the fifth one did their luck change. Plains Freighting, in fact, had a sign posted, seeking drivers. One of the requirements—and this was underlined—was that men must be armed.

"That's us," Mac said.

They crowded into the small office, each of them six feet or over, dressed in range clothes. Thonged down on each rider's hip was a .44–40 single-action Colt, purchased in Wichita, and all they had to show for four months' trail wages. A middle-aged woman sat behind a desk, and they quickly removed their sweat-stained hats.

"Ma'am," said Mac, "we're lookin' for work. Your sign outside—"

"You'll want to talk to Hiram Yeager," she replied. "Just a minute."

She walked down a hall and knocked on a door at the end of it. They heard a gruff voice answer the knock, and she disappeared inside. In seconds she returned, and with her was a nearly bald man in a town suit, wearing wire-rimmed spectacles.

"I'm Hiram Yeager," he said. "Come on back to my office."

The four of them followed him, their boots clunking on the wooden floor. When they had all entered the office, Yeager closed the door and took the chair behind his desk.

"Have a seat," he said, nodding to half a dozen chairs to the right of the desk.

"We'll stand, if you don't mind," said Buck McLean. "We're from Texas, and we're all partial to lookin' a man in the eye, when we talk business. You're wantin' drivers who can use guns. We got the new Winchesters and matchin' Colts."

"Texans," Yeager said. "You've come a long way looking for work."

"Oh, we had work as far as Wichita," said Red McLean. "We come up with a Texas herd, and we're . . . well, financially embarrassed. We're lookin' to earn grub money to get us back to Texas."

Yeager laughed at their frankness. "Perhaps I have something that will interest you," he said. "This particular assignment will take you all the way to Austin, Texas. Each of you will be paid a hundred dollars and your expenses, including food."

"Pardner," said Haze Sanderson, "it ain't often we drop our loops on such good luck."

"I hope you still feel that way after I've told you the rest of it," Yeager replied. "Are you familiar with the new 1873 Winchester, and the .44–40 single action U.S. Army Colt, chambered to take the same cartridges?"

"I reckon we are," said Haze. "They're the answer to a man's prayer in an Indian fight."

"Then you can appreciate the value of the weapons," Yeager said. "The U.S. Army's repeating-rifle trials have been completed, and the government has adopted the new 1873 Winchester, whose shells interchange with the .44–40 single-action U.S. Army Colt. We've been commissioned to freight six hundred of these Colts, six hundred Winchesters, and a hundred and twenty thousand rounds of ammunition to Austin, Texas. These weapons are for use by the military in the state of Texas. There will be six wagons, for which we will provide teamsters. It will become the duty of you men to protect these wagons. Do you all have a saddle mount?"

"Yes, sir," said Haze.

"These six wagons will be loaded at the ordnance depot at Fort Leavenworth," Yeager said. "These wagons will then be loaded on railroad flatcars and taken to Dodge City, Kansas. From there, it will be wagons all the way to Austin, Texas. I'm sure you men, being Texans, can appreciate the potential danger of such a journey."

"My God, yes," said Mac Tunstall. "If Quanah Parker and his Comanches managed to get their hands on all that firepower, they could run the U.S. Army plumb back across the Mississippi."

"That's just part of it," Red McLean added. "Don't forget all them owl hoots roostin' there in Indian Territory, looting wagons and killing the drivers."

"I'm glad you appreciate the potential danger," said Yeager. "Now how do you feel about taking on the assignment?"

"We've fought Indians and outlaws before," Mac Tunstall said, "besides ridin' all over hell after stampeded longhorns. If you're satisfied with us, I reckon you've hired yourself some Texans. Am I right, pards?"

"Right!" the three of them answered in a single voice.

"Good," said Yeager. "The train bearing the loaded wagons will leave here at six, on the morning of September fifteenth. My son-in-law, Watson Brandt, will be in charge of loading the wagons here, and unloading them in Dodge. Once the wagons take the trail to Austin, Watson will be wagon boss. You will take your orders from him. I'm going to pay each of you a twenty-five-dollar advance today. Watson will pay you the balance when the wagons reach Austin. For the rest of the time you're in Kansas City, you may stable your horses in our barn. I'll put you up in the Drover's House, and you may take your meals in the hotel restaurant."

The four friends departed Yeager's office in a high state of jubilation. Each of them had twenty-five dollars, the freight line would stable and feed their horses, while they had a signed letter from Yeager granting them free room and board while they remained in Kansas City.

"I reckon the big Boss up yonder is lookin' after broke and hungry Texans," Haze Sanderson observed.

But that was before they met their trail boss, Watson Brandt.

Kansas City, Missouri. September 15, 1873.

Mac, Buck, Haze, and Red reached the railroad yards at five o'clock, in time to have their horses loaded into a boxcar. The six loaded wagons were already there, and two were being taken aboard each of the three alotted flatcars. The railroad men seemed to know exactly what they were doing. The wheels of every wagon were chocked, and to prevent possible tipping over on curves, all four wheels of each wagon were chained to the side of the flatcars. The six bullwhackers Yeager had hired were there, and the Texans noticed all six men had a Winchester under his arm.

"Let's go say howdy to the bullwhackers," Mac Tunstall suggested.

The Texans were greeted with enthusiasm by the teamsters. There was Port Guthrie, Lafe Beard, Emmett Budd, Saul Estrella, Gourd Snively, and Smokey Foster.

"Good to have you gents on our side," said Smokey Foster. "From what I've seen of this Watson Brandt, I purely don't like the varmint."

There was a rumble of assent from the other teamsters, and the four Texans focused their attention on Brandt. He was squat, heavy-muscled, with a bristly black beard, and had busied himself offering unnecessary guidance and shouting commands at the railroad employees who were securing the wagons on the flatcars. The train consisted of the locomotive, a tender, a boxcar, a passenger car, the three flatcars, and a caboose.

"I don't like the way this train's bein' made up," Mac Tunstall said. "Whose idea is it to put the passenger car and caboose on the tag end of the train? Damn it, the passenger coach should be coupled behind the tender. Then two of us can watch the rails ahead, and the other two can keep their eyes on the backtrail, from the caboose."

"I suspect the varmint responsible for the makeup of

the train is Watson Brandt,'' said Port Guthrie. ''He seems to be havin' his way in everything else.''

''There's Hiram Yeager,'' Saul Estrella said. ''Why don't you talk to him?''

''I will,'' said Mac.

He sought out Yeager, who had just arrived, before he could reach Watson Brandt. Yeager listened while the Texan talked, nodding his head in understanding.

''Come on,'' Yeager said, when Mac had finished. ''Watson can have the position of the cars changed. I'm sure he hasn't considered the possibility of trouble between here and Dodge City.''

''Well, he should,'' said Mac. ''Outlaws who know about this can dynamite the track and stop the train.''

''This shouldn't be common knowledge,'' Yeager replied. ''I have instructed Watson to observe the utmost secrecy.''

But before they could reach Watson Brandt, a tall man in town clothes confronted them. He spoke to Yeager.

''I'm Kevin Watts, from the Kansas City *Liberty-Tribune.* We understand this is the first shipment of the 1873 Winchester recently adopted by the U.S. Army, and the new .44–40 single-action army Colts. Where are they going, and how many are being shipped?''

''I have nothing to say,'' Yeager replied angrily.

He went on, Mac right behind him, and when they reached Watson Brandt, Yeager did not bother introducing Mac Tunstall.

''Watson,'' Yeager said, ''I specifically *told* you not to breathe a word of this to the newspapers. Why are there reporters here, asking questions?''

''I don't know,'' said Brandt, shrugging his shoulders.

Brandt turned away, obviously dismissing Yeager, who refused to be dismissed.

''Watson!''

Irritated, Brandt again faced Yeager, who wasted no time.

''This is Mac Tunstall, one of the outriders,'' Yeager

said, "and he has a suggestion which I believe has merit. He believes the passenger coach should be coupled on behind the tender, instead of to the caboose."

"Oh?" said Brandt, seeming to notice Tunstall for the first time. "I suppose you have a reason."

"I do," Mac replied, his eyes meeting Brandt's. "We aim to post two men with Winchesters in the passenger coach to protect the front of the train, and two in the caboose, to protect the rear of the train. A mite difficult, with both the passenger coach and the caboose coupled together, at the tag end of the train."

"That will take time," said Brandt. "The train's already made up, and to change it now will throw it off schedule. This is a damn-fool, unnecessary change."

"Take the time," Yeager said. "The idea has merit, and I happen to agree with Mr. Tunstall. This is not a regular run, but a special. There's a two-hour gap between it and the eastbound, which should allow you plenty of time to reach the siding in Dodge. Now whatever it takes, get with it and couple that passenger car on behind the tender."

Brandt's face was crimson with anger, and before he turned away, he cast a look at Mac Tunstall which said he wasn't going to forget.

"Position your men as you see fit, Mr. Tunstall," said Yeager.

Yeager headed for the dispatcher's office, while Tunstall returned to his companions and the teamsters, all of whom had been watching with interest.

"We couldn't hear the words," Port Guthrie said, "but it looked mighty like the little coyote got a dressin'-down."

Mac laughed. "He did. The passenger car will be coupled behind the tender. Turned out that Mr. Yeager agrees with me. He was also givin' Brandt hell, because word of this shipment of arms has been leaked out to the newspapers. Three reporters are here, and our Mr. Brandt denies any responsibility."

"None of us has said a word to anybody," Emmett Budd declared.

"And none of us," Buck Prinz said. "Hell, but for Yeager himself, we don't know anybody in this town."

"However it happened," said Mac, "the cat's out of the bag. If these hombres from the newspaper found out, so could anybody else. We'll have to keep a close watch ahead and behind, from here to Dodge. Anybody of a mind to snatch these wagonloads of guns and shells can dynamite the tracks and stop the train."

Whatever Watson Brandt's objections, he had the passenger coach uncoupled from the caboose and coupled on behind the tender. Once it had been done, he approached Mac with an arrogance that did little to impress those who beheld it:

"I hope you're satisfied," he told Mac. "If you don't like this particular locomotive, I can swap it for another."

"The truth is, I don't like *you,* Brandt," Mac said, "but I'll try to tolerate you. Just don't push your luck."

Tunstall's three companions and the bullwhackers looked on in amusement, trying hard to suppress their grins. Nobody spoke until Brandt had stomped angrily away.

"The more I think about it," said Port Guthrie, "the more likely it seems that there might be outlaws who'll try to stop the train between here and Dodge."

"It's a likely enough possibility that I'm going to talk to the engineer," Mac said.

He headed for the locomotive, which sat chuff-chuff-chuffing, awaiting the command to depart.

"I need to talk to you," he shouted to the engineer.

The engineer pointed to the iron rungs that made a ladder up the side of the cab. Mac climbed up, careful to stay out of the way, as the fireman fed wood into the firebox to keep up steam.

"I'm Mac Tunstall. My pardners and me are along to see that nobody makes off with the freight on those flat-cars."

"I'm Will Herbert," the engineer said. "Welcome aboard."

"What would you do," Mac asked, "if outlaws dynamited the track ahead?"

"Stop the train," said Herbert.

"I don't aim to try and tell you how to run the train," Mac said, "but can I offer a suggestion?"

"Sure," said the engineer.

"If outlaws should dynamite or barricade the track, go ahead and stop the train. Then can you reverse it and backtrack to the nearest town?"

"Yes," Herbert said, "but that will throw us off schedule. We may end up on the same track with the eastbound."

"Better that than have outlaws make off with the wagons riding those three flatcars," said Mac. "Won't there be a sidetrack at every town?"

"Yes," Herbert replied.

"Then back up to the nearest town, and if we have to, we can wait on the sidetrack until the eastbound passes."

"My God," said Herbert, "if we don't get back to a station with a telegraph in time, the eastbound could be derailed where damaged track was intended for us."

"You're getting the idea," Mac said. "If outlaws stop the train, don't waste any time. Get it into reverse, pronto."

That taken care of, Mac climbed out of the cab in time to be confronted by Watson Brandt.

"What business do you have here?" Brandt demanded.

"None that concerns you," said Mac, his voice cold.

"If you're going with this train," Brandt said, "get aboard. We're leaving."

Watson Brandt entered the passenger car, followed by the six bullwhackers. The last to enter were Haze Sanderson and Red McLean. They stationed themselves at the rear of the car, with their Winchesters. They noted with approval that the six bullwhackers sat three on one side of the aisle, and three on the other, their Winchesters across their knees. In the caboose, Mac Tunstall and Buck Prinz sat with Andy DeVoe, the brakeman.

"You gents lookin' for trouble?" DeVoe inquired.

"Not us," said Mac. "We never look for it. It generally finds us soon enough."

Some ten miles west of the little town of Newton, Kansas, a dozen men had hidden themselves in a thicket near the tracks. Their horses were picketed nearby, cropping at the little graze there was.

"I've heard it said dynamite shouldn't be allowed to lay too long, once the charge is set," one of the men said. "Why don't we go ahead an' blow the track?"

"Damn it, Turk," a companion said, "the wind's out of the west. Somebody in Newton could hear the explosion and figure out what's goin' on. We got to wait till the train's so close, it won't make no difference who hears the blast."

"Since we got to wait," Turk said, "why don't we go over it one more time, just what we're aimin' to do?"

"We're follerin' Brandt's orders," said Tucker, the boss of the gang. "Slack, Price, Oden, Driscoll, and Shelby will be with me on the north side of the tracks. Turk, you'll be with Simpson, Welter, Coggins, Phelps, and Malone to the south of the track. Accordin' to what we been told, the passenger coach an' the caboose will be at the rear of the train. I want one man coverin' the locomotive cab, when she stops. Slack, that'll be you. The rest of us will advance on that passenger coach and the caboose. Gun down anybody comin' out of either of 'em."

"I'd feel better about all this," Phelps said, "if we'd got some money up front. Hell, we got to take all the risk, we still owe for them mule teams, and we don't know how long we'll have to wait for our share of the loot."

"We ain't all that far from Fort Dodge," said Coggins. "They could send soldiers after us. We can't make any time, with them wagons loaded to the bows."

"You don't get a chance at a haul like this, without

some risk,'' Tucker said. ''If we're able to pull this off, we'll be set for life.''

''You're forgettin' somethin','' said Slack. ''Brandt gets half, just for settin' this up. If we split the balance twelve ways, I don't see all that much for my share.''

''That's because you always see things cockeyed, like they're supposed to be,'' Tucker said. ''Suppose we take the whole thing and split it twelve ways?''

Slack laughed. ''You aim to double-cross Brandt?''

''Why not?'' said Tucker. ''What's he goin' to do, tell the law we cheated him out of his share?''

There was much laughter, and their good humor restored, they settled down to wait for the train.

The train bearing the six wagons loaded with government cargo stopped at the little town of Newton, Kansas, for the locomotive to take on water.

''We ain't that far from Dodge,'' said Lafe Beard, one of the bullwhackers. ''If there's any varmints of a mind to stop us, it'll have to be soon.''

''I'll be glad when we get to Dodge,'' Saul Estrella said, ''so's we can mount them wagon boxes and be on our way. I purely don't like this kind of freightin', where we got to depend on the railroad. I don't feel like we got control of nothin'.''

''Once those wagons roll out of Dodge,'' said Red McLean, ''we'll have control over it all. That is, as much control as Watson Brandt will allow.''

''Once we get out of reach of his daddy-in-law,'' Haze Sanderson said, ''we'll show Watson Brandt how the cow et the cabbage. Once we get to Austin, I reckon he can telegraph Mr. Yeager in Kansas City, tellin' him we've been bad boys, but what can Yeager do? We'll be in Texas, then, and our work for Yeager Freight Lines will be done.''

''I just hope when we get to Dodge,'' said Gourd Snively, ''we ain't told the livery had no luck findin' enough mules to pull them wagons. From what Yeager said, they was havin' a problem.''

"That ain't your worry," Haze Sanderson said. "If they ain't enough mules in Dodge, we'll just wait there until Yeager can send us a boxcar load of the varmints from Kansas City.''

"Let's don't worry about problems until they become problems," said Red McLean. "We're not in Dodge yet."

The locomotive's whistle bellowed twice. With a jerk, it tightened the couplings of the cars and the train lurched into motion. Once out of Newton, there was little to see except the flat Kansas plain that seemed to roll on to infinity.

"My God," said Red McLean, "I ain't seen a bush big enough to shelter a horn toad, and there ain't a tree nowhere. This kind of country must drive dogs crazy."

The train rolled on, and they were only a few miles west of Newton, when the earth shook with the force of an explosion. There was an immediate blast of the locomotive's whistle and a grinding, shuddering sensation as the brakes were applied.

"They're out there!" Haze Sanderson shouted.

But as suddenly as the locomotive had ground to a halt, it just as suddenly reversed itself and began backing toward Newton! There were shouts from the outlaws, as they all galloped after the departing train. But Haze Sanderson and Red McLean were outside the passenger coach, on the iron and steel platform. They cut loose with their Winchesters, and had the satisfaction of seeing two of the outlaws pitch from their saddles. From the rear of the train, from atop the caboose, Mac Tunstall and Buck Prinz were firing, and two more of the pursuing outlaws were shot out of their saddles. That was more than enough for the others, and they fell back out of range. Haze and Red stepped back inside the passenger coach, to be confronted by Watson Brandt.

"What is going on here?" Brandt demanded.

"A gang of outlaws blew the track ahead," said Haze,

"and were about to take those government wagons off the flatcars. We shot four of them, and the others changed their minds."

"You . . . killed them?"

"Hell, yes," Red replied. "What would you have done, spanked them?"

But Brandt was furious. "Who gave the order to reverse this train?"

"Mac Tunstall, probably," said Haze, "but what does it matter? Would you have preferred that it hit that broken stretch and be derailed?"

Brandt said nothing, slouching down in his seat, while the teamsters grinned at one another in delight. The train soon reached Newton, backing in to the depot. The dispatcher was waiting on the platform, and the engineer leaned out the window of his cab, shouting.

"Outlaws dynamited the track maybe fifteen miles out. At least four of 'em dead. Get on the wire and try to stop the eastbound."

Mac Tunstall and Buck Prinz stepped down from the caboose and approached the depot. Watson Brandt was standing there as though uncertain about his next move.

"Brandt," said Mac, "are you going to telegraph Mr. Yeager, or must I do it?"

"I am in charge of this expedition," Brandt snapped, "and if there's telegraphing to be done, I will do it."

"Then do it," Mac snapped back. "It's unlikely that track will be repaired in time for us to reach Dodge today. Since you're in charge, make some arrangements for us tonight, including grub. If you don't have that much authority, then telegraph Mr. Yeager."

If looks could have killed, Mac Tunstall would have been dead. Brandt stalked away to the railroad depot, and Tunstall laughed behind his back.

CHAPTER 1

❧

Newton, Kansas. September 16, 1873.

Mac Tunstall, his three pardners, the six bullwhackers, Watson Brandt, and the train crew remained at the hotel in Newton until the following day. When the damaged track had been repaired, the train bearing the six loaded wagons continued on to Dodge. There was no evidence of the outlaws, and the train reached Dodge in the early afternoon. When Mac and his three pardners stepped down from the train, they were surprised to find a sheriff waiting for them.

"Tunstall and friends, I reckon," the lawman said.

"I'm Tunstall," Mac said. "This is Buck Prinz, Haze Sanderson, and Red McLean."

"I'm Sheriff Harrington. I have a telegram from the sheriff in Kansas City, sent at the request of Hiram Yeager, of Yeager Freight Lines."

"We're working for him," said Mac. "There are six wagonloads of military goods going to Austin, Texas, and it's our responsibility to see that they arrive safely. We've had a bunch of outlaws stop the train on the way here."

"I heard about that," Harrington replied, "and you persuaded that bunch it wasn't a good idea. Yeager wants me to offer you hombres as much support as I can. He believes there might be an attempt during the night to shanghai those wagons you're guarding. He didn't say what led him to that conclusion, but I promised to do what I can."

"We aim to spend the night with the wagons," said Mac. "While we're obliged, I don't know what you can do, short of being a fifth man."

"What I have in mind," Harrington said, "is deputizing the four of you. We're fifty miles from Indian Territory, and during the summer and fall, there are trail herds from Texas, so we have our share of hell-raising. There have been so many killings, the town council is on the prod. If you have trouble tonight, we'll all come out of it lookin' better if the four of you are lawmen. *Comprende*?"

"*Sí*," said Mac. "Can you do it here? We need to keep an eye on those wagons."

"Yes," Harrington replied. "Let's go into the depot waiting room. There's no reason for the entire town to know what we're doing."

The swearing-in was done quickly. Harrington presented each of them with a deputy's star and then shook their hands. He then went on his way, and when the four Texans left the depot, they came face-to-face with Watson Brandt.

"What is the meaning of this?" Brandt demanded, his eyes on the stars they wore.

"Why don't you telegraph Mr. Yeager and ask him?" Mac suggested.

Brandt said nothing, and the four of them positioned themselves near the wagons on the flatcars. In less than an hour, the six bullwhackers returned to the train.

"We won't have the necessary mules until sometime tomorrow," said Port Guthrie. "I see we've gained some lawmen while we were gone."

"Sheriff Harrington's idea," Mac said. "Has Brandt arranged a place for you to sleep, and grub?"

"Not yet," said Guthrie. "We're thinking of sleeping in the passenger coach, with our Winchesters handy. We figure if these owl hoots are that damn determined, we'll have to fight 'em sooner or later."

"We'll appreciate the company, gents," Red McLean said.

"It's likely to be a long night," said Gourd Snively. "When it's time to eat, two of you can go with three of us. Then when the first five is done, they can come back and guard the wagons while the others eat."

"That's mighty generous," Mac said. "Have you cleared that with Watson Brandt?"

"No," said Snively. "We didn't feel the need to."

"Neither do we," Mac replied. "It's up to us to get these wagons safely to Austin, and I get the feeling we may have to do it in spite of Mr. Brandt."

"That's pretty much how we feel," said Port Guthrie. "I reckon there'll be plenty of shootin' between here and Austin, and it ain't uncommon for a bothersome jasper to be shot accidental, by his own outfit."

"I've heard of that," Mac replied. "It happened some during the war."

They had no idea what had become of Watson Brandt, and by eating five at a time, all had a good meal at Delmonico's. With the train and its wagons loaded with priceless cargo on a sidetrack, the ten men commissioned to get the wagons safely to Texas settled down for the night. Lamplight streamed from windows, and from a distant saloon there was the tinkle of a piano and the laughter of women.

"This is Tuesday night," Red McLean said. "This must be some hell of a town, come Saturday."

"I've heard tell it is," said Lafe Beard. "Fort Dodge is maybe eight miles downriver, and them soldiers is a bunch of wampus kitties. I hauled freight there long before the railroad come through. I wouldn't be sheriff of this town for all the money in Kansas."

Watson Brandt had rented a horse at the livery and, under the cover of darkness, had ridden to Fort Dodge.

"Sorry, sir," said the sentry on duty, "but civilians are not allowed to enter the fort after dark."

"I only want to see a friend of mine," Brandt pleaded. "He's Sergeant Jernigan, the quartermaster. If I can't go in, can't you send somebody to bring him to the gate?"

"I'm not sure, sir," said the sentry. "I'll find out. Sergeant of the guard, post one!"

"This is Sergeant Cooper," the sentry said, when the sergeant of the guard arrived.

"I'm Watson Brandt, Sergeant, and I want to see a friend of mine, Sergeant Jernigan. I've been told I can't go in. Is Jernigan allowed to come out and visit a few minutes?"

"If I can find him," said Sergeant Cooper. "Wait here."

"Much obliged," Brandt said. "Durin' the war, we fought together for the Union."

It was true, up to a point. Brandt had deserted under fire and had done time, after a court-martial. Jernigan had been too seriously wounded to run, and had remained in the service. Following the war, Brandt had discovered Jernigan had become a sergeant, and was in charge of buying beef for Fort Dodge. It had been a simple matter for Brandt to organize a gang, rustle cattle in Texas, and sell them to the military through Jernigan. He had conspired with Jernigan to steal the weapons and ammunition, promising a split he had never intended to make, had the robbery of the train been successful. Now it was neck meat or nothing, and one plan having failed, he must depend on an alternate plan devised by Jernigan. Jernigan soon arrived, joining Brandt outside the gate.

"Damn it," Jernigan said, "what are you doing here? I told you never to come here."

"I had no choice," said Brandt. "That bunch I had lined up to take the wagons from the train failed, and four of them were killed. Yeager hired some gun-throwing Texans, and they're guarding the wagons tonight."

"You spent weeks planning to take those wagons," Jernigan said, "and now that you have failed miserably, you expect me to do the job in ten hours."

"All right," Brandt snarled, "I'm admitting I failed. I'm offering you a chance to prove your plan is better than mine, and I'm willing to take a lesser cut, if you can pull it off."

Jernigan laughed. "How much less?"

"Twenty-five percent, instead of fifty," said Brandt.

"And what are you going to do to earn that twenty-five percent?" Jernigan demanded.

"Whatever I must," said Brandt.

"Ah," Jernigan said, "that's what I wanted to hear. I have a bunch waitin' in Indian Territory that would slit their own mothers' throats for the kind of loot we're after. I got a pass to get me out of here, and it'll be sometime after midnight before I can get this bunch to Dodge."

"Just get them there," said Brandt. "I don't want to lose out on this."

Brandt mounted his horse and rode away, and Jernigan went immediately to the post orderly room for his pass. He had a hard ride to Indian Territory and back, but within his reach was a veritable fortune in guns and ammunition. A fortune he had no intention of sharing with Watson Brandt.

Fourteen men followed Jernigan back from Indian Territory. Milo Quince, the leader of the bunch, rode alongside Jernigan, and the two talked.

"There's ten hombres guardin' the six wagons," Jernigan said, "and from what I've been told, they're a salty bunch. Four of 'em have been deputized by Sheriff Harrington. I reckon we'll have to kill them all, and the sheriff, too, if he gets froggy."

"I reckon we understand one another, then," said Quince. "We don't leave nobody alive that's got the sand to come after us."

"My sentiments exactly," Jernigan replied. "We won't move in until after midnight, so the town will be mostly closed up."

They rode in from the east, and by the time they were

within half a mile of the town, the night wind brought them the unmistakable sound of a locomotive with steam up. There was a chuff-chuff-chuffing, and they could see sparks billowing from the stack.

"Damn it," said Quince, "the train crew must still be there."

"No matter," Jernigan replied. "It's easier, keepin' up steam in the boilers, than havin' to fire it up in the morning. Besides, that gives me an idea. Why don't we just get the drop on that gent that's firin' the engine, and take the whole damn train?"

Quince laughed. "You won't get no argument out of me. I'd as soon be shot for a sheep as a lamb. We'll be a while, gettin' them wagons off the flatcars, and if we're a few miles away from Dodge, all the better."

"Ever'thing depends on us gettin' the drop on that gent that's firin' the boilers," said Jernigan. "I'm takin' care of him. When I got him covered, I aim to use him to force them hombres out of hiding that's been hired to guard the wagons. Once they're out where you can see 'em, you know what to do."

"We'll cut them down to the last man," Quince said.

"That's it," said Jernigan. "Then the lot of you mount your horses and follow after that train, until we're safely away from Dodge. Keep an eye on your backtrail, and if anybody—such as the sheriff—decides to follow, shoot to kill."

Mac Tunstall and Buck Prinz were in the caboose, at the end of the train, while Haze Sanderson and Red McLean had remained in the passenger coach, directly behind the tender. Of the teamsters, Port Guthrie and Lafe Beard were awake, while their companions all slept.

"I ain't used to bein' closed up like this," Haze Sanderson said. "I think I'll go up to the engine and chew the fat with the fireman."

"I'll go with you," said Red McLean.

There was no moon, and it being past midnight, most

of Dodge City slept. There was only an occasional distant
light.

"Them bullwhackers is a good bunch," Haze said, "but
they all like to light up their Durham. I don't smoke the
stuff, and it's hell on me."

"Me, too," Red replied. "Wasn't but two of 'em lit up,
but with all the smoke, you'd of thought the coach was
afire."

Suddenly, over the sound of the engine blowing off
steam, they heard a voice.

"I got you covered, bucko. I want.you to walk along
the track, toward that passenger coach. One bad move, and
I'll kill you."

Haze and Red moved quickly away from the track,
drawing their Colts. Two sets of footsteps came toward
them, for they could hear the crunch of cinders and ballast.
They waited until the captive railroad man had walked past
them, and Red challenged the man with the gun.

"Drop the gun, *amigo*. You're covered."

But the challenge went unheeded. There was a roar, followed by an answering blast, as Red McLean fired at the
muzzle flash. An agonized groan told him what he. wanted
to hear, and he eased down the hammer on his Colt. Gravel
crunched as the trainman ran back the way he had come,
toward the locomotive. Finally there was the distant sound
of galloping horses.

"The bastards," grunted the man Red had shot,
"they're . . . runnin' out . . . on me."

Among those drawn by the shooting was the brakeman,
and he approached from the caboose, with a lighted lantern.

"You with the lantern," Red called, "stay back. He
may be playin' possum."

"No," said the man on the ground, "I . . . I'm hurt. I
need a doc."

"Come on with the lantern," said Red.

By the time the brakeman arrived with the lantern, followed by Mac Tunstall and Buck Prinz, the bullwhackers

were there with Winchesters. There was a clatter of hooves, and Sheriff Harrington reined up.

"I've seen this varmint around town," Harrington said. "What was he trying to do?"

"Him and a gang of owl hoots was after the wagons on the train," said Red.

"Yeah," the fireman said, "this one on the ground snuck up behind me with a gun. He said he'd kill me if I made a bad move."

"A couple of you tote him to jail," said Harrington. "I'll have the doc patch him up, and in the morning, I'll ride to Fort Dodge. Considering the nature of what he was about to do, I reckon the Federals will be interested in him."

"I ain't takin' . . . all the rap," the wounded man said. "This . . . was Brandt's idea."

"Watson Brandt?" Mac Tunstall asked sharply.

"Yeah," the wounded man replied.

"Tarnation," said Buck Prinz, "he's son-in-law to Hiram Yeager, owner of the freight line that hired us. He's in charge all the way to Austin, Texas."

"He won't be, after this," Mac Tunstall said. "I reckon the post commander at Fort Dodge will be telegraphing Mr. Yeager."

"Who are you, mister?" Sheriff Harrington asked the wounded man.

"Jernigan is . . . my name, and I . . . ain't sayin' . . . no more."

"After we get him to jail," said Haze, "let's roust out Watson Brandt. I'm just plumb anxious to hear what he's got to say."

"Hell, yes," one of the teamsters said. "This wagon caravan to Austin is shapin' up to be right interesting."

Watson Brandt had taken a room at the Dodge House, and became abusive when he was awakened by Sheriff Harrington.

"I won't be pushed around by a hick-town sheriff," he

bawled. "I represent the Plains Freight Lines, and I'll tele-graph—"

"You won't have to telegraph," said Mac Tunstall, who had accompanied the sheriff. "We just shot a friend of yours—an hombre named Jernigan—who claims you're behind his trying to take those wagons off the train. I'm going to ask the post commander at Fort Dodge to contact Mr. Yeager."

"Damn you," Brandt bawled, "I had nothing to do with this. I know nothing about it."

"Then how did Jernigan learn of these wagons?" Mac demanded.

"He's quartermaster at Fort Dodge," said Brandt.

"That's why he looks familiar," Sheriff Harrington said. "I go to the fort occasionally, and I've seen him in town."

"But that doesn't mean Brandt's telling the truth," said Mac. "From what Mr. Yeager said, word of this arms ship-ment has been kept quiet, except for a leak to the news-paper in Kansas City. I think we need to play Mr. Brandt against Jernigan, and see who's the most willing to talk. Jernigan don't seem like the kind who's willing to risk court-martial, if he can talk his way out of it."

"Whatever he says, he's lying," Brandt cried desper-ately.

"We'll get some answers in the morning," said Sheriff Harrington. "Brandt, if you got ideas about running, just bear in mind that the law considers that an admission of guilt."

"I'll be here," Brandt said grimly.

He slammed the door and bolted it, leaving Mac and Sheriff Harrington in the hall.

"You believe he's guilty, then," said Sheriff Harring-ton.

"I do," Mac replied. "Somebody got word of these arms and ammunition to the newspaper in Kansas City. I think that was done so that Brandt could draw suspicion from himself, after the robbery. He's going to argue that if the newspaper people could learn of these arms and ammunition, then so could Jernigan or anybody else.''

"That could have been the case,'' said Sheriff Harrington. "It's going to be interesting when Brandt and Jernigan come together.''

"Sheriff,'' Mac said, "I have an idea. Why don't you see if Brandt rented a horse at one of the liveries sometime after the train arrived here? I believe he went to Fort Dodge and talked with Jernigan.''

"If Brandt rode to the fort,'' said Harrington, "he likely would have waited until after dark. Civilians are not allowed to enter after dark, so Brandt would have had to ask for Jernigan at the gate. The officer of the guard will remember.''

"Do it your way, Sheriff,'' Mac said, "but we're not leaving Dodge with those wagons, as long as there's any doubt of Brandt's involvement.''

Mac Tunstall returned to the train, and although every man remained awake the rest of the night, there was no further disturbance.

"We'll eat five at a time, like we did at supper,'' said Port Guthrie, "if that's suitable to everybody.''

"I reckon we can all agree on that,'' Mac replied. "It's been a long night, and we can all stand some breakfast and hot coffee.''

By the time the ten men had eaten and were all again with the waiting train, Sheriff Harrington arrived.

"You were dead right, Tunstall,'' he said, dismounting. "Brandt rented a horse last night, just after dark. He was denied entry at Fort Dodge, and the sergeant of the guard sent Jernigan to the gate. After Jernigan's conversation with Brandt, Jernigan picked up a pass and rode out. I reckon that answers some questions.''

"It does,'' said Mac. "Brandt and Jernigan are both neck-deep in it. On the way here, some outlaws blew up the track just this side of Newton, and we killed four of them. Now I'm wondering if Brandt didn't plan that.''

"If he did," Harrington said, "you'll never get it out of him. But you won't need that. His involvement with Jernigan will be enough to finish him. I took the liberty of telegraphing Yeager, at Plains Freight Lines, and waited for an answer. Here it is."

Jail Brandt and Jernigan stop. Inform Tunstall and companions wagons to remain in Dodge until I arrive.

The message had been signed by Hiram Yeager, of Plains Freight Lines.

"That means Brandt won't be segundo from here on to Austin," Red McLean said.

"I'd gamble that you're right," said Sheriff Harrington. "This is shaping up like Brandt and Jernigan are going to implicate one another. I'm going to suggest to Yeager that we have a hearing before the judge, taking testimony from the fireman who was taken hostage, from those of you who captured Jernigan, and finally, from Brandt and Jernigan. I'll see that personnel from Fort Dodge are on hand to identify Brandt and testify to his meeting with Jernigan last night."

"You're a thorough man, Sheriff," Mac said, "and we're obliged. I believe Mr. Yeager will be, too."

Hiram Yeager arrived that afternoon. The train was a special, consisting of the locomotive, the tender, a passenger coach, and a caboose. It was sidetracked behind the train that waited with the wagons. When Yeager stepped down from the passenger coach, he was followed by two army officers. There were captain's bars on the epaulets of their blue coats. The ten men Yeager had hired to protect and deliver the arms and ammunition were there to meet the train, accompanied by Sheriff Harrington. Harrington introduced himself.

"Sheriff," said Yeager, "this is Captain Meeker and Captain Oliver, from Fort Leavenworth. They are here because one of the men you are holding—Jernigan—is career military. They wish to meet with the post commander at Fort Dodge, prior to any hearing before the judge."

"Suits me," Sheriff Harrington said. "We'll do it in

whatever manner you like. All I'm doing is holding this pair in jail, until their day in court. The gents you have to thank are those over yonder beside those flatcars, with the wagons. They caught Jernigan as he was about to capture the train with a band of renegades. Mr. Tunstall figured there had to be a connection between Jernigan and Brandt, and I established the truth of that, by riding out to Fort Dodge. Brandt and Jernigan had met early last night, before Jernigan and a gang of outlaws attempted to take the wagons.''

"Thank you, Sheriff,'' said Yeager. "Now, if all of you will excuse me, I need to talk to those men who are waiting for me.''

Yeager approached Tunstall and his companions, and the teamsters he had hired to drive the wagons from Dodge to Austin. One by one, Yeager shook their hands, and it was Mac Tunstall who spoke first.

"Sorry we had to send you bad news, Mr. Yeager.''

"All you men acted in the best interests of Plains Freight Lines,'' Yeager said, "and I am more than satisfied with your performance. It appears that we may be here for several days, until the law takes its course. Among yourselves, set up a schedule for sentry duty, so that these wagons are secured twenty-four hours a day. I will arrange for quarters and food at one of the hotels.''

With that, he turned away. Sheriff Harrington had provided a buckboard, and he led Yeager and the pair of army officers to it.

"Well, damn,'' Red McLean said, "I was hopin' he would tell us what he aims to do about Watson Brandt. It'll be just our luck for the slippery varmint to weasel his way out of this, and give us hell from here to Austin.''

"I don't think so,'' said Mac. "I've already seen Brandt try to blame it all on Jernigan, and I can't see Jernigan getting maybe ten years at hard labor, while Brandt goes free. I'd say each is going to implicate the other.''

* * *

An hour before sundown, Hiram Yeager returned to the railroad siding where the men he had hired stood watch over the six loaded wagons still on flatcars. Every man gathered around to hear what Yeager had to say.

"A hearing has been scheduled for Friday, the nineteenth," said Yeager. "I've arranged for rooms for all of you at the Dodge House, when you're not on watch, and you may take your meals at Delmonico's."

Just when it seemed Yeager wasn't going to tell them anything more—when he had turned to leave—he changed his mind.

"From what I have already heard, I have seen fit to make one change. Watson Brandt has been relieved of any further responsibility insofar as this expedition is concerned. You, Tunstall, will be in charge, and to compensate you for the added responsibility, you are to receive an additional hundred dollars. The rest of you—when the wagons have been safely delivered to Austin—will receive an additional fifty dollars. You will be paid by an officer at the ordnance depot."

With that, he was gone, and it was all the assembled men could do to avoid cheering.

"It's surprising that he made such a decision before the hearing," Port Guthrie said.

"Not if he's talked to Jernigan," said Mac. "I don't believe Brandt can lie his way out of this."

"Neither do I," Red McLean said. "If we hadn't caught Jernigan, there wouldn't be any connection to Brandt, but like Mac says, each will likely convict the other."

The men continued standing watch over the loaded wagons, but there was no trouble. On Thursday, the day before the hearing, there was some excitement when the westbound arrived. Four women exited the passenger coach, and stood looking around.

"Tarnation!" said Red McLean, "prettier than speckled pups, and not a one older than twenty-two or -three."

"Out of our reach," Buck Prinz said. "Way they're

lookin' around, they're all bein' met by somebody. Soldiers from the fort, likely.''

But the four looked in vain, for nobody paid the slightest attention to them, except the men who guarded the six loaded wagons.

"Whoever they're lookin' for ain't here," said Haze Sanderson.

"No," Mac Tunstall said, "and it's downright ungentlemanly of us not to offer to help them in any way we can. Come on."

"You gents go ahead," said Port Guthrie. "They'd likely fall into a faint, if all of us was to go troopin' over there."

Mac led the way, and was the first to speak.

"Ladies, is there anything we can do to help?"

"Perhaps," said the girl with red hair and blue eyes. "Is there a carriage available that can take us to a hotel?"

"Nothing short of the livery," Mac said, "and they'd expect you to pay. All of us have horses, and if you don't mind riding double, each of us could take one of you."

"We aren't exactly dressed for it," said the blonde with brown eyes. "Besides, there's our trunks."

"Maybe the Dodge House can send somebody for the trunks," Buck Prinz said.

"Come on," Red urged. "We're almost bearable, once you get to know us."

"But we don't know you," said the girl with black hair and green eyes.

"That's easy to fix," Mac said. "I'm Mac Tunstall, the gent with red hair is Red McLean, the varmint with sandy hair is Haze Sanderson, and the *paisano* with the hole in the crown of his hat is Buck Prinz."

Despite themselves, they laughed.

"I'm Trinity McCoy," said the girl with red hair and blue eyes. "This," she said, gesturing toward the blonde with brown eyes, "is Hattie Sutton. Next to her," she said, with a nod toward the girl with curly black hair and green eyes, "is Rachel Price. And this is Elizabeth Graves," she concluded, pointing to the girl with brown hair and hazel eyes.

"Now that we're acquainted," Buck Prinz said, "are you ready to ride on to the Dodge House?"

"We're not dressed for it," said Hattie. "It would be indecent."

"Oh, darn," Rachel said, "nobody here's ever seen us before, and when we're gone, they'll never see us again. Let's do it."

"We can lift you up in front of us," said Mac, "so you won't straddle the horse."

"Bring on the horses, then," Elizabeth said.

"It's not too early for supper," said Red. "Delmonico's is just across the street from the hotel. Will you ladies do us the honor of eating with us?"

"I will," Trinity said. "I'm half-starved."

"So will I," the others answered in a single voice.

CHAPTER 2

⌒∿⌒

Dodge City, Kansas. September 18, 1873.

*T*he four women were hungry, and not until the meal
was over did conversation seem appropriate. Mac
Tunstall spoke.

"May we ask why you ladies are here in Dodge, unes-
corted? That is, unless we're just pryin' into something
that's none of our business."

"You are, and it is," Trinity replied, her eyes twinkling,
"but I suppose we have to trust someone, and so far, we
haven't had a lot of choice."

"That don't say much for this town," said Haze Sanderson, "overlookin' four pretty girls."

"We're here looking for men," Hattie Sutton said, "but
not in the way it may seem."

"We're looking for our husbands," said Trinity.

"Oh?" Red McLean said. "What would they be doing
here in Dodge?"

"They're not here," said Rachel Price. "This is as close
as we could get to them by train. They're somewhere in
Texas, we think."

"We hope," Elizabeth Graves added. "They were part
of a scouting party from Fort Griffin, and the army reported them missing, almost a year ago."

"Begging your pardon, ma'am," said Haze Sanderson,

"but if the army can't find 'em, how do you ladies expect to?"

"We don't exactly know," Trinity replied. "We finally learned that their scouting party was believed to have been attacked by Quanah Parker and his Comanches."

"That's bad news, ma'am," said Mac. "In fact, it couldn't be much worse. Does the commanding officer at Fort Griffin know you're coming?"

"No," Elizabeth said. "We feared the military would just try to talk us out of it."

"That, or forbid us to come at all," said Trinity.

"They would and should have done exactly that," Buck Prinz said. "Quanah Parker and his bunch of Comanches are gettin' desperate, and the danger is three times greater than it was a year ago. How do you expect to get from here to Fort Griffin?"

"We have enough for a wagon, teams, and supplies," said Trinity. "We're hoping that we can find another train going south, and travel with them."

"There likely won't be any wagon trains going south, until Parker and his Comanches are under control," Mac said. "There may be an occasional military payroll going to the Texas forts, but it would be under heavy guard, and you ladies certainly wouldn't be permitted to go."

"They could go with us," Red McLean suggested helpfully.

"I'm afraid that won't be possible," said Mac, glaring at Red.

"Why not?" Rachel Price demanded. "We don't have a lot of money, but we can pay."

"Several reasons," said Mac. "We are already committed, and we've given our word. If that's not enough, our wagons will likely draw Parker and his Comanches like flies are drawn to honey. That's the last thing you want."

"Quanah Parker and the Comanches will be a problem for us, either way," Elizabeth Graves said. "Do you think they won't bother us if we're alone?"

"Alone?" said Buck Prinz. "My God, you can't go through Comanche country alone."

"Oh, but we can," Trinity said, "if that's the only way."

"Ma'am," said Mac, "what you're suggesting is as foolish as it is impossible."

"Perhaps," Rachel Price said, "but we didn't come this far just to be turned back for fear of a bunch of troublesome Indians."

"They're more than troublesome," Red McLean said. "Do any of you have any idea what they'll do to white women?"

"We're getting away from the subject," said Rachel Price. "We're going to Texas, if we have to go alone. If our wagon can't travel with yours, and there's no other train, then we'll have to go alone."

"No decent white man would allow you to do that," Mac said.

"No decent white man would deny us help," said Hattie Sutton. "I'm ready to return to the hotel."

"We'll walk you back," Red McLean said.

"Thanks," said Rachel Price, "but you've done enough for us."

"Yes," Trinity snapped, "we're perfectly capable of finding our own way."

Without another word, the four of them got up and stalked out of the restaurant.

"I reckon," said Red, "we got on the bad side of them."

"It won't make no difference," Buck said. "They all got husbands."

"Wrong," said Mac. "They all *had* husbands. How many bluecoats have been captured by the Comanches and lived to talk about it?"

"You're dead right," Haze said. "It's just a damn shame they're risking their lives for a cause that's already lost. Maybe if the post commander at Fort Dodge—"

"Whoa," said Mac. "We've done our best to change

their minds. They didn't trust the judgment of the post commander at Fort Griffin. Anything we say or do will only result in them disliking us all the more. We'd best quit while we're ahead.''

''Yeah,'' Red agreed. ''Tomorrow, when that hearing's over, we can be on our way.''

Dodge City, Kansas. September 19, 1873.

At the request of the army officers who had accompanied Hiram Yeager, the hearing was private. It was also brief. As expected, Jernigan and Brandt convicted each other.

''There is no doubt in my mind that these men are guilty,'' Judge Calder said. ''Since Mr. Jernigan is active military, it has been requested that he be returned to Fort Dodge, where he will remain until the time of his court-martial. Mr. Brandt will be returned to Kansas City, where he is to be prosecuted in federal court for his participation in a crime against the Union. This court stands adjourned.''

Hiram Yeager looked relieved, for Watson Brandt had run afoul of federal law, and it was out of his hands. The ten men he was depending on to take the wagons to Austin had gathered in the hall, outside the courtroom, and Yeager went to them.

''I'm counting on you men,'' he said. ''The livery will have your teams ready in the morning. There is room in each wagon for two hundred pounds of grain, and necessary supplies for the journey. Get your supplies and grain from the mercantile across the street from the livery and wagon yard.''

''One thing we ain't discussed,'' Port Guthrie said. ''We got no particular reason for goin' to Texas, except as whackers for your wagons. What becomes of them and the teams after we reach Austin an' unload?''

''Return to Dodge empty,'' said Yeager, ''and that's where you'll leave the mules. The wagons are to be left near the depot, where they'll be returned to Kansas City by rail. If you men want to remain with Plains, telegraph me from here, and I'll arrange for all of you to take the train back to Kansas City."

With that, Yeager was gone.

"Well," Mac said, "I reckon we'd better enjoy this town grub and the hotel beds while we can. But for now, we'd better get back to the depot and relieve those men Mr. Yeager left guarding the wagons."

Later that afternoon, Sheriff Harrington rode to the depot, where he visited with the men he had come to know and like.

"I reckon it all worked out to suit you gents," said Harrington. "Jernigan will likely catch hell from the military, and with Brandt to be tried in federal court, he'll be lucky to get off with ten years. Now all you have to bother you is the several hundred renegades hidin' out in Indian Territory, and them seven hundred Comanches out yonder with Quanah Parker."

All the men laughed, for it was gruesome frontier humor at its worst.

"You're a real comfort, Sheriff," Mac said. "Wish you was ridin' with us."

"Thank God I'm not," said Harrington. "I'll stay here in civilization, where all I have to bother me is the possibility of bein' shot in the back by some drunk or tinhorn cardsharp. Good luck."

Dodge City, Kansas. September 20, 1873.

At first light, Mac Tunstall gathered his nine men, prior to unloading the wagons from the flatcars.

"Go on to the wagon yard for the mules," Mac said. "First thing, after unloading the wagons, we'll go to the mercantile for our supplies and grain for the mules."

Mac and his three companions waited with the wagons until the teamsters returned with the teams of mules and harness. The flatcars were then uncoupled, and with a ramp

at one end, mule teams were backed up to each wagon.
Once all the wagons were unloaded, the teamsters drove
to the mercantile. Mac and his companions followed, and
as soon as they were in sight of the mercantile, their eyes
were drawn to the wagon yard across the street. Four very
familiar women were harnessing teams of mules to a
wagon.

"Well, by God," Red exclaimed, "would you look at
that."

"I'd say they aim to join us, whether we want 'em or
not," said Buck.

"Not by a jugful," Mac replied. "We'll have all we can
say grace over, without those troublesome females along."

"Suppose they follow us," said Buck. "What do you
aim to do?"

"Ignore them," Mac said.

Haze laughed. "That won't be easy, if the Comanches
attack. You aim to stand by and watch them hostile varmints have their way with white women?"

"Damn it," said Mac, "I don't know what I'll do, until
the time comes. If Comanches attack, don't expect them
to ignore us. We won't be standing around watching them
have their way with those foolish females. We'll be fighting for our lives."

"Somebody ought to suggest they arm themselves,"
Red observed.

"Go ahead," said Mac. "They don't value my advice
all that much."

Red trotted his horse over to the wagon, and the women
seemed not to see him. He spoke as calmly as he could.

"If you're bound to go, you need weapons."

"Oh?" said Trinity. "You mean these?"

Reaching under the wagon seat, she brought out a Winchester and jacked a shell into the firing chamber.

"Yeah," Red replied.

He heard them laughing at him as he rode away, and
when he reached his companions, they greeted him with
delighted grins.

"That's what happens," he gritted, "when a man tries to do the right thing."

"Now that you've done your good deed," said Mac, "let's help the bullwhackers load the grub and grain into the wagons."

"They didn't leave us much room," Port Guthrie said, as he loosened the drawstring to the canvas pucker at the rear of his wagon.

"We can pack some grub behind our saddles, if need be," said Mac.

They loaded the grain first, and by carefully packing the supplies, managed to get all of them into the space that remained. Sheriff Harrington reined up, and hooking a leg around his saddle horn, watched them complete their task. Gesturing toward the women across the street, Harrington spoke.

"What do you know about the ladies hitching mules to that wagon?"

"That when it comes to stubborn, they're six notches below the mules," said Mac.

Harrington laughed. "I heard you hombres was havin' supper with 'em last night, and then I heard they're goin' to Texas, so I just reckoned they'd be goin' with you gents."

"They reckoned the same thing," Haze said, "but Mac set 'em straight."

"Hell," Red observed, "they got at least one Winchester."

"They have four," said Sheriff Harrington. "The gunsmith come and told me."

"For their sake," Mac said, "I hope they can shoot. I don't reckon there's anything you can do to keep them from followin' us?"

"Not a thing," said Harrington cheerfully. "Since they're hell-bent on goin', I was kind of hopin' you'd allow them to trail with you. I'd feel better about them."

"Plains Freight Lines is paying us," Mac said, "and I

doubt Mr. Yeager would take it kindly if we had a wag-onload of gypsy females followin' us.''

"Yeager's gone," said Harrington, "and I can't see that it would matter to him, just so you reach Austin safely with his cargo. But that's your business."

Sheriff Harrington rode away. When the supplies and grain had been loaded, the six teamsters climbed to their wagon boxes and the big wagons rolled south. Crossing the railroad tracks, they were soon just moving dots on the endless Kansas plain. The wagon with the four determined women followed, and not being nearly as heavily loaded, it managed to catch up to within a few hundred feet of the six wagons ahead of it.

"They're followin' us," Red observed.

"No law against that," said Mac. "When our mules get used to one another, and used to the trail, we'll leave them behind."

"Don't count on it," Red said. "Their wagon ain't loaded like ours. They'll be on our tail ever' jump of the way."

"Don't sound so damned pleased," said Mac irritably.

"Come on, Mac," Haze said, "you know their men are dead and their bones are likely bleaching in the Texas sun. Sooner or later, they'll have to accept that. They're all young enough and pretty enough to make some lucky var-mints a real handful. Me, I got my loop set for that little blonde with the big brown eyes."

"Haze," said Mac, "you're a damned romantic fool. That pack of females will all hang around some fort and end up gettin' hitched to some bluecoats just as broke and unlucky as them four the Comanches took care of."

But the determined women kept up with the heavily laden wagons, and when the men made camp for the night, the lone wagon that had trailed them all day was but a stone's throw away. Worse, a light breeze brought the taunting smell of dutch-oven biscuits, as the women pre-pared supper. When the men began cooking their own meal, they made an alarming discovery. For all the supplies they had loaded into the wagons, they had failed to bring any coffee. That same breeze that tortured them with freshly baked biscuits added to their misery by wafting the odor of strong, black coffee.

"Damn it," said Mac, "in the morning, I'll ride back to Dodge and get some coffee."

"But I want coffee tonight, and in the morning," Haze Sanderson said.

"So do I," said Buck.

"Me, too," Red added.

"Hell," said Emmett Budd, one of the teamsters, "I'm goin' over there and askin' them females fer some coffee. All they can say is no."

Taking his tin cup, he headed for the distant wagon. Not to be outdone, his five companions took their tin cups and followed. Red McLean laughed, while Buck, Haze, and Mac watched with interest, expecting the brash teamsters to get their comeuppance. But it didn't happen. The six men returned with cups of steaming coffee, eating fresh-baked dutch-oven biscuits.

"Tarnation," Red growled, "how'd they manage that?"

"We told 'em we didn't have any coffee," said Lafe Beard, "an' asked if we could have a cup of theirs. They said we can have some more at breakfast, an' we got biscuits, too."

"Well, by God," Haze said, "I ain't got too much pride to go beggin' hot coffee."

"Me, neither," said Red. "Let's go."

"Damn right," Buck said. "You goin', Mac?"

"I reckon not," said Mac. "I got on their bad side, and I doubt I'd be welcome."

Mac remained with the wagons, while his three companions went to try their luck. To Mac's surprise, when they returned, Red had brought an extra tin cup of coffee for him. He got a freshly baked biscuit, too.

"They ain't holdin' a grudge," Haze said. "They was a lot nicer to us than we was to them. They told us we can have coffee for breakfast, too."

"One of you can ride back to Dodge in the morning and get a supply of coffee," said Mac, "and we'll replace some of theirs."

"I think they'd be insulted if we done that," Buck said. "The coffee they sent you is in one of their cups. When you're done with it, why don't you return it? While you're there, eat some crow and invite them to trail their wagon with ours."

"Hell, why not?" said Haze. "They'll follow us anyhow, and who'd have ever thought they'd know how to bake dutch-oven biscuits?"

"I won't be a bit surprised if they know how to handle them Winchesters," Red said.

"I'll talk to them, damn it," said Mac.

He put it off as long as he could, waiting until they had finished the coffee and all the cups had been washed. Then, like a condemned man with his borrowed cup, he took the walk to the wagon. The first stars were blooming like silver daisies in a meadow of deep purple, and the four women watched him approach. They said nothing, and he realized the next move was his.

"We're obliged for the coffee," he began. "I don't know how we could have been so damned—"

Embarrassed, he caught himself, and the women laughed.

"We're not shrinking violets, Mr. Tunstall," said Trinity. "We don't expect a man to talk and act like he's in Sunday school."

"One of us will ride back to Dodge in the morning," Mac said, feeling a little more at ease. "We'll get enough coffee to replenish your supply."

"You owe us nothing," said Hattie. "You needed coffee, and we have plenty. Let that be the end of it."

"You're generous," Mac said, "and kinder to us than we deserve. I reckon it's time I admitted I was wrong in not allowing your wagon to trail with ours. I still believe yours is a dangerous and probably hopeless journey, but if you're determined to go, then I have no right to stand in your way. We'll see you to Fort Griffin, if that's where you're wanting to go, and help you in any way that we can.''

"We all have our shortcomings," said Trinity. "I suppose we seem forward at times, and I believe we should forget past misunderstandings and go on from here. Do you have any objection if we move our wagon closer to yours?''

"None," Mac said. "I'll harness your teams for you.''

"No," said Trinity. "We'll pull our own weight. Go on back and tell your men there'll be hot biscuits and coffee for breakfast.''

Mac found the lot of them waiting for him, grins on their faces. He said nothing, but when the women had harnessed the teams and the lone wagon joined theirs, his men looked upon Mac Tunstall with approval.

The following morning, when the teams were being harnessed, Mac sent Red back to Dodge for a supply of coffee.

"Get us thirty pounds of beans, and a coffee grinder," Mac said.

"Yeah," said Haze Sanderson. "If we run out of anything, don't let it be coffee.''

Red returned from Dodge and caught up to the wagons well before noon. In addition to the coffee, he had brought six dozen eggs.

"I reckoned these would be good with hot biscuits," he said, passing the eggs up to Hattie Sutton, on the wagon box.

For the second day, the train was forced into dry camp, relying on the pair of twenty-gallon kegs mounted on the side of each wagon.

"Time we make coffee in the morning and give these mules a swig of water, we'll all be thirsty," said Mac, as they gathered around the supper fire. "From the map at the railroad depot in Dodge, it's at least fifty miles to the

Cimarron River. We're doing well to make ten miles a day."

"We're in trouble, then," Buck said. "Even if we could last three more days without water, these horses and mules can't."

"We have plenty of empty barrels," said Red. "If all our wagons weren't loaded to the bows, we could take a wagonload of barrels to the Cimarron, fill them with water, and then rattle our hocks back here."

"Too risky," Mac said, "even if we had an empty wagon. We couldn't spare more than two men, and it could mean sending them to their deaths. We're not that far from Indian Territory, and against a gang of renegades, two men wouldn't have a chance."

"But we must have water," said Buck. "You got any better ideas?"

"No," Mac admitted.

"You could use our wagon," said Trinity, "if the journey wasn't so dangerous."

"Dangerous or not," Buck replied, "we must have water, even if we have to return to Dodge. In either case, I'll go."

"That wouldn't make any sense," said Red. "We got to be at least halfway to the Cimarron. If you ladies are serious about the use of the wagon, I'll volunteer to go on to the Cimarron, startin' right now."

"Trinity spoke for us all," Hattie Sutton said. "We must have water, and so must our teams. If you men are willing to take the risk, the least we can do is offer the wagon. Our belongings are a few changes of clothing. That and the supplies might be distributed among your wagons until you return with the water."

"I still say it's too risky," said Mac, "but I'll agree we must have water. Buck, if you and Red are willing, then we'll accept the use of the wagon. Ladies, if you'll remove your belongings and your supplies, we'll manage to fit them into the other wagons. Risky as this may be, we don't want that wagon bearing any more weight than it has to.

Buck, you and Red take a horse with you. You can take turns driving the wagon, leaving one of you with a horse, to keep watch ahead and behind."

"We'll take some jerked beef with us," Buck said, "and by resting the teams, we'll get to the Cimarron sometime early tomorrow."

"We should cover another ten miles tomorrow," said Haze. "That'll shorten the return trip to maybe twenty miles. We'll then be two days from the Cimarron, and the barrels of water should see us through."

"It's a courageous thing to do," Hattie said, her eyes on Red. "We never expected anything like this."

"We certainly didn't," said Rachel, "and we won't forget."

Just for a second her eyes met those of Buck Prinz, and his heart beat faster, for he saw some interest there.

"Hitch up the teams, load the barrels, and get going," Mac said. "Travel as far as you can tonight. We'll roll at first light tomorrow, taking as many miles from your return as we can."

Quickly, the women removed their belongings from the wagon, while Mac and Haze removed the supplies and one sack of grain. Buck and Red then began harnessing the teams while Port Guthrie and the teamsters loaded empty barrels into the wagon. Within minutes, Buck was on the wagon box and was headed south. Red loped his horse alongside.

"Oh, I hope nothing happens to them," said Elizabeth Graves.

"They know the risk," Mac said. "There may be even greater risks for us all, before we reach our destination."

"In our haste," Trinity said, "we overlooked something. With our wagon gone, all of us are afoot."

"Not quite," said Mac. "I reckon Port and three of his teamsters will be glad to have you share a wagon seat, until Red and Buck return with your wagon."

"You're all more than welcome," Guthrie replied. "We

need water, too, and it's comin', thanks to you offerin'
your wagon.''

"Port," said Mac, "we're far enough south to concern
ourselves with renegades. We'll stand watch in pairs. Haze
and me will take the first three hours. Can we count on
the rest of you to take the next three watches?"

"You got it," Guthrie replied.

In anticipation of tomorrow's early start, the party took
to its bedrolls. Haze took his position at the north side of
the camp, while Mac kept his eyes to the south. Between
the two sentries were the wagons and the grazing horses
and mules. There was no moon, and the silver pools which
were the stars seemed far away. The sound, when it came,
was more sensed than heard. In an instant, Mac's Colt was
in his hand, cocked and ready.

"Please," came a whisper, "it's me. Trinity."

"Damn it," Mac gritted, "I could have shot you. Don't
ever come up on me like that."

"I'm sorry," she replied. "I . . . I couldn't sleep."

Mac said nothing, and uninvited, she sat down, her back
against a wagon wheel. Mac hunkered down, facing her.
He could see only the white oval of her face in the darkness, and had no way of reading the expression in her eyes.
But she was as handicapped as he, and they faced one
another uneasily, dependent on words. Finally she spoke.

"At first, I thought you were opposed to us traveling to
Texas because you believed we are weak—and probably
helpless—females. But after this . . . situation . . . lack of
water . . . I can see there are dangers such as we never
imagined. You really *don't* believe the men we are seeking
are alive, do you?"

"No," said Mac, "and it's more than just my opinion.
A soldier's pay is less than half that of a teamster, yet he
may be called upon to spend months in the field, wet, cold,
and hungry, risking his life for a cause some politicians in
Washington thought was a noble idea at the time. When
soldiers die, the army must put the best face on the situation that it can. It's the diplomatic thing to do, announcing

that a man is missing. It's less harmful to the army's image, and a little easier on the feelings of the folks back home."

"Even when it is known for a fact that the man is dead?"

"Even then," Mac replied. "The Comanche isn't known for his compassion, and when a soldier isn't slaughtered and scalped immediately, it's generally because they have plans for him later on."

"What kind of plans?"

"You don't want to know," said Mac.

"Yes," she said, "I do want to know."

"Torture," said Mac. "A captive may be burned at the stake, or spread-eagled naked, on the ground, and a fire built in his crotch. Or he may be turned over to the squaws for torture, to be killed when they tire of him."

She caught her breath and choked back a sob.

"Sorry," Mac said. "There's no easy way of answering your question."

"I wanted to know. Thank you for telling me. In the end, knowing—and accepting—the worst isn't as terrible as *never* knowing, never being sure."

"That's the way I feel," Mac replied.

"Then you don't believe we're wasting our time, undertaking this perilous journey for nothing?"

"No," said Mac, "if it takes that to ease your mind, it's something you must do."

"Thank you," she said softly.

CHAPTER 3

✺

*A*fter a while, Buck took to the saddle, swapping places with Red. There were a dozen empty water kegs within the wagon, and two more outside, one mounted on either side of the wagon box. The Texans kept the teams moving as fast as they dared, stopping hourly to rest the faithful mules.

"We're makin' good time," Buck said, during a rest stop. "There's a chance we might reach the Cimarron by first light."

"We might not do so bad on the return trip," Red replied. "I don't think this wagon will have near the load as one of them piled to the bows with them boxed Winchesters and canisters of shells."

But when first light came, there was only the endless plain stretching before them. On the eastern horizon, tendrils of gold crept across the gray of the heavens. Without water, even the late-September sun could be unmerciful. The mules might last another two hours. But the terrain grew progressively rougher, which was a promising sign. Finally, far ahead of them, was what appeared to be a ridge stretching from east to west.

"Treeline," Buck shouted. "That has to be it."

Red eased up on the reins, allowing the teams to slow to a trot. As it was, the rattle of the wagon could be heard for a great distance in the early morning air.

"I'll ride on ahead," said Buck. "We'll need to back the wagon down as close to the water as we can. It'll be a job, loadin' them full kegs."

There was more to it than that, however, and Red reached under the seat, where he had placed his Winchester. If their luck played out and they attracted the attention of some Comanches or white renegades, the best they could hope for was to die fighting. Red kept his eyes on Buck, and saw nothing to alarm him. Reaching the river, Buck rode west, trying to find a bank that had a gradual slope down to the water. When Buck reined up and waved his hat, Red flicked the reins. Their first duty was to water the thirsty mules, when they were ready to drink.

"They're stubborn varmints," said Buck, "but they're smart enough not to drink until they've cooled off enough not to founder. A damn shame horses don't have that kind of smarts."

"Yeah," Red replied. "You'd better tie that jug-head of mine to a wagon bow, or he'll slide down that riverbank and commit suicide. By the time we get the teams unharnessed, they should be ready to drink."

Swiftly they unharnessed the mules, and by the time the animals had drunk their fill, Red's horse had rested enough to drink safely.

"Now," said Buck, "let's hitch up the mules, back this wagon as near the water as we can, and fill those water kegs."

They were soon sweating, wrestling the filled kegs into the wagon. Finally, there were only the empty kegs mounted on either side of the wagon box.

"This water we're loadin' is almighty muddy," Red observed, "but there's no help for it. You purely can't wade into water that's deep enough to fill a keg, without muddyin' it."

"It'll settle, the mud goin' to the bottom," said Buck. "Time we meet our wagons, I'd bet we could haul a dead skunk out of every keg, and the water would still be drinkable."

Red laughed. "Some of the best water I ever tasted come out of a buffalo wallow, and that was after it had fermented over buffalo droppings for a while."

They had spent less than an hour at the river, and both men breathed sighs of relief as they headed north, Buck at the reins. Red rode behind, his eyes constantly on the backtrail. Despite it being late September, the sun was hot, and they were forced to rest the teams more often.

"I believe we'll meet our outfit before sundown," Buck said.

"Maybe," said Red, "but if we don't, we'll have to keep goin' until we do, because they'll be hurtin' for water."

Slowly the sun slipped toward the western horizon, and when it was but an echo of dusty rose, Red and Buck again stopped to rest the teams. Quickly the earth cooled, as a breeze crept in from the northwest, caressing their sweaty faces. They listened, for the wind could also bring the welcome rattle of approaching wagons. But they heard nothing. Wearily they resumed their journey, as the first twinkling stars became distant points of silver in the purple vastness of the heavens.

The six wagons rumbled to a halt, and the sweating mules stood there in harness, too exhausted to move. Their sweating hides trembled. Port Guthrie got down from the wagon box, his eyes on the western sky. There would be only a few more minutes of daylight. Mac Tunstall reined up his tired horse and dismounted.

"Mac, the teams can't go on. They're ready to drop. We got to have water."

"We'll stay here for the night," Mac said. "Have the men unhitch the teams and turn them out to graze. There'll be a little dew, maybe, and that'll help some."

Mac released Buck's horse, which had trailed Guthrie's wagon on a lead rope. There was but one choice, and that was to spare the mules until Red and Buck returned with the water. Trinity, Hattie, Rachel, and Elizabeth climbed down from the wagon boxes, and it was Trinity who spoke.

"Mac, since there's no water, should we try to cook supper?"

"No," said Mac. "I reckon we're all so dry, we'd choke. Let's wait a while. Maybe Red and Buck will make it."

Nobody said anything, but strong on their minds was the possibility that their companions had met with foul play and lay dead on the barren plains somewhere short of the Cimarron. Darkness had settled over the land, and the only sound was the crunch-crunch-crunch of the mules and horses cropping grass. There was no conversation, for as long as they didn't speak their fears aloud, there was always hope that they wouldn't become cold, hard reality. Suddenly one of the horses nickered, and even against the northwesterly wind, there was a distant answer.

"It's them!" Hattie said, in a reverent whisper.

"Maybe," said Mac, seizing his Winchester.

Haze was quick to follow his example, as were Port Guthrie and the other teamsters. But they relaxed when they heard the rumble of the approaching wagon.

"Listen," Buck cried, reining up the teams. "I can't see a damned thing, but my horse nickered and another answered. That's got to be them."

"I don't hear any wagons," said Red.

"The teams likely gave out," Buck replied, "and they had to stop for the night. Ride on ahead of me, and hail the camp."

"Hello the camp," Red cried. "This is Red and Buck comin' in."

"Come on," Mac answered.

Red dismounted, staggering with weariness. Buck almost fell off the wagon box.

"The water's there," said Red, "but you'll have to unload it. We're about used up."

"We'll take care of it," Port Guthrie said.

"Do we risk a supper fire?" Haze asked.

"Yes," said Mac, "whatever the risk. Port, while the rest of us get supper under way, you and your men spread a couple of kegs of water among the mules."

"Don't forget our horses," Haze said.

"We'll water them along with the mules," said Guthrie.

Supper was prepared quickly and the fire doused.

"Red, you and Buck will take the last watch," Mac said. "You've had a hard ride, and it'll allow you a little more rest."

The wagons took the trail shortly after first light. There was a light wind from the northwest, and Mac Tunstall didn't like the feel of it. He slowed his horse, waiting until the lead wagon caught up to him. Port Guthrie looked at him questioningly.

"Port," said Mac, "you're more familiar with these plains than I am, but I feel a shift comin', a change in the weather. What do you think?"

"It's near October," Guthrie said. "and there's been snow in Colorado and Montana for more'n a month. We're overdue for it to come skalleyhootin' out of the mountains and across the plains. Might start as rain, but it'll change to snow. We got to reach the river and find us some shelter. Some shelter and some wood."

It was what Mac expected and feared. When they paused to rest the teams, he asked them all to gather around.

"We'll stop before dark, cook supper and eat, then push on," said Mac. "There'll be a change in the weather soon, with snow blowin' in from the mountains. We must get to the river, where there's shelter and plenty of wood. Buck, you and Red took a wagon to the river after dark. With six wagons, loaded heavy, how far can we safely travel in darkness?"

"About as far as the teams can hold out," Red replied.

"He's right," said Buck. "We could likely travel all night, but with these wagons full to the bows, we'd have to lay over tomorrow, just to rest the teams."

"Port," Mac said, "how do you feel?"

"We might push 'em an extra four or five miles," said Guthrie, "but Buck and Red is right. The harder you push the teams tonight, the less you can expect of 'em tomorrow."

"Then we'll only drive them two hours past sundown," Mac replied. "It's still going to take the better part of two days."

After supper, the teams were watered. There was no moon, and the extra two hours in darkness gained them little. Again, while Mac was on watch, Trinity McCoy joined him for a while. This time, she was careful to warn him of her approach.

"There's been lightning far to the west," she said. "What does that mean?"

"Rain, beyond the mountains," said Mac. "By the time it reaches us—if it does—I'm lookin' for snow."

"How soon?"

"Likely by tomorrow night," Mac replied.

"I can understand us finding more wood near the river, but what about shelter?"

"Sometimes," said Mac, "if the water's not too high, there'll be an overhang beneath a riverbank. On the plains, it's worth a lot just to have a windbreak. Even if we're unable to find an overhang along the river, there'll be some undergrowth. Maybe a thicket or a stand of trees. It's goin' to be almighty uncomfortable if we can't get somethin' between us and the wind."

"The more I learn about the West," Trinity said, "the more foolish I feel about the four of us coming here to face these dangers alone."

"Nothing to feel foolish about," said Mac. "You must come to terms with this country if you aim to understand it, and you understand it by learning its habits, good and bad. I take that as a favorable sign, you wanting to learn."

"I do want to learn," Trinity said, "and so do Hattie, Rachel, and Elizabeth. If we've been told the truth by the army—if our journey west is fruitless—we want to stay here. Is there a place for women on the frontier, besides—''

''Whorehouses and saloons?''

''Yes,'' she said.

''A few,'' said Mac. ''As the West becomes more settled, there'll be a need for nurses, teachers—''

''And for those of us not so inclined?''

''Wives,'' Mac said. ''Women are scarce on the frontier. A good woman is practically worth her weight in gold.''

She laughed softly, with just a hint of bitterness. When she finally spoke, her voice was soft.

''I came west looking for a man whose hero was George Armstrong Custer, a seeker of glory on the field of battle. A man who, I am told, lies dead at the hand of hostile Indians. My future—if I have one—lies with the possibility of my becoming the wife of yet another man as unpromising and as unfortunate as the first.''

''The long shots are always the ones that pay,'' Mac replied. ''If you want a life without risk and a man who's home every night, then why in tarnation are you planning to stay on the frontier?''

''Oh, I don't know,'' she said, exasperated. ''I could have remained in Indiana, married again, and been secure, I suppose. I could be cooking, scrubbing, and having children until I'm old and used up, with nothing to look forward to except the grave. For those of us who fear living, it's the security for which we've labored all our lives.''

''But you didn't remain in Indiana,'' said Mac, ''and you don't fear living. If you did, you wouldn't be here. You and your three friends have had a taste of security, and that's been enough. You've learned what many a man or woman never learns. A comfortable rut and a grave are very much alike. The only real difference is the dimensions.''

''I've never thought of it that way,'' she replied, ''and I can't deny that it makes a lot of sense. But it still gets back to the inescapable fact that a woman on the frontier is as much a drudge as ever, dependent on a man.''

"Not necessarily," said Mac. "Once, when I was in New Orleans, my nose led me to a little shop operated by a pair of ladies old enough to have been my grandmother. They had freshly baked cakes, pies, bread, sandwiches, and coffee. They had a few tables with benches and chairs, and I never seen so many hungry men in my life. I had to stand to eat my pie and drink my coffee. I don't see why a little bake shop like that couldn't work just as well or better in any Western town. Dodge City, for instance."

"But Dodge City has restaurants."

"So does New Orleans," Mac said, "but they never have fresh-baked goods like that little shop on the corner."

"It's something to consider," said Trinity, "and thank you for telling me. But we have questions that need answers, before we begin looking for a new direction for our lives."

Their conversation ended on a melancholy note, and when she departed, Mac hated to see her go. She was an attractive woman, and he found himself thinking of her more and more often.

"Tunstall," he said under his breath, "you are a damned fool."

"I reckon we can forget about the rain and jump right into worryin' about snow," said Port Guthrie, as the men hunkered around the breakfast fire. "I never seen wind this cold that didn't have sleet and snow pretty close on its heels."

The wind from the northwest whipped the fire into a frenzy of smoke and sparks, and looming closer on the western horizon were banks of dirty gray clouds.

"We ain't got enough wood fer another good cook fire," said Lafe Beard, "unless the other wagons has some. My wagon's possum belly is plumb empty."*

The rest of the teamsters nodded their heads in gloomy

*A possum belly was a cowhide stretched beneath a wagon, for storing firewood.

assent, and as every man of them knew, when a blue norther swept across the plains, there was need for considerably more than a cook fire.

"Hitch up the teams," Mac said. "Our only hope is to reach the river, and even then, we'll need some time to find shelter and gather wood."

But time and their luck ran out. The ominous clouds drifted ever closer, pushing before an increasingly chill wind, and before the sun was noon-high, it was swallowed up in a roiling gray mass of clouds. Sleet rattled off wagon canvas like buckshot, and the only thing favoring them was the wind at their backs. The mules needed no urging, voluntarily picking up their gait, while braying their discomfort. Mac waved his hat, beckoning Buck, Haze, and Red to him. He had to shout to be heard above the rising wind.

"Red, come with me. We'll ride on to the river and begin looking for shelter and firewood. Haze, you and Buck tell the others where we're going, and keep them moving."

Even as Mac and Red rode away at a gallop, snow began mixing with the sleet. Their situation was worsening by the minute.

"Ain't more than two more miles," Red shouted, veering his horse to the left.

"I hope you're right," Mac shouted in reply, "but how can you be sure?"

"We just circled a buffalo wallow," Red answered. "Buck and me run into it on the way to the river, in the dark."

Mac understood. It was a huge depression in the earth, often thirty feet and more across. It could prove dangerous if a heavily loaded wagon lurched into it unexpectedly. Mac could only hope that Buck would remember, and would guide the wagons around it.

"There's the river," Red shouted.

Mac allowed Red to take the lead, and he sought the low bank where he and Buck had filled the water kegs. He rode down to the water, Mac following. As they followed the river westward, the banks gradually became steeper, until they were out of the wind, with its sleet and snow.

"Not enough overhang," said Mac, "even if we could get the wagons down here. We'll have to ride back the other way."

They followed the Cimarron eastward for as long as they dared, without finding overhang suitable for a camp.

"We'd best give up on the river," Red said, "and look for somethin' beyond. Maybe a stand of pine, or an arroyo."

"No sense in that," said Mac, "until we find a place shallow enough, with the banks low enough to cross the wagons."

"Well, hell," Red growled, "unless we push on to Fort Elliott, in north Texas, we got no choice but to find shelter here."

"Fort Elliott's out of the question," said Mac. "It's a good thirty miles ahead, somewhere to the southwest. Yeager figured the most direct route from Dodge, and that takes us through western Indian Territory."

"Damned considerate of him," Red replied, "since there's owl hoots holed up in there with looting and killing on their minds."

"You're right about one thing," said Mac. "Yeager was considerate. While there may be some danger from outlaws, there's some cover, too. If nothing else, we must find a stand of trees thick enough to offer some protection from that norther."

"I'll buy that," Red replied. "Where there's trees, there'll be some fallen ones we can use for wood."

Eventually Mac and Red found the river crossing they were seeking. The river flowed over rock, and the sandy banks had eroded and caved in.

"We won't find any better than this," said Mac. "Now let's find some shelter."

They rode across the Cimarron, following it eastward until it dipped sharply toward the south. The undergrowth became more dense, and beyond the riverbank, a stand of pines had grown to a substantial height.

"Not bad," Red suggested.

"No," said Mac, "except that where trees are dense enough to offer shelter, there's no way to get the wagons into them. Let's ride on a ways and see if there's a break where we can get the wagons through."

The south bank of the Cimarron was clear enough for the wagons and teams, and they would have little choice except to follow the river until there was a break in the trees. But their desperate search yielded something better. They came up on a canyon that angled off to the south, obviously a runoff from the Cimarron in times of high water. Reining up on the rim, they sought a way down.

"It's an answer to a prayer," said Mac, "if we can find a way to get the wagons down there. Let's follow it a ways. It'll have to shallow down."

The arroyo's rims soon began to slope as they followed it away from the Cimarron. A stream meandered down the sandy bed of the arroyo.

"Not much of a runoff," Red observed, "but it'll do. There's still some trees in the way of us gettin' the wagons down here."

"Hiram Yeager didn't overlook anything," said Mac. "In every wagon there's an axe. We'll ride back for a pair of them, and clear some of the trees off this arroyo rim."

When they rode out of the protection of the trees and crossed the river, the storm struck them with all its fury. They faced the storm-bred wind with their hats pulled low, yearning for their coats which were stashed in one of the wagons. By the time they met the lead wagon, Mac had to shout to be heard above the wind. All the wagons drew up abreast of one another.

"An arroyo leads off to the south of the Cimarron," Mac shouted. "Maybe three more miles. Follow the river east to the first shallows. Cross there, keeping to the south bank until you reach the arroyo. Follow it south. We're goin' to fell a few trees to make way for the wagons."

Two of the teamsters reached under their wagon boxes and brought out axes, which they passed to Mac and Red. Wheeling their horses, they again rode south toward the Cimarron. Behind them, they could hear the rattle of the wagons and the shouts of the teamsters, as they pushed on with renewed hope. So heavily had the snow begun to fall, Mac and Red could no longer see their tracks that had led back to meet the wagons. Their horses increased their gait to a slow gallop, the driving wind and snow at their backs being all the motivation they needed to seek the shelter that lay ahead. Mac and Red crossed the Cimarron, rode to the arroyo's rim and dismounted. They looped the reins of their horses to low-hanging limbs, so the animals wouldn't stray. Then each man attacked one of the trees that stood in the way of the wagons. Fortunately, the trees hadn't reached their full growth, and Mac and Red had the way clear almost to the shallow end of the arroyo by the time the wagons crossed the Cimarron. There were shouts from the teamsters as the wagons rattled along the arroyo's rim. When the wagons could go no farther, Buck and Haze seized axes and attacked the remaining trees. When the way was clear, the teamsters guided the wagons to the arroyo's low end, toward the protection of the high rims. The last wagon to enter was driven by Trinity McCoy.

"Come on," Mac shouted to his three companions.

Red, Haze, and Buck needed no urging. The four of them rode in among the pines in search of windblown or lightning-struck trees. They must have wood to see them through the storm. Providence was with them, as they quickly found a multitude of fallen trees, a few of which had rotted away to leave hearts of resinous pine. With their lariats they began dragging the dead wood into the arroyo. The wagons had been drawn in close to the banks and the teams unhitched. Port Guthrie and his teamsters seized axes and began cutting the logs into firewood lengths, and splitting the resinous pine into splinters. The four Texans immediately rode out for more wood. When they returned, there were two roaring fires, and the women were filling the coffeepots with water. For almost two hours, the four riders worked frantically, snaking wood into the arroyo. When they finally dismounted and unsaddled their weary horses, they were half-frozen. Gratefully they accepted tin cups of scalding black coffee, and gathered around the fires. The high rim of the arroyo effectively shut out the howling wind and swirling snow.

"Thank God you found this arroyo," Port Guthrie said. "It'll save our bacon. I've seen these northers blow for three days and nights."

Mac's eyes met those of Trinity McCoy. She said nothing, but Mac believed her mind was strong on what she had told him of her increasing awareness of the dangers on the Western frontier. Despite the independent spirit and determination of the four women, their lives would have been in real peril had they faced the raging storm on their own. Darkness seemed to fall early, and after supper there was little to do except keep the fires burning.

"Normal watch tonight," said Mac. "The two of you on watch will keep the fires going and the coffee hot."

The storm became more intense and the temperature continued to drop. The horses and mules gathered as close to the fires as they could. Red and Buck took over the watch at midnight. The wagons were strung out along the arroyo as near the west rim as they could be driven. Red stood watch near the head of the arroyo, while Buck remained at the lower end. They met occasionally, replenishing the wood when the fires burned low, filling their tin cups from the two-gallon coffeepot that hung over the fire. While Red poured his coffee, Hattie Sutton approached the fire with her own cup. She spoke.

"I'm tired of lying there listening to the wind. May I get some coffee and join you for a while?"

"Come on," Red replied.

They sat down on a wagon tongue, their backs to the arroyo wall.

"This is unlike anything I ever expected," said Hattie. "The four of us have been talking, and we've begun to realize the truth of what Mr. Tunstall said, before we left Dodge. The frontier is no place for a woman alone. God knows what would have become of us, if we hadn't been with your outfit.''

''Well,'' Red replied, ''for your sakes, I'm glad you've come to understand the dangers facing you. I reckon it's none of my business, but I can't help wonderin' what the four of you will do, if you find the army's been telling you the truth.''

''Before we left Dodge,'' said Hattie, ''I'd have been the first to agree that our future is none of your business.''

''But you've changed your mind,'' Red guessed. ''Why?''

''Because Trinity changed hers,'' said Hattie, ''and she talked to the rest of us. It was Trinity's idea that we come west, and we've . . . well . . . followed her lead. We were all angry at first, when Mr. Tunstall refused to let us travel with you. We believed he was being unfair to us because we were women. But then, when there was no water, when you and Buck had to travel ahead to the river, we began to see . . .''

''I reckon the storm helped,'' Red said.

''It did,'' said Hattie. ''If we had been caught on the plains, we wouldn't have known what to do. As it was, when we reached this shelter, we were half-frozen. Alone, we could have died out there. No, Mr. McLean, when you wonder what's to become of us here on the frontier, we take your concern as a kindness, and I can't tell you how indebted we are to all of you.''

''One thing you can do for me,'' Red replied, ''is to stop referrin' to me as mister. I'm just plain Red, to friend and foe.''

Hattie laughed. ''Red it is, if you'll call me Hattie.''

''It's a deal, Hattie. Now, since you ain't told me to mind my own business, what *will* you do, if it turns out the army's telling you the truth?''

''Trinity says you—all of you—care what happens to us. Do you?''

"I care," Red replied, "and I reckon the others do, too. Mac Tunstall's tough as whang leather, and he talked hard to all of you, but that's because he feared what might happen to you."

"We understand that now," said Hattie, "and to answer your question, I have no idea what I—or any of us—will do if we confirm what the military has already told us. I'll try to start a new life, I suppose."

"If it comes to that," Red said, "will you consider somethin' . . . I have to say?"

"I will," said Hattie. "I truly will."

CHAPTER 4

❧

The Cimarron River, Indian Territory.
September 30, 1873.

*A*fter two days and nights, the storm blew itself out, but because of the depth of the snow, movement was impossible. The wind howled across the plains, and the temperature dropped even more. Keeping the fires going required enormous amounts of wood, making it necessary for Mac and his three companions to fight their way through drifted snow to still-standing dead pines.

"Some of us can mount mules and help you," Port Guthrie suggested.

"No," said Mac. "I want all of you to remain here and guard the camp."

"This weather ain't fit fer man nor beast," Gourd Snively said. "Won't be nobody out to bother us."

"Maybe not," said Mac, "but the six of you are responsible for those wagons, and I'll feel better if you're right here with your Winchesters."

Accustomed to cattle drives, to withstanding the worst the elements had to offer, the four Texans had heavy mackinaw coats and wool-lined leather gloves. Thonging down their hats against the fury of the wind, they rode down to the shallow end of the arroyo. Their horses fought the drifted snow, eventually reaching the thick stand of pines, where the tall trees had blunted the storm's fury. While the snow had drifted, it wasn't as deep, allowing the horses to move more freely. There were many standing dead pines whose bark had peeled off, leaving them gaunt and naked among their more fortunate companions. Quickly the Texans dismounted, and swinging their axes, felled a number of the dead pines. The wind tugged at their hats, blew its frigid breath beneath their coats, and numbed their hands and feet. Each man looped his lariat over the butt end of a fallen tree, dallied the loose end around his saddle horn, and lit out for camp. Within the shelter of the arroyo, they loosed their lariats from the logs and hurried to the fires. The women handed them tin cups of scalding coffee, which they accepted gratefully.

"Maybe three more trips," Mac said. "The trees are down, and it won't take as long out in the cold."

But when they rode out for the fourth time, the snow had started anew. The stand of pines was only a blur in the distance, and the trail they had beaten out was rapidly disappearing. Suddenly Mac's horse nickered and reared, and he fought the reins, trying to calm the animal. When Mac had brought the frightened horse to a trembling standstill, the other horses were equally spooked. In vain the men looked for the cause, but couldn't see more than a few feet in the swirling snow.

"We'll lead 'em the rest of the way," Mac shouted.

Like phantoms, the prairie wolves came out of the swirling snow. Mac drew his Colt and shot one of the brutes, missing another when his horse spooked. His three companions fared no better, as their horses reared and plunged. One of the wolves sank its fangs deep in Red's thigh, and he smashed the beast's skull with the muzzle of his Colt. The vicious attack ended as abruptly as it had begun. Three wolves lay dead, while three more vanished into the blinding swirl of snow. Slowly the trembling horses settled down.

"How bad, Red?" Mac asked.

"Bad enough," said Red. "Anybody else hurt?"

"No," Haze replied. "Buck and me didn't get a scratch."

"Mount up," said Mac. "Let's get back to camp. Red's wound needs attention, and the teamsters need to know of these wolves. The varmints could leap off the arroyo rim onto the mules. We'll have to build another fire and double the watch."

"We thought we heard shots," Port Guthrie said, as the Texans rode in, "but you was downwind from us."

"You did hear shots," said Mac. "Prairie wolves jumped us. We killed three, but three more escaped. One of them chomped down on Red. Port, you and all your men take your Winchesters and get out there among the mules. Keep your eyes on the arroyo rims. Lose just one mule, and we're in trouble. Haze, you and Buck start another fire up yonder near the head of the canyon. Red, get over there near the fire and peel off your Levi's. We'll have to get some disinfectant into that wolf bite, pronto."

"I've had nursing experience," Rachel Price said. "Bring me any medical supplies that you have. Hattie, come help me."

Mac dug around in Port Guthrie's wagon until he found the medicine chest that had become a necessary addition to a freighter's supplies. Rachel had spread a blanket near one of the fires, and had already removed Red's boots and Levi's. Hattie had a pot of water on the fire. Rachel took the medicine chest from Mac, opened it and began sorting through the items within.

"I don't see any bandages," said Mac.

"We won't need them," Rachel replied. "My father was a doctor, and always preached against binding animal bites. They're puncture wounds, and must heal from within, and it's impossible for them to drain properly if bandaged."

"Ma'am," said Mac, "I never stand in the way of somebody that knows more than I do. Go on and patch old Red up."

"Reach me that quart of whiskey," Red said, his eyes on the open medicine chest.

"No," said Rachel. "Not unless you become feverish."

"I'm already feverish," Red complained.

"I don't think so," said Rachel, touching his forehead.

"Damn," Red growled, "no consideration for a wolf-bit man."

Mac laughed, while the women pretended not to have heard him. Hattie brought the pot of boiling water and Rachel cleansed the wound. She then poured whiskey over the puncture wounds.

"Lie there and let the alcohol soak in," said Rachel. "In a while, I'll pour on some more of the whiskey. There may still be infection, but it's all we can do."

Buck and Haze had a third fire going, and the horses and mules needed no urging, for they gathered in as close as they could.

"The varmints are still out there," said Haze, "and they're upwind from us. The wolf smell's ridin' the wind."

"We'll have to keep our eyes on the rims," Mac said. "Let a couple of wolves leap off among these mules, and they'll light out down this arroyo like hell wouldn't have it."

"Yeah," said Buck, "and the damn wolves wouldn't ask for nothin' better. Snow bein' deep as it is, they'd drag them mules down pronto. Come the thaw, we wouldn't find anything but mule bones."

When Mac returned to see about Red, he was asleep, his head on his saddle, a blanket spread over him. Rachel wasn't there, but Hattie was.

"We gave him some laudanum," Hattie said.

"I'm glad he's in good hands," said Mac. "The rest of us will have to look out for the wolves."

There were distant howls during the night, borne on the wind, but the wolves didn't appear. The day dawned cold and gray, with no evidence the snow would let up anytime soon. Hattie Sutton had spent the night at the fire, with Red, but there was no fever.

"All our luck ain't bad," Haze observed. "Old Red could of come down with a raging fever and drunk all the whiskey."

"I wouldn't be crowin' about our good luck just yet," said Port Guthrie. "If this snow was to let up this very minute, we'd be stuck here a week 'fore we could move these damn wagons."

"Maybe longer," Saul Estrella observed. "If it don't warm up, the stuff could just lay there for two or three weeks."

These gloomy possibilities did nothing to raise morale within the camp, and in the late afternoon the wolves began howling again.

"Lord," said Trinity, "I've never heard anything so mournful, so terrifying."

"Stay in between the wagons and the arroyo overhang," Mac cautioned. "It'll likely take all of us to keep them away from the mules and horses."

"We have rifles," said Hattie.

"I'll be able to get up and stand watch," Red said.

"I don't think so," said Mac. "I think you'd better stay off that leg for another day or two. How about it, Rachel?"

"I think so, too," Rachel said. "Hattie can stay with you."

"In that case," said Red, "I'll set here as long as I can. Just hand me my Winchester, and I'll shoot wolves, layin' on my saddle."

Three times during the night, the wolves ventured close enough for the watchful men to see their eyes looking down from the arroyo rims. They fired, but there was no reason to believe their shooting had been accurate. Sometime before dawn, the snow ceased and in the faraway vastness above them, a few stars crept out of hiding, their silvery brilliance exploding into tiny points of light. Nobody had slept much as long as the wolves had been a threat, and during the long nights, Rachel Price and Elizabeth Graves had spent some time getting to know the Texans. Elizabeth had shared coffee with Haze Sanderson, while Rachel had talked at length with Buck Prinz. Buck spoke to Mac about them.

"Them females is talkin' more and more like they believe the army told it straight, and they likely won't find their men alive. If they don't, and they end up at Fort Griffin all alone, what's goin' to become of them?"

"If they show up at Griffin with no men in sight," Mac said, "soldiers will be fighting over them. Are you gettin' ideas?"

"Maybe," said Buck. "If nobody's there to claim Rachel, who's gonna stop me from droppin' my loop on her, if I can?"

"Not me," Mac said, "but you're a fiddle-footed Texan with nothin' but a horse, your saddle, and the hundred dollars you'll have, if we reach Austin alive. That ain't a hell of a lot to offer a woman."

"Hell," said Buck, "you think I don't know that? She'll be gettin' *me*, Buck Prinz."

Mac only grinned at him in a manner that was downright insulting. Buck swore under his breath and silently vowed to begin spending more time with Rachel Price.

The dawn broke clear and cold, with the sky so intensely blue, the eyes ached, just looking at it. The wind had died, and when the sun rose in golden splendor, its warmth came as a welcome surprise.

"I think," said Port Guthrie, "when a little of this snow melts, we'd better drive these mules out on the plains so's they can get at some grass. This twice-a-day ration of grain is ruinin' us."

"We can likely buy more at Fort Worth or Fort Griffin," Emmett Budd said.

"Likely we can," said Guthrie, "if we're willin' to pay for it out of our pockets."

"I reckon you're right," Budd said. "We'd best get them jug-headed varmints to some grass, an' cut back on the grain."

"We'll have to take them back across the river, to the

Kansas plain," said Mac. "Snow will begin meltin' there first. That'll mean splitting our force, some of us staying with the wagons, the rest ridin' herd on the mules."

"With snow drifted so deep we can't move the wagons," Port Guthrie said, "nobody else can move 'em, either."

The women had heard most of the conversation, and Trinity McCoy spoke.

"We have weapons. We can remain with the wagons."

"No," said Mac. "Too dangerous. For this cargo, there are hostile Indians and outlaws who would murder their own mothers."

"The problem with grazin' the mules," Buck said, "is that a dozen Indians flappin' their blankets, or some renegades firin' over their heads, could scatter them mules from hell to breakfast. If we was all out there watchin' the mules, there wouldn't be enough of us to prevent a stampede."

"He's right," said Mac. "It's a risk we'll have to take. If we lose the mules, we'll be as bad off as if we'd lost the wagons. The hostile Indians and outlaws will be as aware of that as we are."

The temperature didn't rise much, but two days of sun made a marked difference in the snow on the plains. The snow hadn't drifted deep, for the incessant wind had swept it away. There was grass enough to reduce the graining of the mules to once a day. Guthrie and his teamsters—each man riding a mule—drove the animals back across the Cimarron to the Kansas plain. Mac and his companions remained with the wagons. It was Trinity who approached Mac with a request.

"None of us have had a bath since Dodge. We'd like to go down the canyon a little way and wash ourselves in the runoff. May we?"

She caught Mac totally off guard. She was actually asking his permission.

"I don't like the idea," Mac said. "With Port and his

men watching over the mules, we must stay close to these wagons. Indians or outlaws could grab you and be gone before we could get to you.''

"Don't think we don't appreciate your concern," said Trinity, "because we do. But we are all in need of a bath, and nobody's bothered us but the wolves.''

"All right," Mac said, "but it's against my better judgment. Take your weapons, and if you see anybody, fire a warning shot and we'll come running.''

They started down the arroyo, and a bend soon lost them to view.

"I'm with you," said Red. "I don't think they ought to be down there alone. How can I keep an eye on 'em, without losin' my status as a gentleman?''

Haze laughed. "I didn't know you was.''

"I reckon I'm as much of one as some other Texas polecats I could name," Red said.

They waited three-quarters of an hour without hearing anything, and without the return of the women. Red finally broke the silence.

"I'm goin' down there and fetch them back to the wagons.''

"Sure," said Buck, "go blunderin' down there and catch 'em all stark naked. That'll do wonders for their feelings toward us.''

"I reckon we'll have to risk that," Mac said. "It's still cold enough to be uncomfortable without something coverin' your backside. They've been down there long enough.''

"They was supposed to fire a shot if anything went wrong," said Haze.

"If anything went wrong," Red added, "maybe they wasn't able to get to a gun. Let's get down there pronto.''

They rounded the bend on the run, and their worst fears became reality. The women were nowhere in sight. Their Winchesters lay with their clothes near the small pool where they had been bathing. In the sand near the water there were tracks of six shod horses.

"My God," said Buck, "renegades got 'em."

"Yeah," Red growled, "and they wasn't even allowed to take their clothes."

"Well, let's go after the varmints," said Haze. "What are we waitin' for?"

"We can't leave the wagons unprotected," Mac reminded them. "Haze, ride over across the river for Port Guthrie and his teamsters. Tell 'em to round up the mules and light a shuck back to the wagons. We have to track these varmints down before dark."

The anxious Texans lost an hour before Guthrie and his men could round up all the mules and return to the arroyo.

"Keep your Winchesters handy," Mac cautioned. "They'll be expecting some of us to follow them, and that'll mean splitting our forces. This could be a means of drawing some of us away, so they can attack the camp."

"We'll be ready with a proper welcome, if they try," said Port Guthrie.

The six renegades had appeared so suddenly, the startled women were speechless. Not a word was spoken as four of the men dismounted. The women were seized, and each was clubbed unconscious with the muzzle of a revolver. Without regard to the cruel horn, each of the women was flung belly-down across a saddle, with one of the renegades mounted behind her. The six horses were kept to a walk until they were a mile downstream. From there they continued at a lope until they reached a distant boxed-end canyon. Two men on watch at the shallow end were armed with Winchesters.

"Hey, Russ," shouted one of the sentries, "send somebody to relieve me. I want me a better look at them females."

"You'd best keep your mind on your business and your eyes on our backtrail," Russ replied. "We'll be havin' company pronto."

The renegades rode on to the blind end of the canyon, to a squat log cabin without windows. The canyon ended at the mouth of a cave, and the cabin extended two-thirds into it. With the canyon overhang above, the stronghold was virtually impregnable except from the front. At the very front of the cabin was a mud-and-stick chimney, and wood smoke curled from it. Another sentry stood on each side of the cabin, with a clear field of fire for three hundred yards. The six riders reined up, dismounted, and the four bearing the women carried their captives inside. A dozen men surged to their feet.

"Sit down, damn it," Russ shouted. "This ain't a party. They're goin' in that last room on the left, at the end of the hall. Any of you that's got gear in there, move it out."

Several of the men hastened to obey, while the rest stared at the four naked women who were regaining consciousness. Flung over the shoulder of the renegade Russ, Trinity seized the man's revolver. But Russ was too quick for her. He flung her to the hard floor flat on her back, and the weapon skittered away from her. Dazed, she tried to sit up, but could not.

"Chug, Wilkerson, Gillis, and Taylor," Russ commanded, "take 'em into that back room and kindle 'em a fire, and no messin' around. Bar the door when you're done, and grab your Winchesters. We got company comin'."

The room was small, with no furnishings. Four bunks had been built against the log walls. There was a thin straw-tick mattress over wide, crisscrossed strips of cowhide. In a fireplace along an outer wall, there were a few live coals. One of the renegades produced a blaze with a few resinous pine splinters, adding larger logs as the pine caught.

Chug laughed. "I reckon they're goin' to need that fire, without clothes."

"Yeah," Taylor agreed. "I wonder how Russ managed that, bringin' 'em back naked as skint coyotes?"

"Hell," said Wilkerson, "I'm wonderin' if we're all goin' to have our way with 'em. I ain't had contact with a woman since we was run out of Wichita."

"You ain't likely to have contact with these, either," Gillis said. "Russ aims to use 'em as hostages so's we can take over them wagons. He ain't the kind to mix business with pleasure."

"Hey," said Chug, "they're wakin' up."

Trinity McCoy glared at them from the bunk where she lay, and there was no fear in her. She was furious.

"Haw, haw," Wilkerson said, "we better git out of here. That one's poison mean, and she's ready to strike."

They left the room, and Trinity heard a heavy bar drop in place.

"Oh, God," Elizabeth cried, "I've never been so mortified. The brutes could at least have brought our clothes."

"Not much point in it," said Trinity. "I'd not complain if all we had to worry us was the humiliation of being dragged in here naked. I think we have bigger problems. After we have been used and abused, I doubt we'll ever leave here alive."

"But they're holding us as hostages," Rachel said. "You heard them. They're expecting Mac, Red, Buck, and Haze to come for us."

"I'm expecting them, too," said Trinity. "I imagine they're on their way. But whatever happens to us, they can't surrender those wagons and their cargo to outlaws. Even if they gave up the wagons to save us, I don't trust this bunch. They could still have their way with us, murder us all, and then attack the men at the camp."

"My God," Hattie said, "we know our men would save us if they could, but there's so many of these outlaws . . ."

"Impossible as it all seems," said Trinity, "those four Texans will get themselves shot down, trying to save us. I don't intend for that to happen. We must do something to even the odds."

"But what?" Rachel cried. "We're naked, locked in, without a weapon."

"Oh, but we *do* have a weapon," said Trinity. "Fire. We're going to give this bunch a choice. They can go out and fight, or have this place burned down on top of them."

"Perhaps on top of us, as well," Rachel said.

"Perhaps," said Trinity, "but is that any worse than being used as whores, only to die later, when they're tired of us?"

"You're right," Rachel sighed. "When do we start?"

Suddenly there was a distant shot.

"That answers your question," said Trinity. "Listen. Perhaps we can hear a little of anything that's said."

They listened, and while they could hear nothing from the Texans, they could hear the outlaw leader as he laid down an ultimatum.

"Ride off and leave them wagons," Russ shouted, "and we'll let the women go. If you don't, we'll have our fun with the girls, and then we'll *take* the wagons. We got three men to your one. You got maybe an hour, until the sun is noon-high."

The two sentries, having fired a warning shot, had withdrawn to the cabin. Mac, Red, Haze, and Buck had reined up just out of rifle range. It was Mac who responded to the outlaw ultimatum.

"Turn the women loose, and then we'll talk."

"Go to hell," Russ shouted. "They're our ace in the hole. You got maybe an hour."

"Damn," Red grunted, "they got an open field of fire, with protection at the flanks and behind. How in thunder do we get to 'em?"

"That open field of fire could be used against them," said Mac, "if we could somehow drive them out of that cabin. I can see at least two chimneys, both showin' smoke. If one of us could get to the cabin roof, we could plug the chimneys and smoke 'em out. Get 'em out in the open, and we can cut 'em down from the canyon rims."

"The rest of you circle around to the rims and get as close to the cabin as you can," Red said. "Usin' a lariat, I'll try to swing down to the roof of the cabin and block one or both chimneys."

"It's our only chance," said Mac.

Inside the cabin, the women were making their own desperate move.

"We'll fire the outside wall first," Trinity said. "Perhaps the fire will eat through it before our time runs out."

"We could pile these straw ticks against the door and burn it down," said Elizabeth.

"We could," Trinity agreed, "but it would almost immediately attract the attention of the outlaws. Starting with this outer wall, we could have an entire side of the cabin afire before they discover it. We must create enough of a distraction to take their minds off us and to force them into the open."

The logs were powder-dry, with resinous knots, but the flames seemed to move painfully slow. Ripping open one of the ticks, the women stuffed straw into cracks where log ends touched the chimney. There the fire took hold more readily, and flames quickly swept toward the shake roof. Partially sheltered by the canyon overhang, the shakes caught, and the flames soon burst through the roof. Burning debris began raining into the room, and the four frightened women stood with their backs to the barred door. While the renegades were unaware of their peril, Mac and his Texas companions were on the canyon rims, and trying desperately to reach the roof of the cabin.

"By God," said Mac, "That'll drive the outlaws out, but before we can deal with them, those women will be fried to a crisp."

"It's got to be the women who started that fire," Haze said. "That part of the roof that's afire may be right over their heads. When it's burned enough of it away . . ."

"Knot a couple of those lariats together," said Red, "and lower me to that roof. I'll take an extra rope with me, and lift them out of there. It'll be up to the rest of you to haul them up here."

"We're fighting against time," Buck said. "That roof's gettin' weaker by the second, and your weight may drop you right on through."

"I'll risk it," said Red.

"So will I," Mac replied.

"No," said Red. "The longest haul is from the roof up here. It'll take all of you at this end of the rope."

"We'll knot this end of the rope to a saddle horn," Haze said.

Quickly, Red looped the end of the rope under his arms, and they lowered him toward the roof of the flaming cabin. Some of the outer wall remained, and Red perched on those logs that hadn't burned. He could see the frightened women, their backs against the door, as flaming shingles rained down from the burning roof. From his precarious perch on the log wall, he could never rescue them in time. They must be lifted directly from where they stood to the canyon rim. Quickly Red knotted the third lariat to the two that extended from the canyon rim. In the loose end, he made a loop that must go under the arms. Such a lift would be painful, and cause rope burns, but there was no other way. The women had seen Red, and lifted their arms in a desperate, silent appeal. There was enough length to the lariat for Red to throw it, and he did. It went over Hattie's head, and she quickly snugged it under her arms. Red waved his hat to his companions above, gritting his teeth as they lifted the girl off her feet. He knew what the rope was doing to her breasts, her back, and shoulders. It seemed a painfully long time until Hattie was safe and the rope was lowered a second time. More of the roof collapsed, flaming fragments raining down on the helpless women below. Trinity was the last to be lifted to freedom, but time had run out.

"Thunderation," one of the outlaws bawled, "the whole damn place is afire."

The lariats were dropped for the last time. Red slipped the loop over his head, under his arms, and snugged it tight. The outlaws slammed the door open to the burned-out room where the women had been imprisoned. Red shot two of them, but a third fired, and a slug flung the Texan off the wall. But his comrades from above had taken up the slack, and Red was lifted to safety.

"My God," cried Hattie, kneeling beside Red, "he's dead."

"Not quite," said Mac, "but he's hard hit. The hell of it is, we can't take him or any of you back to camp, until we discourage those renegades. Sorry about your clothes, but there's blankets in our bedrolls."

"Damn the blankets," Trinity said. "I'm burned in so many places, I couldn't stand for anything to touch me. Get me a gun."

"Take Red's," said Mac.

"All of you have revolvers and rifles," Hattie said, "and you can't use both at the same time. Let us have the one you aren't using, and let's shoot some renegades."

The outlaws had left the burning cabin, rescuing their clothing and saddles, but were perfect targets from the canyon rim. Trinity, Mac, Buck, and Haze fired Winchesters, and Hattie, Rachel, and Elizabeth cut loose with Colts.

CHAPTER 5

✺

*T*he renegades, shaken by the burning of the cabin, were without cover. The range was close enough for revolvers, and the women proved themselves accurate. Besides the two Red had shot, a dozen more of the outlaws were gunned down. While some were only wounded, their wounds were sufficient to take them out of the fight. Those who were able leaped on their horses without saddles and rode for their lives. Wounded comrades were left to shift for themselves.

"We ought to put them that's wounded out of their misery," said Haze.

"Leave 'em lay," Mac said. "There's only three, and if they're shot up so they're not able to ride, they won't survive. We have to get Red back to camp and see to his wound."

"Before we go," said Trinity, "I'd like one of those blankets. My modesty's gone forever, but the wind's cold, and I'm freezing."

"Just old Red's luck," Buck said. "Four beautiful ladies jaybird naked, and he's out of it with a gunshot wound."

"He saw us first," said Trinity, "and I think he was as shocked to see us as we were to see him. He shot two of those men, and I think he could have shot the one who shot him if he hadn't been distracted by us."

"I can't fault him for that," Mac said. "You ladies *are* downright distracting."

"Now that you've all had a good look," said Hattie, through chattering teeth, "can't we get those blankets?"

"Yes," Mac said. "Haze, you and Buck loosen the bed-rolls and get those blankets. Save one for Red, too. I'll see how hard he's been hit."

Mac knelt over his friend and felt for a pulse. It was steady but weak. He breathed a sigh of relief when he opened Red's shirt, for the wound was high up. Serious enough, but the lead hadn't struck anything vital. Hattie, a blanket draped about her and concern in her eyes, knelt beside Mac.

"He was hit high up," Mac said, "so there's likely no internal damage. He'll make it, if we get him back to camp, disinfect the wound, and keep him warm."

"Put him in our wagon," said Hattie. "What he did was magnificent."

"No more magnificent than what you ladies did," Mac replied. "If you hadn't set that place afire, some of us— and maybe some of you—would have been killed. There were too many of them, and they'd have been shooting from cover."

"The fire was Trinity's idea," said Hattie. "The rest of us went along, because we'd have preferred being burned alive to being used by that bunch of brutes."

Haze and Buck led the horses. Trinity, Rachel, and Elizabeth, draped with blankets, followed.

"One of you ladies will have to ride Red's horse," Mac said. "You'll have to set far back in the saddle and hold him in front of you."

"I'll do it," said Hattie.

"I'll help you to mount," Mac said, "and then we'll lay Red across in front of you. It's a poor way for a man to ride, but the only way to keep him on the horse. We'll take it slow, so we don't jounce him around too much."

"It's not easy, wearing a blanket and straddling a

horse," said Hattie, as the troublesome blanket rode up above her thighs.

Quickly the other women were lifted astride the horses and the men mounted behind them. They set out toward camp, riding along the rim of the canyon. The cabin was in ashes, and the few tendrils of smoke were whipped away by the wind. The three renegades lay where they had fallen, unmoving.

"Will those who escaped leave us alone?" Trinity asked.

"Maybe," said Mac, who held her in front of him. "It depends on whether or not we killed the segundo. As far as we know, Red killed two, and those three there in the canyon are done for. Nine of those who rode away were hit. If they're hurt badly enough, and if the leader of the outfit is dead or wounded, we may be able to travel beyond their reach before they're able to regroup. But we can't count on that. We'll have to be damned careful. That means no more wandering away alone, for any reason."

"If we ever take another bath, or even go to the bushes," Hattie said, "one of you—or maybe all of you— will have to go with us."

Buck Prinz laughed. "It'll be our pleasure."

They rode slowly, for the sake of the wounded Red and the women. Mac regarded the four of them with more appreciation than he had at any time since leaving Dodge. They all had their faces, arms, hands, and bodies smudged with soot, and their hair was ragged and matted, tufts of it having been burned away.

"After what we've all been through," said Elizabeth, "I know this is going to sound awfully unwelcome, but we must wash ourselves."

"I reckon you do," Mac agreed. "You can use that same pool where you were before."

"I won't feel safe there," said Hattie. "You're not going to leave us alone?"

"No," Mac replied. "We'll stand watch. As improper as it seems, we can't afford the risk of leaving you alone."

"I don't see anything improper about it," said Trinity, "after what we've all endured. I feel like a plucked chicken, passed through the fire and ready for the dinner table. No man has ever seen me in such a mess, and a week ago I'd have swooned at the very thought of it."

"We all would have," Hattie added. "We're changing, adapting to a much harder life than any of us has ever experienced. Would any of us ever have left Kansas City, had we known we'd be dragged naked into a cabin full of outlaws, and then lifted up the side of a cliff at the end of a rope?"

"I don't mean to sound ungrateful," said Rachel, "but that rope may have scarred me for life in some important places. From the waist up, I'm so sore I can barely breathe."

"Sorry about the rope," Buck said, "but we didn't have any better way. There'll be sulfur salve in the medicine chest for the rope burns, but you'll just have to live with the soreness until it goes away."

They reached the shallow end of their arroyo, reining up near the pool of water that had resulted from the runoff from the Cimarron.

"You ladies go ahead and wash up," said Mac. "Haze and Buck will stay with you until I get back. I'm taking Red on into camp, and I'll leave him in your wagon. I'll have Port Guthrie put on some water to boil, so we can tend to Red's wound."

"Please bring us some salve for the rope burns," said Trinity.

Mac walked Red's horse on into camp. Concerned, Port Guthrie and the teamsters met him, every man armed with a Winchester.

"We was commencin' to worry about you hombres," Guthrie said. "Is Red—"

"No," said Mac. "Wounded, high up. Will one of you hang a pot of water over the fire, so we can tend the wound? We all came out of it alive, but the women are skinned up some. They need some salve from the medicine chest.''

"I've had considerable experience with gunshot wounds,'' Guthrie said. ''You want me to take care of Red?''

"I'd be obliged,'' said Mac. "I'll be back to help you.''

Mac returned to find all the women kneeling in the shallow pool, dousing themselves with water, passing around the soap.

"Here's the salve,'' Mac said, "when you're ready for it.''

"I'm ready now,'' said Trinity. "You can put some on my back. I . . . I suppose I'd best do the . . . front.''

She blushed and Mac laughed. "I reckon you had,'' he said.

The wind had a bite to it, and the washing was done quickly. The women scrambled out of the water, and after salving their rope burns, hurriedly, dressed.

"I'm going to see how Red is,'' said Hattie.

The others weren't far behind. The water was hot, and Guthrie was cleansing Red's wound.

"The slug passed on through,'' Guthrie said, "so it didn't hurt nothin' vital.''

"Maybe not,'' said Red, who was conscious, "but it's dealin' me some misery.''

"I'll give you a slug of laudanum, after I disinfect and bandage the wound,'' Guthrie said. "Tonight will be the worst, and you can sleep through that.''

"I'm so glad you're going to be all right,'' said Hattie, kneeling beside Red. "I'll stay with you tonight.''

"That'll help a powerful lot,'' Red replied. "Did all of us get out of it alive?''

"Yes,'' said Mac, "thanks to you. Besides the two you shot, we plugged a dozen of those renegades, leavin' three more dead.''

"You were magnificent,'' Hattie said. "We owe our lives to you.''

She leaned over and kissed him just in time for Haze and Buck to witness it.

"Damn it," said Buck, "next time, I get to shinny down the rope."

"I wouldn't count on them outlaws just ridin' away and leavin' us alone," Red said.

"That ain't your worry," said Haze. "The rest of us will be watching careful, and if they pay us another visit, we'll be ready for them."

"I think we'll stay here another day or two, until Red begins to heal," Mac said.

"I reckon we'd have to do that, even if Red hadn't been shot," said Guthrie. "Most of the snow's melted, but it'll take two or three days of steady sun before we can move the wagons. Mud's axle-deep."

"We'll be safer here than on the trail," Haze said. "If those outlaws regroup and come after us, we'll still be outgunned. We'll need all the cover we can get."

"Haze, you and Buck come with me," said Mac, "and we'll drag in some more logs for wood."

"In view of this outlaw threat," said Port Guthrie, "do you aim for us to go on takin' the mules to graze?"

"Tomorrow," Mac said. "We'll take them out at first light and bring them back in at noon. We can't crawl in a hole and hide from those damn renegades."

The renegades, shaken by the loss of their cabin and the deaths of their comrades, had reined up a dozen miles east of their old stronghold. Of the original gang, five were left dead or dying at the burned-out cabin, and five more would be dead before another day dawned. Of the remaining twelve, four were wounded, including Russ, the leader.

"Haw, haw," one of the outlaws cackled, "four damn women and four bull-of-the-woods gun-throwers, an' they chased us out like we was yellow dogs."

"Shut up, Irvando," Russ snarled. "We ain't whipped. Even a damned ignorant Indian has sense enough to back off, once his medicine's gone bad. We'll camp here until we've buried our dead and our wounds have healed. Them of you that ain't wounded, gather up some firewood and get some water on to boil.''

"Hell," said Wilkerson, "them wagons will be long gone before we're able to ride. It's you, Chug, Gillis, an' Taylor that's wounded. There's eight of us that's ready, willin' an' able to go after them wagons right now. We can do that while the rest of you are layin' around here doctorin' one another.''

"Damn you, Wilkerson," Russ gritted, "I ought to gut-shoot you. I'm boss of this outfit, and we ride when I say. If you don't like it my way, then *you* ride out alone, and don't come back.''

Wilkerson laughed. ''I'll stay until I'm ready to ride out, and I ain't ready yet.''

For a long moment Russ stood there, the left sleeve of his shirt bloody, his right hand near the butt of his Colt. His hard eyes met those of the remaining ten men, and when he spoke, it was in a savage growl, through gritted teeth.

"If any of the rest of you bastards is feelin' froggy, now's the time to jump. You got two choices. You do what I say, or you saddle up and ride.''

Not a word was spoken. Even Wilkerson looked down at the toes of his boots. Russ relaxed, and when he spoke again, it was in a more genial tone.

"Now gather up some wood and get a fire going. The sooner these wounds are taken care of, the sooner they'll begin to heal. Them wagons won't be movin' out for a couple more days, because of the mud. When they are able to move, they'll be slow. We can ride 'em down on the trail, if we have to.''

The weather had warmed up to the extent that Mac ordered only one fire after dark, large enough to accommodate two coffeepots. There would be hot coffee throughout the night for the men on watch. But there was little sleep for the women, for by sundown, Red had a raging fever which lasted most of the night. The concern of the four women for his comfort was almost comical, and didn't go unnoticed by Red's companions.

"Damn it," said Haze, "I never thought I'd envy a varmint who'd been shot, but I'm purely beginnin' to wish it had been me, instead of Red. Laid up in a wagon with four beautiful females fussin' over him."

"Yeah," Mac said, "and he don't know a thing about it, 'cause he's sweatin' off half a bottle of whiskey and a burnin' fever."

Buck sighed. "That's one of the most unfair things about the frontier. A man don't ever get a bait of whiskey or women until he's too shot up to appreciate either of 'em."

But because of the narrow confines of the wagon, only one of the women at a time was comfortably able to remain with Red. The others divided their time among Mac, Haze, and Buck. After all they had endured together, there was an easy familiarity among them. Despite having spent most of a day with four stark-naked females, the Texans had in no way bully-ragged them or laughed at their expense.

"They've been perfect gentlemen," said Trinity, "and I'm not in the least ashamed of my experience with them."

"Neither am I," Hattie said.

"Nor I," said Rachel and Elizabeth in a single voice.

"You know," Trinity said, now that they were alone, "I've been thinking. We've come all the way west to search for men the army swears are dead, while these Texans are very much alive. Maybe we should take another look at our priorities."

Elizabeth laughed nervously. "Trinity, what a brazen thing to say."

"I think Trinity's right," said Hattie. "I've never been more comfortable or felt more secure with men than with these."

Rachel laughed. "Especially the wounded one, there in the wagon."

"Yes," Hattie said. "Especially Red."

"Does he know that?" Rachel asked.

"Yes," said Hattie proudly, "he knows. He's already asked me if he can talk to me, provided our search doesn't work out."

"And you agreed," Elizabeth said.

"I did," said Hattie, "and after today, I'm ready to say to hell with the search, and go with Red, if he'll have me."

"Hattie," Elizabeth cried, "how shocking."

Rachel laughed. "I don't find it shocking at all. With just a little encouragement, I'd share Buck's blankets tonight."

"My God," said Elizabeth, "this wild, wicked country has taken our very souls. We're behaving like . . . like—"

"Whores," Hattie finished.

"No," said Trinity, "that's not the word. We've found ourselves. We're taking life as it comes, without begging for allowances because we're weak, unpredictable women. Think how easy it would have been, had all of us swooned, throwing ourselves at the mercy of a band of outlaws. But we stood up to them, risked being burned alive, and I believe that it meant something to these four men who rescued us. After today, they might have seen us only as four naked bodies, intended for the pleasure of men, but I'm convinced they did not. We have won their respect, and we won't keep it by rushing to share their blankets."

"You're talking sense," Hattie said. "I . . . I've never been so happy as I was when I saw Red standing on that wall, but I can't . . . throw myself at him. What should we do?"

"Red told you what he expected of you," said Trinity, "and I think that holds true for the rest of us. We'll go on to Fort Griffin and have our confrontation with the army. If we really are free, we won't have to throw ourselves at these men. They'll come to us, and that's as it should be."

"I suppose you're right," Rachel said. "If you're that sure of Mac Tunstall, then I've no reason to be concerned about Buck Prinz."

"Who said anything about me and Mac Tunstall?" Trinity demanded, blushing.

Rachel laughed. "Nobody has to say anything, Mrs. McCoy. It's in your eyes, when you look at him. He'd have to be blind not to see it."

"I didn't know it was that obvious," said Trinity.

In the wagon, Red groaned.

"My God," Hattie whispered, "I hope he hasn't been awake, listening to us."

"Get back in there and find out," said Trinity. "If his fever hasn't broken, he may be in need of more whiskey."

With Red wounded, and only nine men, Mac had divided the night into three four-hour watches. The teamsters, three at a time, would take the first and second watches, while Mac, Haze, and Buck took the last and most critical watch. While Hattie remained with Red, Trinity, Rachel, and Elizabeth dozed, waking occasionally to add wood to the fire and put on a fresh pot of coffee. When the stars said it was two o'clock in the morning, the three teamsters on watch awakened Mac, Buck, and Haze. They were surprised to find Trinity, Rachel, and Elizabeth near the fire, drinking coffee from tin cups.

"What are the three of you doing, still awake?" Mac asked.

"Several reasons," said Trinity. "We're awfully sore, and those blankets awfully thin. That, and I suppose we're still a little nervous about what happened yesterday. We just . . . need someone to talk to . . . besides one another."

"We'll welcome the company," Mac said, "as long as you can stand losing the sleep. I'll be at the north end of the camp, Haze at the south end, while Buck will be here close to the middle, near the fire. It's up to him to keep the fire alive and the coffee fresh and hot."

"I'll stay here and help him," said Rachel.

"Elizabeth," Haze said, "I hope you'll join me at the south end."

"I intend to," said Elizabeth. "Trinity would pull out

what's left of my singed hair, if I stayed with her and Mac.''

''I might do it anyway,'' Trinity said, trying to sound as angry as possible.

Mac laughed, took his tin cup of coffee, and started toward the north end of the camp. Trinity followed, aware that Haze and Elizabeth were laughing at what Elizabeth had said. Trinity sighed. What did it matter? If Mac Tunstall was so thick-headed that he still wasn't aware of her interest in him . . .

''We'll perch here on the wagon tongue,'' Mac said. ''Beats hunkerin' on the ground, and four hours is a long time to stand.''

''Sitting or standing, I feel like I've taken a beating,'' said Trinity, ''but lying down is the worst of all.''

''I'm sorry we didn't have time to rig somethin' a little more gentle than a cowboy's lariat,'' Mac said, ''but after you set that cabin afire, we didn't have much time.''

''We realized that,'' said Trinity, ''and we're just thankful to have gotten out of there alive. I just feel like my . . . my bosom is higher up than it's ever been.''

She laughed nervously, and Mac laughed with her, enjoying her frankness.

''It all looked pretty much in the right place and holdin' its own,'' Mac replied.

''I was afraid . . . after that . . . none of us would be able to look any of you in the eye,'' said Trinity, ''but you were all so nice. We looked so terrible, blackened with soot, and so much of our hair singed and burned, you could have laughed at us.''

''All of you are ladies to us,'' Mac replied, ''and if nothing else, we'd have admired you for the courageous thing you did. I've considered you a beautiful woman from the first day I laid eyes on you, and you'll never be more beautiful than the moment you were lifted out of that burning cabin.''

She was silent for so long, he feared he had offended her. When she tried to speak, her voice broke, ending in a sob. She dropped her tin cup, threw her arms around Mac, and he could feel her tears soaking the front of his shirt. His heart pounded like a nine-pound hammer on a blacksmith's anvil, and he didn't care that her hair still smelled of wood smoke from the burned-out cabin. When her tears ceased and she tried to draw away, he wouldn't allow it. He tilted her chin, kissing her long and hard. She didn't fight him, but responded with a fervor of which he had only dreamed. When they finally parted, they were gasping for breath.

"Oh, God," she said, "you no sooner called me a lady than I behaved like . . . like a . . . fallen woman, a whore."

"No," said Mac. "Get that out of your head. You're real, Trinity McCoy, and I never, ever had such an experience in my life. Only one thing bothers me. You know as well as I that this is more than just a one-time thing. If I can't follow it to the end, I need to know . . . before I decide I can't live without it."

She leaned toward him, taking his face in her hands, and when she spoke, it was only a whisper.

"I want you to follow it to the end, but I feel compelled to travel on to Fort Griffin, to receive that final word from the army. The others—Hattie, Rachel, and Elizabeth—are wanting to accept the army's decision, but it was I who convinced them we must take it to its conclusion. But I'm weak, and I don't have the strength of my own convictions. I tried to be strong, to encourage the others, but there was nobody to encourage me. I needed to hear the words you said, to shed the tears that had backed up in me since we were taken by those outlaws. It's difficult for a woman to comfort another woman, and I believe Elizabeth, Hattie, and Rachel feel the same way. I asked them to hold back their feelings until after . . . Fort Griffin, and . . . I couldn't hold back my own. I feel like I'm being unfair to you, like I've cheated you, but God help me, I didn't mean to. I want you to take me, body and soul, but I . . . I can't turn loose until I know . . . I'm free. Until after . . . Fort Griffin . . ."

The words had been torn from her heart, and Mac held her close as she wept. Only when there was but an occasional sniffle did he bring her tear-streaked face near his own.

"I'll respect your wishes," he said, "but until we reach Fort Griffin—whatever should happen there—don't hide from me. Talk to me, allow me to stand beside you in any way that I can. Am I being selfish when I say that if I can't have all of you, that I still want the little that you feel comfortable sharing with me in the time that remains?"

"No," she said. "Oh, no. I want that, and oh, so much more than that. My fear is . . . that things may turn out all wrong at Fort Griffin, and I . . . we . . . your rainbow will die. If it does, part of me will die with it."

Mac said nothing, and while he trusted the army's decision, he was still plagued by a lingering doubt that couldn't be resolved until they reached Fort Griffin.

Rachel Price had driven from her conscious mind all that might take place when they reached Fort Griffin. She knew Buck was interested in her, and she wasted no time fanning the flames.

"I was positively mortified," Rachel said, "having you see all of us naked, but there didn't seem to be any help for it. What did you think?"

"Well, I, uh," Buck stammered, choosing his words carefully, "I didn't pay all that much attention to the others. My eyes were on you."

"What do you think of me?" she asked, enjoying the moment.

"Before or after I—"

"Before you saw me naked, and afterward." she said.

Buck realized she was enjoying his discomfiture, and seizing her by the shoulders, he kissed her long and hard. She started to say something, and he repeated his performance. Only then did he speak.

"Damn it, Rachel, the first time I saw you, clothes and all, I thought you was near the prettiest girl I'd ever seen. I ain't what people call handsome, and I purely didn't know what to say to you, to have you know that I care for you. Now I know that you like me, I can't stop thinkin' about you goin' to Fort Griffin, and why you're goin'. Suppose, when you get there, you learn the army was wrong? Am I goin' to have to give you up, with nothin' to remember except a few kisses and seein' you jaybird naked?"

"I want to forget all about Fort Griffin," said Rachel, "and so do Hattie and Elizabeth, but Trinity won't let us."

"I wish you could," Buck said, "but I can understand Trinity's thinking."

"Oh, I understand her thinking," said Rachel, "but I don't agree with it. Would it be a shock, if I told you that you're ten times the man Virgil Price ever was?"

"Yes," Buck said, "if you're sayin' that, it is a shock. Whatever kind of bastard he was, you took him for better or worse, didn't you?"

"I had to say that," said Rachel, "but I didn't mean it. Daddy caught us up in the hayloft and, using a shotgun, persuaded Virgil to marry me. Two weeks later, he joined the army, and I haven't seen him since. Even if he's alive, damn him, I'll divorce him."

"But you . . . didn't he . . . ?"

"He never laid a hand on me, before or after I married him," Rachel said. "I'm in no way used goods, if that's what you mean."

"Damn it," said Buck, "that wouldn't make any difference, as long as you ain't tied to him legal. If you'd take me for what I am—just a Texas cowboy—then I'd take you with no questions asked."

"Then let's do it Trinity's way," Rachel said. "We'll go on to Fort Griffin, and I'll be sure I'm free. Then if you still want me, we'll go from there."

"I'll still want you," said Buck.

"Then let's don't worry about Fort Griffin until we have to," she said.

She came to him then, and Buck Prinz selfishly hoped that nothing would take place at Fort Griffin to rob him of the girl in his arms and the dream in his heart . . .

CHAPTER 6

*A*n hour before first light, Red's fever broke, and Hattie slept until breakfast. There wasn't a cloud in the sky, and for early October, the sun was hot. Armed with their Winchesters, Port Guthrie and his men again drove the mules out to graze. Before the sun was an hour high, Red was awake. He had a towering hangover and a thirst to match. Hattie filled a tin cup with water five times before he was satisfied.

"That's why I've never been a drinking man," said Red. "The damn stuff tastes like an almighty awful medicine, and the goin' up ain't never been worth the comin' down."

Hattie laughed. "A strong man never needs strong drink. Besides the hangover, how do you feel?"

"Like somebody's been beatin' me with a singletree. But I reckon no worse than you're feelin' after being hoisted out of that burning cabin with a rope cuttin' you in half."

"I'm awfully sore," Hattie said, "and I'll have to agree with Trinity. She claims her bosom is higher up than it was, and I believe mine is, too."

Red laughed at her frankness, enjoying the easy familiarity that had blossomed between them. Without being asked, she brought him a tin cup of steaming coffee.

"Hattie," said Red, as she knelt beside him, "you're

the kind of woman a man dreams about. Why couldn't I have found you before you was roped and branded?"

It was Hattie's turn to laugh. "I was roped yesterday, and I was stripped down to the hide. Did you see any brand?"

"Come to think of it, I didn't," Red replied, "but I was busy shootin' outlaws. I only got to see the front, since you had your back to the wall. A brand is usually on the left flank. I'll have to examine the flank sometime, I reckon."

"Perhaps that will be part of your reward for saving us," said Hattie, "but here's something you can claim right now."

She kissed him once, twice, three times.

"Lordy," said Red, when he came up for air, "I reckoned I was gonna heal, but now I find out I've died and gone to heaven. That leaves me needin' just one thing."

"What's that?" Hattie asked, holding her breath.

"Grub," said Red. "I'm starved."

"I can take care of that," Hattie said.

When she had gone, Red managed to get up, and was easing himself over the tailgate of the wagon, when Mac spoke.

"You reckon you ain't bein' a mite hasty about gettin' up? I thought Hattie was doin' for you."

"She is," said Red, "but she can't go to the bushes for me. Besides, she's gone after some grub. I'm near starved, and I got to rid myself of that damn whiskey taste."

Mac laughed. "You ungrateful varmint. You drunk all the whiskey we had."

"If them renegades come after us again," said Red, "it'll be your turn to get shot, and then *you* can drink all the whiskey. What happened after they plugged me?"

"We hoisted you up to the canyon rim," Mac replied, "and then we went after those renegades. They seemed to forget about us, and were trying to save their saddles and bedrolls from the burning cabin. We caught 'em in the open and killed three more that we know of, and wounded probably a dozen others.''

''My God,'' said Red, ''that's some shootin', for three hombres. Even Texans.''

''Oh, we had some help,'' Mac said. ''Those four naked females begged the use of our Colts, and they're better shots than you'd think. I don't know if any of their shooting was fatal, but they accounted for some of the wounded.''

''Tarnation,'' said Red, ''ain't they somethin'?''

''They're all that, and then some,'' Mac agreed.

There was no laughter in the renegade camp. The five mortally wounded men had died during the night, and only eight of the remaining twelve weren't wounded. It fell to their lot to dig graves and do the cooking. After the burying was done and the men were drinking hot coffee, attitudes improved a little. Bilbo, one of the renegades who hadn't been hurt, had a suggestion.

''Russ, I can't abide just settin' here doin' nothin', while some of you hombres nurse a few bullet holes. I been thinkin'.''

''Don't do too much thinkin', Bilbo,'' said Russ sourly. ''You ain't equipped for it.''

''Was I you, Bilbo,'' Wilkerson said, ''I wouldn't get too snotty with them that's been wounded. The time may come when you got some bullet holes in you that need healin'.''

''I been thinkin' we ought to do something,'' said Bilbo, as though he hadn't heard the criticism. ''Why can't some of us ride over to that wagon camp, throw some lead in there, an' stampede them mules to hell an' gone?''

''Bilbo,'' Russ said wearily, ''use your damn head for somethin' besides holdin' your ears apart. When we finally take them wagons, how do you reckon to move that cargo? In your saddlebags? We'll need them mules, and they won't be no good to us, scattered all over Indian Territory.''

Some of the men laughed, and Bilbo's hand dropped to the butt of his Colt.

"Go ahead," Russ growled. "There's plenty of room for another grave."

The leader of the bunch was on his feet, his left arm bandaged, but his right wasn't injured, and his hand was near the butt of his own weapon. Bilbo dropped his hand to his side, away from his Colt.

"We'll ride when I say," said Russ, his hard eyes on Bilbo. "Them of us that's been wounded gets time to heal. Any of the rest of you that ain't satisfied with that, you got to answer to me."

"You're the boss, Russ, and I ain't leadin' up to gun play, but sometimes you do all the wrong things," McCarty said.

"I reckon you aim to point some of 'em out," said Russ.

"Just one particular thing that rankles my hide," McCarty replied. "When you drug in them four naked females, why didn't you let us have our way with 'em? When we was done with 'em, they sure as hell wouldn't of had the ambition to set our cabin afire."

"I done what I thought was best, McCarty," said Russ. "I ain't always right, but I can see farther than pleasurin' myself with the first available female. Now back off. I ain't in a mood for any more damn complaints."

The Cimarron River, Indian Territory. October 5, 1873.

"I reckon the sun's sucked up enough water," Port Guthrie allowed. "Mud shouldn't be a problem. I figure the wagons can take the trail anytime."

"We'll move out in the morning at first light," said Mac. "Red, how do you feel?"

"I could say I ain't doin' well," Red replied, "and that I need to lay here at least for another week, with Hattie fussin' over me. But you wouldn't believe that, would you?"

"No," said Mac, "I wouldn't. I think she's been feeding you about six times a day. If we leave tomorrow, we may run out of grub before we reach Austin."

"That's not fair," Hattie protested. "I've been feeding him from our supplies."

"Then *you* may run out of grub before we reach Austin," said Mac.

"You're forgetting something," Hattie said. "We're only going as far as Fort Griffin."

"I haven't forgotten," said Mac.

Nobody said anything. All eyes were on Mac Tunstall, and he just walked away.

When the wagons again took the trail, the event didn't go unnoticed. Russ had sent Stewart and Pryor to observe and report any movement.

"I reckon Russ will have to do somethin' besides set on his hunkers," Stewart said, as they watched the wagons turn south and disappear in the distance.

"Yeah," said Pryor. "Let's mosey on back and break the news."

"We'll follow 'em a ways," Russ said, when Stewart and Pryor had reported. "They'll likely be expecting a visit from us. We won't make our move until they've decided we ain't comin' after 'em. They'll reach the North Canadian today and the Canadian tomorrow. We'll strike near dawn, before they leave the Canadian."

Mac scouted half a dozen miles ahead without seeing any living thing. He had no idea how far they were from the North Canadian River. He rode on, knowing he must decide whether or not they could reach the river before dark. The level Kansas plain had been somewhat predictable, while the terrain of Indian Territory was constantly changing. He had no illusions about continuing after dark, for there were obstacles that would be hazardous and unavoidable. There were stone-studded hills and sudden drop-offs that could snap an axle or splinter a wheel, either of which could cost them a day far from water and decent graze. Mac rode on, with a growing awareness that they weren't going to reach the North Canadian before dark. The distance was too great for the heavily loaded wagons. He reached the river, and by his estimation, he had ridden fifteen miles or more. He watered his horse and began the ride back to meet the wagons. What he must report to them—*dry camp*—were two of the most dreaded words on the Western frontier. However, he had the satisfaction of knowing they were prepared. Amid some grumbling, he had seen to it that each of the two water kegs aboard each of the wagons had been filled before leaving the Cimarron. There would be water for the horses and mules and water for cooking, until they reached the North Canadian, sometime the following day. However, he soon found that things hadn't gone well in his absence. When he came within sight of the wagons, his first thought was that they had stopped to rest the teams. But drawing closer, he could see that wasn't the case. They were all gathered around Gourd Snively's wagon, and not for conversation. The rear of the wagon box sagged precariously close to the ground, for the left rear wheel was missing. The hub was there, but the wooden spokes and shattered rim lay on the ground. A huge stone had split it in half. Mac reined up, and Snively spoke, almost apologetically.

"When she rolled across the rock, it split. The wheel dropped. Wasn't no help for it."

"I can see that," Mac said, "but why is nobody working to replace it?"

"It ain't happened more'n ten minutes ago," said Snively. "We'd have to half unload this wagon to git at the spare wheel an' the wagon jack. Port's checkin' the other wagons, thinkin' he might find a wheel an' wagon jack easier to git to."

"We don't have a hell of a lot of time to devote to

changing this wheel," Mac said. "As it is, we're facing a dry camp tonight."

Before Mac could go in search of Guthrie, the teamster returned.

"The damn army ordnance people don't know doodly about loadin' wagons," said Port. "Ever' wagon's loaded the same. Have to move half the load, just gettin' at the jack and the spare wheel."

"Use the extra wheel from our wagon, if it will fit," Trinity suggested.

"We'd be obliged, ma'am," said Guthrie. "Gourd, you and Emmett have a look at it."

"We're a good fifteen miles from the North Canadian," Mac said, "and this busted wheel won't help. We'll be until noon tomorrow, getting there."

Gourd Snively and Emmett Budd returned, bearing a wagon wheel and wagon jack.

"Trinity," said Mac, "when we reach Fort Griffin, we'll unload one of these wagons and return your wheel."

Replacing the wheel required less than an hour, and the wagons moved on. Sundown found them half a dozen miles shy of the North Canadian River.

"We don't have enough wagons for a circle," Mac said, "but we can half-moon them with the arch to the north. If we're attacked, I expect it to come from there. Just one fire, for the sake of hot coffee during the watch."

After supper, that first night after leaving the Cimarron, Mac called the outfit around the fire for a permanent change in sentry duty.

"Starting tonight, Port, I want you and your men to take the first and second watch, three men at a time. Buck, Haze, Red, and me will take the third watch. If there's trouble, I look for it in the small hours."

"So do I," Guthrie said. "The third watch is the most dangerous. If that's how you aim to work it, then we'll keep our Winchesters close, and won't shuck nothin' but our hats."

"I'm obliged," said Mac. "That's how we did it on the

trail drives. While we did have some surprises and a few stampedes, every man had a gun in his hands within seconds of an attack. We always held our own, and gave 'em more hell than they gave us.''

"Bueno," Guthrie replied. "That's how a man lives to the ripe old age of thirty-five on the frontier.''

Despite the revelation that might lie ahead at Fort Griffin, each of the women continued a late-night rendezvous with one of the four Texans. While none of the men spoke of these meetings, they were hardly secret, and whatever Port Guthrie and his teamsters may have thought of the arrangement, they kept it to themselves. Conversation was subdued, and after leaving the security of the arroyo near the Cimarron, each of the women came armed with a Winchester. Mac had chosen a clearing for their camp, allowing them to see in all directions the approach of a potential enemy. He and Trinity sat in the shadow of a wagon, and it was she who spoke.

"Even with just the starlight, nobody could take us by surprise. You're expecting that bunch of renegades to follow us, aren't you?''

"Yes," Mac said. "If they don't, we'll be pleasantly surprised, and if they do, we'll be ready. Besides, we can't overlook the possibility of a fight with Quanah Parker and his band of Comanches.''

"I remember reading somewhere that Indians don't attack at night," said Trinity.

"Whoever wrote that wasn't familiar with Comanches," Mac replied. "Some tribes do believe that if they die in battle at night, their spirits will wander forever in darkness. But Comanches either don't believe that, or they're willing to take the risk. They're not called horse Indians for nothing. A Comanche will trail a man for days, and they generally don't take prisoners, unless it's for torture.''

"Dear God," said Trinity, "how can the army expect men to face that kind of brutality just for food and virtually no pay?''

"Most career men—jack leather army—are in it for the

glory," Mac said. "I believe they're yearning for the days of King Arthur and the knights of old, and the army's about as close as they can get."

"It's strange you should say that," said Trinity. "That's almost exactly what my . . . the man I married . . . once said about General Custer. He perceived Custer as noble, the kind of man, had he been English, who would have been knighted by the queen."

"I don't know a lot about knighthood and the queen," Mac replied, "but I know a hell of a lot about Custer. Him and his U.S. Seventh Cavalry murdered Black Kettle, a chief of the Cheyenne, and the best friend the white man ever had."

"That's terrible," said Trinity. "Why?"

"Glory," Mac said. "It happened on the Washita River, somewhere north of where we are now. Custer gave the order, and they attacked a sleeping camp, killing every man, woman, and child."*

"May God have mercy on the soul of a man so heartless and cruel," Trinity said. "If that's how the whites have treated the Indians, I'd not blame them for anything they do or have done in retaliation."

"They're guilty of that, and worse," said Mac, "and somebody's going to pay. Before the Indians are beaten, they'll be flying Custer's scalp from the point of a lance."

"As uncivilized as it sounds," Trinity said, "I think he deserves the very worst they can do to him."

"So do I," said Mac. "Trouble is, other soldiers—decent men—will die for the few, like Custer, who are building reputations on the bodies of the dead."

"Red," said Hattie, "what will you do after you reach Austin, and these wagons are no longer your responsibility?"

---

*On November 23, 1868, Custer and the U.S. Seventh rode from Camp Supply, south. Five days later, they wiped out the Cheyennes in what is now western Oklahoma.

"A month ago," Red replied, "I could have answered that. With money in my pocket, I'd have rode the grub line, hoping I could sign on with another trail drive in the spring. Now, I just don't know. I reckon it'll depend on what you learn at Fort Griffin."

"Oh, God," said Hattie, "you make me feel so . . . so . . . oh, I don't know *what* I mean."

"Frustrated?"

"I suppose that will do," Hattie said. "I'd give up this foolish search at Fort Griffin, but I fear that I'd always feel guilty, not knowing the truth."

"The truth will set you free," said Red.

"Or enslave me forever."

"I don't think so," Red replied. "I believe the army's tellin' you the straight of it. I'd say that if they've given you their official verdict, they'll stick to it. Being the self-ish varmint that I am, I hope they do."

"If you're selfish, then so am I," said Hattie. "I want to leave that part of my life in the past, where it belongs. I want to be with you, but not with a cloud of guilt hanging over my head. Does that make sense?"

"It does to me. You're an honest, decent woman, and I respect you for it."

"Even if you lose me?" Hattie asked softly.

"Even then. When you're buildin' something to last, you don't build on the sand."

"I know," said Hattie. "I tried. Mama died when I was young. Daddy never was the same, and after he took to drinking, everything just went to hell. We were sharecrop-pers and never had much more than our pride. Daddy died three days past my eighteenth birthday. Drunk, he fell off the wagon seat, and the front wheel broke his neck. Jack Sutton was the son of a preacher, and old man Sutton believed I was trash, because of what my daddy had been. Like a fool, I defied the Sutton family and married Jack. He was twenty-two, and couldn't—or wouldn't—stand up to his father. I don't know whose idea it was that he join the army, but he did, and that's the last I ever saw of him."

"When you decided to come west to look for him, how did his family take it?"

"I didn't bother asking them how they felt," Hattie said, "but word got back to me that old man Sutton would rather have Jack dead than tied to me. I was tempted to get myself in the family way, and swear Jack had done it."

Red laughed, despite himself. "That would have only hurt you, linking you forever to a family who didn't want you."

"I understood that," Hattie replied, "and I wasn't the trash the Suttons believed I was. Jack Sutton's sin was that he was weak, and I couldn't think of anything less appealing than having his child, even if I could have used it to destroy his high-handed old daddy. I could never hate anybody that much, and even if Jack's alive, I'm not here to claim him."

"Suppose you find that he is alive?"

"Then I'll find some legal way to rid myself of him," said Hattie. "I'll be going on to Austin with you, and wherever you go beyond there, if you'll have me."

"It seems like we've been on the trail forever," Elizabeth Graves said. "How far are we from Fort Griffin?"

"I don't know," said Haze. "Anyhow, I ain't all that anxious to get there. I reckon I'm afraid you'll find that bluecoat the army says is missing. I'm selfish, damn it."

"Then so am I," Elizabeth replied, "and you needn't worry. I'm not hunting him for the reason you would expect."

"Then why *are* you hunting him?"

"If he's still alive," said Elizabeth, "I want to be legally free of him."

"Then why did you tie yourself to him?"

"He . . . wasn't what I thought he was," Elizabeth replied. "Oh, damn, I might as well be honest. I was a foolish girl, just seventeen, and Bud was six years older. He did things . . . daring things that were . . . well, dishonest.

He quickly made a believer of me. He started seeing other women, and he didn't care who knew it, me included. But that wasn't why he joined the army. He was a thief, and when some of his friends were arrested for stealing mules, Bud ran for it. By the time his friends went to trial, Bud was gone, and not until a year later did I learn he was in the army. I got a letter from him, but I heard nothing more until the army notified me he was missing and presumed dead."

"So if he was all you claim, why are you looking for him?"

"Certainly not to live with him," said Elizabeth. "What I'm about to tell you, none of the others know, not even Trinity."

"Then maybe you'd better not tell me," Haze said.

"But I want to. You'll feel a lot better about me. The newspapers printed a story that told about Trinity, Rachel, and Hattie coming west to search for their missing men. Well, I had one missing, too, and I used that as an excuse to come with them."

"You left your family to come west, with no good reason?"

Elizabeth laughed softly. "Oh, I had a reason. I wanted out of that godforsaken little village where I grew up. Nobody actually said anything, but they laughed at me for the fool I was. I was tied to a man who was a thief, who openly consorted with other women, and God only knows what else."

"If they laughed at you then," said Haze, "imagine how they must be laughing today, thinkin' you're out here looking for the no-account varmint."

"But I know better, that I'm here to make a new life for myself," Elizabeth said, "so what do I care what anybody thinks, that I left behind? I only care what *you* think. That's why I've been honest with you. Now that you know I'm a conniving, hard-hearted, and mean-spirited woman, do you want me to go away and stop bothering you?"

"No," said Haze. "I'm obliged to you for easing my

mind. All I could think about was you gettin' to Fort Griffin, findin' this bastard, and me losing you.''

"It doesn't matter to you that he had me first, that I'm used goods?''

"From what I've seen of you, there's plenty left,'' Haze said. "Just save the rest of you for me.''

"I plan to,'' said Elizabeth. "Will you keep my secret? I'd as soon Trinity, Hattie, and Rachel didn't know my *real* reason for coming west with them.''

"I won't say a word,'' Haze replied. "Now lean that Winchester against the wagon and come set beside me.''

The night passed without difficulty. The horses and mules were given a small ration of water from the kegs. It would be sufficient to see them to the North Canadian. But before they reached the river, they could see buzzards circling ahead. They were harbingers of death, and with each spiral, they were closer to the ground.

"Something or somebody's dead or dying,'' Mac said. "Come on, Red.''

Long before they reached what had attracted the buzzards, they could see that it was a man. Or the remains of one.

Several buzzards flapped away as Mac and Red dismounted. The body was that of an Indian dressed in buckskin, and he lay belly-down.

"Easy enough to see what happened to him,'' Red observed. "Shot in the back. Twice.''

"He's alive, but just barely,'' said Mac, as he felt for a pulse. "Stay here and keep the buzzards away from him, until the wagons get here. I'll ride back and hurry them along.''

"Trinity,'' Mac said, when he met the wagons, "there's an Indian who's been hurt. We will take him on to the river with us and do what we can for him. We'll have to put him in your wagon, if that's all right with you.''

"It's all right with us,'' said Trinity. "We'll trot our

teams on ahead. Why don't you get the medicine chest from Port's wagon?''

Mac did so, making the rest of the outfit aware of the wounded Indian. He then rode on, catching up to the rattling wagon. When it reached the Indian, Red let down the tailgate. Trinity and Hattie were shoving their belongings aside, making room for the Indian. By the time Mac and Red got him to the wagon, Hattie was spreading a blanket. Quickly the wagon rattled on toward the river, Mac and Red riding alongside it.

"I'll start a fire," said Red. "Did any of you think to bring a pot to boil some water?"

"We have several in our wagon," Trinity said. "I'll get one."

"We'll have to move him out of the wagon, so we can see what we're doing," said Mac. "Red, when you get the fire going . . ."

When Mac and Red lifted the wounded man, Hattie took the blanket and spread it on the ground beneath a poplar tree, a few yards from the river. Within minutes, the rest of the wagons arrived, Port Guthrie in the lead.

"Port," Mac said, "you're our authority on gunshot wounds. Why don't you have a look at him?"

"Get that shirt off him, then," said Guthrie, "while I wash my hands."

The rest of the teamsters were unharnessing the mules, while Haze and Buck had taken the reins of the horses. They must not be allowed to drink too soon.

"God," Red observed, when the Indian's buckskin shirt had been removed, "he's been hit hard and low down."

"No exit wounds," said Guthrie. "The lead's still in him. Takin' it out may finish him for good."

"No more certainly than leaving it in," Mac said. "It'll be uphill all the way, but it has to come out. He's a *bueno* hombre, or he wouldn't have survived this long."

Guthrie spent an hour removing the lead, and when he had finished, he fell back on the ground, sweating and exhausted. Without being asked, Hattie passed an unopened quart of whiskey to Mac. He poured it into the wounds.

"We have a bolt of cotton muslin in our wagon," said Trinity. "We brought it for—"

She blushed, and the rest of the women laughed.

"Get it," Mac said. "We'll save enough for whatever need you have. Cut or tear me a couple of pads, each thick enough and large enough to cover these wounds. Then rip some strips long enough to reach around him, to hold the pads in place."

Mac soaked the pads with whiskey and placed one over each of the wounds in the Indian's back. With Red lifting the wounded man, Mac passed the long strips several times around him, tying the ends tight.

"It's not the most comfortable position," said Mac, "but we'll leave him belly-down, so we can keep an eye on those wounds. They're still recent enough that he doesn't have a fever, but it'll come."

"Move him back in our wagon before dark," Trinity said, "and we'll look in on him during the night. If fever takes him, we'll dose him with whiskey."

So began the long night of watching the critically wounded Indian, of pouring whiskey down him when he burned with fever, of changing the whiskey-soaked pads covering his wounds. At dawn the fever left him and his pulse seemed stronger. But then, riding from the west in a column of twos, the soldiers came . . .

CHAPTER 7

✧

The patrol consisted of ten men. A lieutenant and a sergeant were in the lead, and the rest of the men reined up behind them. The officer spoke.

"I am First Lieutenant Weems, and this is Sergeant Gilbert. We're on patrol from Fort Elliott. Yesterday, a few miles west of here, we flushed an Indian. We got some lead in him, and just after sundown, shot his horse from under him, but we lost him in the darkness."

"I'm Tunstall," Mac said. "We're bound for Austin. Why were you after the Indian? What has he done?"

The officer laughed. "He's guilty of being an Indian. There's nobody left except Parker and his hostiles, so he has to be part of that band. We've been ordered to shoot Indians on sight. Any Indians."

"Any Indians?" Red asked. "Without knowing if they're friendly or hostile?"

"Mister," said Lieutenant Weems, "as far as the army is concerned, every Indian is hostile. I am authorizing you to shoot any Indian you may encounter. Failure to do so will be considered an act of insubordination against the government of the United States. Have I made myself clear?"

"Yes, sir," Mac said. "You have, sir. Abundantly clear, sir."

The lieutenant interpreted the response exactly as Mac

had intended, and he rode away in silence. The sergeant and the rest of the men followed, the privates trying mightily not to grin. Finally, when they were lost to distance, Red laughed.

"You, sir," said Red, "are guilty of harboring a fugitive. Aren't you ashamed of yourself?"

"I am," Mac said, "and I'm shaking in my boots."

"He was high-handed, spit-and-polish, by-the-book," said Port Guthrie, "but I'd say he's right about one thing. This wounded man is almost surely one of Parker's band."

"But we don't know that," Mac replied, "and neither does Lieutenant Spit-and-polish."

"What would they have done, had you surrendered the Indian to them?" Trinity asked.

"Finished what they started," said Mac.

"Then I'm glad you didn't let them have him," Trinity said. "Whatever he is, he's a human being."

"He is," said Hattie, "and soldier or not, I'd have shot any man trying to take him."

"That's precisely why I said nothing about him," Mac said. "We have enough enemies without adding the army to the list."

"He's tough as a hickory nut," said Haze, "and he'll live. Question is, what will we do with him?"

"Turn him loose, I reckon," Mac said, "when he's able."

"I hope he'll remember this," said Buck, "when Quanah Parker and his bunch come after our scalps."

"When it comes to Indians," Red said, "you can't count on anything but your fingers and your fast gun."

"That's gospel," said Port Guthrie.

"This is as confusing as anything I ever heard," Elizabeth said. "Why are we saving and protecting a man who may later return with his friends and murder us?"

"It just rankles the hell out of me, seeing a man shot in the back," said Mac, "even if he is an Indian, even if I have to kill him myself, the next time we meet."

"That's about the way I feel," Red said.

"Well, I'd like to know what we're goin' to do," said Saul Estrella. "Do we spend the night here, where there's water, or move on?"

"I think we'll spend the night here," Mac replied. "I'll ride on ahead and see how far we are from the Canadian River. It could be as much as twenty miles."

"That's a good two-day drive," said Gourd Snively. "Another dry camp."

"We have water barrels, and there's the river," Mac said.

Part of Mac's decision to remain at the North Canadian another day had to do with his consideration of the wounded Indian. It was a critical time, and being tumbled about in a moving wagon might mean the end of him. Besides that, it seemed about time for that troublesome bunch of renegades—those who remained—to make their move, and the terrain was especially good near the river. As they traveled south, toward the Red, the possibilities of an ambush increased as the country became more broken. Danger of Indian attack would be great enough, without adding to it the almost certain ambush by outlaws. Mac went to the wagon where the Indian lay. The drawstrings had been loosened and the canvas drawn back to provide light and air. The wounded man's breathing was no longer ragged and irregular, and as Mac looked at the solemn face, he was shocked. Obsidian eyes stared back at him without expression. Just as suddenly the eyes closed, and Mac turned away. Hattie stood a few paces away, watching him.

"I think you'd better avoid getting into the wagon for a while," Mack said. "Just for a few seconds, his eyes were open. As he gains strength, there's no telling what he may do or how he may react."

"After all we've done to help him," said Hattie, "I can't believe he'd harm me."

"Believe it," Mac replied. "You're white, and that means you're the enemy."

"Why . . . that's ridiculous," said Hattie.

"Is it? You heard what the lieutenant said about Indians. They've been forced to see us as the army regards them."

After breakfast, Mac prepared to ride south, to the Canadian River. He had a parting word for the outfit.

"Use this day to wash and mend clothes or anything else that needs doing. Port, I'm depending on you to see that every water barrel is filled. Draft as many men as you need. Until I know, one way or the other, we must prepare for a two-day drive from here to the Canadian River."

"Mac," Trinity asked, "may I ride with you?"

"You don't have a horse," said Mac, "and it's too far to ride double."

"Red says I can ride his horse," Trinity replied.

Red grinned and winked when Mac looked at him.

"All right," said Mac. "Saddle him, Red."

Red laughed. "He's already saddled and the stirrups raised."

"You take a hell of a lot for granted, don't you?" Mac said.

The sun wasn't more than an hour high when Mac and Trinity rode south.

"I didn't know you could ride," said Mac.

"Of course I can," Trinity responded. "I grew up in farm country. I can handle a mule or horse hitched to a turning plow, too. I know all the cuss words."

"That's a relief," said Mac. "I could just see me bringing you back belly-down across the saddle, your behind a mess of saddle sores. How are you at milking cows?"

"That's a foolish question. I can milk any damn thing that gives milk. Why?"

Mac laughed. "A Texas man won't have a woman that can't milk. We have a fondness for milk in our coffee, but we'd be disgraced if we were caught milking a cow. If it ain't written somewhere in the Bible or the Constitution of the United States, I'm sure it's part of Texas law, on file at Austin."

"Texas men are crazy as loons," she said, with as straight a face as she could maintain. "I want a man who doesn't chew, dip, or smoke, and only gets drunk on Saturday night.''

"I reckon that rules me out, then," said Mac. "I can't stand Texas red-eye, even on a Saturday night. It's been aged about ten minutes, and it's so strong it'd gag a llano buzzard."

"But that's not all," Trinity said. "I'll want two milk cows, a flock of chickens, and a big red rooster."

"That's a relief," said Mac. "I was afraid you'd want a house with a parlor, a bed, a cookstove, a table, eatin' tools, and maybe a carpet on the floor."

"Oh, I'm a primitive woman," Trinity said. "I'd not expect any more finery than any Texas man could comfortably provide."

"Good," said Mac. "All we'll need is a one-room line shack with a cowhide hung over the open door to keep out wind and rain, and a water hole not more'n a mile distant."

"Aren't you Texans afraid of spoiling a woman, being so lavish?"

"Oh, hell," Mac said, "you got it all wrong. The shack's for the cows, chickens, and the big red rooster. You and me will take our bedrolls and bunk out in the brush."

It was perfectly foolish conversation. They laughed until they could laugh no more, until their horses snaked their heads around, wondering what had come over these strange humans. Even for October, the sun was hot.

"We'd better stop and rest the horses," Mac said.

They dismounted, loosened the saddle cinches, and sat down beneath a pine.

"How far do you think we've ridden?"

"Maybe ten miles," said Mac. "I'm sure it'll be a good two days' journey, as slow and as loaded as the wagons are. I just hope it's no farther."

"I'm not used to it being this warm in October," Trinity said. "It's warm enough for a swim in the river."

"Maybe," said Mac, "but it's not safe enough. Remember what happened the last time you took your clothes off and got in the water?''

Trinity sighed. ''Yes, I remember. But it seems so peaceful.''

''That's generally the way it is in the West, just before all hell busts loose,'' said Mac.

It was time to go. Mac snugged up their saddle cinches. They mounted, riding south.

Far behind Mac and Trinity, careful not to raise any dust, a pair of the renegades—Russ and Gillis—followed.

''I got my doubts,'' Gillis said. ''You really think if we grab these two, the rest of 'em will abandon them wagons to us?''

''They will, if they want this pair to go on livin','' said Russ.

''You'd turn 'em loose?''

''No way,'' Russ said. ''Once we get control of the wagons, we'll have to kill 'em all. But they don't have to know that.''

''Why don't we go ahead and take them?''

''Don't be a damn fool,'' said Russ. ''They'll be watchin' their backtrail, and would see our dust long before we could get close enough. We'll find a good place, take cover, and get them as they return.''

Everything seemed peaceful along the North Canadian. The women had followed Mac's suggestion and were at a shallows in the river, washing clothes. Upstream, Guthrie and his teamsters were filling water barrels. Red, Buck, and Haze were helping. It was Red who first saw the riders approaching from the north, and before he could utter a word, the others could see the alarm in his eyes. Slowly they turned, and what they beheld sent chills at a fast gallop up their spines. The landscape was alive with mounted Indians!

''Lord amighty,'' Port Guthrie groaned, ''there must be five hundred.''

"Don't nobody pull a gun," said Red quietly. "We're at their mercy."

"Hell," Buck said, "if they're Comanches, they don't know the meanin' of the word."

Hattie, Rachel, and Elizabeth, up to their knees in the river, had just become aware of the Indians. They stood there, pieces of wet clothing in their hands, shocked into silence. Then a miracle took place. From the wagon where the wounded Indian lay, there came a shout. It was a guttural sound that none of them understood, but the mounted Indians had heard. Somehow the wounded Indian had gotten to his feet and was holding to the rear wagon bow, speaking to the mounted men who surrounded the wagon. One of the mounted Indians trotted his horse to the wagon's tailgate, extended his hand, and the wounded man stepped from the wagon onto the horse. The horde of mounted Indians turned their horses and rode north, in the direction from which they had come. One rider fell back, and for just a moment, faced the men and women at the river. He then whirled his horse and rode after his comrades.

"By God," said Red, "I got a feeling we was just face-to-face with Quanah Parker, the chief of the Comanches."

Hattie, Rachel, and Elizabeth had forgotten their wash, and came on the run.

"They took him away," Hattie cried. "How did they know he was here?"

"They didn't," said Port Guthrie. "They were here because they had plans for us. That wounded Indian in the wagon changed their minds. It was our kindness to him that saved our bacon."

"If Mac Tunstall never does anything right again, this will be enough," Buck said.

"There was one of them who turned back and looked at us," said Hattie. "He looked young, almost a boy."

"That likely had to be Quanah Parker himself," Red said, "and he is young. He had a white mother. Cynthia

Ann Parker was taken by the Comanches, and became the wife of a Comanche chief."*

"I reckon that'll be some relief to Mac," said Haze. "Now all we got to bother us is what's left of that band of renegades."

"You really think they'll come after us?" Elizabeth asked.

"Yes," said Haze, "for the same reason Mac does. We dealt 'em too much hurt. They want the wagons, but they want us just as bad. I'd say we're a hundred and forty miles north of the Red River. Once we cross it, we'll be in Texas. I look for that bunch to come after us somewhere between here and the Red."

"Unless they've picked up some more men," Buck said, "there can't be more than a dozen of 'em. That means an ambush."

"Mac and Trinity've been gone for more than three hours," said Hattie. "I hope nothing has happened to them."

"I can't imagine anything happenin' to Mac Tunstall," Red said. "Not when he's armed and on a good horse."

But something could happen, and did. Russ and Gillis had positioned themselves three hundred yards apart, and when Mac and Trinity rode within rifle range, Gillis fired. While it was only a warning shot, it kicked up gravel. With the force of a bullet, a fragment of it struck the horse Trinity rode, and the animal spooked. It was as wicked a piece of luck as Mac Tunstall had ever experienced, for the horse ran directly toward the thicket where Russ, the renegade leader, was hiding. He leaped to his feet, seized the reins, and brought the horse between himself and Mac Tunstall. Mac had his Winchester cocked, but he had no target. Russ laughed. He then shouted a challenge.

"Drop the rifle, mister, and then your pistol rig. Do it quick, or the lady gets it."

*Quanah Parker was born in 1852.

Mac had no choice. He dropped the Winchester, then unbuckled his cartridge belt and dropped it.

"Now you ride on up here," Russ commanded, "and do it slow. Gillis, gather up his weapons."

Mac reined up a few yards away. He could see the fear in Trinity's eyes. Russ waited until Gillis arrived with Mac's weapons.

"You," Russ commanded, pointing to Mac, "put your hands behind you. Gillis, tie his hands and tie them tight."

Gillis tied Mac's hands and then looked to Russ.

"Tie the woman's hands the same way," said Russ.

The renegades then rode north, their captives' horses following on lead ropes. When they reached the camp, there was jubilation among the men.

"She don't look near as tasty, all gussied up, as she did buck naked," Bilbo observed. "What do you aim to do with 'em?"

"Swap them for those wagons," said Russ. "Come sundown, I'll ride close enough to their camp to make an offer. We get the wagons by dawn tomorrow, or these two will die. That is, if the eleven of you can keep them from escaping until I get back."

"Haw, haw," Bilbo said. "We'll keep the woman busy, and the hombre can watch."

"You'll keep your hands off the woman," said Russ.

"I don't hold with this hostage takin'," Wilkerson growled. "It's already cost us ten men and a damn good hideout."

"He's dead right about that," said Tull. "You got until in the mornin' to make your play. After that, the rest of us aim to ambush that outfit and take the wagons."

Russ looked from one to the other, and in their eyes he saw the same discontent, the smoldering rebellion.

"All right," Russ agreed. "If this don't work, we'll attack the wagons."

"Now you're talkin'," Bilbo shouted.

There was a chorus of agreement from the others.

"Now," said Russ, "take this pair over yonder and rope

'em to a tree. If they manage to get loose, damn it, I'll have somebody's head on a plate.''

Mac and Trinity were forced to sit with their backs against a pair of young pines not more than a few feet apart. Their arms were passed around the trunk, their wrists bound behind it, and only their legs were free.

''You're damned poor excuses for men, subjecting a lady to this,'' Mac said.

Bilbo laughed. ''This is downright pleasurable, compared to what the lady will likely be facin' tomorrow mornin'. There ain't nothin' much worse'n bein' dead.''

Mac and Trinity were left alone, staring helplessly at one another.

''What do you suppose the others will do,'' Trinity asked, ''when these outlaws try to make a deal for the wagons?''

''Red, Haze, and Buck will try to buy some time,'' said Mac. ''One of these varmints will have to take the message to our outfit. I figure Red, Haze, or Buck will follow him back here. Then they'll try to rescue us.''

''But how? Won't these outlaws be expecting something like that?''

''Maybe,'' Mac replied. ''I reckon we'll just have to wait and see.''

They soon had their answer, and it was what Mac had feared. Near sundown, one of the renegades saddled a horse for Russ, and he rode near where Mac and Trinity were held captive.

''I'm takin' word to your *compañeros*,'' said Russ, ''and you'd better hope they've got enough smarts to listen to what I got to say. Don't get any ideas about 'em findin' the two of you by follerin' me back, 'cause I won't be gettin' there until after dark.''

He rode away and was soon lost to their view. Trinity looked at Mac in silent despair, and he could think of nothing to say that might lessen it.

*   *   *

"Something's wrong," Haze said. "Even if the Canadian was thirty miles away, they've had time to ride there and back twice."

"We can't wait any longer," said Red. "I'm riding south to look for sign."

"Whatever you discover," Buck said, "don't try to handle it alone. Light a shuck back here, and let's make some plans. If Mac and Trinity's in trouble, you getting sucked into it will just make it tougher for the rest of us to help you."

"If it involves Indians or outlaws," said Red, "there's no way I can handle it alone. I'll get back here as quick as I can."

"Please be careful," Hattie said.

Red rode at a fast gallop, stopping only to rest his horse. Tracks of the horses Mac and Trinity had ridden were easy enough to follow, and before Red had ridden more than a few miles, he came upon the tracks of two other horses trailing Mac and Trinity.

"Damn," Red swore aloud. "I know what I'm goin' to find."

He had no trouble finding the place where the two outlaws had holed up, and there was an empty shell case where a shot had been fired. Finally there were tracks of the two horses from the south, and the place where all four horses had come together. The four had not followed the original trail north, but had angled off to the northeast. Red followed the new trail a ways before reining up. He must make a decision. The sun was hardly more than an hour high. If he returned to the wagons, as he had promised, darkness would fall before they could take this new trail. But he had given his word, and with a sigh, he took the trail north. When he reached the wagons, everybody gathered around. While they all wanted to know what he had discovered, they dreaded what he might say.

"They were ambushed and taken prisoner," said Red. "Less than ten miles south of us. The trail leads northeast."

"Indians or outlaws?" Buck asked.

"The varmints that took them rode shod horses," said Red. "It's got to be those damn renegades."

"There won't be enough time to trail them before dark," Buck said.

"No," said Red. "I should have trailed them instead of coming back here, but you had me promise."

"They're plannin' to bargain with hostages again," Haze said, "and that means they'll have to contact us. When they do, we can trail them to their camp."

"Not if they contact us after dark," said Red. "I have a feeling, after what we did to them before, they won't be very patient with us."

"What can we do?" Hattie cried.

"Nothing until morning," said Red. "Unless they contact us, all we have is the tracks of their horses, after they took Mac and Trinity captive."

"It's gonna be an almighty long night," Haze said.

But they didn't have that long to wait. Less than an hour after darkness had fallen, a taunting voice hailed them.

"You, with the wagons. We got some friends of yours, and we're ready to trade."

Red had been about to pour himself some coffee. He set the tin cup down and moved into the shadows before replying.

"How do we *know* you have them?" Red shouted.

"You know we have," came the response. "They ain't come back, have they?"

"What do you want?" Red responded.

"You know what we want. Them wagons. You have until first light. When you leave the wagons, your friends go free."

"What proof do we have of that?"

"You got our word," Russ shouted. "Some of us will be watching you. You got just one hour after first light. Then we shoot your friends, and somewhere along the trail, you can look for us to be waitin' for you."

That was the end of the exchange, and it was Red who finally broke the silence.

"I was afraid of that. They don't aim to allow us enough time to plan a rescue."

"We could split up and ride in a circle, lookin' for their camp," Haze suggested.

"They'll counter that by dousing their fire," said Buck. "Besides, they might be ready for us to do exactly that. If we stumbled on them in the dark, they might just go ahead and shoot Mac and Trinity."

"My God," Elizabeth said, "we must do *something*."

"We will," said Red. "We'll abandon these wagons, if we have to."

"Sorry," Port Guthrie said, "but we can't go along with that. We got nothin' but high regard for Tunstall and the young lady, but we give our word to Mr. Yeager."

There was an uneasy silence, for without Guthrie and the teamsters, Mac and Trinity didn't stand a chance against the outlaws . . .

When Russ returned, he had nothing to say to Mac and Trinity, and when he spoke to his comrades, the conversation was for their ears only.

"I'm dying for a drink of water," Trinity said. "One end's dry and the other's wet. I needed to go to the bushes hours ago."

"So did I," said Mac, "but that's the least of our problems. Obviously they don't aim to feed us, but maybe I can get us some water."

The fire had been doused, and there was only a soft mumble of conversation from the outlaws.

"You hombres," Mac shouted, "we're in need of some water."

"Shut the hell up," Russ growled. "Open your yap again, and I'll bend a pistol barrel over your skull. Pryor, take them some water."

The outlaw brought two tin cups of water. Trinity drank

first, then Mac. Within a few minutes, the outlaw camp became silent.

"If I ever get loose from this tree," said Trinity, "I'll never be able to use my arms or hands again."

"I'm in about the same shape," Mac said. "Try to sleep, if you can."

"I don't think I can," said Trinity. "How do you rest when you may be spending your last night on earth bound to a tree?"

"I don't know," Mac replied. "I don't know what Red and the others can do, but I'll gamble a horse and saddle they'll try something. As somebody once said, a Texan is never at his best until he's down to one cartridge and surrounded by Indians or outlaws."

"Well, I'm not a Texan," said Trinity, "and I'm scared to death."

The night wore on, and nobody within the wagon camp slept. In their subconscious, each of them could hear a ticking clock, with every second, every minute, every hour, drawing them closer to the appointed time when Mac Tunstall and Trinity McCoy had been sentenced to die. There was no moon, and the stars—distant points of silver—all seemed cold and far away. When the first gray light of dawn painted the eastern horizon, Red, Buck, and Haze had their horses saddled, prepared for they knew not what.

In the outlaw camp ten miles away, the men were silent, their eyes on Russ. There was no fire, no morning coffee, no breakfast. Russ saddled his horse, mounted, and without a word, rode away. The outlaws watched in silence. Mac and Trinity looked at each other, wondering what the next hour might bring. The Indians struck without warning. A veritable wall of mounted horsemen descended on the camp. Arrows whipped through the early morning silence, and while some of the outlaws died with guns in their hands, not a shot was fired. Within seconds the fight was over. Indians moved among the fallen outlaws, driving lances through those yet alive, taking their weapons and ammunition. Two of the Indians trotted their horses near where Mac and Trinity were bound.

"One of them is the Indian we doctored in the wagon," Trinity whispered.

"I'd gamble the other is Quanah Parker, chief of the Comanches," said Mac.

The Indians dismounted, and for a moment stood there looking at Mac and Trinity. The wounded Indian whom Mac had saved from the army nodded. His companion drew a knife and swiftly slashed the rope that bound Mac and Trinity. He backed away, and only then did he speak.

"You give Little Wolf his life, and now Little Wolf gives you your own. Take your woman and go. Quanah Parker commands it."*

*Quanah Parker and the last of the Comanches surrendered on June 2, 1875.

CHAPTER 8

❦

*W*ithin minutes the Indians had vanished, leaving only the two horses Mac and Trinity had been riding. Their Winchesters were in the saddle boots, and looped around a saddle horn was Mac's pistol belt with its Colt.

"In a small way, I reckon this proves what I've always believed," Mac said. "Indians treated fairly will respond in kind."

"Why can't the army and the politicians in Washington be told of this?" Trinity asked. "Why can't they depend on kindness, rather than killing?"

"Because they all live under a double standard," said Mac. "Washington has broken every treaty ever signed with the Indians, and for one reason or another, reclaimed every acre of land ceded to them."

"It's all so sad," Trinity said. "Back east, we believed what we were told, that Indians are savages who kill without cause, and must be eliminated. I have seen more compassion among these savages than I knew existed. Through the years, we have lost something we may never regain. God help us, and them."

"It's too late for them," said Mac, "and maybe for us. Let's ride. One of these owl hoots has gone to try and trade us for the wagons. I can't wait to get my hands on him."

Unaware of the Indian attack, Russ reined up within sight of the wagons, but out of rifle range. Red, Buck, and Haze were expecting him.

"Time's run out," Russ shouted. "Your friends for the wagons. Is it a deal?"

"No deal," Red shouted back.

"Then we'll shoot your friends and take the wagons anyhow," Russ shouted angrily.

"You can try," said Red.

Russ wheeled his horse, riding back the way he had come. Haze brought two saddled horses for Red and Buck.

"Damn it," Haze said, "if we had another horse, I could ride with you."

"We need somebody with the wagons besides the team-sters," said Red. "Besides, we're already so outgunned, three of us probably wouldn't make any difference. I don't know what Buck and me can do, if anything, but we can't just do nothing. Come on, Buck."

Red and Buck had no trouble following the trail Russ had left. It was testimony to the outlaw's confidence in his position and superior numbers.

As Russ rode away, he seethed with anger, for he now must concede that he had misjudged the men with the wag-ons. He must now do what his comrades had urged him to do from the start, and it rankled him. That bunch with the wagons would now be expecting an attack, and they were no short-horns. Suddenly there was a shot, and lead burned a fiery furrow under the outlaw's left arm. A sec-ond shot lifted his hat off his head, and he kicked his horse into a fast gallop, veering to the east. Something had def-initely gone sour, for the shots had come from the direction of the outlaw camp! Looking over his shoulder, he could see two horses pounding after him. Mac Tunstall rode the lead horse, a blazing Colt in his hand. Russ rode for his life, unsure as to what had happened to his comrades, aware only of the vengeful rider who seemed to be gaining on him.

"Listen," Red shouted. "Shots!"

"I'd say the varmint that laid down the law to us is havin' problems of his own," said Buck. "Maybe we can hand the bastard some more grief."

But there were no more shots. Russ pushed his tiring horse and managed to reach a dense thicket. Mac reined up, Trinity behind him.

"I can't see trying to root him out of there," Mac said. "He could stand us off all day and then escape in the dark."

"Then let's forget him," said Trinity. "I never expected us to escape with our lives. Let's not press our good fortune."

Turning their horses, they rode back the way they had come, and within just a few minutes, met Red and Buck.

"My God," Red shouted, "are we glad to see the two of you."

"There's quite a story to tell," said Mac. "Let's get on back to the wagons, and we'll ease everybody's mind. Then we'll share somethin' you'll find hard to believe."

"We got somethin' you may find hard to believe," Buck said. "Yesterday, we come face-to-face with the godawfulest bunch of Indians I ever seen at one time. They took the wounded Indian and rode away."

"We know," said Trinity. "The Indian we helped was Little Wolf. We saw him just a little while ago."

There was jubilation among the outfit when Mac, Trinity, Red, and Buck rode in. They all listened in amazement and delight of the Indian raid on the outlaw camp.

"Trinity and me owe our lives to Quanah Parker and his band of Comanches," Mac concluded. "The only one of the outlaws to escape was the varmint that rode over here to try and swap Trinity and me for the wagons."

"Nothin' he can do alone," said Haze.

"That was somethin', them Comanches comin' through for us," Port Guthrie said. "But I can't help wonderin' if they'd rode away and left us, had they knowed these six wagons is loaded to the bows with weapons and ammunition."

"You're wondering if they'd have put greed ahead of honor," said Mac.

"Yeah," Guthrie said.

"No," said Mac. "Could you have stopped them, if they had chosen to look into the wagons, to see what they were giving up?"

"No," Guthrie replied. "We was at their mercy. I reckon we've learnt somethin' about Indians. It's just a damn shame this kind of thing couldn't have happened often enough for that bunch in Washington to learn from it."

"I'll tell it wherever I go," said Trinity, "to anybody who will listen."

"Speaking of going," Mac said, "it's time to move these wagons. It's a good two days from here to the Canadian River."

"The water barrels is all full," said Port Guthrie. "We're good for at least one night in dry camp."

"If we don't get rolling, it'll be more than one night," Mac said. "Move 'em out."

Russ didn't have to wonder what had happened, for the bodies of his comrades fairly bristled with arrows. Not a horse, scrap of food, or arms and ammunition remained.

"What I can't figger," said Russ aloud, "is how them two from the wagon outfit got loose and escaped the Indians. You can count on one thing, Mister Wagon Boss. You ain't shut of me. We'll meet again, and when we do, you'd best have your iron in your hand."

The Canadian River. October 10, 1873.

"I'd reckon us to be a hundred and twenty-five miles north of the Red River," said Port Guthrie. "That's two weeks, if we can hold to ten miles a day."

"I'd say we can rule out any threat by the Comanches," Mac said, "so that leaves only the renegades."

"After we just got rid of one gang," said Trinity, "you're expecting another?"

"Maybe more than one," Mac replied. "The trouble we had gettin' these wagons out of Kansas City to Dodge, I can't believe there isn't a Judas of some stripe in Washington who hasn't telegraphed ahead."

"You're more right than you know," said Port Guthrie. "We're in more danger from the army itself than from Indians and renegades combined."

"My God," Buck said, "how do you figure that?"

"Remember Jernigan, from Fort Dodge?"

"Yes," said Buck. "He wore the gray."

"Well, I'm tellin' you Union ranks is shot full of former Confederates who took the pledge, just like Jernigan," Guthrie replied. "They was beat, but they ain't bowed. They're short on hope but long on hate. I ain't sure we should even stop at Fort Griffin."

"But we're going to," said Mac. "Hell, we can't pick up these wagons and put 'em in our pockets. If everybody knows we're out here, it's just a matter of time until they find us."

"I got an idea that's why Mr. Yeager didn't recommend us stoppin' at any of the outposts," Guthrie said.

"He didn't recommend it," said Mac, "but he didn't forbid it. This is the kind of thing where Yeager can't sit in Kansas City and call the shots. If he didn't know it already, he got the message after what happened in Dodge. Success or failure depends almost entirely on our judgment."

The wagons crossed the Canadian without difficulty, and spirits rose, for it seemed that much of the trouble might be behind them. But it was time for the elements to again take a hand, and big gray thunderheads began stacking up on the western horizon.

"There's gonna be one hell of a snowstorm blowin' in off the high plains," said Saul Estrella.

"It won't reach this far south," Port Guthrie said, "but there'll be rain. We might as well find us a place to rest for two or three days, until the sun's had a chance to dry up the mud.''

"Perhaps we can find a place like the arroyo, near the Cimarron,'' Elizabeth said. "It's nice to have shelter and a fire.''

"I'll ride south a ways,'' said Mac, "and look around. Port, before we leave here, see that the water barrels are all filled. Red, why don't you ride along the Canadian and see if there might be an overhanging bank or cave we can use for shelter? That's in case there's nothing suitable ahead of us that we can reach before the rain begins.''

"May I ride with you?'' Trinity asked.

"I reckon,'' said Mac, "but you know what happened the last time you rode with me.''

"I know,'' Trinity said, "but I'd rather have been with you than left behind, worrying about you.''

"Come on, then,'' said Mac. "See if Haze will allow you to ride his horse.''

"I already did,'' Trinity said. "He's saddling it now.''

Mac and Trinity rode south, while Red rode eastward, along the bank of the Canadian.

"What will we do for water between here and the Red?'' Trinity asked.

"We'll have to depend on springs and creeks,'' said Mac. "I believe that's one reason Yeager routed us through western Indian Territory. After leaving the Canadian, I know of no sure water until we reach the Red. But when I say that, I'm thinking of Texas. Here in Indian Territory, the terrain is entirely different. It's the kind of country where there'll be springs, maybe artesian water. I reckon that's why it's such a haven for renegades.''

"I can feel a dampness in the wind,'' Trinity said. "How long until the rain begins?''

"It'll hit us sometime tonight,'' said Mac. "If we don't find shelter today, we're in for a soaking. The weather—rain and snow—is one of the real hardships on the plains. It's difficult to keep a fire for food and coffee, and nobody sleeps much. When there's snow on the ground or the water and mud is deep, there's nowhere to spread your blankets.''

"It seems like the freight lines would allow room in each of the wagons for teamsters to sleep," Trinity said.

Mac laughed. "You don't know freight lines. They begrudge the space it takes for the two hundred pounds of grain each wagon must carry to feed the mules. When it comes to consideration, the teamster's three or four notches below his mule teams.''

Mac and Trinity had ridden almost fifteen miles before finding water. Following a runoff, they reached a more-than-adequate spring.

"Good water," said Mac, "but the trees and rocks surrounding it won't offer decent shelter. Not even for a cook fire. We might as well ride back and see if Red's found anything."

Red rode along the river, keeping to the south bank, where vegetation was sparse. He soon gave up finding a decent riverbank overhang. While there was some overhang, and the water was low, a day or two of continuous rain would raise the water level dramatically. Their shelter—if they had any—couldn't be anywhere near the river. Even along the bank where he rode, Red could see debris and signs of flooding. When he turned in his saddle and looked westward, the thunderheads seemed bigger, blacker, and closer than ever. The wind had a bite to it, and while there likely wouldn't be any snow, there would be a cold rain which might continue for several days and nights. Red realized he was riding deeper into Indian Territory, but riding westward would have taken him to the virtually barren plains of the Texas panhandle. He reined up, studying the ground. There was just a hint of a trail that angled off to the southeast. Long unused, but a trail of sorts, and for the lack of a better choice, Red followed it. Something or somebody had used the trail to get water from the river, for the bank had angled down to the water.

"Deer trail, maybe," said Red aloud.

But it was considerably more than a deer trail. Beyond

a stand of mostly leafless trees Red could see part of a
shake roof. Dismounting, he looped the reins of his horse
around a pine limb and continued on foot. From the outside, the cabin appeared substantial, with a mud-and-stick
chimney. A leather-hinged door stood open, moving in the
wind. Shutters over the windows were closed. There was
no sign of life. There was a stoop sheltering the entrance,
and dead leaves had piled up beneath it.

"Hello the cabin," said Red. "Anybody here?"

Only silence greeted him. His Colt in his hand, he
kicked the dead leaves away from the door and swung it
inward. The cabin was even larger than it appeared from
the outside. Red could see an entrance—without a door—
into another room. He stepped inside and was greeted with
a musty odor. There was firewood stacked on both sides
of the fireplace, and a dozen crude bunks—six upper and
six lower—anchored at intervals to three walls of the
room. There was only a dirt floor, and no furnishings of
any kind. His boots crunching on blown-in fallen leaves,
Red made his way to the curtainless, doorless opening that
led to the next room. Suddenly he halted, the macabre
thing on the dirt floor drawing from him an involuntary
gasp of surprise.

Lying on its back, arms outflung, lay the skeleton of a
man. The bony fingers of the right hand still gripped a
Colt, and just above the eyeless sockets of the skull, there
was what could only be a bullet hole. The gruesome thing
still wore the clothing in which the man had died. There
were scuffed, run-over boots, faded Levi's, and a red flannel, out-at-the-elbows shirt. A tattered black hat lay partially under one bony leg. The only other item in the
squalid room was ripped-open saddlebags. They appeared
empty, but when Red picked them up, a piece of paper
fluttered out. It was a strip that banks used to band their
currency, and on it was printed "Bank of Wichita."

"Looks like a fallin'-out among thieves," Red said,
"and pardner, you was ridin' with some damned sorry
companions."

Red had seen enough. He left the cabin, returned to his horse, and rode back the way he had come. By his estimate, the cabin was maybe two miles from where the wagons had crossed the river.

"Well?" said Haze, as Red dismounted.

"I found a cabin," Red replied, "as long as none of you are superstitious. In one of the rooms there's the bones of a dead man. There's a bullet hole in the skull."

Hattie shuddered. "Let's wait until Mac and Trinity return. Maybe they've found us a shelter somewhere up ahead."

"Oh, I don't aim to make a move until Mac's had a look at this," said Red. "This had to be a fallin'-out among thieves. I found a strip of paper that says 'Bank of Wichita.' It's the thing banks use to band currency."

"A cabin used by outlaws," Buck said. "There's always a chance they could return."

"I reckon there's always a chance," said Red. "Somebody put an almighty lot of work into that place, just to ride away and leave it. But the gent they left behind has been there a good six months, I'd say. It looks like his pardner or pardners in crime took the money and vamoosed."

There was more speculation, but they were all of the same mind. They would wait for Mac and Trinity to return, and an hour later, they did.

"The nearest water's a good fifteen miles," said Mac, "and as for shelter, there's only an occasional stand of trees. Find anything, Red?"

"Yeah," Red replied, "but before we all go rushin' downriver, you might want to have a look at the place."

Red quickly told Mac what he had already told the others.

"I'll ride down there with you," said Mac, "and we'll dispose of Mr. Bones before the wagons arrive. If outlaws built the cabin and they return, there'd better be enough of them to throw us out."

"Port," Red said, "follow the river until you come to

a dim trail leadin' off to the southeast. From there you can see part of the shake roof of the cabin. You may have to fell a few trees to get the wagons up close."

"We'll be along, then," said Guthrie.

Without further ado, Mac and Red rode out.

"God," Rachel said, "I've had enough of outlaws."

"Honey," said Trinity, "you haven't had nearly as much of them as I have, but I feel the same way Mac does. Until enough of them show up to run us out, then that cabin will belong to us."

"Amen to that," Buck said. "I've never slept worth a damn, standin' in the rain, and I purely don't like it waterin' down my coffee. That is, if there's a fire, and we *have* coffee."

Port Guthrie's wagon led out and the others followed. Trinity's wagon came last, with Haze and Buck riding behind it.

With Red leading the way and Mac following, they soon reached the cabin. Everything was as before. The open door swayed in the rising wind, and dry leaves swirled at their feet.

"Well," said Mac, "it's plenty big enough, and there's a bunk for us all."

"The skeleton's in this next room," Red said.

But when they entered the back room, Red was more shocked than when he'd found the bones. The skeleton was gone! So were the saddlebags, the tattered hat, and even the scrap of paper with "Bank of Wichita" printed on it.

"By God, that tears it," said Red. "He wasn't in no shape to get up and walk away."

Mac looked at his friend with some concern. "Are you *sure* there was a pile of bones in here?"

"Why, hell yes, I'm sure," Red growled. "You think I don't know a skeleton when I see one? The damned thing still had a Colt in its hand."

"Well, either it wasn't as dead as you thought," said Mac, "or it's got friends around here close by."

"I doubt they're friends," Red replied, "but for some

reason, they hauled what was left of him out of here. How's that going to affect us usin' this cabin?"

"We're still going to use the cabin," said Mac, "and to avoid fanning the fires of anybody's superstitions, we're not goin' to tell them your skeleton disappeared. Let them think we dragged it away and got rid of it."

"I reckon you're right," Red replied. "Hattie's eyes got big as tin plates when I told 'em about the bones."

"I may have to confide in Haze and Buck," said Mac, "because we don't know what all this means. I think one of us will always have to be waitin' just inside this cabin door with a cocked Winchester."

"Well," Red said, mollified, "I'm glad you're takin' me serious. This could be trouble."

"Anytime there's an unexplained dead man, it means trouble for somebody," said Mac. "I expect there's been a lot of hombres who came to Indian Territory and never left, and I don't want us addin' to their numbers."

There was the thunk of axes as the teamsters felled enough of the smaller trees to get the wagons to the cabin. There was a clearing around it ample enough to secure the wagons, and beyond that, decent graze for a few days. Once the wagons had reached the cabin, it was time to seek firewood.

"Buck, Haze, and Red, come with me," Mac said. "We'll take some axes and cut us a supply of firewood while it's still dry. There's plenty of room for all of us in the front room of that cabin. We can pile our wood in the second room, and not have to drag it in during the storm."

It was good that they wasted no time, for the rain began well before nightfall. There was a chill, driving wind, and the horses and mules took shelter in a stand of pines that were within sight of the cabin. The chimney drew well, and a roaring fire did wonders to lift the spirits of the outfit.

"One thing is certain," Port Guthrie said, "if it's rainin' to the south of us anything like it's rainin' here, we won't have a water problem from here to the Red. There'll be a blessed plenty of wet-weather springs and streams."

Mac had a few candles in his saddlebags, and when he lighted one, they all looked at him curiously.

"There's plenty of light in here from the fire," said Buck.

"Not in the back room," Mac replied. "I aim to poke around back there."

"I'll go with you," said Red.

They got no argument from any of the others, for they all knew that Red had found the bones of a dead man there. Some of the firewood had been piled just beyond the door to the room, but not enough to hinder their search.

"I don't like things left dangling, where there are no answers," Mac said. "There may be no answers here, but it won't cost us anything to look around. That strip of paper you found from the Bank of Wichita tells me there were some thieves here, and that they must have had a saddlebag full of stolen bank greenbacks."

"Yeah," said Red, "and the gent I found had a fallin'-out with the others. He bought more than he could pay for. Somebody else was a dead shot, and a hell of a lot quicker. I just wish I'd had the sense to go through the dead hombre's pockets while I still had the chance."

"I doubt you'd have found anything of value," Mac replied. "Whoever shot him would have picked him clean before leaving him."

"Maybe," said Red, "but they left him his Colt. It was still in his hand. When he was left here, they must have figured he'd never be found. Now I'm wonderin' why they came back, and why they went to the trouble of takin' him away from here. Nobody's lived in this place for months, yet the minute I discover it, they show up and take his bones away. Where have they been, and why have they returned?"

"I have a powerful hunch we need to know the answer to that last part," Mac said. "I got a notion they've returned because there's somethin' here that they want. Or at least they believe there is. But you showed up before they could accomplish what they intended to do."

"While I don't take kindly to the thought," said Red, "they could have just shot me."

"If they knew or suspected you weren't alone, that wouldn't have solved anything," Mac said. "They were likely gambling that you wouldn't return, and just on the off chance that you might, they took the skeleton away. If you did come back, maybe bringin' somebody with you, there'd be no evidence of what you had seen. You might have some trouble convincin' anybody else that you hadn't had too much red-eye, that you wasn't just seeing somethin' that wasn't there."

"I ain't had a drop of nothin' stronger than coffee," said Red, "but I'm about ready to admit my eyes was playin' tricks on me."

"No," Mac said, "I believe you found a man's bones in here, and that for reasons we can only suspect, those bones were taken away. The hombres who took the bones may be watching this cabin right now, waitin' for us to leave. I think we'll have a look at these log walls, and if we find nothing there, we'll check out the dirt floor."

"We don't know that what we're lookin' for is in this room," said Red. "It may be in the next room."

"Maybe," Mac replied, "but we'll start our search in here. There's no point in getting the others involved in this, if we don't have to."

"I reckon you're right," Red conceded. "It'd scare hell out of the women, if they got the idea a whole new bunch of outlaws was lurkin' around here."

Red lighted a candle off Mac's, and they went over the log walls thoroughly, finding nothing. A careful examination of the floor revealed nothing except a reddish-brown stain that might have been blood, long since dried.

"Nothing in here," said Red. "Do we tell the others what we suspect, and start in the next room?"

"Not yet," Mac said. "This storm may be with us a while, and we should have plenty of time. Let's not feed anybody's superstitions unless we have to."

The storm raged on, unabated. By suppertime, there was a rumble of distant thunder.

"Ever'body better load up on hot coffee," said Port Guthrie. "That thunder's gettin' closer by the minute, and it'll bring lightning with it. I look for us all to be out there with the horses and mules, tryin' to convince the varmints there's nothin' to git spooked over."

"Good advice," Mac said.

Guthrie's prediction proved all too true, and came to pass within the hour. There was a crash of thunder that shook the cabin, followed almost immediately by the frightened braying of mules and the nickering of horses.

"Come on," Mac shouted. "They're gettin' spooked!"

Every man with a pair of catch ropes, they surged out into the storm. Mac, Red, Haze, and Buck went after the horses first, for they were creating more commotion than the mules. By the time the rearing, nickering horses had been secured, panic had spread to the mules, and some of the animals lit out back toward the river. Then, on the heels of a clap of thunder, like an echo, came the unmistakable bark of a Winchester. Three more of the deadly weapons added their voices to the fury of the storm, and taken by surprise, the teamsters and outriders tried to fight back with their Colts. Then, as suddenly as it had begun, the fusillade ended. The thunder had diminished, and in the lightning flashes there were revealed three huddled bodies.

"Mac!" Red shouted.

But Mac didn't answer. He lay facedown in the mud and driving rain. Slipping in the mud, Red managed to shoulder his friend and started toward the distant cabin. By the time he reached it, Port Guthrie and Lafe Beard were there. Each had brought in a wounded man.

"Mac's hard hit," Red panted.

"So is Buck and Haze," said Guthrie, "and we don't know who else."

"Go after the others," Trinity said, "but one of you bring the medicine chest first."

With trembling hands, Trinity unbuttoned Mac's shirt.

Blood welled from a wound in his side, and when she felt for a pulse, there was none.

"Oh, God," Elizabeth cried, "Haze has no pulse."

"Neither does Mac," said Trinity. "We must get them out of these wet clothes and see to their wounds."

"It's too late," Rachel wailed. "Buck's been hit twice."

"It's not too late," Trinity snapped. "Move, damn it."

CHAPTER 9

❧

*A*mong the teamsters, only Lafe Beard and Smokey Foster had been wounded. Lafe had been hit in the shoulder and Smokey in the thigh.

"Some of us better take our Winchesters and stand watch outside," Port Guthrie said. "There's at least four of the varmints, and they're better than average with them rifles."

"Port," said Red, "you've had experience with gunshot wounds. If you'll see to the wounded, I'll stand watch outside."

"Near 'bout all the mules stampeded," Gourd Snively volunteered.

"Damn the mules," said Red. "Trinity, is there anything else you need, anything any of us can do . . . ?"

"Say some prayers," Trinity said. "The bullets are still in Buck, and that goes beyond the experience any of us have had."

"You ladies see to the others," said Port Guthrie, "and let me work on Buck. He ain't hurt no worse than that Indian was, and I saved him."

Red stepped out the door and stood under the stoop, staring grimly into the rain-swept darkness. He marveled at how rapidly events could take a turn for the worse. They were suddenly free of any threat of a troublesome band of renegades, and through an act of kindness, had been spared by the Comanches, only to see everything go straight to hell within a matter of seconds. His three companions lay grievously wounded, while the damn jug-headed mules would end up God knew where. But the worst of it was that there were at least four men out there somewhere who would kill to keep strangers out of this cabin where a man had been murdered.

"You varmints went about it all wrong," said Red softly. "We'd have overlooked the dead man, and after the storm we'd have moved on. Now, by God, we got three men near dead, and we ain't movin' until they can ride. Until then, I aim to always have this Winchester in my hand. Show your slimy heads, and I'll blow 'em off."

The door opened and Hattie stepped out, a tin cup of steaming coffee in her hand.

"I thought you might be needing this," she said.

"I do," said Red. "How does it look for Mac, Haze, and Buck?"

"I feel better about Buck, with Port seeing to him," Hattie replied. "The man has a good touch. He's even managed to get Rachel and Elizabeth settled down. What do you suppose was the cause of this attack?"

"This cabin may have been built and used by outlaws," Red replied. "That's about all I can figure. I reckon we took a chance coming here, but we needed shelter, and the place looked to have been abandoned for months."

"I don't understand the reason for the attack," said Hattie. "If they wanted us out of here, why didn't they just leave us alone? After the storm, we would have been gone. Now we have five men wounded, three of them so seriously they won't be able to ride anytime soon."

"I can't make any sense of it, either," Red said. "They went about it like they intended to kill us all. That's why I'm out here. If they have killing on their minds, we don't know when they'll attack again. That's a good reason for you not lingering with me."

"I had to get out of there," said Hattie. "With Port,

Trinity, Rachel, and Elizabeth all tending the wounded, I was in the way.''

"How about Mac and Haze?''

"Neither of them had a pulse at first,'' Hattie said, "but Trinity never gave up. First she got them out of their wet clothes and then began massaging them all over. Elizabeth and Rachel helped, and soon they had a pulse. Port showed them how to stop the bleeding, using cobwebs he found in the cabin's corners.''

While the thunder and lightning had ceased, the rain seemed to become more intense. From somewhere upriver, sounding faint and far away, a mule brayed.

"Port's as worried about the mules as he is about the wounded,'' said Hattie.

"With good reason,'' Red replied. "We're downwind from that varmint you just heard brayin', so he could be five miles away. Without mules—two teams per wagon—we'll be finished.''

At that point, Port Guthrie stepped out into the night, and Hattie went back inside the cabin. Red waited for the teamster to speak, and he did.

"With plenty of rest, they'll all make it. I reckon they'll have plenty of time. It'll take us a week to round up them damn mules. Maybe longer.''

"You're right about that,'' Red agreed, "because all of us can't look for the mules. We have to count on those varmints who tried to kill us having another go at it. Some of us will have to keep watch.''

"Lafe and Smokey ain't hurt all that bad,'' said Guthrie. "They can stay with you and stand watch while the rest of us hunt for the mules. But we can't do nothin' until this rain lets up.''

"There won't be all that much graze, this time of year,'' Red said, "and those mules have been getting grain. Some of them may wander back on their own.''

"True,'' said Guthrie. "It's a wonder the horses didn't run with 'em.''

"Those bushwhackers expected us to go after the

horses," Red said. "That's how they nailed three of us. Will you stand watch for a while? I'd like some more coffee, and I want to see how the wounded are doing."

"Go ahead," Guthrie replied. "I'll be here."

Mac, Buck, and Haze lay around the fire, clothed only in bandages. Trinity was soaking the bandages with whiskey. Lafe and Smokey sat on one of the bunks, their wounds already bound. Emmett Budd, Saul Estrella, and Gourd Snively stood in the shadows, concern on their weathered faces. Rachel sat beside Buck and Elizabeth beside Haze.

"If some of you will bring in their bedrolls," Trinity said, "we'll move Mac, Buck, and Haze to bunks."

"Saul and me will get 'em," said Gourd Snively. "Come on, Saul."

When the teamsters returned with the bedrolls, Trinity, Rachel, and Elizabeth made up a lower bunk for each of the seriously wounded men. They were then carried to the bunks and covered with blankets.

"Is there any more whiskey?" Trinity asked. "We used a quart of it, disinfecting and dressing the wounds."

"Should be plenty, ma'am," said Lafe Beard. "There was two quarts to every wagon, strictly for medicinal purposes. I'll go round up some more."

"You've been wounded," Saul Estrella said. "Gourd and me will get it."

"Good thinking," Red said, "going two at a time. For as long as we're here, nobody goes out alone. Those of us who haven't been wounded will take turns standing watch outside the door. Trinity, we'll depend on you, Hattie, Rachel, and Elizabeth to take turns at seeing to the wounded. Sometime before dawn, they'll likely all be burning with fever, and in need of whiskey."

The storm continued unabated, a strong west wind slapping sheets of rain against the log walls and shake roof of the cabin. Gusts of wind swept down the chimney, sending showers of sparks and smoke into the crowded room where the wounded slept fitfully. On the hearth, on a bed of coals, a big black coffeepot bubbled. Hattie was awake, going from one wounded man to the other, feeling their foreheads for fever.

"Hattie," Rachel said softly, "lie down and rest for a while. I'll take over."

"I'll stay up with you, Rachel," said Elizabeth. "I can't sleep until their fever breaks."

Red was on sentry duty outside the door, and suddenly there was the roar of a Winchester. Port Guthrie and the rest of the teamsters were immediately awake, on their feet, their Winchesters ready.

"Red," Guthrie said, "are you there?"

"Yeah," said Red. "I saw somethin' out yonder."

"Rain's still comin' down like a cow waterin' a flat rock," Guthrie said. "You sure it wasn't one of the mules?"

"It wasn't a mule," said Red, "and I may not have hit it. Come mornin', we'll take a look. Nobody goes back out there tonight."

An hour before dawn, Mac's temperature rose, and Trinity forced a dose of whiskey down him. After breakfast, Haze and Buck began running fevers, and were given whiskey.

"Port," Red said, "come along with me and let's see if I hit anything or anybody last night. If I killed one of the mules, you can shoot me."

"I reckon them mules is scattered for miles," said Guthrie.

The rain hadn't let up much, and the two men were soaked for nothing. There was no evidence that Red's shot had accomplished anything.

"I saw something or somebody last night," Red insisted. "I'm sure enough of it that I will personally stand watch today. You can't see ten feet in all this rain."

"It's a real handicap in more ways than one," said Guthrie. "Anybody comes skulkin' around, he's got to leave some sign. But not in this rain. Them four varmints could be all over us 'fore we knowed they was there."

"My point exactly," Red replied. "That's why we must have somebody on watch outside the cabin all the time."

The day dragged on. The sky lightened up just a little, but more storm clouds swept in from the west, and the rain continued.

"Mac's fever's broken," said Trinity.

"*Bueno*," Red said. "This time tomorrow, he'll be awake and talking to us."

"Buck won't be," said Rachel. "His fever hasn't let up, and I'm afraid that it won't."

"Double the dose of whiskey," Port Guthrie said. "His wounds was worse, so he's got maybe twice the infection. What about Haze?"

"Still feverish," said Elizabeth, "but he's resting well."

"They should all be takin' a turn for the better by suppertime," Guthrie said.

It was what Guthrie left unsaid that bothered them most. A wounded man who didn't respond to treatment and showed no improvement could only continue to slip away from the living until he became one of the dead. But Guthrie's prediction was accurate, and well before suppertime, the fever broke. Buck and Haze were judged to be out of danger. When Port Guthrie had eaten, he took his Winchester and went to relieve Red. But no sooner had the teamster opened the door than a slug slammed into the log wall just inches from his head. Guthrie dropped to his knees, cocking his Winchester, but Red was already firing.

"Back inside," Red shouted.

Guthrie needed no urging, for in quick succession there were three more shots, and all were chest-high. Had he been on his feet, Port Guthrie would have been a dead man. He threw himself back through the cabin door, Red right behind him. Red kicked the door shut just as another slug tore into it. The rest of the teamsters—even the wounded—had their Winchesters ready.

"We'll have to abandon that outside watch as long as this storm's roarin'," Red said. "When we open the door, we're presenting them with a target, and thanks to the storm, we're not even gettin' a muzzle flash to return the fire.''

"Yeah," said Guthrie, "but with nobody on watch, they can kick in the door and blow us all to hell and gone, before we can fight back.''

"Maybe not," Red said. "We'll pile all the extra firewood in front of the door. It's not all that thick, and if they throw enough lead through it, some of it could get to us.''

"I just want the storm to be over, so we can get out of here," said Hattie.

"We'll likely be here another week, storm or not," Guthrie said. "We got wounded men, and we'll need a good three days of sun before we can move the wagons.''

"Not even then," said Gourd Snively, "if we don't find them mules.''

While their prospects were grim enough, things promised to get worse. There came a crash of thunder. Yet another storm was moving in, and the continual pounding of wind-driven rain on the shake roof and log walls of the cabin became a dirge. Twice, since the five men had been wounded, they had been fired upon by unknown, unseen adversaries, and with no effective means of retaliation, their nerves had become frayed almost to the breaking point.

"I suppose we should be thankful for the continual rain," Trinity said. "If it wasn't for that, they could burn us out.''

"That's the one thing we don't have to worry about," said Red. "There must be something in this cabin they want, somethin' they can't get to while we're here. At least, that's what Mac thought.''

"So that's what you an' him took candles and was searchin' for in the other room," Gourd Snively said. "Didn't find nothin'?''

"No," said Red. "We didn't make a big thing of it, because we didn't want the rest of you gettin' rattled.''

"After gettin' shot, an' havin' all that lead throwed at

me by varmints I don't know, can't see, an' can't shoot at," Smokey Foster said, "I'm commencin' to git rattled anyhow."

"I reckon I can understand that," said Red. "It's time you knew the straight of it. Mac and me didn't take that skeleton out of here. When we came back to remove it, the thing was gone. Bones, hat, saddlebags, and Colt."

"More damn outlaws," Emmett Budd said, "and they knowed we was lookin' for some place to hole up durin' the storm."

"Yes," said Red, "but we had no idea they wouldn't just wait for us to leave. Damn it, how could we know they planned to kill us?"

"I reckon we can't fault you and Mac for goin' ahead and takin' this cabin," said Port Guthrie. "It's good shelter, but it's a real skookum house."*

"What . . . what's happened?" Mac mumbled.

"Nothing you should think about until you're better," said Trinity, kneeling beside his bunk. "Go back to sleep."

"No," Mac said weakly. "I've . . . been awake . . . heard the talk. Water . . . bring me water . . ."

Trinity brought him a tin cup of water, and when he drank that, brought more.

"Red," said Mac, his voice stronger, "tell me . . . what happened."

Trinity shook her head, but Red McLean appeared not to notice. He hunkered down beside Mac's bunk and began to talk.

"The horses and mules were spooked by the lightning. When we all ran out to try and hold 'em, four rifles cut down on us. Lafe and Smokey have flesh wounds, but Haze, Buck, and you caught some bad ones. Buck was hit twice, but him and Haze survived the fever. They'll make it, and so will you."

"The shooting," Mac said.

*A Chinook word meaning devil or evil spirit.

"Since that first time, when you were hit, they've fired on us twice," said Red. "Port and me was takin' turns standing watch outside the door, and they damn near got the both of us. The door ain't that strong, so we piled all the extra firewood against it. You can't see ten feet, with all the rain. We couldn't return the fire, because we couldn't even see a muzzle flash."

"None of you are to go out there again," Mac said, "until the storm lets up and you can see to defend yourselves."

"We haven't been out," said Hattie. "Since we couldn't get to the bushes, we've been going to the back room. It's beginning to smell like there's something dead back there, for sure."

Despite his wound, Mac laughed, and it ended in a coughing fit.

"Enough talk," said Trinity. "See what it's doing to you?"

"It's . . . not . . . the talk," Mac wheezed. "It's that . . . damn rotgut . . . whiskey. More water . . ."

Trinity brought him another cup of water.

"How are . . . you getting water?" Mac asked.

"By opening the door just enough to set a pot or pail out there," said Red. "It's been raining for three days and nights, like pourin' it out of a boot."

"Bring me . . . my Colt," Mac said.

Trinity started to say something, but her eyes met Red's, and she changed her mind. Red brought the weapon and Mac took it.

"All of you . . . keep your guns ready," said Mac. "There's no use . . . fooling ourselves. I believe this bunch has . . . no . . . intention of us leaving . . . here . . . alive. I just wish . . . I'd been . . . savvy enough to consider that, before . . ."

"We needed shelter," Red said, "and there was nothing else. Just this cabin. So I'm as much to blame as you are, if anybody's to be blamed."

. But Mac hadn't heard, for he was again asleep, the Colt gripped in his right hand.

"He's one *bueno hombre*," said Port Guthrie.

"Water," a weak voice cried from the other side of the room.

"Buck," Red shouted joyously.

Quickly Rachel brought a tin cup of water, and so eager was Buck that he strangled. It cost him, in his condition, but he emptied the cup three more times before he was satisfied.

"God," he croaked, "I feel . . . like . . . my gullet's been . . . salted . . . with gunpowder . . . and set afire. More . . . water . . ."

Rachel brought more water, and gathering his strength, Buck spoke again.

"Red, I . . . heard what you . . . told Mac. Bring me . . . my gun . . ."

"Buck," said Red, "you took two slugs. You're in no shape . . ."

"I'll be the . . . judge of . . . that," Buck growled. "Now bring me . . . my damn . . . gun . . ."

Without another word, Red brought the Colt and gave it to Buck.

"Red . . ."

Haze Sanderson's eyes were open. He tried to speak again, but his voice was raspy, a dry croak. Without a word, Elizabeth brought a tin cup of water, and Haze drank it gratefully. Again he tried to speak.

"More . . . please . . ."

His thirst satisfied, he again spoke to Red.

"I . . . I've . . . been listening, Red. Bring me . . . my . . . Colt."

Elizabeth's eyes met Red's in silent appeal, but he didn't hesitate. He took the Colt from its holster and handed it to Haze. The wounded man then closed his eyes as though in sleep, the weapon gripped in his hand. The gesture wasn't lost on the teamsters. They grinned in appreciation and Port Guthrie spoke for them.

"More and more, I'm gettin' the feelin' we'll come out of this alive."

Sometime during the night, the rain ceased. But the wind still screeched around the cabin like a live thing, and the dawn broke gray and dismal.

"By God," said Gourd Snively, who had eased the door open a little, "looky yonder."

The four horses had remained near the cabin, and grazing with them were a dozen of the all-important mules.

"That means we only got to find twelve of the varmints," Saul Estrella said, "and God only knows where they are."

"Saul," said Guthrie, "I reckon it's time we went looking for the missing ones. It'll be you, Emmett, Gourd, and me. Smokey, you and Lafe bein' wounded, I want you to stay here and help defend the cabin. Red, does that suit you?"

"I reckon," Red replied. "It's the only sensible thing to do. You gents ride careful. If that bunch is determined to gun us down, they'll start with you four, once you're away from the cabin."

"One more day," said Mac, who was stronger, "and I'll be on my feet. We must find those missing mules and, as soon as the sun dries up the mud, be on our way."

"There's nothin' I'd like better than gettin' out of here," Red said, "but the way these varmints has been gunnin' for us, you really think they'll allow us to leave?"

"I don't know," said Mac. "Everything points to there being something here that they want, something for which they've returned, and they're behaving like they believe we might have found it."

"Then damn it, let's find whatever it is," Red said. "It's got to be in this front room. Maybe it's under the hearth."

"That's too obvious," said Mac. "Did you ever hear of anything hidden in a house that wasn't under one of the hearthstones?"

"If it's so obvious, perhaps that's all the more reason

to look there," Hattie said. "Why don't we begin there, and spend the day looking?"

"The rest of you can do that," said Red. "Now that the storm's blown itself out, I'll keep watch outside the door. The horses and mules are out there, and those loaded wagons, as well. The freight on those wagons is worth ten times whatever those hombres are looking for."

A dozen miles away, under a shelving rock, four men sat around their breakfast fire. There were the brothers, Eldon and Ebeau Darrow, Keno Norris, and Antoine Burke. Their bearded faces still retained a prison pallor, and every man's temper was on a short rein.

"Just don't fergit," Ebeau said, "me an' Eldon's bossin' this outfit."

"How could we *ever* forget?" Keno Norris snapped. "It was you varmints that killed Ab Winkler before he told us where he hid the twenty-five thousand we took from that bank in Wichita."

"The double-crossin' bastard took the money an' run out on us," said Eldon. "We got no reason to believe the money's anywhere but in that cabin."

"Hell," Antoine said, "when we caught up to Winkler, the posse wasn't more'n a mile behind us. We should of took Winkler with us, lost the posse, an' then worked our way back to the cabin. But you damned Darrows wanted Winkler dead so bad, it cost us the bank loot an' near two years in jail."

"Winkler had his Colt out and would of kilt Ebeau," said Eldon, "if I hadn't shot him quick. I didn't know the posse was that close."

"I reckon that's all water down the creek," Keno Norris said. "I got another crow to pick with you Darrow varmints. Somethin' more recent. It was you Darrows that was hell-bent on gunnin' down that bunch that's squattin' in the cabin. By God, if we'd just left 'em alone, they'd have moved on after the storm. Unless they're a bunch of damn fools, after all the lead we've throwed at 'em, they've likely decided they're settin' on somethin' mighty valuable.''

"Yeah," said Burke, "an' thanks to the Darrows, they got plenty of time for a search. They ain't about to go nowhere with wounded men. Hell, they'll likely be squattin' there for another week."

"Oh, I don't think so," Ebeau said. "Some of 'em will have to go searchin' for their mules. That means them that ain't been wounded will be away from the cabin. There'll be just the wounded hombres an' the women. I say we bust in there, finish what we started with the wounded men, and take the women hostage. When them mule hunters come back, we'll be waitin' for 'em."

"Maybe some of them hombres in the cabin ain't been wounded as bad as you think," said Keno Norris. "We could go waltzin' in there and git shot to doll rags."

Ebeau laughed. "You scared, Keno?"

"Yeah," Keno said. "I'm scared of you Darrows with your damn fast guns. You shot Winkler, cost us twenty-five thousand, and now you've as good as told that bunch in the cabin there's somethin' in there worth killin' for."

"Saddle up," said Eldon Darrow. "We're goin' to clear out that cabin, just as soon as some of them hombres are out of the way. We know five, maybe six of 'em, was hit, and they won't be in no shape to fight."

"And you aim to go chargin' in there with guns blazing," Keno said.

"Yeah," said Darrow, "and when the others come back, we'll cut 'em down from the cabin."

"You damn Darrows is too kill-crazy to suit me," Antoine Burke said. "I ain't gonna be a party to such a fool scheme. I say we wait on that bunch to leave the cabin and then do our searchin' in peace."

"I'm of the same mind," said Keno Norris. "Robbin' banks is one thing, but leavin' a trail of dead men is the way, quick and sure, to find yourself at the business end of a hangman's rope."

"You don't aim to help us bust into that cabin," Ebeau

said, "but you still aim to git a share of the twenty-five thousand that's hid there."

"Why not?" Keno said. "I spent near two years in the *juzgado* for it."

"Damn right," said Antoine. "It was a Darrow slug that killed Winkler and landed us all behind bars. I ain't takin' a rap for any more Darrow killing. The storm's over, and I'm waitin' for that bunch in the cabin to move on. Then we'll take it apart one log at a time, if we have to."

"Well, by God, Ebeau an' me's goin' back there and takin' it apart one log at a time, right now," Eldon said. "You don't ride with us, then you don't share the money."

Keno and Antoine reached for their Colts, but the Darrows had been expecting just such a move. With a fiendish light in their hard eyes, Eldon and Ebeau Darrow drew their revolvers and shot dead their companions with whom they had long ridden the owl-hoot trail. Leaving the dead men where they lay, the Darrows saddled their horses and rode to a ridge overlooking the cabin. They reined up within a thicket in time to see Port Guthrie, Emmett Budd, Gourd Snively, and Saul Estrella mount mules and ride away.

"That's the ones that wasn't hurt in the shootin'," Eldon Darrow said. "That leaves us with the wounded men and the women."

"Them that just rode away is still close enough to hear the shootin'," said Ebeau.

"Hell," Eldon said, "that's what we want. Let 'em come skalley-hootin' back here, and we'll git shut of the whole bunch. 'Cept the women, of course."

"Let's git on with it, then," said Ebeau. "You circle around an' come in from the west and I'll come in from the east. We'll meet outside the cabin door and bust in together."

When Port Guthrie and the teamsters had ridden away, Red McLean had been called to breakfast.

"I ought to be eatin' out there on the stoop," Red said. "Hostile as that bunch of owl hoots has been, I can't believe they won't try somethin', now that the storm's passed and we're four men shy.''

''Not much they can do,'' said Mac, ''unless they bust in here with their guns blasting. All of you move back, and stay out of line with the door. It's not that strong, and a slug from a Winchester can penetrate it.''

Mac sat up, his feet on the floor, his Colt within reach. Haze Sanderson assumed the same position, and while Buck wasn't quite up to such movement, he had his Colt in his hand. Hattie was kneeling by the fireplace, readying a fresh pot of coffee. Trinity, Rachel, and Elizabeth had lighted candles and were searching the walls for a loose section of log or some other possible place of concealment. Suddenly the door slammed open and in the hand of each of the Darrows was a Colt spitting lead . . .

CHAPTER 10

❧

*W*hen the Darrows crashed the door, Hattie was the only one in line with it. One slug wrecked the coffeepot while a second struck the girl's right thigh. The force of it threw her sideways on the floor, saving her life. Mac's Colt was like rolling thunder, and three slugs ripped into Eldon Darrow. Red shot Ebeau Darrow twice, and the outlaw died on his feet. Without a second look at either of the dead men, Red rushed to the wounded Hattie and knelt beside her. Mac was on his feet, unsteady but facing the open doorway, expecting other outlaws. But for the groaning of Hattie, there was only silence. Without a word, Red lifted her, placing her on one of the lower bunks. Trinity, Rachel, and Elizabeth were instantly by his side, and he turned to them.

"See to her, please."

"We will," Trinity said. "Don't worry."

Haze and Buck, despite their wounds, sat on their bunks, their Colts ready. Suddenly there was a pounding of hooves, and Red moved to the door, his Colt ready.

"It's Port and the boys," said Red. "They must have heard the shooting."

The teamsters hit the ground running, halting at the sight of the two dead men lying on the cabin floor.

"What happened to the other two?" Guthrie asked.

"That's all there was," said Red, "but they wounded

Hattie before we nailed them. If you gents will help me, we'll haul these varmints out for the buzzards and coyotes. I hope it don't make the critters sick.''

Once the dead men were removed, the teamsters hung the door back in place as best they could.

"Red," Guthrie said, "don't you reckon we ought to backtrack them two? There was four of 'em, and if the others is still skulking around, we ought to know it.''

"I think you're right," said Red. "Mac, we're goin' to do some trailing.''

"Boys," Guthrie said, turning to his teamsters, "stay close until we get back. Them mules, wherever they are, can wait till we settle with these owl hoots.''

"Saddle us a couple of horses, Port," said Red. "I'm not handy at ridin' a mule. I'll be along after I see Hattie.''

Hattie lay on her back, stripped from the waist down. Trinity had a pot of boiling water and was about to cleanse the wound.

"How bad?" Red asked. Her teeth clenched, Hattie said nothing.

"It missed the bone," said Trinity. "It ripped through the fleshy part of her right thigh and made a bloody mess of part of her behind. We're going to turn her on her belly and she'll be that way for a while.''

It was serious enough, painful in the extreme, but not life-threatening. Red went out and joined Port Guthrie.

"How bad is she hurt?" Guthrie asked.

"No broken bones," said Red, "but she'll be on her belly for a while.''

"All the more reason for us findin' out what happened to those other pelicans," the teamster said. "We'll be here a few more days, until the wounded can travel.''

"I think so," Red agreed. "I'd hate to slam Hattie around in that wagon box. We've killed so much time here, another three or four days won't hurt.''

Red and Guthrie had no trouble backtracking the outlaws. They reined up when Red's horse nickered and another answered.

"That gives us away," said Guthrie.

Both men dismounted, took their Winchesters, and proceeded on foot. They came out above the shelving rock, and from their position, could see only the two grazing horses.

"They're camped under the bluff," Red said quietly. "You ease down this side, and I'll take the other. We'll have them in a cross fire."

The descent was difficult, for there was thick underbrush and stones that might easily dislodge and send a man tumbling. Guthrie was first to reach a position where he could see the sprawled bodies of the dead men.

"They're down there, Red," Guthrie shouted, "but their owl-hootin' days are done."

Reaching the camp, Red and Guthrie silently regarded the grim scene for a moment.

"This don't make a hell of a lot of sense," said Red. "The pair that come chargin' into the cabin must have killed these two, but why?"

"Whatever the reason, it flat didn't help their cause none," Guthrie said. "The four of 'em could have staked out the cabin and picked us off, one or two at a time."

"I reckon these two might have favored doin' just that," said Red. "That would explain the varmints that tried to rush us. There's got to be somethin' in that cabin they purely was afraid we'd find."

"They ain't gonna be needin' their horses," Guthrie said. "We might as well take them with us, and pick up the other two we saw as we rode out."

"Smart thinking," said Red. "I can't see leavin' good horses running loose as bait for wolves. We'll take the saddles, too."

When Red and Guthrie approached the cabin leading the four horses, Mac came out to meet them. He didn't ask any questions, for the led horses said it all.

"For an hombre that's been shot, you're up and about a mite soon," Red observed.

Mac laughed. "I've come down with somethin' more

deadly than lead poisoning. Cabin fever. I don't see any
bullet holes in either of you."

"We wasn't exposed to any lead," said Guthrie. "Them
other two hombres was graveyard dead when we found
'em. We reckoned they was gunned down by the same two
that busted into the cabin. Don't make no sense at all."

"Maybe it does," Mac said. "Come on in and have a
look at what we found while you and Red were gone."

"I want to see how Hattie is," said Red.

"She's asleep," Mac replied. "Trinity dressed her
wound and gave her a powerful dose of laudanum so she
can sleep through the worst of the pain."

"All right, then," said Red, "what have you discovered?"

"Elizabeth and Rachel found what the outlaws were
looking for," Mac said. "There was a loose log head-high,
near the chimney. Rachel, light a candle so Red and Port
can see."

Rachel lighted a candle and held it over one of the bunks
where there was a mass of what appeared to be paper rem-
nants.

"Why, that's just chewed-up paper," said Guthrie.
"The rats has had hold of whatever it used to be."

"We believe it used to be thousands of dollars in greenbacks," Mac said. "Sure don't seem worth the lives of
five men, does it?"

"It's the cruelest kind of joke," said Red, "but consid-
erin' the four varmints involved, I reckon justice has been
done."

"Yeah," Guthrie said. "We come out of it considerably
better than them owl hoots. We got four good horses and
saddles."

Red found Hattie asleep, belly-down.

"She was in a lot of pain," said Trinity. "I gave her a
big dose of laudanum, and by the time she comes out of
that, she may have a temperature and be ready for whiskey."

"My God," Red replied, "I don't envy her that. The

hangover from that whiskey's far worse than bein' shot.''

Even with Hattie being wounded, the mood of the outfit was much improved. Buck and Haze were able to sit up, could eat, and the healing process had begun.

"Tomorrow," said Port Guthrie, "we'll go after the missing mules."

"I'll go with you," Red said. "With Mac, Buck, and Haze here, and with that bunch of outlaws out of the way, the cabin should be secure enough."

Port Guthrie, Emmett Budd, Saul Estrella, Gourd Snively, and Red McLean rode out the following morning in search of the missing mules.

"We had rain for two days after the varmints lit out," Guthrie said, "so we can forget about follerin' a trail. We'll just have to ride along the river and look for 'em."

"There was enough rain to fill ever' dry creek an' water hole for a hunnert miles," said Gourd Snively. "We may be wastin' our time huntin' 'em along the river."

"Maybe," Guthrie agreed, "but it's a good place to start. There's generally more graze close to the river, especially this time of the year."

"We'll likely find all of 'em or none of 'em," said Saul Estrella. "They'll usually bunch together, whether they're grazin' or driftin'."

"When they stampeded," Red reminded them, "they were running into the storm, and no horse, mule, or cow will do that for long. After the thunder and lightning let up, I'd not be surprised if they all drifted with the storm."

"That makes sense to me," said Saul Estrella, "and if that's the case, we're ridin' this river the wrong direction."

"Maybe," Port Guthrie said, "and if we don't find some mule sign within the next few miles, we'll take Red's suggestion. We're tryin' to do it the easy way, follerin' the river. If this don't work, the hunt's goin' to get considerably more complicated."

"I hope the jug-heads don't wander too far into Indian Territory," said Emmett Budd. "There was just a hell of a lot of them Comanches, and with the buffalo gone, some mule meat might tickle the fancy of Quanah Parker and his bunch.''

"I wish you hadn't brought that up," Red said.

"It's a possibility we may have to consider," said Port Guthrie, "if all else fails. We can make do with eight of the critters, by harnessin' them four extra horses to one of the wagons, but we sure can't manage with no less."

"Many a good saddle horse ain't worth a damn in harness," Red said. "We'll find the missing mules, unless they've been carved into Comanche steaks and eaten."

After a two-hour westward ride, Port Guthrie reined up.

"Red's idea is makin' more sense all the time," Guthrie said. "We've come twenty mile at least. If we're goin' to find them missin' critters, we'd as well ride back the way we come. They must of drifted with the storm."

They rode on in silence, every man of them aware of the consequences of losing half their mules. They rode past the cabin, following the river eastward. Having ridden almost fifteen miles, they discovered the first mule tracks.

"They been waterin' here, where the riverbank is low," said Guthrie, "and they've been here more'n once, from the tracks. That means they ain't too far off."

Some of the tracks were fresh and the animals had been to the river often enough to have left a broad trail. It led to the south, away from the river.

"They've found some good graze somewhere," Gourd Snively observed.

The riders topped a rise, and from there they counted all twelve of the missing mules. Downwind from the mounted men, the mules lifted their heads, aware that they were being watched.

"Don't nobody move," said Guthrie. "Give the varmints time to get used to us being here. They been loose long enough they're likely to scatter like wild turkeys if we move suddenly."

The riders waited until the wary mules resumed their

grazing. They hadn't been free long enough to spook at the sight of mounted men.

"Let's ride a mite closer," Port Guthrie said. "If they act skittish, rein up and wait for 'em to settle down again."

With Guthrie leading, the men rode a few yards closer, and again the mules ceased grazing and lifted their heads. The riders reined up until the mules again settled down.

"A mite closer," said Red, "and we can rope five of 'em."

"No," Guthrie said. "That would scare hell out of the others. We got to get among 'em, so's we can bridle 'em. They ain't used to bein' roped, but they'll all remember what a bridle is."

Guthrie's mule sense worked to perfection, and after five of the animals were bridled, the others submitted meekly, as though they believed it was expected of them.

"Port," said Red admiringly, "when there's mules to be reasoned with, I'll shut my mouth, get out of the way, and stand back and watch."

Guthrie laughed. "I've been around mules more'n I have people. I reckon the varmints has accepted me as one of them."

The mules followed willingly on lead ropes. As the riders neared the cabin, there was a ragged cheer from the men who had remained behind. The return of the elusive mules was their assurance that they would again be taking the trail, leaving behind the cabin that had at times seemed a prison.

"From now on," Guthrie said, "we're goin' to picket these critters. Emmett, Saul, and Gourd, help me settle 'em down and grain 'em."

Red dismounted and hurried to the cabin, anxious about Hattie. He found she was still belly-down and still sleeping.

"She's had her first dose of whiskey," said Trinity. "Rachel and Elizabeth had to hold her while I poured the stuff down her."

"The wound didn't weaken her," Mac said. "She fought like a bobcat."

"I reckon that's a good sign," said Red. "We'll be waiting for her to heal enough for us to take the trail."

"I'm still a mite sore," Buck said, "but I'm ready to get out of here."

"So am I," said Haze. "This was a great shelter when we needed one, but I want to be away, out on the plains."

"When Hattie's fever breaks," Trinity said, "we'll see how she feels about leaving. If she can lie belly-down in the wagon as well as she can in this bunk, then we can go."

The Canadian River. October 20, 1873.

"I can't see us remaining here another day on my account," Hattie said, when she had slept off the effects of the whiskey. "Spread me some blankets in that wagon and let's be on our way."

The teamsters harnessed the mules, mounted their wagon boxes, and the big wagons again lumbered south. Each of the first four wagons had a horse loping behind on a lead rope. Trinity's wagon was last in line. Red and Haze rode beside it, while Buck rode ahead of Port Guthrie's lead wagon. Mac had ridden ahead to scout for water, having made sure all the water barrels had been filled before leaving the Canadian.

"Whoa up!" Guthrie shouted. It was time to rest the teams.

Hattie twisted around and raised her head above the wagon's tailgate.

"Well," said Red, "you've made the first two hours. Maybe eight more, and you can get out of there."

"Lying belly-down, I can't imagine the ground being any better than a wagon bed," Hattie grunted, "except that the ground won't be moving up, down, and sideways."

When the teamsters were about to take the trail again,

Mac rode in, and they waited for his report about the terrain ahead.

"The storm replenished some water holes and dry creeks," said Mac. "There's a good spring with a runoff that we should reach before sundown."

"How about graze?" Guthrie asked.

"Close by, and not bad for this time of year," said Mac. "It'll do for tonight."

Again the wagons moved on, Mac riding ahead.

"Rachel," Trinity said, "take over the reins for a while. I'm going to ride one of the extra horses."

"I suppose you should," said Rachel devilishly. "Mac looks terribly lonesome."

"Oh, shut up," Trinity said, "or I'll tell Buck you're having trouble with the teams and you're wanting him to take the reins for you."

"Oh, would you?" Rachel asked, in a pleading way.

Trinity could hear them laughing as she rode away, and it sounded like Hattie had taken part in the merriment. She trotted her horse alongside Mac's, and he didn't seem surprised to find her there.

"Tired of the wagon seat?" he asked.

"That, and Hattie's grunting and groaning," said Trinity. "Perhaps just tired of female company in general."

"Come, now," Mac said, "you're betraying your own kind."

"There's times when my own kind can be a bother," said Trinity. "Why is it that a man can be mortally wounded and die without a whimper, while a female with a scratch on her behind . . ."

Mac laughed. "You said it was a bloody mess when you first looked at it."

"There was a lot of blood," Trinity said defensively, "and it looked worse than it was. The bullet was mostly spent from having passed through her right thigh, but I'd swear her bottom bled worse than your wound."

"Given a choice," said Mac, "I'd rather be shot just about anywhere else. I reckon it's hell, not bein' able to sit. How much longer do you think she'll be on her belly?"

"Two or three more days, at least," Trinity replied. "Isn't there something else we can talk about?"

"Yes," said Mac, "but you won't like that any better."

"We've survived two outlaw gangs," Trinity said. "You're expecting worse?"

"Maybe," said Mac. "Indian Territory's infested with renegades of every stripe, but we may encounter others as bad or worse in Texas."

"I suppose you have a reason for believing that."

"I do," Mac replied. "You know the kind of cargo we're taking to Austin. Before we left Kansas City, word had leaked out regarding these arms and ammunition, and before we even reached Dodge, there was a gang—a dozen strong—trying to stop the train. Then after we reached Dodge, the son-in-law of the owner of the freight line pulled a Judas and had his own bunch of outlaws try to steal the wagons."

"That's serious enough," said Trinity, "but what does that have to do with Texas and the trouble you're expecting there?"

"If word of this arms shipment leaked out in Kansas City," Mac said, "I believe it all could have been common knowledge in Washington. Thanks to the telegraph, there's a good possibility that every fort in Texas knows about us. I know Mr. Lincoln wanted us all to be one nation again, and with all due respect to him, there's a bunch of varmints wearin' Union blue that ought to be backed up against a wall and shot."

"You believe we're in danger from the military in Texas?"

"I don't have any proof," said Mac, "but after what happened in Dodge, I don't trust even the military."

"Then you're taking some risk in going to Fort Griffin," Trinity said.

"If they already know about us," said Mac, "our stopping there won't make any real difference. Anybody looking for us can find us."

"My God," Trinity said, "if we can't trust our own soldiers . . ."

"I'm not saying we can't trust any of them," said Mac. "There's a mix of good men who fought on both sides, but there's some renegade Rebs who took the pledge that won't forget and won't forgive. They're watching and waiting for an opportunity to pull off a coup that will cripple the Union, and the loss of this initial shipment of arms would just about do it. Especially if they fall into the hands of the nation's enemies."

"What do we do, how do we protect ourselves?"

"I'm not sure," Mac said, "because I don't know from what quarter such a move might come. I hope when we reach Fort Griffin I can meet with the post commander and see how much he already knows about where we're going and what we're hauling."

"But we're still a long way from Fort Griffin."

"Yes," said Mac, "and you're wondering what might happen before we get there. I'm wondering the same thing. We're just goin' to have to keep our eyes open and our guns handy."

"When are you going to warn the others?"

"Most of the men already have their suspicions," Mac replied. "It's something we'll have to discuss before we cross the Red River. Please don't involve Hattie, Elizabeth, and Rachel in this just yet."

"You're a trusting man, Mr. Tunstall."

"Only when I believe that trust is justified, Mrs. Mc-Coy."

"Please don't call me that."

"Whatever you say," Mac said. "But until we reach Fort Griffin, and you know—"

"Oh, damn Fort Griffin," Trinity cried. "I've told you how I feel."

She wheeled her horse and galloped away, riding wide of the wagons so the teamsters wouldn't see the tears on her cheeks. Circling in behind her own wagon, sleeving the tears away, she dismounted. She climbed into the mov-

ing wagon and tied the horse's reins to a wagon bow.
Hattie wriggled toward the front of the wagon, making
room, and it was she who spoke.

"You've been bawling. What did the brute do to you?"

"I have *not* been bawling," Trinity snapped.

"Don't lie to me," said Hattie. "There's streaks in the
dirt on your face."

"He called me Mrs. McCoy," Trinity said.

"Oh, that *is* serious," said Hattie, in mock sympathy.
"He still thinks of you as used goods, a married woman."

On the wagon box, Rachel and Elizabeth had been all
ears, and they joined Hattie in a burst of laughter. Trinity
responded with some choice words that might have embarrassed Mac Tunstall, had he heard, but Trinity's three
mischievous companions laughed all the harder.

As Mac had predicted, the wagons reached the spring before sundown, allowing them time to gather wood and prepare supper before dark.

"We'll leave the fire burned down to just coals, to keep
the coffee hot," Mac said. "I don't know who might see
the fire after dark, but we can't afford to take chances.
We'll continue with three watches, as before. Port, you
gents take the first two watches, three of you at a time.
Red, Buck, Haze, and me will take the last watch."

A few minutes after the third watch began, Hattie, Rachel, and Elizabeth quietly left the wagon. Trinity knew
where they were going, but she stubbornly refused to follow their example. Let Mac Tunstall wonder where she
was, and if he cared enough, perhaps he would come looking for her. But when an hour had passed, there was no
sign of him. She stamped her foot, swore under her breath,
swallowed her pride, and stalked to the farthest wagon
where she expected him to be. Only he wasn't there. She
started around the wagon, but froze at the sound of a Colt
being cocked behind her.

"Damn you," she hissed, "you knew it was me."

"How was I to know?" he taunted. "It's black as the

underside of a stove lid, and you could have been a Comanche.''

''Well, you *could* have come to me,'' she snapped.

''Oh, but I couldn't'' said Mac. ''I'm on watch, and the rest of the camp's covered. Besides, it was you that got a burr under your tail and run off.''

''I did *not* run off. I simply returned to my wagon.''

''Then why are you so hacked off at me?''

''You called me Mrs. McCoy, after all I've . . . all we've . . .''

''I don't know how old you are, and I don't care.'' Mac said, ''but you're old enough that you have no business playing games.''

Seizing her by the shoulders, he kissed her long and hard.

''How dare you,'' she said, breaking his grip. ''I . . . I'll . . .''

''You'll do *what*?'' he demanded.

She threw her arms around him, returning his kiss twofold.

''That's your best answer so far,'' he said, when she finally let him go.

Elsewhere within the camp, Red leaned against a wagon and Hattie stood beside him.

''I'm so glad to be off my belly and out of that wagon,'' Hattie said, ''I'll never tire of standing. I'm hoping by tomorrow I'll be able to sit.''

''Will you have a scar?'' Red asked.

''Perhaps,'' said Hattie. ''Will it bother you?''

''I reckon not,'' Red replied, ''if mine don't bother you.''

''I don't know,'' she teased. ''It depends on where they are.''

''You'll have to wait,'' said Red. ''The time ain't right.''

''When will it be right? After Fort Griffin?''

''I reckon,'' Red said. ''Some things deserve a man's

undivided attention, and I reckon I can't devote all mine to you until we get these wagons to Austin.''

"That's a relief," said Hattie. "I was afraid . . . something else . . . was coming between us.''

"Not what you're thinking," Red said. "I'm expecting trouble either before we get to Fort Griffin, or somewhere between Fort Griffin and Austin.''

"Oh, I hope not," said Hattie, "after the trouble we've had. How many more outlaws can there be?''

"Entirely too many," Red replied.

"I was scared to death when you were shot," Rachel said. "Don't ever do that to me again.''

Buck laughed. "It ain't the kind of thing a man chooses. You was all that fearful, just for a galoot like me?''

"I was," said Rachel. "I was so afraid, my eyes were out of focus, and I couldn't have found my backside with both hands. If it hadn't been for Trinity and Port Guthrie, you'd have bled to death.''

"This is the frontier," Buck said. "You got to get over that. Next time I'm shot, Port and Trinity may not be there. It may all depend on you.''

"I'll try," said Rachel, moving closer to him. "Lord, I'll be glad when we finally reach Fort Griffin.''

"Why?" Buck asked. "So you can track down Private Price?''

"You *know* why," said Rachel. "You must be good for something more than sittin' on a wagon tongue teasing me.''

Buck laughed. "Not much. You're seein' my best side right now.''

"Something's botherin' you," said Haze. "What is it?''

"When there's shooting," Elizabeth said, "must you always jump right in the middle of it?''

"If you're referring to back there at the cabin," said Haze, "when the stock is about to stampede, it's every man's duty to get out there pronto. There won't always be a pack of outlaws waitin' with Winchesters. Hell, I only got hit once. Poor old Buck took two slugs, and might of died.''

"My sympathy to poor old Buck," Elizabeth said, "but my concern is for you."

"If you want me," said Haze, "you'll have to accept the good and the bad. Can you?"

"Ah reckon," she said, imitating his Texas drawl.

CHAPTER 11

⌖

The Red River. November 5, 1873.

*W*hile resting the teams, the teamsters had climbed down and were stretching their legs. To relieve the boredom of the trail, the outriders and the women had joined them.

"If my reckonin' is anywhere close," Port Guthrie said, "we should be in Texas this time tomorrow. We can't be more than a few miles from Doan's Crossing."*

"What's there?" Trinity asked.

"Just a shallows in the Red," said Guthrie. "Lots of northbound cattle drives cross there. There's good water and graze, and sometimes friendly Indians camp there."

"And sometimes, not-so-friendly whites," Lafe Beard said.

"It's too late in the season for cattle drives," said Mac, "and it's a mite far south for owl hoots from Indian Territory. There's Texas law just across the river."

"We don't need to scout for water," Red said, "but it might be handy knowin' if we'll have company at the crossing."

"I'll find out," said Mac. "I aim to ride on ahead. If

---

*Doan's Crossing is fifteen miles north of the present-day town of Vernon, Texas.

anybody's there, I want to know who they are and *why* they're there.''

Mac rode out, and found Guthrie's estimate to be correct. He reached the river somewhere west of the crossing, and as he rode downriver he could see the dirty gray of smoke in the sky ahead of him. Mac rode only a little farther before dismounting and proceeding afoot. He wished to see without being seen. For convenience, the fire was near the river, in a clearing that surely must be the crossing. There was little cover, and Mac had to satisfy himself with what he could observe from a distance. Four men were gathered around the fire, and were obviously preparing a meal. Mac could recognize none of them from so great a distance. He watched the camp for a while, finally deciding the party consisted of only the four men he could see. He returned to his horse, and after leading the animal for almost a mile, he mounted and rode north.

''Rein up,'' Port Guthrie shouted.

It was time to rest the teams again, and an opportunity for the outfit to hear what Mac had to say about the Red River and Doan's Crossing.

''Four hombres had a cook fire goin',''' Mac reported. ''I wasn't close enough for them to see me, and I couldn't identify any of them. If they're unfriendly, I reckon we can hold our own.''

''Them bein' on the north bank of the Red is reason enough to make me suspicious of them,'' said Guthrie. ''Leavin' Texas, the Red is the jumpin'-off place. Even the Rangers won't chase a man into Indian Territory.''

''We won't start a fight, even with hostiles,'' Mac said, ''but if they start one, we'll finish it. When we're near the crossing, Red, I'll want you, Haze, and Buck riding with me.''

Nobody said anything. After their recent experiences with outlaws, they understood his caution. The teamsters mounted their wagon boxes and the caravan moved on. There was no sign of smoke as they approached the river.

Red, Haze, and Buck rode on ahead of the wagons, joining Mac. Warily they trotted their horses into the clearing that led to the crossing, but there was no sign of the men Mac had seen.

"Maybe they just stopped long enough to eat, and then rode on," said Haze.

"That's possible," Mac replied, "but not likely. It's too near sundown. They built their cook fire close to the river for convenience, but they've drifted back into the brush for the night. We'll set up our camp as near the river as we can, leaving most of this clearing behind us. They'll have to cross some portion of it to get to us, even if they approach from up- or downstream."

"There should be a moon later tonight," Red said. "Maybe, instead of allowing Port and his boys to take the first two watches, we ought to be awake, settin' on ready."

"I kind of feel the same way," said Buck. "I don't want any more surprises like we had back at the cabin."

"My sentiments, exactly," Haze said. "Ever since that outlaw segundo escaped Quanah Parker and his Comanches, I've had the uneasy feeling we'll be meetin' the varmint again."

"I kind of hope we do," said Mac. "It's like walkin' through tallgrass, knowin' there's a sidewinder in there somewhere. You want him to go ahead and strike, and be done with him."

There was time for supper before dark, and afterward, Mac explained the strategy he and his companions had already discussed.

"Red, Buck, Haze, and me will be watching for anything that moves, and that means nobody gets up and wanders around. Stay put until dawn."

"Suppose we have to go to the bushes?" Hattie said.

"Suppose you do," said Mac, "and behind the bushes there's an outlaw with a gun? Don't spread your blankets so close to one another. Leave enough space to squat where you are."

"And afterward," Trinity said, "try not to thrash around too much."

Though embarrassed, Hattie laughed with everybody else. But they took Mac seriously and there was no moving about during the night, nor was there any sign of the expected visitors. They showed up next morning, before breakfast. Red saw them first.

"Mac, here they come."

The four stepped out of the brush, well out of Colt or rifle range.

"He didn't disappoint us," Mac said. "One of them is the varmint whose *compañeros* had a bad experience with Quanah Parker and his Comanches."

"A damn shame he wasn't there, himself," said Buck. "You recognize any of the rest of them?"

"No," Mac replied, "but he's had time to throw in with others of the same caliber as those who tangled with the Comanches. Stand fast, until we know what they have in mind."

The four came on, but Mac didn't allow them to come within range.

"That's far enough," said Mac. "Who are you and what do you want?"

"You know who I am," Russ replied, "and I want *you*, wagon boss."

"Take me, if you can," said Mac. "The rest of you, don't buy more than you can pay for. Only a damned fool gets gunned down in somebody else's fight."

"We ain't doin' nothin' but seein' he gits an even break," one of the trio siding Russ replied.

"Fair enough," Mac said, "and my three *amigos* are here to see that I get one. Red, Buck, Haze, if any one of those three pulls a gun, kill him."

Russ came on, but his three companions didn't accompany him. Russ wore his Colt low on his right hip, thonged down. His hand swung freely, hovering nearer the weapon as he came closer. Mac went to meet him, leaving Red,

Buck, and Haze out of the line of fire and in a position to face the outlaw's three companions.

"My God," Trinity cried, "Mac could be killed."

"He could," said Port Guthrie, "but he won't be. He's doin' what he has to do, if he's to go on standin' on his hind legs like a man. Watch him."

Trinity did watch, unable to turn away. Mac halted, his hands at his side, and at that moment Russ went for his gun. Chills of terror swept over Trinity, for Mac Tunstall had made no move! The outlaw's gun rose, spat flame once, and lead kicked up dust at the outlaw's feet. Mac hadn't seemed to move, but the smoking Colt was in his hand, the roar of his second shot seeming part of the first. Russ stumbled backward, and when his knees buckled, he fell on his back, the Colt still in his dead hand. A west wind sent his old hat tumbling away, while his three companions watched it in morbid fascination. Only then did Mac speak.

"Unless the three of you aim to take up where he left off, mount up and ride."

"We'll ride," said one of the three. "He got a fair shake."

The trio turned and walked back the way they had come, disappearing in the brush. In a matter of moments, there was the sound of hoofbeats as they rode away.

"Oh," Trinity cried, "oh!"

Not caring what anybody thought, she ran to Mac, throwing her trembling arms around him.

"Whoa," said Mac, "I don't have any bullet holes in me."

"He didn't even come close to gettin' ventilated," Red said.

"Trinity," said Elizabeth, "turn him loose. It's your turn to make biscuits."

"Yeah," Mac said, "we can do this anytime. I'm starved."

"You're an insensitive brute," said Trinity, letting go of him.

They all laughed as she stalked away, toward the wagons.

"You'll have plenty of time to sweet-talk her tonight," Buck said. "Looks like we're fresh out of outlaws."

After breakfast, they crossed the river into Texas.

"I'll ride on ahead," said Mac. "We're good for a night or two of dry camp, but I'd prefer fresh water."

Mac saw Trinity watching him, and just for a moment he thought she was going to go with him. But she resisted the temptation and he rode south alone. He mentally pictured a map of Texas Hiram Yeager had shown him, and he believed they were not more than sixty miles from the White River. But if nothing went wrong, the heavily loaded wagons would need a week to cover that distance. He rode fifteen miles without finding water, and that meant a dry camp. A second night in a dry camp would see them in trouble, for the Texas sun was hot, and there was a limit as to how long the mules could last on a small ration of water from the barrels. When he met the wagons, they were at a standstill, and at first he believed they had stopped to rest the teams. But as he drew closer, he learned otherwise. In the shade of one of the wagons lay a man dressed in Union blue.

"He stumbled into us afoot," Red said, as Mac dismounted. "He's been shot."

"Have you learned who he is, or what post he's from?" Mac asked.

"No," said Red. "He's burning with fever and talkin' out of his head. Trinity's gone to the wagon for the medicine chest."

The man lay belly-down. Port Guthrie had removed his shirt, revealing the wound. It was high up, encrusted with dried blood.

"I'll need hot water," Guthrie said. "It's been maybe three days since he was shot, and it may be too late to save him. I've seen wounds after blood poisonin' had set in, and this looks like one of 'em."

Hattie had taken wood from the possum belly beneath

one of the wagons, and had a fire going. Elizabeth was dipping water from one of the barrels.

"I reckon this ain't a good time to bring it up," said Mac, "but it's dry camp tonight, and maybe tomorrow night. I rode a good fifteen miles without a sign of water."

"The more time we lose today, the more we'll have to make up tomorrow," Red said.

"That's it," said Mac. "We have to get this hombre patched up, into the wagon, and be on our way."

Trinity returned with the medicine chest, and Port Guthrie took it.

"This ain't goin' to be pretty," Guthrie said. "Them of you with a weak stomach best not stick around. I'll do what I can."

Mac backed away and sat down in the shade of one of the wagons. To his surprise, Trinity sat down beside him.

"I'm sorry," she said. "I'm a silly goose."

"Honk, honk," said Mac.

"Damn you," she said, "you don't make it easy, do you?"

"If I did," said Mac, "you'd come to expect it and would give me a hard way to go more often, wouldn't you?"

She laughed, surprising him. "I suppose I would. What do you think happened to that soldier?"

"If I had to guess," Mac replied, "I'd say he's been shot."

"Oh, damn it," she said wearily, "you *know* what I mean. Why do you think he was shot? Indians?"

"No," said Mac. "Indians would have ridden him down and he never would have made it this far. He's likely from Fort Worth, and likely a deserter. He may have been confined to a guardhouse or stockade, and may have been shot while escaping."

"The army would shoot a man for that?"

"They would, without hesitation," Mac said. "The army takes discipline seriously. If a soldier runs—deserts— under fire, he's subject to being shot by his own men. Then if he escapes and is later captured, the sentence is almost always death before a firing squad.''

"My God, that's cruel," said Trinity. "It's no crime, being afraid."

"It is when a man's a soldier," Mac replied. "A chain is never any stronger than its weakest link. A soldier who yields to cowardice or fear imperils the lives of others."

"I suppose you've never been afraid."

"You suppose wrong," said Mac. "I've been afraid most of my life. Only a fool is without fear. Fear can keep a man alive or be the death of him, dependin' on how he can relate to it."

"Mac Tunstall, sometimes you strike me as the most brilliant man I've ever known, and at other times, the most . . . most—"

"Ignorant," Mac finished.

"Yes," she said. "That's it."

"Trinity McCoy, every man is a mix of ignorance and brilliance. What you get, and how much, generally depends on what you're askin' for. A man rises or falls accordin' to what's expected of him."

Trinity had a sharp response on the tip of her tongue, when she saw the merriment in his eyes. She was about to prove his point, and they both knew it. Moreover, they seemed to have attracted an audience.

"My God," said Buck reverently, "we're about to lose old Mac. Next thing we know, he'll be wearin' a derby hat, teachin' school, and rollin' in money. I hear that them with his kind of learnin' makes as much as forty dollars a month."

"He's mighty deep," Red agreed, "and he's had me fooled all these years. Told me his daddy always took him to school. Mac was in the fourth grade, and his old man was in the fifth. Now I know he was just tellin' me that so's I wouldn't feel ignorant alongside him."

They all roared with laughter. Especially Trinity.

"Damn fine lot you are," said Mac. "A man can't carry

on a private conversation without all of you gatherin' around like a flock of geese.''

The merriment ended as abruptly as it had begun, when Port Guthrie approached.

''This young hombre's got the worst case of blood poisonin' I've ever seen,'' Guthrie said. ''If I'm any judge, he'll be leavin' us sometime tonight.''

''Then we'll have to search him for some identification,'' said Mac. ''He'll have a family somewhere who deserves to know of his death. We can report it at Fort Griffin, but we'll need to at least know his name.''

''I found a letter in his shirt pocket,'' Guthrie replied. ''It was wrote to him from Ohio and looks to be from his ma.''

''Hold on to it then,'' said Mac. ''We'll do for him what we can, and failing in that, see that he's properly buried. The army will be responsible for notifying his family.''

''Do you honestly believe they will?'' Hattie asked.

''It would be the right thing to do,'' said Mac.

''Mr. Guthrie,'' Trinity said, ''before you turn that letter over to the army at Fort Griffin, I want his family's address from it. As soon as I reach a place where I can post a letter, I'll write to his mother, tell her of his death, and that we buried him.''

''I think that would be a fittin' and proper thing to do, ma'am,'' said Guthrie.

''If there's nothing more to be done for him,'' Mac said, ''put him in the wagon and we'll move on. We can't afford to lose any more time, if we're to have any hope of reaching water sometime tomorrow.''

The wagons rolled on, and near sundown Mac halted them on a plateau where, if there was no water, at least there was good graze.

''We'll dig a fire pit,'' said Mac, ''so we can bed the coals for hot coffee during the night. I don't know that anybody would be attracted to our fire, but there's no point in taking chances, when we don't have to.''

Just before supper was ready, Port Guthrie broke some sobering news.

"The young hombre in the wagon is dead. It'd be easier, buryin' him in the cool of the evening."

"I think you're right," said Mac. "We'll hurry supper, dig a grave, and lay him to rest before dark."

"I hope we didn't hasten his death by bouncing him around in the wagon," Trinity said.

"I doubt it," said Guthrie. "He wouldn't have lasted any longer if we'd left him lay in the shade of a wagon, instead of bringin' him on. When a man's flesh is rottin' away and death is just a matter of time, it's a blessin' when the end comes quick."

Supper was a somber meal. Red and Haze were the first to finish, and taking a pair of shovels, they began digging a grave on a hummock a hundred yards from the wagons. The first stars were winking silver in a field of deep purple when they wrapped the soldier in a blanket and lowered him into the lonely grave.

"It's so sad," Hattie said. "He can't be a day over twenty, and he's being laid away by strangers, hundreds of miles from his family and all that he must have held dear."

"He's more fortunate than some," said Guthrie. "Many a man has come west, only to leave his bones bleachin' on the plains where he breathed his last, with not even a stranger to bury him and send word to his family."

Swiftly they filled the grave, and when it was done, Guthrie recited the Twenty-third Psalm. Reaching the wagons, Hattie refilled the coffeepot with water and added coffee. It would be a long night, with only the water in each wagon's kegs.

"We'll resume sentry duty as it was before," Mac said, "with Red, Buck, Haze, and me takin' the last watch."

The night passed uneventfully, and the next morning after breakfast, Mac rode south in search of water. Trinity took one of the extra horses and soon caught up with him.

"Haven't you noticed you always end up in trouble when you ride with me?" Mac asked.

"I'm tired of woman talk," said Trinity. "As opposed to more of that, I'd welcome trouble with you."

"What's wrong with woman talk?" Mac asked.

"Since we buried that soldier," said Trinity, "there's been a whole new sympathy outburst. I'm afraid I know three females who are beginning to think of our quest as some noble undertaking. Soldiers are looking more desirable, and brave beyond the call of duty."

"I reckon you don't share that feeling," Mac said.

"No," said Trinity, "I don't. The country's not at war, and service is voluntary. After the experience I've had, I think too many men join the military to escape trouble at home. Then when soldiering becomes more difficult and dangerous than they had imagined, they become misfits and deserters."

Mac laughed. "You're startin' to think and talk like a man."

"I suppose one has to on the frontier," said Trinity. "It's a man's world here, and it's all grim reality. Back East, women are pampered. We've never had to tend a man who's been shot, or watched a young man barely out of his teens die of blood poisoning. And do I have to tell you what people would have said, had the four of us been dragged naked into the presence of a dozen men, and then viewed in the same state by the four men who came to our rescue?"

"Tell me," Mac said.

"We'd have been disgraced," said Trinity. "No decent man would have ever given us a second look. Back East, reputation is everything, and one who is exposed to sin is forever branded as having partaken of it."

"What a lot of hogwash," Mac said. "The only reputation that matters on the frontier is the good sense to stay alive by whatever means may be necessary. Many a Western man has taken a wife out of a whorehouse. By Western standards, the four of you are as pure as driven snow."

Trinity laughed. "I can see that now. We didn't die of mortification, and we haven't compromised our reputations. That's all the reason I need to remain in the West."

"If there are no more delays," said Mac, "we should reach Fort Griffin within two more weeks."

"Suppose we can't reach the next nearest water by sundown tomorrow?"

"Then we may be in trouble," Mac replied. "Provided we cover ten miles today and ten more tomorrow, we'll still be forty miles from the White River. When we left Texas in the spring on a trail drive, there hadn't been a lot of rain. That often is the promise of a dry summer, with the possibility of the only sure water being the rivers."

"If we can reach the White River, what's beyond that?"

"The Colorado," said Mac, "and maybe another dry trail of about sixty miles. But we can follow the Colorado right on to Austin."

The terrain grew rough, with occasional draws, but no sign of water.

"We're not riding due south anymore," Trinity said.

Mac laughed. "You're becoming a Western woman, ma'am. You're right, we're veering to the southeast. You'll notice there are more hummocks and arroyos, the rougher the land becomes. In Texas there are some mighty good springs in some unlikely places. Usually at the deep end of some arroyo, flowing from beneath solid rock."

They had ridden only another mile or so when Mac reined up.

"What is it?" Trinity asked.

"Bees," said Mac. "Look."

At first Trinity saw nothing, but then one of the tiny winged creatures caught her eye and her vision followed it until it disappeared in the same general direction they were riding.

"I saw one," Trinity said. "What does it mean?"

"Water," said Mac, "and not too far off. Let's ride."

They soon reached the mouth of an arroyo, and there

was a dampness where the runoff had been swallowed up by the sand.

"We'll dismount and lead the horses," Mac said.

But they had trouble holding the horses, for the animals had smelled the water. When they reached the blind end of the arroyo, they found the water tumbling from a crevice in the rock into a clear pool a dozen feet across.

"What a beautiful sight," said Trinity. "To think we could have ridden within a mile of this and never have known it was here. How did you know to watch for bees?"

"It's just somethin' you learn on the frontier," Mac said. "It never fails during a dry season, if you have patience. I'd been looking for bees for an hour before I finally sighted one."

"I feel so foolish. I thought we were just riding until we stumbled on water."

"Don't ever rule out that possibility," said Mac. "We might have found this water on our own, but when I saw the bees, I knew it was here."

"My God, I shudder when I think of Hattie, Rachel, Elizabeth, and me setting out for Fort Griffin on our own. There's so much we didn't know, and would have had no way of learning."

"It's been the death of many an Easterner, I reckon," Mac said. "The things you most need to know are the things you never learn until you get here, until you experience them. Experience is a hard teacher, especially when that experience may leave your bones whitening somewhere on the plains."

"Is it safe for the horses to drink? This fellow's about to drag me into the spring."

"Yes," said Mac, "they can drink, and we'll take ourselves a long drink before we ride back with the good news."

"The canyon's too narrow to bring the wagons in here," Trinity said.

"We'll leave the wagons on the rim and post our sentries there," said Mac. "Even if the arroyo was wide enough, we couldn't bring the wagons in, nor could we ever be safe down here. We'll eat here, near the water, water our horses and mules, and then spread our blankets on the rim, near the wagons. Tomorrow morning, we'll repeat the procedure and fill all the water barrels.''

"I suppose this is another important thing a tenderfoot would overlook," Trinity said.

"Usually," said Mac. "An enemy with rifles could cut you down from the rims before you could fire a shot."

Mac and Trinity mounted and rode back to meet the wagons.

"How far do you think we rode before finding the water?" Trinity asked.

"More than ten miles," said Mac. "Probably closer to twelve."

"Perhaps the thought of fresh water will excite everybody enough to cover the extra miles before dark," Trinity said.

"We'll have to," said Mac. "The terrain's rough, with stones and dropoffs. We can't risk splintering a wagon wheel or snapping an axle in the dark."

The teamsters reined up to rest the mules, allowing them an opportunity to learn what Mac had to report.

"An arroyo with a spring," Mac announced, "but it's maybe twelve miles. We'll have to travel a mite to the southeast, but it'll be worth it."

"I reckon it will," said Red. "My coffee had mud in it this mornin'."

"Sorry," Hattie said. "We did the best we could with what we had. Since there'll be a spring with good, clear water, suppose some of you rinse out those water kegs before you refill them? There's still mud in there from the Cimarron."

"Red, I reckon you've been assigned a worthy task," said Mac. "I hope you can enlist some help. Those kegs are heavy when they're full."

"Everybody to your wagons," Port Guthrie ordered. "If we're to reach that spring today, we'll have to make up some time."

CHAPTER 12

✣

*T*he wagons reached the arroyo, remaining on the rim. The stock was led down to the spring and watered and returned to scant graze on the rim. Supper was prepared near the spring, but after the outfit had eaten, the fire was doused and they returned to the wagons on the rim.

"If my memory serves me right," Red said, "we'll have to swing back toward the southwest to reach Fort Griffin. It's on the clear fork of the Brazos River."

"How would you know that?" Mac asked. "We went up the Chisholm Trail when we took the herd north."

"There's a big map on the wall at the courthouse in San Antone," said Red. "It's got all the Texas forts and rivers. We crossed the Red almost due north from Fort Griffin, and somewhere before we reach the fort, we'll be crossing the Brazos."

"I never been to Texas," Port Guthrie said, "but if there's another river between us and Fort Griffin, there ought to be some creeks feedin' into it."

"I don't know," said Red. "The map I was lookin' at only had the rivers on it. I think after we leave here, we'd better turn back to the southwest, else we'll come out somewhere to the east of Fort Griffin."

"Well, hell," Mac said, "so we're a mite off course. We needed water, and this was the closest. We'll get back in line as we travel south."

"Don't get your hackles up," said Red. "Damn it, I'm only tryin' to be helpful."

"Then why don't *you* scout ahead for water?" Mac said. "Yeager had a map with the White River on it, but I don't remember seein' the Brazos. That tells me Yeager's map wasn't all that accurate. Maybe you'll have better luck than I've had."

"I don't think this is the time for a disagreement among us," said Buck.

"No disagreement," Mac replied. "I said Red can scout ahead for water, instead of me. For that matter, so can you. I've never been through this part of Texas before, and if any one of you knows it better than I do, then speak up."

"Since we're going to Fort Griffin," said Haze, "and Red knows for sure it's on the clear fork of the Brazos, then we got to pull back to the west. Instead of Mac doing all the scouting, why don't we take turns? Red can go tomorrow, Buck can ride out the next day, and the day after that, I'll take a turn. Then Mac can go again. What's wrong with that?"

"I'm the damned wagon boss," Mac said irritably, "and it's my responsibility."

"At the risk of speakin' out of turn," said Port Guthrie, "I can only tell you what Mr. Yeager told me. He said you gents have equal responsibility for the safety and well-bein' of this outfit. Bein' wagon boss don't pile all the responsibility on one man's back, nor does it mean he's the only one with savvy enough to scout the trail ahead. Let me remind you that if Mr. Yeager's plans had worked out, Watson Brandt would of been wagon boss. Can any one of you imagine *him* ridin' into unknown country lookin' for water, or anything else?"

For a moment they looked at him in silence. Red laughed and everybody else joined in. Mac laughed the loudest of all, and it was he who spoke.

"It's hard arguing with that, Port. If Brandt had re-mained in charge, we wouldn't even be going to Fort Griffin. I'll go along with sharing responsibility. Red, ride out tomorrow and see what you can find.''

Everybody sighed with relief, especially Trinity McCoy, and while Mac was on watch, she made it a point to spend some time with him.

''Port Guthrie's a valuable man, isn't he?''

''Sometimes,'' Mac agreed.

''I'm referring specifically to tonight,'' said Trinity.

''That's what I thought,'' Mac replied. ''If Red, Buck, and Haze don't like the way I've been bossin' the outfit, why didn't they say so before?''

''Perhaps because they expected you to . . . to—''

''Raise hell,'' Mac finished.

''I didn't intend to use those words,'' said Trinity, ''but yes, that's exactly what I mean. I didn't know this Watson Brandt, but I get the idea he wouldn't have been much of a wagon boss.''

Mac laughed. ''I haven't told you about him. Maybe I ought to, so you can appreciate even more the point Guthrie made.''

He proceeded to tell her of Watson Brandt's attempt to steal the wagons loaded with Winchesters, Colts, and ammunition.

''So that's why you believe there are some within the military who would steal these wagons loaded with weapons and ammunition,'' said Trinity. ''Because of this Jernigan, at Fort Dodge.''

''Yes,'' Mac said. ''Jernigan was a former Reb.''

''For a Texan, aren't you being a little hard on the ex-Confederates? These weapons and ammunition must be worth thousands of dollars. I'm sure there are men motivated by nothing more than greed.''

''I reckon you're right,'' said Mac grudgingly.

''I know I am,'' Trinity said, ''and I'm feeling much better about you.''

''Because I've admitted to being wrong twice in one day?''

''Yes,'' said Trinity. ''A strong man isn't afraid to be

wrong. Weaklings and cowards have the need to prove themselves every day.''

"I never thought of it that way,'' Mac said. "I've always heard you can't teach an old dog new tricks.''

"You can, if the old dog's willing to learn,'' said Trinity.

The next morning when the wagons again took the trail, Red McLean rode out to look for water and learn what lay ahead. Not surprisingly, Hattie rode with him.

"Is it true you've never been in this part of Texas?'' Hattie asked.

"Yes,'' said Red. "We've all been north with trail drives, but up the Chisholm Trail. Mac, Haze, Buck, and me are all from around San Antone. This is about the biggest thing we've ever done, outriding for these wagons into Austin.''

"The freight line didn't ask about your experience?''

"No,'' Red replied. "Yeager was looking for men well-mounted, who could use a gun. That's all he asked for, and we didn't volunteer anything more. Among the four of us, we didn't have the price of a meal, and we needed money to get back to Texas.''

"After we reach Fort Griffin, are you sure you know the way to Austin?''

Red laughed. "The Colorado River runs right through it. Austin's maybe a couple of axe handles north of San Antone. Once we're shut of these wagons, we can all be home by sundown.''

"When you say 'home,' do you mean your own place?''

"I was referrin' to San Antone,'' said Red. "The only home any of us has got is with our kin. After the war, Texas was picked clean. We're just now startin' to get back on our feet, thanks to the cows and the railroad buildin' west. I ain't sure any one of the four of us will live enough years to have a place of our own.''

"You don't look that old to me,'' Hattie said innocently.

"How old do you reckon I am?''

"Eighteen," said Hattie.

"Close," Red replied. "Actually, I'm a hundred and eighteen."

"You're too old for me, then," said Hattie.

"Let me say that a mite different," Red said. "I *feel* like I'm a hundred and eighteen. Actually, I won't be twenty-four until next April. Buck's twenty-five, and the oldest. Mac and Haze are a year younger than me."

"I'm twenty-four," said Hattie, "and I dare not tell you the ages of Trinity, Elizabeth, and Rachel. I can only say they're not as old as me."

"I reckon, after we're finished in Austin, it'll be time for Mac, Haze, Buck, and me to start thinkin' about what we aim to do. Give it another year and sodbusters will be goin' west, claiming the open range, and the trail drives will be done."

"What *is* there to do in Texas? Could you start your own freight line?"

"I doubt it," said Red. "There's already talk about railroads into Texas, and that'll be the end of freighting by wagons. That leaves nothin' but ranching or farming."

"Somehow I can't see you as a farmer."

"Neither can I," Red said. "Mac, Haze, Buck, and me all learned cow together, and we don't really know anything else."

"Suppose all of you joined in together and started your own ranch?"

"When we reach Austin and get the rest of our pay," said Red, "we'll have no more than seven hundred dollars among us. That won't go far."

The conversation ended on a somber note. They were riding southwest, and to their surprise, came upon a creek.*

"I reckon this is proof enough that we can't rely too much on maps," Red observed. "This creek ain't even ten miles from last night's arroyo."

*Beaver Creek.

"But suppose we ride beyond this," said Hattie, "and it's too far to the next water to reach it today?"

"We'll stay here tonight," Red said. "Now that we know we'll have water for tonight's camp, we'll ride a few more miles beyond this. If we can stay two days ahead on water, we can breathe a little easier."

"I like that," said Hattie.

"We'll ride on another ten miles or so," Red said. "We didn't know this creek was here, so maybe there's another."

While they didn't find another stream, there was a spring sufficient for their needs.

"Maybe a dozen miles beyond the creek," said Red. "The wagons can make it in a day's drive. After that, we can't be too far from the Brazos."

Hattie laughed. "We'll have some exciting news, won't we? We're assured of water for the next two days, and perhaps it won't be too far to water for a third day."

As Red and Hattie approached the oncoming wagons, Mac rode to meet them. Red explained what they had discovered.

"Well, by God," Mac said, "that's good news. You sure you haven't been through this part of Texas before?"

"It's all new to me," said Red, "but with all the twists and turns of the Brazos, there has to be some streams feeding into it. After we leave the spring, why don't we travel due south?"

"I'm willing," Mac said. "The closer we get to the Brazos, the more likely there'll be fewer streams or springs."

Port Guthrie halted the wagons to rest the teams, and during the interval, Red passed the word on to the rest of the outfit about the nearness of the creek and the spring to the south.

"Short drive today," said Red, "maybe a little longer tomorrow, but plenty of fresh water."

After resting the teams, the caravan rolled on. Spirits were high, and Red was a hero for discovering water for the next two days. He lagged behind, much embarrassed. Since they reached the creek a good two hours before sunset, there was time to water all the mules and horses and to prepare and eat supper.

"Buck," Mac said, "tomorrow you can ride ahead, checking out the terrain and looking for water. We're expecting you to do at least as well as Red did."

"He did so well today," said Buck, "I think he should be our permanent scout, all the way to Austin."

"Oh, no you don't," Red shouted.

The night was clear, and except for an occasional distant coyote, there wasn't a sound to disturb the tranquility. Silver stars winked down, adding their light to that of a pale quarter moon. Sometime after midnight, Trinity crept away to join Mac on watch.

"It's too nice a night to waste it sleeping," said Trinity.

"I reckon the short drive today was what we all needed," Mac said. "Are you sure it's the moon and stars keepin' you awake, or is it the nearness of Fort Griffin?"

"What do you mean?"

"You know what I mean," said Mac. "Is it not botherin' you just a little, what you might learn there?"

"Perhaps just a little," she conceded. "The others feel a little spooky, too. Despite all our brave words and resolutions, we can't help wondering what we'll do if . . . if things aren't like we were told."

"You're having some doubts because of that soldier we buried, I reckon."

"I suppose that's it," said Trinity. "Before coming west, we . . . well, we didn't know anything about the grim realities. We just . . . never thought of the army shooting its own men, I guess."

"It's a hard life," Mac said, "and it takes strong men to survive. The others . . . well . . . they fall out. They're generally the first to die on the field of battle. Surviving that, they usually don't accept discipline well, and spend a lot of time in the stockade. Finally they'll throw caution to the wind and run for it. Now you're wondering if the man you're searching for might not have yielded to temptation and met a predictable end."

"Yes," said Trinity. "I've been talking to Hattie, Elizabeth, and Rachel, and there's one thing on which we all agree. For one reason or another, our men all ran away. We believe if they did it once, they'd do it again, so we believe we haven't been told the truth."

"So if you learn they deserted under fire and were gunned down by their own men, will it make you feel better?"

"In an odd sort of way, yes," Trinity said. "When a woman marries, regardless of how irresponsible the man is, she can't help wondering if there wasn't something she could have done to save him."

"So you're wondering if he was truly beyond redemption, unable or unwilling to conduct himself as a man among men."

"Yes," said Trinity. "You've put our feelings into words. When a woman marries, she wants to believe in her man, and to respect him, even if he's dead. Is it wrong for us to feel that way?"

"I don't believe it is," Mac replied. "If these men died under less than honorable circumstances, then you'll know their answer to any difficulty was to just run away."

"But what are our chances of learning the truth? Do you think the post commander will be honest with us?"

"I don't know," said Mac. "If he hasn't told you the whole truth, it's likely because it isn't a pretty picture, and he's tried to spare you."

"We don't want to be spared," Trinity said. "We already suspect the facts are going to be ugly, but we deserve to hear them."

"In that case," said Mac, "if you get the runaround, I'll do what I can to get to the truth for you."

"Thank you," Trinity said. "All of us want to put this part of our lives behind us, and we can't do it until we know the truth."

*　　*　　*

The next morning, as the wagons were about to move out, Buck saddled his horse.

"Saddle me a horse," said Rachel, "and I'll ride with you. Trinity and Hattie have had all the fun."

"I don't know how much fun it'll be," Buck replied, "but you're welcome to go along and find out."

They rode out, taking some hoo-rawing from Mac, Red, and Haze. Trinity, Elizabeth, and Hattie just looked at one another and smiled.

"Are we going to try and find two days' worth of water?" Rachel asked.

"I don't know," said Buck. "We'll see how far the next water is from the spring Red found. If we can find water a day's drive beyond the spring, then maybe we'll try and find some for a third day. That'll equal what Red did, and it might take us within a day or two of the Brazos River."

"How will we know it's the Brazos?"

"I hear it's so crooked it doubles back and almost meets itself," Buck said, "and it'll be plenty wide."

Keeping their horses at a mile-eating slow gallop, they soon reached the spring Red had located. They dismounted well before reaching it.

"We'll have to hold the horses a few minutes," said Buck.

"Why?"

Buck laughed. "Tenderfoot. If they don't cool down first, the jug-heads would gorge on water and kill themselves."

"I'm sorry I seem so dumb," Rachel said, "but there's so much to learn."

"But you're willing," said Buck, "and that's all that matters."

After watering their horses and drinking their fill, they continued riding south.

"How much farther are we going to ride?" Hattie asked.

"Not much farther," said Buck. "I had hoped we might—"

Somewhere ahead, a horse nickered, and Rachel's horse answered. Buck reined up and caught the bridle of Rachel's horse. Seizing his Winchester from the saddle boot, he dismounted. Rachel slid out of her saddle and stood beside him.

"Who could it be?" Rachel asked quietly.

"I don't know," said Buck, "but whoever it is, they know we're here. Stand fast."

The horsemen—soldiers—rode into a clearing in a column of twos and reined up.

"Advance and identify yourselves," one of the lead riders shouted.

"We're friendly," Buck shouted back, but he kept the Winchester under his arm.

"Maybe they're from Fort Griffin," said Rachel.

"I reckon," Buck said. "Come on."

Leading their horses, Buck and Rachel went to meet the soldiers, who had remained in their saddles. There were ten men, the lead riders being a lieutenant and a sergeant. They waited for Buck to speak, and he did.

"I'm Buck Prinz, and this is Rachel Price. We're part of a six-wagon outfit, and we're on our way to south Texas. We're scouting ahead, looking for water."

"I'm Lieutenant Beale, and this is Sergeant Adler," the officer said. "We're on routine patrol from Fort Griffin. You're maybe four or five miles north of the Brazos, and beyond that another forty miles is the fort. Will you be stopping there?"

"Yes," said Buck. "It's good to know the Brazos and the fort are that close. We're obliged."

"Have you seen any Indian sign?" the lieutenant inquired.

"Considerable," said Buck. "In Indian Territory, we met Quanah Parker and maybe five hundred Comanches, but they left us alone."

"My God," Lieutenant Beale said, "the post commander will want to hear about this."

"I reckon our wagon boss will meet with him when we

reach the fort," said Buck. "We should be there in another week. How is the water situation between the Brazos and the fort?"

"Several streams and a good spring," Lieutenant Beale said. "Just continue due south."

He gave a command, wheeled his horse, and the soldiers followed him back the way they had come.

"I'm surprised he didn't have more questions," said Rachel.

"So am I," Buck replied. "It was fortunate, you being with me. They must have taken us for settlers."

"But they'll know better, once we reach the fort," said Rachel.

"Yeah," Buck said, "thanks to the damn telegraph."

Buck and Rachel rode back to meet the wagons, and the rest of the outfit was amazed to learn of their nearness to the Brazos and Fort Griffin beyond.

"I'm glad the army didn't ask our business in south Texas," said Mac. "Maybe we can get into and out of Fort Griffin without everybody there knowing of our purpose and our freight."

"You know better than that," Red said. "That lieutenant will have figured us out by the time he reaches Fort Griffin. South Texas wasn't exactly the garden spot of the world, in its prime, and there ain't a damn thing there now to lure settlers. They're all ridin' the Union Pacific, looking for range in Colorado, Wyoming, and beyond."

"Red," said Haze, "you sure know how to take a little good news and plumb turn it around. If Fort Griffin's aware of these arms and ammunition being wagoned to Austin, they got no reason to expect those wagons to go out of their way gettin' there. I think we can all agree that if we'd traveled a mite more to the southeast, we could have bypassed Fort Griffin entirely."

"Damn it," Buck said, "there's no sense in us gettin' hot over what we're *expecting* to run into at Fort Griffin. My old granny always said don't fret about tomorrow. If you'll just think on it, there's a blessed plenty of things to worry about today."

"I reckon we'd better take that advice," said Mac, "and move on to our water for tonight. We're still a week from Fort Griffin, even if everything goes well."

Fort Griffin, Texas. November 20, 1873.

"I think we'll make our camp here on the Brazos," Mac said, "and be sure some of us are with the wagons at all times. I'll ride to the fort and talk to the post commander."

Trinity bit her tongue. She wanted Mac to ask for permission for herself, Hattie, Rachel, and Elizabeth to meet with the officer in charge, but thought better of it. There was much at stake here, with a possibility of trouble because Mac had gone out of his way to bring the wagons to Fort Griffin, when he might have taken a shorter trail to Austin. They were close enough to the fort for Mac to walk, and he did so. The sentry at the gate had seen the wagons approaching, and he was waiting for Mac.

"I'm Mac Tunstall, wagon boss, and I'd like to talk to the post commander."

"That'll be Captain Stockton," the sentry said. "Sergeant of the guard!"

"This is Sergeant Lassiter," said the sentry, when the sergeant arrived. "Sergeant, Mr. Tunstall, the wagon boss, wants to talk to Captain Stockton."

"Come on," Lassiter said.

The commanding officer's quarters was an old log house. Lassiter knocked, received permission to enter, and did so. The captain stood up, Lassiter saluted, had it returned.

"At ease, Sergeant," said Captain Stockton.

"This is Mac Tunstall," Lassiter said. "He wants to talk to you."

"Very well," said Stockton. "You're excused, Sergeant."

Lassiter went out, closing the door behind him. Stockton nodded toward a trio of oak ladder-back chairs that faced his desk. Mac took one of the chairs, while Stockton sat in the leather-upholstered chair behind his desk.

"I've heard of you, Tunstall," Captain Stockton said, "but frankly, I'm surprised to see you here. This is hardly the shortest way to Austin."

"I'm aware of that," said Mac, "and I have a reason for coming this way. I had a vain hope that the nature of this drive might not become common knowledge."

"The . . . ah . . . nature of your drive was leaked in Kansas City," Captain Stockton said. "I do not believe this represents negligence on the part of the military."

Mac thought the man was overly defensive and a little smug, but there was nothing to be gained by antagonizing him. There was another way to get in a dig or two.

"Like I told you," said Mac, "I had a reason for traveling this way. We encountered four ladies in Dodge City who had business here. Being Easterners, they had no business undertaking such a journey alone. We allowed them to travel with us, and since they've come this far, I believe you should at least talk to them."

"I'll be the judge of that," Captain Stockton said, all civility vanishing. "Who are these, ah, ladies?"

"Maybe you'll recognize the names," said Mac, with a hint of a smile. "Trinity McCoy, Hattie Sutton, Rachel Prinz, and Elizabeth Graves."

"Yes," Captain Stockton said, "I feel as though I know them well. I have nothing to say to them that I haven't already said by letter."

"They have the feeling," said Mac, twisting the knife, "that you haven't told them the whole truth, and that's why they're here. They're not satisfied."

"The men in question—their husbands—are dead," Captain Stockton said, "and that's my final word on the subject. Since you brought these people here, Tunstall, I'll expect you to take them with you, when you depart. Good day."

"Not so fast, Captain," said Mac. "If you refuse to cooperate, a complaint can be filed in Washington, with the Department of the Army. Why don't you go ahead and dispose of this, ah, obvious misunderstanding before it becomes more complicated?"

"Since you have taken such an interest in this unsavory affair," Captain Stockton said, "suppose I supply you with the gruesome details these ladies are so desperately seeking. It will then be up to you to satisfy their curiosity, telling them as much or as little as you see fit. But there is a condition. The subject will be closed, and you will take these ladies with you when you leave this area. Agreed?"

"Agreed," said Mac.

"Very well," Captain Stockton said. "As I have already told you, the men in question are dead. Or perhaps I should be totally honest, and say they are *presumed* dead."

"Meaning that you aren't completely sure," said Mac.

"I am satisfied they are," Captain Stockton said. "However, I'm going to relate to you the events as they took place that day these men disappeared. Then you decide."

"Go on," said Mac. "I'm listening."

"Privates McCoy, Sutton, Price, and Graves were part of a seven-man patrol. Indians attacked, and while under fire, the four men in question deserted. By the time reinforcements arrived, two of the remaining men were dead. The third—a private—lived just long enough to tell us of the desertions. He had watched the Comanches surround the men who had deserted. Mortally wounded himself, he did not witness their eventual fate, but knowing the ways of the Comanches, I didn't hesitate to declare them dead."

"Missing, I believe," said Mac.

"Damn it," Captain Stockton snapped, "I tried to spare their kin, to put as kind a face on the situation as I could. It could have been far worse. Had they escaped the Comanches and later had been captured by us, I'd have per-

sonally seen to it that the four of them were sentenced to
die before a firing squad.''

"But they escaped that," said Mac, "and you feel
cheated. Why?"

"When these four left their comrades to face the fury
of the Comanches," Stockton said, "they condemned three
men to certain death. One of those men—the officer in
charge of the patrol—was my kid brother."

His eyes looked beyond Mac into a hell only he could
see. He didn't even notice when Mac left, closing the door
behind him . . .

CHAPTER 13

*W*hen Mac reached the gate, the sentry who had admitted him was there. The sergeant of the guard was there also.

"Is there any reason my outfit can't visit the sutler's store?" Mac asked.

"None that I know of," said the sergeant, "but you're not allowed beyond there without permission from Captain Stockton."

"That's as far as we'll be going," Mac replied.

The sutler's was within sight of the gate. After the unpleasant meeting with Stockton, Mac had no intention of remaining at Fort Griffin any longer than necessary. Now he had to relate to Trinity, Hattie, Rachel, and Elizabeth what Stockton had told him, keeping his word to the captain. As Mac left the post, two men stepped out of the sutler's store and watched him go.

"Seven wagons instead of six," one of the men said, "but that's got to be them."

"Yeah," said his companion, "and it's a long trail from here to Austin. Anything can happen. We'll stay here until they move out, makin' sure which way they go. Makes sense they'd travel south to the Colorado and foller it to Austin."

"Whatever direction they take, we'll have plenty of time to get ahead of them and plan a reception."

*   *   *

By the time Mac reached the wagons, everybody had gathered to hear what he had to report. He didn't beat around the bush.

"Captain Stockton admitted our freight bound for Austin is common knowledge, and he blames the leak in Kansas City for that."

"Hell, we know Watson Brandt was responsible for that," Red said, "but what would have been his reason for usin' the telegraph to alert the entire frontier?"

"None, that I know of," said Mac, "but Stockton wasn't in a good mood. He got on the bad side of me by insisting on knowing why we had come here to Fort Griffin, instead of taking a more direct route to Austin. So I told him."

"You had trouble with him because of us," Trinity said.

"He had a burr under his saddle before I even mentioned any of you," said Mac. "He wanted to be ornery, so I just laid it on the line. I told him he'd been speaking with a forked tongue, and that the four of you were here for the truth. He told me a story that had the ring of truth. Do you want to hear it in private?"

"No," Trinity said, "and I believe I'm speaking for us all. Each of you knows why we are here, and for putting up with us and our ignorance all the way from Dodge, I think you deserve to know what really happened."

Mac told them, except for the captain's last few words, repeating what Stockton had told him. For a long moment, there was only silence. Hattie spoke.

"There must have been other deserters. Why is the captain so bitter toward these four men, and so angry with us for wanting the truth?"

"I wasn't going to tell you all of it," Mac said, "unless I had to. When the four men deserted during the Comanche attack, one of the three soldiers who remained was Captain Stockton's brother, the lieutenant in charge of the patrol."

"I reckon Stockton has a right to some ill feelings," said Red, "but I get the idea this bunch of Comanches was enough in number to have wiped out a seven-man patrol to the last man, if they'd all stood their ground.''

"I felt the same way, while Stockton was talking,'' Mac said, "but he's jack leather army. Our discussion would have gone to hell and beyond.''

"I believe I understand his feelings,'' said Trinity. "It's a matter of responsibility, of honor, and the four men who deserted were lacking in both.''

"That's exactly how I feel,'' Hattie said. "That was justice, the Comanches capturing them.''

Rachel and Elizabeth quickly agreed, and Mac sighed with relief. The worst of it was over, but there was still one condition upon which Captain Stockton had insisted.

"Trinity, Hattie, Rachel, and Elizabeth,'' Mac said, "Stockton demanded that all of you leave Fort Griffin. He insisted that since I brought you here, I should take you away when we move on. Do any of you object to going on to Austin with us?''

"I think you know the answer to that,'' said Trinity. "When do we start?''

"I have permission for us to visit the sutler's store,'' Mac replied. "I reckon we'll stay here through tomorrow. But nobody goes in alone.''

"We've used nearly all our muslin for bandages,'' said Trinity, "and unless there's some whiskey that I don't know about, there's only part of a bottle left.''

"We'll need plenty for snake bite,'' Gourd Snively said. "I got the snake in a jug, in my wagon.''

It was graphic frontier humor, and drew a laugh, even from the women.

"Some of us will have to stay with the wagons at all times,'' said Mac. "Port, you and your boys can go in a group. When you're done, and return to the wagons, the rest of us will go in. Let's wait until the morning. We'll stand watch as usual tonight.''

For the first time since leaving Dodge City, Mac realized he could think of Trinity as a widow, a single woman, without the specter of a no-account husband coming between them. He doubted any of the women would sleep much during the coming night, for they would be making plans for Austin, and each would be tasting freedom as a result of what they had learned at Fort Griffin.

Mac and his outfit had just finished breakfast when two riders left the fort and rode away to the southeast.

"They was sure lookin' this way," Red observed, "like they wanted to know somethin' about our business."

"According to Captain Stockton," said Mac, "everybody already knows about us, our destination, as well as our cargo. Remember, all of you, if anybody at the sutler's comes on strong, back off. We'll answer no questions."

"None of us will be there long enough to arouse any curiosity," Port Guthrie said. "We're just needin' some plug and some Durham."

"You gents go ahead, then," said Mac. "We may be there a while."

The teamsters were gone less than an hour.

"The place was packed with soldiers," Port Guthrie said, "and they looked at us like we wasn't very welcome. You'd best keep that in mind."

"We will," said Mac. "Thanks."

"I reckon we need to talk some, before we visit the sutler's," Red said. "We're playin' with dynamite, taking four women into a fort where there's likely nothin' but men."

"We don't have to go," said Trinity. "We know the post commander doesn't want us here."

"All the more reason you should go," Mac replied. "You'll go with me, Hattie will go with Red, Rachel will go with Buck, and Elizabeth will go with Haze. As far as Stockton is concerned, each of you will have an escort. If anybody starts trouble, we'll finish it."

"I like that," said Hattie. "Let's go."

Port Guthrie had been right about one thing. The sutler's was teeming with soldiers. Mac wondered if Captain

Stockton had forbidden the men to leave the fort and approach the wagons. That would account for the sudden interest in the sutler's store, especially if the word had spread there were women with the wagons. Since the teamsters had already been to the store, there was reason to believe the women might come later.

"Let's not become too widely separated," Mac said, as they were about to enter the store. "There's undoubtedly a saloon in here."

There was a saloon, and it seemed that every soldier who could arrange to be there was on hand. They spilled out of the saloon and into the store, and for a few moments they stared in silence. But all that changed in an instant.

"By God," a burly private shouted, "she-males!"

He seized Hattie in a bear hug, and she retaliated with a knee in his groin. Grunting like a wounded grizzly, he doubled over just in time for his bearded chin to collide with Red's fist. Another soldier went after Trinity. Seizing the only thing handy—a kerosene lantern—she slammed it into his face. Mac already had his hands full, slugging it out with a sergeant who outweighed him by fifty pounds. When Mac went down, his assailant straddled him with the intention of slamming his head into the wooden floor, but Trinity got her hands on an axe handle and clubbed him unconscious. Buck and Haze had their shirts ripped off, and were beaten to the floor by sheer numbers.

"Stop it!" Trinity shouted. "You're killing them!"

She was ignored and the brawl continued, becoming more brutal by the minute. With Trinity leading the charge, the women went to the defense of their outnumbered men. A long-handled shovel became a deadly weapon in the hands of Hattie, and men bawled curses as they were battered and bloodied. A display of tinned goods was toppled, and Elizabeth and Rachel began throwing tinned tomatoes and peaches with unerring aim. Trinity clutched the bail of a kerosene lantern in each hand, slamming the lanterns against the heads of the struggling, cursing soldiers. Finally even the women went down under the onslaught.

When it seemed nothing could stop it, there was the thunder of a shot and a bawling voice of authority that struck terror into the heart of every soldier, drunk or sober.

"Damn it, on your feet, every man of you!"

There were ten military policemen with billy clubs. Captain Stockton stood there with a smoking Colt in his hand, his weathered face flaming with fury. Slowly, painfully, the soldiers got to their feet, those who were able. Some of those struck by Trinity's lanterns lay unconscious, their heads bloody. Mac got to his hands and knees, his shirt in shreds, and found Trinity beside him. She had fared no better, and was half naked. Red was helping Hattie to her feet. There was a nasty cut above her eyes, and her face was a mask of blood. Rachel leaned weakly on Buck, while Haze leaned over Elizabeth. She appeared to be unconscious. At that point, Captain Stockton said exactly the wrong thing.

"Tunstall, I am holding you responsible for this."

Beaten and bloody as he was, Mac stumbled to his feet. He said nothing until his face was only inches from Stockton's. When he spoke, his voice was barely more than a whisper, but it was cold, deadly.

"Stockton, we defended ourselves when we were attacked, nothing more. Now if you are hell-bent on punishing somebody, there's blue bellies all around you. If you try to lay the blame for this on us, after your men started it, you'd better go ahead and shoot me. If you don't, by God, I'll see you cashiered out of the military, if I have to crawl to Washington on my hands and knees."

"Captain," said the sutler, "he's right. The soldiers started it by molesting the women. The bar's been six-deep with soldiers, ever since I opened the doors. The men was totally snockered, and they just went crazy."

Captain Stockton looked about him. Only four of his men stood unsteadily on their feet. The others—either beaten unconscious or in a drunken stupor—still lay sprawled on the floor. Stockton then spoke to the sergeant in charge of the military policemen.

"Sergeant, these men are to be taken to the guardhouse. Have the medic see to those who are injured. I'll deal with them in the morning."

With Haze supporting her, Elizabeth was able to stand. Stockton looked from one of the women to the other. They were battered and bloody, their clothing ripped or missing to the point of indecency, but they held their heads high, glaring at Stockton in undaunted, fire-eyed defiance.

"I don't consider you blameless, Tunstall," Captain Stockton said, "but I'll settle for you leaving this post immediately, with your assurance that you won't return."

"Captain," said Mac, "I promise you we won't come here again, if we're pursued by Comanches. But we came here for a few things we needed, and we won't be leaving until we get them."

"Then have the sutler get them for you," Stockton said stiffly. "I'm standing here until I see the lot of you out that gate."

The sutler made a list and quickly gathered the requested items. Mac paid, and without a word, he led his battered outfit from the store, past the sentry, and through the front gate.

"I've seen some bastards in my time," said Red grimly, "but he takes a prize, the fur-lined slop bucket."

"I reckon we should have left you ladies with the wagons," Buck said.

"I'm glad you didn't," said Rachel. "You needed all the help you could get."

"Under the circumstances," Mac said, "all of you conducted yourselves quite well. I just hope you have a change of clothes in the wagon."

"I can stand being near naked," said Hattie, "but blind is something else. My eyes are full of dried blood."

"Red can lead you to the river," Trinity said, "and you can duck your head."

"I'm glad we're going to be here another night," said Elizabeth. "It'll take us the rest of the day, doctoring our cuts and cleaning ourselves up."

"You sound a little down," Hattie said. "Don't tell me you didn't enjoy that."

"Oh, but I did," said Elizabeth. "I've never been knocked unconscious before, on the floor of a saloon, with three drunken soldiers piled on me."

"You played hell with some of them, before they put you down," Haze said, with some admiration.

Port Guthrie and the rest of the teamsters saw them coming long before they reached the wagons.

"A damn shame we had to stay with the wagons," Lafe Beard observed. "I'd of liked to show that bunch how the cow et the cabbage."

"We give 'em as good as we got," said Red.

"We've been ordered to stay off the post," Mac said. "We'll keep our usual watch tonight and move out tomorrow at first light."

What he left unsaid was far more important than what he said. There was a possibility that some of the soldiers, seeking revenge, might come prowling around the wagons.

"We ought to go downstream, out of sight of the fort, and dunk ourselves in the river," said Trinity.

"No," Mac said. "Build a fire, heat some water, and do your bathing in your wagon. When you're done, Red, Buck, Haze, and me will do the same."

By suppertime, all the blood had been bathed away and wounds attended.

"Before we got on the bad side of everybody at the fort," said Buck, "we should have learned how far we are from the Colorado."

"We know it's dead ahead of us," Mac said. "We'll have to be satisfied with that."

Mac, Red, Buck, and Haze took over at the start of the third watch, and none of them were surprised to find the women gathered around the bed of coals on which the coffeepot bubbled. Now that the uncertainty of Fort Griffin was behind them, they were ready to commit themselves to a new life with a quartet of Texas cowboys they had known only a few weeks. When Trinity arrived, Mac was waiting for her.

"Back home," Trinity said, "our conduct would have been disgraceful, but I don't feel disgraced. Aside from being bruised and sore, I feel like I've been through the fire. The others feel the same way."

"If anybody should feel disgraced, it's the bunch that jumped us," said Mac. "I'd not be in the least surprised if word gets around, and Captain Stockton has to justify all that happened in the sutler's store. On the frontier, there's nothing disgraceful about defending yourself. You're disgraced if you don't."

"I'd be tempted to accuse Captain Stockton of spreading the word that we were going to be on the post, but how could he have known?"

"Easy enough," Mac replied. "After talking to Stockton, before I left the post, I got permission from the sergeant of the guard for us to visit the sutler's. It would have been proper military procedure for him to have told Stockton. But I can't imagine him having anything to do with that brawl."

"I can," said Trinity. "He hated the four deserters he blames for the death of his brother, and he hates Hattie, Rachel, Elizabeth, and me for coming here and opening old wounds. Wouldn't the rest of the men on the post be equally bitter toward those four who deserted under fire?"

"I reckon they would," Mac agreed, "although some of them might have deserted if they'd been involved in a sure-death fight with Comanches. But what we think of Fort Griffin and what Fort Griffin thinks of us no longer matters. We accomplished what we came here to do. Are you satisfied with what you've learned?"

"Yes," said Trinity. "I've talked to Hattie, Elizabeth, and Rachel, and we believe what Captain Stockton told you pretty well agreed with what we expected of the men we were looking for. If he had been more honest with us at the beginning, our coming west would have been unnecessary."

"And I'd never have met you," Mac said.

"I've thought of that, too," said Trinity, "and in an odd sort of way, I suppose we owe Captain Stockton a debt of gratitude."

"Maybe," Mac agreed, "but I'd be hung upside down over a slow fire, before I'd ever have him know it."

Hattie and Red had put everything having to do with Fort Griffin behind them.

"You're stuck with me now," Hattie said. "I could never go back East."

"But you have family and friends there," Red replied.

"Yes," said Hattie, "in a little town where everybody knows everybody else, along with everybody else's business. I've been in the West only a few weeks, but I'll never leave it. What will *your* family and friends say, when you show up with me?"

"Pretty as you are, I reckon they'll be struck dumb with admiration," Red replied. "In fact, I know they will be, when they learn you can hold your own in a saloon fight."

"Surely you won't tell anyone about *that*."

Red laughed. "Oh, I'll have to. That's the stuff of which legends are made. You'll be the envy of every woman in Texas."

Buck and Rachel were discussing an entirely different matter.

"Now that Fort Griffin's behind us, and you know you're a free woman," Buck said, "you might as well know the truth about me."

"Oh?" said Rachel. "You're not afraid of girls, are you?"

"Only them that can stand their ground in a saloon brawl," Buck said.

"Besides that?"

"I don't own a damn thing except my horse, saddle, and bedroll," said Buck.

"Are you bragging or complaining?"

"Complaining, I reckon," Buck said. "A woman's got a right to expect more than that of a man."

"Who told you that?"

"I . . . well . . . I dunno," said Buck. "What do *you* expect?"

"A man who'll stand beside me, who won't run at the first sign of trouble," Rachel said. "That's all I want."

"I may never have anything else to offer," said Buck, "but you'll have that."

"I know it," Rachel said, "and I'm not exactly empty-handed. I have a little over three hundred dollars. Is that enough to start a ranch?"

"A bull and maybe twenty-five cows," said Buck. "I'll have a hundred and fifty dollars when we finally get to Austin. We can have our own brand."

"We can call it the BR," Rachel said. "Buck and Rachel."

"Or the B-R Connected."

She laughed. "I like that even better."

Hattie, enjoying her newfound freedom, sat beside Red on a wagon tongue. Each had a black eye, and Hattie had a bandage around her head.

"There's one thing I wish we hadn't learned at Fort Griffin," Hattie said. "I wish that everybody didn't know about these wagons bound for Austin, and what they're hauling. I'm just afraid something's going to happen."

"I wish I could tell you that nothing will, and be sure of it," said Red, "but I'll have to admit anything's possible. The war ain't that far behind us, and Texas is full of hombres without a pot and a window to throw it out. We'll have to keep our eyes open and our guns handy."

Haze was having his problems with Elizabeth's misgivings.

"I don't like what I've seen of the military," Elizabeth said, "and I only wish they all didn't know about the guns and ammunition being freighted to Austin. What's to stop some of the soldiers from banding together, shooting us, and taking the wagons?"

"I don't know," said Haze, "but I wouldn't judge all the military, based on what we encountered here at Fort

Griffin. When we reach the Colorado, we'll be assured of water all the way to Austin. That means we can keep the outfit together, tightening our defense."

"Perhaps I'm worrying for nothing," Elizabeth said, "but it seems like every time I try to be happy, things go wrong."

"Maybe not this time," said Haze, but he had his own misgivings.

"It's your turn to scout ahead," Mac told Haze. "If you're fortunate enough to find our water for today within ten miles or less, see what you can find for tomorrow."

When the wagons took the trail, Haze rode south, Elizabeth riding beside him.

"I hope you don't mind," she said.

"I don't mind," said Haze. "Glad to have you."

They had ridden only a few miles when Haze reined up, Elizabeth beside him.

"We'll rest the horses and stretch our legs," Haze said.

They walked about a hundred yards to the east, returned to the horses, and walked an equal distance to the west.

"You're not stretching your legs," said Elizabeth. "You're looking for something. What is it?"

Haze laughed. "You're becoming a Western woman. All right, I am looking for something. I haven't forgotten those two men who rode out early this morning, and I'm looking for tracks. I know they rode to the southeast, but they could just as easily have changed directions, once they were well away from the fort."

"You think perhaps they have a gang somewhere ahead of us?"

"We can't be sure that they don't," said Haze. "I figure the closer we get to Austin, the less likely that we'll be attacked."

"But we're still a long way from Austin, aren't we?"

"Yes," Haze said. "They could hold off, attack us somewhere along the Colorado, and still prevent us from reaching Austin."

"And you told me not to worry," said Elizabeth. "If you're not worrying, what do you call it? Is there a Texas word for it?"

"You'd think of it as worrying," Haze said, "but in Texas, it's not quite the same. We don't actually worry about all hell bustin' loose. We just keep our eyes open and our guns handy, and let the rough end drag."

Elizabeth laughed. "I'm going to like Texas, if I ever get used to its ways."

"It's time we was ridin' on," said Haze. "If we don't find water within the next two or three miles, we may be facin' a dry camp."

Eventually they came upon a clear, fast-flowing creek.

"We'll rest and water the horses," Haze said, "and then I want to scout a ways up- and downstream."

"How far have we ridden?"

"Near fifteen miles," said Haze. "The teams will have to rattle their hocks to get the wagons here before sundown."

When the horses had rested, Haze led them to the creek for water. He helped Elizabeth mount, then straddled his own horse, and they rode upstream several miles. There was no sign, and they returned to their starting point.

"We'll ride downstream a ways, just to be sure," Haze said.

The ground was littered with dead leaves from the trees and bushes that lined the banks of the creek.

"I can't even see the ground, most of the time," said Elizabeth. "If there are tracks, how are you going to find them?"

"I may not be able to," Haze said. "Men who are up to no good can hide their tracks, but if they've spent a day or two in one place, it's hard for them not to leave some sign."

They had ridden almost two miles downstream, along the north bank, when Haze suddenly reined up.

"What is it?" Elizabeth asked.

"Maybe nothing," said Haze. "Wait here."

The creek was shallow enough, and he walked his horse across. Dismounting, he knelt down and picked up something from the clutter of brittle, fallen leaves.

"Come on across," Haze said.

Elizabeth walked her horse across the creek and reined up, studying the oval bit of paper Haze held in his hand.

"Tag from a sack of Durham," said Haze, "and it ain't been here long. Come on."

They rode away from the creek, still heading downstream, but in a half-circle toward the southeast.

"Where are we going now?" Elizabeth asked.

"I'm gambling that somebody rode in from the south," said Haze, "and if that's the case, we should cross the trail."

As they rode farther from the creek, the trees and bushes thinned out, diminishing the fallen leaves that littered the ground. Haze reined up.

"The ground's bare enough for tracks," Elizabeth said, "but it looks hard as stone."

"It likely is," said Haze, "but I aim to look."

He dismounted, hunkered down, and began studying the ground. Finally he mounted his horse, nodded to Elizabeth, and they rode off to the south. Eventually they reached a barren stretch where even Elizabeth could see tracks leading north.

"Perhaps they were soldiers from Fort Griffin," Elizabeth said hopefully.

"Maybe," said Haze, "but I don't think so. There were at least a dozen riders, and at most, there's seldom more than ten men in a patrol. With most forts undermanned, there's usually less. But we'll find out."

They rode back to the point where they had first approached the creek, crossed it, and then began riding a half-circle to the southeast. They crossed several stretches of bare ground where there was no sign, but when they reached a clearing where there were few leaves, Haze reined up. The tracks were plain enough.

"Two horses heading north," Elizabeth said. "Bad news."

"Damn right," said Haze. "That's the two varmints that left the fort this morning."

CHAPTER 14

⌘

"It looks damned suspicious," Mac said, when Haze told him of the sign he had found, "especially when two riders apparently rode on to the fort. That could very well be the same two hombres that rode out early this morning."

"My thoughts exactly," said Haze, "and the fact that they rode southeast could mean that the whole bunch aims to come after us somewhere along the Colorado."

"Maybe," Mac said, "but we can't be sure of that. They need only wait until we're far enough south of Fort Griffin so that there's no chance of being discovered by soldiers on patrol."

"One other thing," said Haze. "I almost forgot about the water. The creek we have to reach is a good fifteen miles south of Fort Griffin. We didn't ride beyond that."

"We've still got ten miles ahead of us, then," Port Guthrie said.

"At least that," said Mac. "The teams have rested enough. Let's move out."

Among the outfit there was only grim determination. The prospect of yet another band of outlaws planning to seize the wagons was enough to sober them all. They pushed the teams as much as they dared, resting less often, and managed to reach the creek barely before dark.*

*Hubbard Creek.

"Go ahead with the cook fire," Mac said. "That bunch knows we're coming. I reckon it won't matter if they smell the smoke from our fire. We'll continue with three watches, same as before."

As she had so often done before, Trinity found Mac at his post shortly after midnight. But this time was different, for she had her Winchester, fully loaded.

"We all talked about it," Trinity said, "and reached a decision. If the third watch is the most dangerous, then we'll stand it with you from here on to Austin. We can shoot, and we're all armed. We were tenderfeet when we reached Dodge, but we weren't as green as we might have been."

"No," said Mac, "and the time may come when you'll be mighty glad you have those Winchesters. There's no guarantee we'll be attacked at night. The attack could come during the day, when we're strung out on the trail. Keep those Winchesters loaded and handy in the wagon, and anytime one of you is riding one of the horses, see that your rifle is in the saddle boot."

"That'll be fourteen guns," Trinity said. "If Haze was right about the number of men, we won't be outnumbered by much."

"Haze is probably the best tracker among us," said Mac. "That's one reason I wanted him to scout ahead today. He can track a lizard across solid rock."

"Then you had your doubts about the two riders who left the fort this morning."

"Yes," Mac said. "That's another way to stay alive out here. You watch for anything that seems out of place, a man where he shouldn't be, a flock of birds that takes sudden flight."

"I haven't forgotten how you and me were captured while searching for water," said Trinity. "That could happen again, to any of us riding ahead of the wagons, couldn't it?"

"Yes," Mac replied, "and I don't know of any sure

and certain way to avoid it, unless the man riding ahead is constantly watching for tracks.''

"We can't depend on that," said Trinity, "with them somewhere ahead of us, can we?"

"No," Mac said. "They could flank us, riders east and west a couple of miles out, and with those riders coming together, catch us in a deadly cross fire."

"It's so frustrating," said Trinity. "All we can do is wait for them to strike, and when they do, we're always on the defensive."

"You've just put your finger on our biggest problem," Mac said. "It's impossible to win from a defensive position, but there's no way we can attack. We dare not leave these wagons undefended, and if we split our forces, we risk having one faction wiped out before the two can come together for an effective defense."

"I think I understand. It sounds like military talk."

"I reckon it is," said Mac. "I wore the gray, riding with John Mosby. They called him the Gray Ghost. Haze and me learned from him, and it's kept us alive on the frontier."

The wagons again took the trail at first light, and it was Mac's turn to scout ahead for water. Trinity rode with him, and he noted with approval that her Winchester rode in the saddle boot. The terrain was partially timbered with post oak, cedar, blackjack, and mesquite, eventually giving way to grassy prairie. They looked in vain for a stream, and after riding what Mac believed was twelve miles, eventually came upon the runoff from a spring that flowed from beneath a stone ledge.

"Not much of a runoff," Mac said, "but there's plenty of water in the spring. I think we'll ride south a ways, and see what we can find for tomorrow."

The terrain changed to a succession of valleys divided by hilly limestone ridges. There was a variety of timber, including live oak, post oak, willow, mesquite, and walnut. In the numerous valleys there was lush prairie grass, and in such a valley was the stream they sought.

"More than a ten-mile drive," said Mac, "but worth it. The graze will be better as we travel farther south. This is the best so far."

The wagons had traveled farther than Mac had expected, and he was quick to praise the teamsters.

"I reckoned it wouldn't hurt if we reached water in time to have supper before dark," Port Guthrie said. "If that bunch is somewhere ahead, they'll expect us to have a fire, but I don't favor allowin' the varmints any kind of edge."

Mac laughed. "That's sound thinking, Port. I reckon the rest of us had better stick to that from here on."

The wagons reached the spring in time for the outfit to water the mules and horses and to prepare and eat supper before dark.

"Starting tonight," Mac said, "I think we'd better keep two men with the horses and mules. Hombres wantin' to draw us away from the wagons could do it easy enough, just by stampedin' our stock."

"On the first and second watch," said Port Guthrie, "that'll mean just one man with the wagons."

"I know," Mac said, "but Red, Buck, Haze, and me are light sleepers. We won't shuck anything but our hats. A shout from any one of you, and we'll be on our feet with guns in our hands in an instant. I still think we need the four of us on the third watch, and I'll want all of you ready to grab your guns in a second. I reckon none of us will be sleepin' much until we reach Austin, but if we allow this bunch to take us by surprise, we may all be down for the long sleep."

Sixty miles south, near the Colorado, a dozen men gathered around a fire drinking their coffee from tin cups. Sloan, the leader of the bunch, was speaking.

"I'm sayin' we don't make our move until they reach the Colorado. If anybody's got any objections, sing out."

"I got no objection to that," Jarvis said, "but I ain't

favorin' what you aim to do with them guns and ammunition.''

"Me, neither," said Ringo. "I don't trust that pair of Mexes—Diaz and Mercado—as far as I could flap my arms and fly.''

"I got my reasons for dealin' with them," Sloan said. "The important one is that when we take over the wagons, we'll be maybe a hundred miles from the border and San Felipe del Rio.''*

"It won't make no damn difference what your other reasons are, if they shoot us all stone dead," Ringo argued. "I say them wagons don't cross the border till we git paid, and I mean in gold, not Mexican pesos.''

There was a shouted chorus of agreement from the rest of the men, and Sloan had to think fast to avoid a mutiny.

"That'll be settled when we git to the border," said Sloan, "and they already agreed to pay in gold. Fifty dollars for a Colt, a hundred for a Winchester, and by God, we'll git no better offer, even if we had somewhere else to go.''

"That's another thing I don't like," Jarvis said. "We got no other place to go, and I'd bet my hoss an' saddle they know it. Once we git there, what's to stop them from backin' down on the price? What if the varmints offer us twenty-five dollars for a Colt, and fifty for a Winchester?''

There were angry shouts from the rest of the men, and Sloan had a difficult time restoring order. When their anger subsided to a murmur, Sloan spoke.

"Damn it, they *want* these weapons, and we won't take less than the prices we agreed on. But just keep one thing in mind. If this deal falls through, we're stuck with six wagonloads of weapons that'll be hotter than a brandin' iron.''

That sobered them.

"Hell," said Carter, "we *got* to deal with the Mexes.

---

*First settlement was begun on St. Phillip's Day. Third—and permanent—was Del Rio.

There's nobody else, except the Comanches, and they've been on the run for months. Where would they get enough gold to buy from us, even it they was willin'?''

There was grumbling among the men as they were forced to consider this possibility. Sloan pressed his advantage.

"Don't forget about the army," Sloan said. "By now, the whole damn world knows of those wagons, of the weapons and ammunition, and that they're on their way to Austin. If they fail to arrive, how long do you reckon it'll take the military to begin searchin' for 'em?"

"By God, he's right," said Dirk. "We got to deal with them Mexes. Let the military catch us with them wagon-loads of guns, and we're dead men. They'll back us up against a wall and pour enough lead into us to sink a steamboat."

"All that's got to be considered," Sloan said, "but first we have to take control of the wagons. We'll wait until they reach the Colorado, until they've spent their first night. Then we'll attack at first light, and we'll have to kill them all."

"They got some right pretty females with 'em," said Rufe, one of the outlaws who had been sent to Fort Griffin. "Ain't I right, Zack?"

"Yeah," Zack said. "We ain't told what they done in the sutler's store."

"Then tell us," said Jarvis. "Them females might be worth keepin' alive. At least for a while. What about it, Sloan?"

"Maybe," Sloan said, not wishing to have another shouting match on his hands. "Our first objective is to get control of them wagons by whatever force it takes. Feisty females can be had in droves, when you got gold in your pockets."

Mac continued taking every possible precaution, but nothing disturbed the tranquility of the nights, as they pressed on toward the Colorado.

"I know better than to suggest it," said Red, "but there's just a possibility that we'll reach Austin without any more trouble."

Haze laughed. "There's just as strong a possibility that there's folks in hell, right this minute, havin' 'em a snow-ball fight."

"Much as I hate to," Buck said, "I'll have to agree with Haze. Since leavin' Dodge, we've had our share of outlaw trouble, but none of it because of the telegraph spreadin' word of these wagons loaded with guns and shells. Now don't that make sense?"

"I reckon it does," said Mac, "as much as I hate to admit it. We'd best be prepared."

But as one uneventful day led to another, even Mac began to hope their fears had all been groundless. It was Mac and Trinity who rode out that memorable day and discovered they were less than fifteen miles from the Colorado.

"Oh, I'm so glad," Trinity cried.

"So am I," said Mac, "but we can't allow our excitement to override our caution. I'll feel better if we ride a ways downstream, toward Austin, without finding outlaw sign. But first, we'll rest and water our horses."

There was a light wind from the west. The horses were drinking, when suddenly there was a faint nicker from somewhere downriver. Trinity's horse raised its head and answered.

"Trouble," Mac said. "Mount up and let's ride."

Trinity sprang into her saddle without question. Mac mounted and they rode at a fast gallop back the way they had come. But they were already too late. A few hundred yards downriver, the band of outlaws knew their presence had been revealed.

"Mount up and ride," Sloan shouted. "That damn horse give us away. Some hombre's on his way to warn them wagons. We got to hit 'em before they got time to group and dig in, or we'll lose our edge."

A dozen strong, they mounted and galloped their horses

upriver, pursuing a distant dust cloud that marked the way Mac and Trinity had ridden.

"They're coming!" Trinity shouted fearfully, looking over her shoulder.

"Our horses can't stand this gait much longer," said Mac. "When I find a place to hole up, I'll hold them off while you ride ahead to warn the outfit."

"No," Trinity cried, "I won't leave you."

"Damn it," Mac shouted, "ride! Warn the others!"

Bearing less weight, Trinity's horse responded with a burst of speed, while Mac could feel his own mount tiring. He looked back, and already he could see individual riders as they materialized from a cloud of dust. While he had no doubt that Red, Buck, and Haze would hasten to his defense, the four of them would be fearfully outgunned. Ahead was a wind blown oak whose root mass had left a waist-deep hole. His horse was heaving now, and he had no time to seek better cover. Grimly he drew his Winchester from the boot and, kicking free of the stirrups, flung himself from the saddle. He rolled into the hole just in time, for the pursuing men had begun firing. Lead kicked up puffs of dust and swirls of dry leaves.

"Come on, you bastards," Mac snarled.

Taking careful aim with his Winchester, he fired once, twice, three times, and had the satisfaction of seeing two of his pursuers flung from their saddles. It had a profound effect on the others, for they hastily reined up. Mac could hear shouted commands, and his fears became reality.

"Dirk," Sloan shouted, "you and Boyd keep this varmint pinned down until one of you can get close enough to kill him. The rest of you come with me. We're goin' to grab us some wagons."

Dirk and Boyd immediately began pouring lead into the upended roots of the oak, showering Mac with dirt. The fusillade was head-high, and he dared not return the fire. He could hear the thud of horses' hooves as the rest of the men rode away, bound for the approaching wagons. Gritting his teeth, he raised his head, unsure as to where Dirk

and Boyd were. He quickly learned they already had him
in a cross fire. Even if he managed to return the fire of
one, the other would eventually pick him off, if only with
a lucky shot. Then, from somewhere ahead, came the
sound of gunfire. Had Trinity warned the others in time,
or was he hearing the sound of their dying? Suddenly there
was a rattle of gunfire and the thunder of hooves. Dirk and
Boyd tried to run for it, but died on their feet, as twelve
bluecoats swept in from the river. A soldier caught up a
horse ridden by one of the outlaws, and galloping near,
threw the reins to Mac. In an instant he was out of the
hole and into the saddle, galloping after the departing soldiers. The shooting from somewhere ahead sounded closer,
more frantic, and Mac hoped they weren't too late . . .

Port Guthrie was the first to see Trinity galloping her tiring
horse madly toward the wagons. He shouted an alarm just
as the outlaws began shooting at Mac. Trinity reined up
and fell from the saddle, gasping. Red, Buck, and Haze
were already in their saddles.

"Mac's trying to stand them off," Trinity cried, her
voice trailing off into a sob, "but there's too many of
them . . ."

All the teams had been reined up and men drew their
Winchesters from beneath their wagon boxes. Hattie, Eliz-
abeth, and Rachel had their weapons, and having brought
Trinity's Winchester, Hattie handed it to her.

"Take cover," Red shouted, swinging out of the saddle.
"Here they come!"

Buck and Haze were forced to follow his example, for
eight outlaws were coming at them in a skirmish line.
Lacking cover, the defenders went belly-down on the
ground, their Winchesters spitting lead. One of the outlaws
pitched out of his saddle, and the rest faltered.

"Damn it," Sloan shouted, "attack."

"Attack, hell," Ringo shouted, "look yonder!"

Sloan whirled his horse just in time to take a slug
through his chest. The men in blue surged ahead, showing

no mercy, until the last of the outlaws lay dead or dying. Mac rode up to the lead wagon and dismounted. Trinity dropped her Winchester and ran to him, her face streaked with tears.

"Pard," Red shouted, "I don't know where you got them soldiers, but I've never seen a more welcome sight."

"I have no idea where they came from, or why they're here," said Mac, "but I reckon we're about to find out."

The officer in charge wore the insignia of a first lieutenant on his blue tunic. He and a sergeant dismounted and approached the wagons. The rest of the soldiers remained in their saddles.

"I'm First Lieutenant Nelson," the officer said, "and this is Sergeant Embler. Mounted are Privates Puckett, Haynes, McCarty, Stearn, Willis, Gerdes, Odell, Konda, Collins, and Corporal Irvin,"

"You couldn't have timed your arrival more perfectly," said Mac. "How is it that you happen to be here?"

"Considering the nature of your freight," Nelson said, "it was decided that you might need an escort the rest of the way. The post commander at Fort Griffin telegraphed Austin that you had left there and were headed south. Were any of you hit?"

"I don't think so," said Mac. "You might as well meet the rest of the outfit."

He then proceeded to introduce his outfit to the soldiers. While they seemed amiable enough, the privates said little, taking their orders from Sergeant Embler or Lieutenant Nelson.

"How far are we out of Austin?" Port Guthrie asked.

"Following the river," said Nelson, "at least a hundred and sixty miles. If you'll get started, you'll reach the Colorado before dark."

The Colorado River. November 27, 1873.

The soldiers had gathered the horses belonging to the dead outlaws, and the animals were driven along behind the wagons. Mac rode ahead of the lead wagon, and Red jogged his horse alongside.

"Seein' as how these hombres got us out of a hole that might have become a grave," said Red, "I'd be an ungrateful varmint, findin' somethin' wrong with 'em, wouldn't I?"

"That depends," Mac said. "What do you find wrong?"

"Maybe nothin'," said Red, "but when somethin' just seems too damn good to be true, it usually is. I can't believe, after we got the bum's rush at Fort Griffin, that Stockton was all that concerned with our well-being. Hell, we beat off two packs of outlaws before we ever left the railroad, and if Yeager had any plans for having a military escort meet us, he could have told us before we left Dodge. Finally, there's somethin' almighty unusual about a twelve-man escort. I've seen army payrolls come into San Antone with maybe half this many soldiers ridin' shotgun."

"I sort of wish you hadn't raised those questions," Mac said. "They're kind of runnin' neck and neck with some of mine. I'd about convinced myself it's just my cockeyed way of lookin' at things. What do you reckon the chances are of us both bein' wrong?"

"I don't ever recall us both bein' wrong about the same thing at the same time," said Red. "Do you?"

Mac sighed. "No, I don't. Have you spoken to Haze and Buck?"

"No," said Red. "I was hopin' you'd convince me my suspicions was all wrong. What do we do now?"

"Not much we can do," Mac said, "unless these gents make some moves that confirm our suspicions. Don't be obvious about it, but speak to Haze and Buck. If there is a joker in the deck and we're forced to call their hand, there won't be much time for explaining."

The wagons reached the river well before sundown, and Lieutenant Nelson approached Mac with a question.

"Are you well enough fixed for grub to accommodate

us? We've had a long ride, and there isn't enough room in a man's saddlebags for more than the essentials.''

"We'll make do," Mac said. "The ladies have been cooking for us all. I'll talk to them about it."

"We were somewhat surprised, finding them with you," said Nelson. "If I'm not being unduly inquisitive, how and why did you acquire them?"

Sparing many of the details, Mac told him.

"Ah, yes," Nelson said. "The army can be cold and insensitive. I've never known one good soldier who hasn't done something worthy of a court-martial."

He turned away, and Mac approached the supper fire where the women had already begun the meal. Trinity and her three companions paused to hear what he had to say.

"Nelson and his men are on short rations, and he's asked if we can feed them from our supplies. Can we?"

"I don't see how we can afford not to," said Trinity, "after what they've done. Tell them we'll cook for them, too."

Mac nodded. He saw some indecision and doubt in Hattie's eyes, and he thought she and Red might have been sharing the suspicions Red had passed on to Mac. But they could do nothing to confirm or deny what Lieutenant Nelson had told them. After supper, Nelson again spoke to Mac.

"It's only fair that we pull our share of sentry duty. How many of my men will you need?"

"None, really," Mac said. "We've had three men on the first and second watches, and four on the third watch. Do you feel there's a need for more than that?"

"No," said Nelson, "that seems adequate. My men won't argue with that."

Mac found it strange and somewhat disturbing that when the soldiers spread their blankets, they were not near one another. Instead, they seemed to have circled the wagons to the extent that they would be aware of any movement within the camp. As usual, Port Guthrie, Lafe Beard, and Emmett Budd took the first watch. Smokey Foster, Saul

Estrella, and Gourd Snively would take the second. Mac, Red, Buck, and Haze unrolled their beds within speaking distance of one another, and were joined by Trinity, Hattie, Elizabeth, and Rachel.

"I know they're part of our camp," Trinity whispered, "but we all feel safer near the four of you, like we've been since we were just two or three days out of Dodge."

When Mac, Red, Buck, and Haze took over the third watch, Trinity and her three companions joined them. To their dismay, they found at least one of the soldiers sleeping near where each of them had their late-night rendezvous.

"It's like . . . they're watching us," Trinity said nervously. "Why?"

"I don't know," said Mac, "unless this is some vindictive scheme cooked up by good old Captain Stockton, at Fort Griffin, to embarrass us. I got the impression he knew there were plans in the making among us, but somehow I don't feel he has the necessary clout to send a dozen soldiers all the way from Austin."

"What are we going to do?"

"We'll have to take them at their word until we have a solid reason for doing otherwise," Mac said. "These wagons and their cargo are important enough to justify a military escort. The part that doesn't ring true is that it was an eleventh-hour decision, and I seriously doubt the army does things that way."

"I'm scared," said Trinity. "I don't really know why, but I am."

Trinity's three companions had their misgivings as well. They were voiced in nervous whispers.

"We owe them for saving us," Hattie said, "but I don't trust them. I have the feeling that when it's time for them to collect, we'll owe more than we can pay."

"We have no proof," said Red. "Whatever you do, don't show any doubts, and keep your suspicions to yourself. Try not to spook the others."

Hattie laughed softly. "They're already spooked."

Haze had said nothing, but Elizabeth had said plenty.

"I wish the soldiers hadn't come at all. I believe we could have defended ourselves."

"We probably could have," said Haze, "but two of them had Mac pinned down, and they'd have killed him in a cross fire before we could have fought our way back to him."

"I suppose you're right," Elizabeth said gloomily, "but I still don't trust them."

"Don't let what happened at Fort Griffin sour you on all the army," said Haze.

Buck listened as Rachel expanded the fears Hattie had shared with her, after talking with Red.

"You wouldn't disagree with Red, would you?"

"Damn it," Buck said quietly, "I can't agree or disagree, because we have nothing but our suspicions. I'm keeping my eyes open and my mouth shut, until I see some proof."

"I suppose you're suggesting I do the same," said Rachel.

"Now that you mention it," Buck said, "I am."

"I find it a bit odd that four of you stand the third watch with a woman at your side," said Lieutenant Nelson, as they waited for breakfast. "Do you not believe such a distraction might jeopardize the safety of the camp?"

"No," Mac said coldly, "I don't. These women each have a Winchester and they know how to use them. Trinity's with me, Hattie's with Red, Elizabeth's with Haze, and Rachel's with Buck, and our interest in them goes considerably beyond their abilities to fire a Winchester. We're not in the military, Lieutenant, and while our ways seem unconventional to you, we're satisfied with them. Are you suggesting we change?"

"Not for the time being," said Nelson.

Without another word he turned away, but most of Mac's outfit had heard the conversation. In their eyes Mac saw doubt and suspicion . . .

CHAPTER 15

The first day on the trail with the soldier escort was uneventful. With water available, the wagons could roll right up to sundown, without fear of a dry camp. Even in November the weather in south Texas was pleasant, but despite the proximity of the river, Mac had forbidden any bathing by the women.

"Heat a big pot of water," Mac told them, "get in your wagon and draw the front and back puckers tight. Do your washing there."

There were no questions or objections, for they understood his reasoning. After their first day of following the Colorado—after supper—Trinity and Hattie hung two big pots of water over the fire. When a pot of water was ready, Trinity and Hattie went first, for there was little room in the wagon. The soldiers watched the proceedings with interest, but that was all. After a while, two of the privates headed for a nearby thicket for reasons nobody questioned. Suddenly there was a screech from Trinity's wagon, followed by the bark of a Winchester. One of the soldiers lay on the ground behind the wagon, blood dripping from his left ear. The second man stood there with his hands raised and his face pale. Mac, Lieutenant Nelson, and half a dozen others arrived at the same time.

"What happened here?" Lieutenant Nelson demanded. "Private Puckett?"

"We just . . . looked in the wagon," said the private with his hands in the air. "That . . . that bitch . . . she shot Haynes without no warnin'."

"This bitch will shoot him again, the next time he pokes his nose in this wagon," the angry voice of Trinity shouted, "and next time it won't be an ear."

To the surprise of everybody, Lieutenant Nelson laughed.

"I fail to find anything funny about this," said Mac, confronting Nelson. "That man on the ground could have been shot dead."

"But he wasn't," Nelson replied, "and I expect he'll think twice before he attempts any such thing again."

"I reckon you don't have any discipline in mind, then," said Red, his voice dripping sarcasm.

"He's been frightened out of his wits," Lieutenant Nelson said. "What do you suggest? The firing squad?"

Trinity descended from the wagon fully dressed. Facing Lieutenant Nelson, she spoke.

"Let him go. If he or any of the rest of you tries that again, a firing squad won't be necessary. I'll do the honors, and I hit what I'm shootin' at."

It was too much for Lieutenant Nelson, and he turned away. Haynes got up off the ground, clutching his bleeding ear, and virtually ran after the others. Dressed now, Hattie climbed out of the wagon.

"I meant what I said," Trinity snapped, her eyes on Mac. "Next time—if there is a next time—I'll shoot the skunk right between the eyes."

"I believe you," said Mac, "and you won't get any argument from me."

Hattie laughed. "It was dark in there, with the front pucker closed. He got his ear shot off, and didn't see a thing."

"For sure, it didn't leave Nelson a leg to stand on," said Red, "but if this bunch ain't on the level and there's a payoff comin', I get the feelin' they'll be holding a royal flush and us a pair of deuces."

"So be it," Mac said. "Until they show their hand, there's not much we can do. We'll stand up to them, because we can't afford not to. As long as they're going through the motions of being military—if that's what they're doing—they'll have to maintain at least some discipline."

The soldiers said virtually nothing the rest of the night, and there was little talk among Mac's outfit, for they had the feeling Nelson and his men were awake, listening. At dawn, breakfast was eaten in silence and the wagons again headed southeast, following the Colorado River. Mac estimated they were traveling at least ten miles a day, and if he was to believe what Nelson had told him, they were about a hundred and forty miles west of Austin, Texas. Despite the coolness of Nelson and his men, there was no more trouble. Mac still talked with the rest of his outfit, usually as they traveled along the Colorado. He often wondered what was on Nelson's mind, for he caught the man watching him. There had to be a showdown coming, and Mac's mind was a turmoil of possibilities. He now had his doubts that they would ever see Austin, but he was at a loss as to what Nelson and his men planned to do with the wagons loaded with Colts, Winchesters, and ammunition. Red, riding along beside him, was plagued by the same questions.

"If they're after the wagons," said Red, "they'll have to make their move somewhere between here and Austin. But those Colts and Winchesters will be hot, and they'll never be able to unload them in this country. I reckon it won't matter to us what they do with the guns, if we're all dead."

"That's what it comes back to," Mac replied. "We must come out of this alive, even if it means losing the wagons and their cargo. If these men are renegades, can you imagine what they'll do to the women, after we're dead?"

"I can imagine it, but I won't allow myself to dwell on it," said Red.

There was a monotony to the days, for there was no scouting ahead, looking for sign and for water. Mac often rode with Red, Buck, or Haze, and occasionally with Trinity, and there was no trouble, but Lieutenant Nelson was always watching.

"He's like a cat watching mice," Trinity said, shuddering. "They don't actually do anything, but all of us are afraid to take our clothes off, even in the wagon."

"I don't look for them to bother any of you, until they're ready to take the wagons," said Mac. "None of us remove anything but our hats when we sleep, and when they try to take us, they'll pay dearly."

"They laugh at us when we go to the bushes," Trinity said, "like they know something that we don't. I feel like they're seeing right through my clothes."

"We've been watching them watching you," said Mac, "and the first time any of them follows, there'll be hell to pay."

The addition of a dozen men began to deplete their supplies, and their fifth day on the trail, Sergeant Embler managed to kill a deer.

"Fifty miles behind us," said Red. "A hundred and ten more miles to Austin. Eleven days. By the time we're five days out, I reckon we'd better not close our eyes. Damn it, the waitin' is gettin' to me. I reckon that's the awfulest thing about the frontier. There's so many ways of dyin', you can't rest even a minute. That old bony bastard with the scythe rides every trail, and you never know when you'll come face-to-face with him."

Even with the short rations, nobody complained. Mac suspected his outfit was more concerned with things other than food, and whatever Nelson and his men had planned, they apparently weren't worried about provisions. Their sixth day with Nelson, Port Guthrie came to Mac with a complaint.

"Them blue bellies are grainin' their hosses with what we brought for the mules. You know them mules ain't up to pullin' heavy wagons when all they got to eat is grass. What can we do?''

"I'll speak to Nelson," Mac said. "Without the mules, we can't move the wagons.''

Lieutenant Nelson was becoming more arrogant and short-tempered by the day, and a complaint from Mac did little for his disposition.

"We're not more than ten days from Austin," said Nelson, "and our mounts are as essential as mules.''

He had nothing more to say, and recognizing the futility of further conversation, Mac said no more. Instead, he spoke to Guthrie and the other teamsters.

"First chance you get," Mac said, "relocate one sack of grain somewhere within the wagons, even if it means concealing it under some of those Winchester cases.''

"I got a better idea," said Gourd Snively. "Since firewood ain't a problem, why can't we stash some grain under the wagons, in the possum bellies?''

"That's good, up to a point," Mac said. "You can't carry too much there, or the hide will sag, giving away the location. But that might be the best place for it, even if you can't hide as much. Movin' things around within the wagons would only attract attention.''

"We'll take care of it tonight, durin' our watch," said Guthrie. "The varmints can't take it if they don't know where it is.''

Mac said nothing to the others of his decision. The hiding of the grain had given him an idea, and he began concealing other things upon which he might rely, if worse came to worst. He waited until the third watch, after Guthrie and the teamsters had secreted part of the grain within the wagons' possum bellies. He then fully loaded his Winchester and slipped it into the possum belly beneath Trinity's wagon. The venison from the deer had been tough, requiring knives. Mac had dropped his in a clump of grass, and he recovered it after dark. It would do in an emergency, and he slipped it into the sack of grain under Trinity's wagon. But his stealth hadn't gone unnoticed. Trinity mentioned it during the third watch, that same night.

"What did you do with your knife after supper?"

"If you're missing one, how do you know it was mine?" Mac asked.

"I noticed your Winchester was missing from your saddle boot," said Trinity, "and I just put two and two together."

"Damn it," Mac said, "I didn't know I was that obvious."

"You aren't," said Trinity. "I'm getting to know you pretty well, Mac Tunstall, and you're as nervous as I am."

"I wasn't goin' to tell anybody," Mac said. "Those damn soldiers have been feedin' our grain to their horses. Port Guthrie and his boys hid some grain under the wagons, in the possum bellies. I decided it wouldn't hurt, havin' some other things secreted away."

"I won't tell your secret if you won't tell mine," said Trinity.

"I can't tell yours, because I don't know what it is," Mac said.

Turning her back to him, she raised her long skirt above her waist.

"It's dark and nobody can see," she said. "Put your arm around my waist and follow the string."

He reached his arm around her and his fingers found the string, but he didn't have to follow it far. Dangling over her belly, the string tied to its haft, was a stiletto. A long, thin dagger.

"How long have you carried it there?" he asked. "I didn't see it when you were—"

"Carried away naked by outlaws," she finished, "but it's been there ever since we were rescued. I made up my mind I'd never be unarmed again."

"I'm glad you have it," said Mac, "but isn't it dangerous, in that particular place?"

She laughed softly. "It would be for you. But I don't have the same body parts, and the string is short."

* * *

Their next day got off to a bad start. The left rear wheel of Lafe Beard's wagon ran over a leaf-filled stump hole, and the wheel dropped with such force, it snapped the axle where it joined the right hub.

"Obviously we're going to be here a while," Lieutenant Nelson said. "Any idea how long?"

"Long enough to fell a tree and fashion a replacement axle," said Mac. "Of course, we have to jack up the wagon, and the wagon jack's somewhere beneath the cargo."

"You're not very amusing, Tunstall," Nelson said, "if your remarks were so intended."

"You asked a question," said Mac, "and I answered it. You can laugh or cry, depending on how it strikes you."

"It's a good half a day's work," Port Guthrie said, hoping to defuse what might easily become an explosive issue.

"Then get started repairing it," said Nelson. "You men may dismount."

The soldiers dismounted, leading their horses downriver where the graze was better. Guthrie and the other teamsters began the back-breaking task of unloading the heavy and cumbersome wooden crates of Winchesters.

"Port," said Mac, "some of us will cut a tree for the new axle. Any preference?"

"Oak, if possible," Guthrie replied. "Get one as near the size of the old axle as you can, so's we only got to fashion the ends."

"Come on, Red," said Mac. "You have a strong back and a weak mind."

Mac took an axe from the disabled wagon and mounted his horse. Red followed. They rode several miles to the north, away from the river, before finding a suitable oak. Mac took first turn at felling the tree, surrendering the axe to Red when he was half through. When the tree fell, Red drove the axe into the stump and sat down to rest.

"That damn lieutenant—if that's what he is—rubs my fur the wrong way, no matter what he says or does," Red said. "He talked like you ought to of pulled a new axle out of your pocket, lifted the wagon and slapped it in place.''

''I'm learning not to let him get next to me,'' said Mac. ''This is the kind of thing you can't blame on anybody, and it takes a real smart mouth to try and make something else of it.''

''When we finally get to Austin, there ought to be somebody we can report Nelson and his highfalutin bunch to,'' Red said. ''I realize they stomped hell out of us durin' the war, but that don't give 'em a license to talk down to us like we was dogs.''

''The privates don't talk much, so I'm not sure about them,'' said Mac, ''but I'd bet a horse that Lieutenant Nelson is a Southerner himself. Likely Virginia or South Carolina.''

''I reckon you're right,'' Red replied. ''The meanest bastard around is always some varmint that sold out his own kind and joined the other side.''

''Let's get this tree topped and trimmed,'' said Mac. ''If the lieutenant don't hear the sound of the axe, he's liable to cut himself a switch and come looking for us.''

When Mac and Red returned to the wagons, dragging the trimmed tree behind Red's horse, Port Guthrie and the teamsters had found the wagon jack.

''We can't raise the wagon with the jack under the old axle,'' Guthrie said, ''because we got to remove the old axle.''

''You've removed most of the load,'' said Lieutenant Nelson. ''Why can't you lift the wagon with the jack under the wagon box?''

''Lieutenant, sir,'' Port Guthrie said in a pitying manner, ''there's still enough weight on this wagon to drive the jack right through the wagon box. What we need is another tree that's at least as long as the wagon box is wide. With that beneath the wagon box, and the jack beneath the tree, we can lift the wagon.''

''Will some of you fetch this man another tree,'' said Nelson, ''or must I resort to a direct order?''

"I ain't military," Red said. "Give me a direct order, and I'll tell you where you can stick it."

There was a chorus of agreement from Buck, Haze, and the rest of the teamsters.

"Come on, Red," said Mac. "Port knows what he's talkin' about."

The implication was that Nelson didn't have the foggiest idea what he was doing. Mac took the axe and mounted his horse. Red followed, and they rode out.

"Port should of thought of this to start with," Red said. "Then we'd have been able to make just one trip."

"I believe Port is just trying to be ornery," said Mac.

They found another suitable oak, not quite as thick as the first, but thick enough to support the heavy wagon without damaging the box.

"This one's about right," Red said, "but I reckon we ought to take our time. I'd not want the good lieutenant to start takin' us for granted."

"Oh, come on," said Mac, "and let's get it done. Delaying will just give the varmint cause to run off at the mouth."

Mac felled the tree, Red trimmed and topped it, and they snaked it back to where the disabled wagon waited. Taking the axe, Port Guthrie flattened two sides of the log, one to rest against the bottom of the wagon box without rolling, and the opposite so that the jack wouldn't slip when the weight of the wagon was upon it.

"Some of you hold that flattened log in place under the wagon box," Guthrie said.

Four of the teamsters—two on each side of the wagon—held the log in place against the underside of the wagon box. Guthrie wrestled the wagon jack into position and, with help from Mac and Red, brought the wagon level, raising the wheel out of the hole. But an unpleasant surprise awaited them. The underside of the wheel rim was splintered, some of the wooden spokes dangling loose.

"Well, by God," said Lieutenant Nelson, "how much longer is *that* going to take?"

"Lieutenant, sir," Port Guthrie said coldly, "we ain't workin' by the hour. I reckon it'll take till we're done with it."

When the wagon had been loaded, it seemed nobody had given any thought to the possibility that the spare wheel and wagon jack might be needed. More of the heavy crates had to be moved to reach the spare wagon wheel. Guthrie unbolted the old axle and placed it alongside the oak log of similar size.

"I don't believe this," said Lieutenant Nelson sourly. "You think you can fashion a new axle without tools, with only an axe?"

"You'd better hope I can," Guthrie said grimly. "I've done it before and I can do it again, long as I ain't distracted with fool questions."

Guthrie began by cutting what was to become a new axle the exact same length as the old one. Taking the axe handle in one hand, near the head, he began the task of sizing one end of the new axle where it would go through the wheel hub. It required almost an hour of tedious work, before he was able to start on the other end. The sun was well on its way toward the western horizon when Guthrie believed the new axle was ready.

"Leave them U-bolts off," said Guthrie, "until we know the wheels is gonna fit. Four of you hold the new axle in place under the wagon box. Mac, you and Red help me hoist these wheels into position."

With Lafe Beard and Emmett Budd on one side of the wagon and Smokey Foster and Saul Estrella on the other, they lifted the new axle flush with the bottom of the wagon box until Guthrie, Mac, and Red could see if the wheels would fit. While the left rear wheel was a good fit, the right rear was not.

"Let 'er down," Guthrie said. "I got to whittle off some more."

While Guthrie continued working on the axle, Lieutenant Nelson folded his hands behind his back and paced the riverbank.

"Look at him," said Buck. "You'd think he was late to somethin' all-fired important, and it was all our fault."

"Maybe that's exactly what's botherin' him," Mac said.

The women had kept their distance from the disabled wagon, and when Trinity finally approached, it was with a question.

"Are we going to be here for the night? Sundown's not far off."

"We'll stay here for the night," said Mac. "You can go ahead and get supper started."

Lieutenant Nelson had approached just in time to hear Mac's decision.

"An incredible waste of time," Nelson said. "We could put another two hours behind us before sundown."

"We could," said Mac, "but we aren't going to. The mules have stood in harness most of the day. Now we're going to unharness them. They can use the extra time to rest and graze. Port, you go on with what you're doing. Red and me will unharness your teams."

The teamsters brought their wagons near the disabled wagon. Mac led Guthrie's teams, and when his wagon was near the others, Mac and Red unharnessed the teams. The grateful mules immediately began to roll.

"We might as well take them to water," Mac said. "Then we'll put them out to graze."

Trinity had brought her wagon near the others. Buck and Haze unharnessed her mules and took them to water. Except for Lieutenant Nelson, the soldiers sprawled on the riverbank and showed no interest whatsoever. Repairs to the wagon were completed and supper was prepared and eaten before sundown. The sun dipped behind a bank of dirty gray clouds, and the wind from the northwest brought with it a hint of rain.

"There'll be snow on the high plains and rain for us," Port Guthrie predicted, "and it won't be long in comin'."

"Exactly what does that mean to us?" Lieutenant Nelson demanded.

"Dependin' on how much rain we get," said Guthrie.

"Rain means mud, and a heavy-loaded wagon mires down. It could slow us down as much as three or four days."

"I think not," Nelson said. "We will continue, keeping to high ground."

"Mister," said Guthrie, "you got somethin' to learn about the freightin' business, and I ain't about to try an' educate you. The mud will do that."

Nothing more was said, and breakfast was barely over the next morning, when the rain started. As it became more intense, it was accompanied by thunder and lightning. The teamsters, anticipating such a problem, had their mules on picket ropes. The soldiers, having taken no such precaution, saw their horses go galloping madly downriver, running before the wind-driven storm.

"I never seen the like," Port Guthrie snorted. "If ignorance was gold coin, that bunch would be filthy rich."

"Here comes his highness, Lieutenant Nelson," said Buck. "He wants something."

"Since you obviously don't intend moving the wagons," Nelson said, "we're going to need some of the mules to round up our horses."

"Oh?" said Mac. "Are you asking or demanding?"

"At this point," Nelson replied stiffly, "I am asking. Do not force the issue to the extent that it becomes a demand."

"You'll be allowed the use of our mules on one condition," said Mac, "and that is that they be returned immediately after you recover your horses."

"They will be returned," Nelson replied. "Just for the record, I might remind you that the military can confiscate every animal you own, should such an act become necessary."

"I don't need reminding," said Mac, "and for your sake, you'd better hope it doesn't become necessary."

Nelson stalked off into the storm, and swearing under his breath, Port Guthrie shook his head in frustration.

"I hate him," Saul Estrella said.

"No more than I do," said Lafe Beard. "I wonder what

the penalty is for shootin' a smart-mouth bluecoat?''

"More than you'd want to pay," Mac said. "I wouldn't swap one of you for him and his whole damn bunch."

Trinity and her companions had remained in their wagon until Lieutenant Nelson and his men had taken mules and gone in search of their horses. Ignoring the storm, the four women joined the men who had gathered near Port Guthrie's wagon.

"What will we do about supper?" Hattie asked. "There's no shelter, no dry wood, and no place for a fire."

"We have plenty of jerked beef, and there's no shortage of water," said Mac. "Nelson and his bunch will just have to make the best of it, like we will."

"I'm sorry they ever showed up," Rachel said. "I miss those camps where we found shelter, where there was a warm fire, and hot coffee."

To everybody's surprise, Lieutenant Nelson and his men managed to find every one of their horses. They returned, leading the mules on picket ropes.

"I never would have believed it," said Gourd Snively. "I'd have bet that bunch would have had trouble follerin' a train if somebody had picked 'em up and set 'em on the track."

The rain began to diminish in the afternoon, and by sundown had stopped completely.

"I'll take an axe and maybe find some dry wood," Buck said. "Who wants to go with me?"

"I'll go along," said Red. "After bein' soaked to the hide all day, some hot coffee will be mighty welcome."

"Damn," Haze said, in mock disappointment, "I was lookin' forward to river water and jerked beef for supper. Not so much for my benefit, but for them blue bellies."

"I reckon we lucked out on this storm," said Port Guthrie, "dependin' on how you look at it. Mud shouldn't be a problem tomorrow."

"Good," Mac said. "Whatever lies ahead, I'd as soon meet it head-on and be done with it."

It was a statement Mac Tunstall was going to regret, in the days that followed.

The day after the storm, the wagons moved on. With only a day of rain, the runoff had been swift. There were no wet-weather springs or streams, and the Colorado only ran muddy for a few hours. Except for Lieutenant Nelson, the soldiers had been mostly silent, and after his heated exchange with Mac during the storm, Nelson seemed to have nothing more to say. But there was something troubling about the prolonged silence, and more than once, Mac felt the eyes of the soldiers upon him and his wary outfit.

"After today," Haze said, during the third watch, "we shouldn't be more than another forty miles from Austin. That is, if Nelson was leveling with us."

"I don't doubt that he was," said Mac. "There's been some kind of change in him and the whole bunch, the last day or two. Can't you tell?"

"Yeah," Haze said, "but I reckoned it was because you had words with him when they wanted the mules to go lookin' for their horses."

"No," said Mac, "it's something more than that. From here on, I reckon we'd better be ready for anything."

The showdown came the next evening after supper, four days west of Austin, and in a manner that nobody in Mac's outfit had expected. Hattie and Rachel had heated several pots of water, and the four women had retired to their wagon for bathing. The soldiers, including Lieutenant Nelson, had left the supper fire and were graining their horses. Suddenly there was a scream from Trinity's wagon. Mac, Red, Buck, and Haze reached it to find Lieutenant Nelson and Sergeant Embler there ahead of them, each man with a cocked Winchester. Nelson spoke.

"That's far enough. Unbuckle your gunbelts and let 'em fall, and that includes all you teamsters. Don't any of you try anything foolish. Four of my men are in the wagon

with the women, and take my word, the ladies will pay
dearly for your mistakes.''

Having no choice, Mac and his companions unbuckled
their gunbelts, while Guthrie and his teamsters were forced
to drop their Winchesters.

''You'll never get away with this, Nelson,'' Mac said.
''We're expected in Austin.''

Nelson laughed. ''The army moves slowly, Tunstall. By
now, they'll have us all down as deserters, but before anybody ties us to these missing wagons and their cargo, we'll
be in another country, with enough gold to last us a life-
time.''

''I reckon it's a waste of time, appealing to a bastard
like you,'' said Buck, ''but what do you aim to do with
us?''

''Do as you're told,'' Nelson said, ''and you'll be al-
lowed to live. You men will be sold to the silver mines in
Mexico, and the whorehouses will welcome the women.
After we're finished with them, of course.''

There was another agonized scream from the wagon . . .

CHAPTER 16

✺

*W*hat followed was a nightmare.

"Puckett, Haynes, McCarty, and Stearn, bring the irons," Lieutenant Nelson ordered.

From saddlebags, the men brought leg irons and manacles for the wrists.

"You first, Tunstall," said Nelson.

Mac's wrists were manacled first, and then the irons were locked about his ankles. He could walk only by taking short steps. Quickly the other men were similarly shackled. Only then were the women allowed to leave the wagon. They all looked terrified and ashamed.

"Willis, Gerdes, Irvin, Odell, Konda, and Collins, gather up all those weapons and put them in that wagon," Nelson ordered. "From now on, you women will ride horseback, and if you know what's good for you, you'll continue doing the cooking. You teamsters will be in charge of your wagons as before, but you will be covered all the time you are on your wagon box. All you men will be manacled at night. Any one of you attempting to escape, be aware that it will go hard on those left behind. Tunstall, Prinz, Sanderson, and McLean, we know the woman each of you are partial to. Escape, or attempt to escape, and she will be shot without mercy. The same goes for you women. Run for it, and your man will die. You ladies will be allowed to continue preparing the meals, since you have been doing it so well. Any questions?"

The very audacity of the man rendered them all speechless, and Nelson continued.

"You may make yourselves comfortable for the night. I must warn you to avoid any activity that might be mistaken by my sentries, lest you be shot. The wagon containing your weapons will be watched, and any one of you approaching it will be shot. You men, I alone have the key to your irons. Good night."

They were left alone, with only the women unshackled.

"Oh, God," Trinity moaned, "I'm so sorry they were able to use us to disarm all of you. What are we going to do?"

"I don't know," said Mac. "Did they . . . harm any of you?"

"They violated us all, like we were whores," Hattie sobbed. "After dark, I'm going to run away, and let them shoot me."

"You'll do no such thing," said Red angrily. "You'll do what you must, to stay alive. Somehow, before we reach the end of this trail, we'll break loose. Then there'll be some dying, but it won't be us."

"They threw all our bedrolls out of the wagon," Trinity said. "We'd better get them, before it gets dark."

"Our bedrolls are in our individual wagons," said Port Guthrie. "Leave 'em there. I'd feel like less of a man if I asked any favors of them skunks."

Trinity brought Mac's bedroll and her own, spreading them away from the others so that she and Mac might have some privacy. Hattie, Rachel, and Elizabeth seemed to have the same idea, for after what had happened, they felt a desperate need to talk.

"Do you think there's any hope for us?" Trinity asked softly.

"There's always hope, as long as we're alive," said Mac. "The most difficult task ahead of us is getting that key from Nelson. We can't fight, chained like dogs."

"I've been thinking about that," Trinity replied. "Suppose I play up to him, beg him not to sell me into a whorehouse, and make him want me?"

"My God, no," said Mac. "I won't have him laying with you, while I'm in chains. Not even to save my life, I won't."

"You'll never know how I treasure hearing you say that," Trinity said, "but you're overlooking something. Four of them took us in the wagon. Don't you suppose the others will demand their turn? If we have to . . . submit to them, can't we use that to perhaps win their confidence, to catch them off guard?"

"I won't have them stripping you of your dignity, of your very soul," said Mac.

"Is it that, or just your way of saying that when they're finished with me, you don't want what's left?"

"If we get out of this alive," Mac said, "whatever happens between now and then will be over and done. I'll still want you, whatever they've done to you, because unless they murder me first, I'll kill every man who's laid a hand on you."

"If you mean that—about wanting me—then let me do whatever I must to get close enough to that rotten lieutenant to get my hands on those keys," said Trinity.

"The very thought of you . . . with him . . . sickens me," Mac said, "but I meant everything I said. But you'd better tell the others what you have in mind. I'd not want them thinking you . . . were serious."

"It doesn't matter what they think," said Trinity. "Nelson's the one who matters, and my act might be more convincing if our outfit seems disgusted. The trouble is, I can't be convincing to him, if I'm spending all my time with you. Can you spare me, until we're all out of this mess?"

"I reckon I'll have to," Mac said, "but I'll need some way to communicate with you."

"Then I'll have to tell Hattie my plans," said Trinity. "I like Elizabeth and Rachel, but I trust Hattie the most.

She'll understand, because once she thinks about it, this is the kind of thing she would do. I'll talk to you through Hattie, and you can talk to me the same way. First I'll talk to Hattie and then I'll get started on that stinking First Lieutenant Nelson.''

It took some doing to lure Hattie away from Red without him knowing the reason. In just a few minutes, Hattie had been won over and sworn to silence.

"It's the same thing I've been telling Red," said Hattie. "If they're going to take what they want anyway, then what do we have to lose, using it to win our freedom? If you're unable to gain his trust, then let me try. We must have those keys. I'll shuck him out of his britches and then bash his head in with a rock.''

Despite their precarious position, Trinity laughed. She threw her arms around Hattie, and for just a moment they held one another tight. Then Trinity went to find Lieutenant Nelson. It still wasn't quite dark, and Nelson saw her coming. He got up off the wagon tongue where he and Sergeant Embler had been sitting.

"What do you want?" Nelson asked.

"I want to talk to you," said Trinity, in as soothing a manner as she could.

"Talk," Nelson replied.

"Not with the sergeant here," Trinity said coyly.

"Take a walk, Sergeant," said Nelson.

Embler stared at Trinity as though he had some idea as to what was about to take place, and she was thankful for the dusky-darkness that hid her embarrassment. Embler got up and, without a word, walked away. Trinity sat down on the wagon tongue where Embler had been sitting. Nelson took the hint and sat down beside her.

"I don't want to be sold into a whorehouse," said Trinity, as earnestly as she could. She even managed to squeeze out a tear or two.

Lieutenant Nelson laughed. "And why shouldn't you be? You're fully equipped for it."

"Because I want to live," Trinity said, "and a whorehouse isn't my idea of living. I'd be willing to make it worth your while, keeping me for yourself."

"Why should I? With the kind of money I expect to have, I can buy any woman that suits my fancy. Any dozen women."

"I'm sure you can," said Trinity, "but what kind of man is it who can only have those women he's bought and paid for? Will you be satisfied with a woman who can never see beyond your money?"

It was dark, and he took advantage of it. One arm around her waist, he dragged her against him. With his free hand, he popped some buttons off the front of her dress. When he found she wore nothing beneath it, he became excited. Trinity forced herself to relax, to breathe normally, hoping he couldn't hear the thudding of her heart or feel the goose bumps on her naked skin. She allowed him to slip the dress off her shoulders, and made no move to halt his exploring hands. Just as she was about to cry out in an agony of revulsion, he let her go. She took her time rearranging her dress, for she couldn't think of a word to say, and she feared her voice would tremble. It was Nelson who finally spoke.

"You're right, to some extent. I've had bought women before, and they usually leave something to be desired. We'll be another week on the trail. That will allow us time to talk again, and perhaps you can convince me you're worth my while."

He got to his feet and walked away in the direction Sergeant Embler had gone. Trinity got up, holding to the wagon box to steady her trembling knees. She had no doubt that Nelson would be watching her, and she dared not go near Mac. She had already moved her bedroll some distance away, and she stretched out. She hadn't been there long when there came a silent shadow to kneel beside her.

"Tell me what happened," Hattie whispered.

Trinity did, sparing no details.

"Dear God," said Hattie, "you have nerve. I don't

know if I could stand that from a man I'd like to see dead.''

"I can stand it," Trinity said, "because that's what it's going to take for us to see this skunk dead. He's putting me off, for some reason."

"He can take you," said Hattie. "He can take everything you have to offer, and still not fall into a trap."

"Perhaps I'll have to let him have it all," Trinity said, "but he'll take it only once, and it'll be the most expensive he's ever had, because I intend to kill him."

"One of us will have to," said Hattie. "It's the only chance we have. I've talked to Rachel and Elizabeth, but I haven't told them what you plan to do. They know we may all be taken by this bunch of deserters, and they can stand that, if they must. I suppose the hardest part has been getting Haze and Buck to accept it. Red finally admitted he'd rather have me alive, even if I've been considerably used. I'm beginning to believe there may be a way out of this for us all, if we can bear the humiliation and indignity."

"We must," Trinity said. "Tell Mac I believe I've made some progress, but try not to tell him *too* much, if you know what I mean."

"I know what you mean," said Hattie. "It's the same thing that's bothering Red. He's treated me like a gentleman, asking nothing more than a kiss, and now he's in chains, with constant thoughts of other men pawing me."

The first long night of captivity came to an end. When it was time for the wagons to again take the trail, Lieutenant Nelson ordered the shackles removed from the men's legs. The teamsters were able to harness their teams and mount the wagon boxes. Mac, Red, Buck, and Haze were able to straddle their horses, even with manacles on their wrists.

"We'll cross the river at the next shallows," Nelson said. "From there, we bear to the southeast. We'll pass to the south of Austin and to the north of San Antonio."

Mac, Red, Buck, and Haze rode near enough together

to talk to one another. Trinity, Hattie, Rachel, and Elizabeth rode well behind the men. Sergeant Embler had taken over Trinity's wagon.

"If we're headed between Austin and San Antonio," said Buck, "these varmints are on their way to the Gulf, somewhere north of Corpus Christi. That means they're aimin' to take us and these guns away on a sailing ship."

"Sounds like it," Mac said gloomily. "How far you reckon it is from here?"

"Near two hundred miles," said Buck. "Don't you reckon, Red?"

"Yeah," Red replied. "Ten days from the gulf. Ten days to escape, if we can."

"We're in need of a plan," said Haze. "There has to be some way we can bust loose from this bunch."

"They'll be expecting that, every waking minute," Mac said. "I reckon all we can do is wait another day or two, and see if they let up on us."

"The women have somethin' on their minds," said Haze, "but Elizabeth won't tell me anything. Ever since she got pawed over in that wagon, she's been mighty quiet."

"It's been hard on her," Buck said. "It's been hard on them all, and we ain't makin' it any easier when we force 'em to talk about what happened."

"It ain't a damn bit harder on them than it is on us," said Haze. "How can a man keep his mouth shut, when his woman's been had by a bunch of no-account deserters, and she don't want to talk about it?"

"She was taken by force, Haze," Mac said, "same as the others. Would you feel any better if Elizabeth had resisted until they shot and killed her?"

"No," said Haze. "I want her alive."

"Then stop holding it against her because she won't try to make you feel better with excuses," Mac said. "You reckon they're goin' to get by with just the four men who took them in the wagon? You reckon the others won't demand their turn?"

"Damn it," Haze shouted, "shut up. We got to escape before that happens."

"Don't count on it," said Red, "and don't make poor Elizabeth any more miserable than she is already. What's happened is almost certain to happen again, and there's not a damned thing we can do about it, in chains like we are, and without weapons."

Casting Red a sour look, Haze said no more. Mac and Red exchanged looks, and Mac almost knew Hattie had told him what Trinity had in mind. Lieutenant Nelson rode back to meet the wagons.

"There's a low bank and shallow water ahead," Nelson said. "We'll cross the wagons there."

In the lead wagon, Port Guthrie said nothing. While he wondered how they were to escape from this predicament, he still had faith in Mac Tunstall and his three companions. Guthrie's wagon crossed without incident and the others followed. Trinity's wagon was the last, and while Sergeant Embler was at the reins, Nelson had ordered Privates Puckett and Haynes to ride behind the wagon. Their camp at the end of the second day of captivity was much like the first. But after dark, that changed. Three of the soldiers came to the place where Trinity, Elizabeth, Rachel, and Hattie had spread their blankets. Private Gerdes took Elizabeth by the arm, while Irvin and Odell seized Hattie and Rachel.

"Not you," said Gerdes, when Trinity got to her feet.

"Damn you," Haze shouted. He stumbled to his feet, fell, and before he could rise, Gerdes drew his Colt and slammed Haze in the back of the head. He slumped down and didn't move again. The sobbing Elizabeth was led away, along with Rachel and Hattie. The three women were taken well beyond the shackled men.

"Now," said Gerdes, "will the three of you strip, or do we do it for you?"

"We'll do it," Hattie said. "We don't have that many clothes."

"Stick with us, girlie," said Gerdes, "and you won't need many."

"Maybe not any," Private Odell said.

The three of them laughed. Taking her cue from Hattie and Rachel, Elizabeth ceased sobbing. She refused to give them that much satisfaction.

"Haze may have a fractured skull," Mac said, for Haze was still unconscious.

"Well, there ain't much we can do," said Red. "Movin' around after dark could get us a case of lead poisonin'."

Haze groaned and, trying to get to his hands and knees, fell facedown.

"Here," said Buck, "let me help you roll over on your back. You can't get up in those shackles."

"They took her," Haze mumbled. "They took her again."

"They took Hattie and Rachel, too," said Red.

"You and Buck didn't do a damned thing," Haze said.

"Our luck wouldn't have been any better," said Red. "We'd have cracked skulls like yours, or some lead in our bellies. You gettin' your skull near busted didn't change the situation."

"Well, something's changed," Haze growled. "Why did they take Elizabeth, Hattie, and Rachel, leavin' Trinity? Why are they makin' whores of the rest of the women, and not her?"

"Haze," said Mac, as kindly as he could, "we're all in this together, and yelling at one another won't help."

The three women didn't return for almost an hour, and when they did, they had nothing to say. Haze shouted at Elizabeth, and she became all the more distant. Hattie and Rachel spoke to Trinity, but that was all. Going to Elizabeth, Trinity put her arms around the stricken girl, while Haze cursed them both.

"Haze Sanderson," Trinity hissed, "shut your mouth! Just shut up. She's hurting, and you're just making it worse. You cuss her one more time, and I'll personally knock you cold."

Surprisingly, Haze said not another word. Rachel sat beside Buck and Hattie beside Red, none of them speaking. Lest Nelson or his men be watching her, Trinity returned to her bedroll. Elizabeth stood there looking lost, and suddenly Haze spoke.

"Elizabeth . . ."

She turned to him, and he could see her pale face in the moonlight.

"Sit beside me," said Haze.

"Are you sure . . . you want . . . what's left of me?" Elizabeth asked.

"Yeah," said Haze. "I want you, whatever happens. I've been a damned fool."

Elizabeth knelt beside him, and it seemed no words were necessary.

The next day, as the women again rode together, Hattie was able to talk to Trinity. "He didn't let them take you," Hattie said. "Your plan is working."

"I don't know," said Trinity. "He hasn't even looked at me, since that first night."

Lieutenant Nelson set the course for the wagons to follow, a southeasterly direction that would take them somewhere between Austin and San Antonio. Nelson rode ahead of the first wagon, while his men were strung out as far as the last wagon, which had been Trinity's. Sergeant Embler still rode the box, and at least one soldier always followed behind. Early in the afternoon, Nelson called a halt. It soon became obvious all was not well with the lieutenant. Refusing food, he took to his bedroll early. He fell into fitful sleep, and when he began talking out of his head, Sergeant Embler went to see about him.

"He's burning up with fever," Embler said helplessly.

"I'll see to him," said Trinity.

It was her opportunity to ingratiate herself with Nelson in a manner that might mean far more to him than the ploy she had in mind. For what it was worth, it was he who held together this ragtag bunch of misfits, and if he died, it might diminish their chances of staying alive. She went to what had been her wagon, where the medical supplies were kept, and was immediately challenged by one of the soldiers.

"Your lieutenant is sick," Trinity said, "and the medicine chest is in the wagon. I'll be needing it."

"Then get it," said Private Willis, "but don't touch nothin' else."

Trinity got the medicine chest, which should have contained two full bottles of the whiskey Mac had bought at Fort Griffin. But when Trinity opened the chest, there was only one quart bottle, and it was less than half full. She approached Sergeant Embler, and he obviously didn't want to talk to her, but Trinity was persistent.

"Sergeant, some of your men have drunk most of the whiskey that I needed to break Lieutenant Nelson's fever. Unless you can get your hands on some more whiskey—and I mean quickly—your lieutenant is going to die."

Trinity had no idea that two quarts of whiskey—or for that matter, any amount—would make any difference to the gravely ill Lieutenant Nelson, but he was the only chance they had. Sergeant Embler seemed indecisive, with little or no control over the rest of the men, and he quickly lived up to the low opinion she had of him.

"I got no authority to go fetch anything, includin' whiskey," Embler said. "It'd take an order from Lieutenant Nelson, and he ain't in no shape to order anything."

"Then you'd better have somebody in mind to give the orders when he dies," said Trinity. "If that fever doesn't break, he's as good as dead."

"Well," Embler said, swallowing hard, "I reckon I could ride to the nearest town . . ."

"Then you'd better get started," said Trinity. "There's about enough whiskey for one good dose. Get at least three quarts, and be quick about it."

Some of the other soldiers had heard Trinity's ultimatum, and they looked expectantly at Sergeant Embler.

"Corporal Irvin," Embler said, "you're in charge till I

get back. I got to get whiskey for the lieutenant.''

Private Stearn laughed. ''Git some for the rest of us, while you're at it.''

''Sergeant,'' said Corporal Irvin, ''ain't you forgettin' what Lieutenant Nelson told us? He said we was to stay out of towns. Any towns.''

''I ain't forgot, damn it,'' Embler replied, ''but we got to keep Nelson alive. He's our contact with . . .''

His voice trailed off, for Mac, Haze, Buck, Red, and some of the teamsters were now listening. Embler seemed to remember something. He knelt beside the gravely ill Lieutenant Nelson for a moment. When he got to his feet, he spoke to them all, but his hard eyes were on Trinity.

''I ain't as trustin' as the lieutenant. I got the keys to the manacles and leg irons, and I'll see that they're returned to Lieutenant Nelson when he ain't out of his head with fever. I ain't near as tolerant as Nelson, neither. I got my own ideas as to discipline, and bein' second in command, I won't hesitate to use 'em.''

Embler saddled his horse and rode north, toward the Colorado. Trinity's heart sank, for it had been her intention to take the key to the manacles and leg irons while Nelson was in the clutches of whatever ailed him. Her eyes met Mac's, and she suspected he was feeling the same frustration. As much as she despised Lieutenant Nelson, she now saw him as their only hope, for Embler had shown no interest in any of the women.

''My God,'' said Hattie, when she and Trinity were able to talk, ''if Nelson dies, we're in real trouble. We won't stand a chance against that coldhearted sergeant.''

''I know,'' Trinity agreed. ''All of you heard what he said, but his words were intended for me. He knows I've tried to gain favor with Nelson, and I'd not put it past him to try and convince Nelson of that. Sometimes fate plays awful tricks on us. I've wished a thousand times that Nelson was dead, and now I'm fighting to keep him alive.''

''He's the lesser of two evils,'' said Hattie. ''Embler has unblinking eyes, like a snake, and despite all we've been through, I don't believe I could stand his hands on me."

"I don't think that'll be a problem," Trinity said. "I just hope he has sense enough to find some whiskey and ride back here as quickly as he can."

"I just hope he has sense enough not to ride into town in uniform," said Hattie. "If he's a deserter, it won't help our cause if he's arrested."

But Sergeant Jake Embler was smarter than that. Before he reached the Colorado, he dismounted and changed into the Levi's and flannel shirt taken from his saddlebags. Still he was ill at ease, for his lust for gambling had often taken him to the saloons of Austin and San Antonio. There was a better than average chance he would be recognized, and since the lot of them had been absent without leave from the outpost at San Antonio for two weeks, the charge would now undoubtedly be desertion. Lieutenant Nelson had lured him into this scheme to steal wagons loaded with the new army issue and sell them through black market profiteers outside the United States. While he respected Nelson's business sense, he was less than enthusiastic about the man's womanizing. Business and pleasure didn't mix, and it was a common thing for a woman to use her favors to influence a man. The redheaded wench with the wagon was playing just such a game with Lieutenant Nelson. Jake Embler was certain of it. Otherwise, why was she trying so hard to keep Nelson alive? Embler, however, was satisfied that he had foiled her plans by taking the key to the manacles and leg irons. The loyalty of the enlisted men whom he had subverted didn't bother him, for they had burned their bridges and could ill afford to jump ship now. If nothing else, the ready availability of the women would keep them there for a while. Embler had become aware of Lieutenant Nelson's infatuation with the red-headed woman when Nelson had forbidden the rest of the men to take her. Now, he thought with satisfaction, while Nelson was out of his head with fever, they could have their way with her. By the time the good lieutenant recovered—if he did—the scheming woman would be pretty well used up.

The soldiers who had remained with the wagons were becoming restless. Corporal Irvin had been elevated to a position of leadership only by virtue of his rank, because he had no real experience. Since he barely outranked the privates and was in trouble every bit as deeply as they, the rest of the men had little respect for Corporal Irvin. Privates Puckett, Haynes, McCarty, Stearn, Willis, Gerdes, Odell, Konda, and Collins openly planned a romp with the women, as soon as darkness concealed their evil deeds.

"Remember," Corporal Irvin cautioned, "Lieutenant Nelson warned against bothering the woman with the red hair."

Puckett laughed. "I plumb forgot all about that, and since he ain't around to remind me, I reckon I'll have my first dance with her."

"Yeah," said Haynes, "they sure ain't nothin' else to do, here in this godforsaken part of the world. I thought that shirttail town in Minnesota, where my daddy drank himself to death, was dead, but it was an absolute beehive compared to this."

"I have a feeling this is going to be a night straight out of hell," Red said, having overheard the plans of their captors.

"I'm afraid you're right," said Mac. "I need to talk to Hattie, and see what Trinity has in mind. We lost our chance when Embler took the key with him that would have freed us from these irons."

"I'll send her your way," Red replied, "when you're alone."

Hattie knelt down beside Mac, and he could see the worry in her eyes.

"I don't like Trinity fussing over Nelson," said Mac. "How much worse off will we be, if the varmint dies?

He's the head of this thing, and without him, it might unravel.''

"Trinity's heard talk," Hattie said. "Selling us into whorehouses and you men to the mines is Lieutenant Nelson's idea. The rest of them favor shooting us all. She still believes she can lure Nelson into a position where she can free all of you from the irons."

"She also knows I can get my hands on a loaded Winchester," said Mac. "Did she tell you that?"

"Yes," Hattie said, "and she believes you would kill some of them, but she knows you could never kill them all before they would kill you. She's going after the key to the irons so all of you can be free. If you can reach that loaded Winchester, you can find cover and draw their fire, while the rest of the men storm the wagons where the weapons are."

"I reckon she's heard the talk, then," said Mac. "With Embler gone and Nelson out of his head, they're plannin' an orgy. Trinity, Elizabeth, Rachel, and you are goin' to be the guests of honor. Or should I say dishonor?"

Hattie sighed. "We all know what's coming, but we believe it's the only way to save some of you. You can't defend yourselves in irons. Trinity says please don't hate us."

"We can never do that," Mac said. "If there was any way, I'd elevate all of you to sainthood."

CHAPTER 17

✧

Trinity forced Lieutenant Nelson to drink what whiskey remained in the one bottle, but if he didn't have additional doses at regular intervals, the first wouldn't matter. There was little to do except listen to the crude comments of the soldiers and the occasional words uttered by the delirious Lieutenant Nelson.

Jake Embler rode warily as he approached Austin. Here were the ordnance people who would be expecting the wagons with their new-issue weapons. It was still early enough in the day that some of the saloons weren't yet open, and in those that were, there was seldom more than a bartender. Embler chose an out-of-the-way joint called the Broken Spoke where he didn't recognize the barkeep, and the man couldn't have cared less who Embler was. He bought three quarts of cheap whiskey. If rotgut couldn't burn the fever out of Nelson, then the lieutenant was just a dead peckerwood, Embler decided. He was about to mount his horse, when a soldier came down the boardwalk. Master Sergeant Townsend was the last man in the world Jake Embler wanted to see, for Townsend was in charge of the very platoon from which Embler and most of his friends had deserted! The men recognized one another immediately.

"Embler, you deserting bastard," Townsend shouted.

Townsend went for his gun, but Embler had ducked behind his horse and fired from beneath the animal's belly. The slug struck Townsend in the chest and he stumbled through the batwing doors of the Broken Spoke saloon. He died there on the floor, and the barkeep was shouting for the law before Jake Embler was in the saddle. Embler rode north, out of town. He dared not immediately ride south, for there was half a day of daylight remaining. Somehow he must conceal his trail, losing any pursuit before riding south. It was ironic, he thought, that he was returning with whiskey that might save Lieutenant Nelson's life. If Nelson knew or even suspected that Embler had killed a man in Austin, the lieutenant would raise holy hell. All the more reason why Embler must elude any pursuers. What the lieutenant didn't know wouldn't hurt him. Reaching a stream that veered south, Embler trotted his horse in the water for half a dozen miles. It was the long way home, for he still must ride forty miles westward to reach the wagons.

Anxiously Trinity watched the sun begin its downward journey toward the western horizon. She believed Embler had been gone long enough to have ridden to town and long since returned, but she had to consider the possibility he had been recognized and arrested by the military. While the rest of the soldiers were in no way negligent in the guarding of their prisoners, they constantly eyed the direction from which they expected Sergeant Embler to return.

"Damn them," said Hattie viciously, "they're hoping he doesn't come back."

"I'm counting on him returning," Trinity replied. "I don't even want to think of what might happen if he doesn't. If Nelson dies, and for some reason Embler doesn't come back, we'll be in the hands of men who only want us dead."

"I don't think Sergeant Embler cares, one way or the other," said Hattie, "but I think he's depending on Lieutenant Nelson to dispose of these wagonloads of guns. But even if Embler comes back with the whiskey, we can't be sure Nelson will live, because we have no idea what's wrong with him.''

''Whatever's ailing him, he has a fighting chance if we can break that fever,'' Trinity said. ''You'd better talk to Rachel and Elizabeth, and try to prepare them for tonight.''

''They're both as prepared as they're going to get,'' said Hattie. ''Elizabeth's gone from being shamed and hurt to as mad as hell. She vows she won't cry again, no matter what they do to her.''

Sergeant Embler reined up on a rise, where he could see his backtrail. The November sun had sucked up the moisture from the most recent rain, and even one horseman would stir up some dust. Embler grunted with satisfaction, for there was no sign of pursuit. He'd have avoided the shooting in town, had it been possible, but he decided it might have been for the best. Master Sergeant Townsend had always given him a hard way to go, and this might have been Embler's only opportunity to even the score. Besides, he reflected, had he avoided killing Townsend, the man would have reported having seen Embler in town. That would have been all the evidence the military needed that Embler—and probably those who had deserted with him—were still in the area. Having allowed his horse to rest, Embler mounted and rode on, confident that he hadn't been trailed.

''Let's go ahead and start supper,'' Hattie suggested. ''It'll give us all something to do besides wring our hands.''

''I'm not wringing my hands anymore,'' said Elizabeth. ''This experience has taught me something. Hate will destroy fear.''

They were halfway through the preparation of supper when Sergeant Jake Embler rode in. He spoke not a word, but passed the sack with three quarts of whiskey to Trinity.

''Hattie,'' Trinity said, ''you'll have to help me get some of this whiskey down him. He may become violent.''

Several of the other soldiers had approached. Anticipating their interest and the reason for it, Embler turned on them.

"That whiskey's for the lieutenant," said Embler. "I'll gut-shoot the first one of you that lays a hand on it."

With sour looks, they returned to their posts near Trinity's wagon, where the outfit's weapons were. With Hattie's help, Trinity poured half a bottle of the whiskey down the feverish Lieutenant Nelson. He coughed, choked, and cursed.

"He's not a drinking man, or he's used to better whiskey," Hattie said.

"If it tastes anything like it smells, I don't blame him," said Trinity.

The whiskey proved to be powerful stuff, for within a few minutes, Lieutenant Nelson was in a drunken stupor.

"You're givin' him too much at a time," Embler protested. "It's near enough to kill a man."

"We know that," said Trinity, "but we must make up for the time you were gone. It's known as the kill-or-cure treatment. If he doesn't die from the whiskey, then we think it'll cure him."

"We'll hold off about two hours," Hattie said, "and then dose him with the rest of that bottle."

Hattie's eyes met Trinity's, and they understood one another. Sergeant Embler seemed inclined to remain there until Lieutenant Nelson died or showed some sign of improvement. Sensing that Embler's presence was making a difference in the bawdy plans of the soldiers, Rachel and Elizabeth had joined Trinity and Hattie at the side of the drunken, feverish Lieutenant Nelson.

"Hey," Private Gerdes shouted, "what about supper?"

"Get your own damn supper," said Sergeant Embler. "Lieutenant Nelson needs help."

Private McCarty laughed. "He needs help to lay there dead drunk?"

McCarty had come closer, and Sergeant Embler moved like a striking snake. His right crashed against McCarty's chin, and McCarty was lifted off his feet. He fell on his back with a thud, and dust puffed up around him. Blood trickled from the corners of McCarty's mouth, and he didn't move. Privates Stearn and Willis backed hastily away.

"The rest of you get back to your posts," Embler snarled.

Nobody spoke. Elizabeth's eyes twinkled and Trinity had to suppress a smile. Guthrie and his teamsters looked upon Sergeant Embler with a little more respect. Mac winked at his three companions. Discord among their captors might help their cause. They realized, however, that this small advantage might be quickly lost when Lieutenant Nelson was again able to assume command. The rest of the soldiers avoided Sergeant Embler and went about completing the supper that had been under way when Embler had arrived. Embler remained near, apparently wishing to be there if and when Lieutenant Nelson was able to talk. Three hours following Nelson's massive dose of whiskey, Hattie checked his temperature.

"No change, as best I can tell," said Hattie.

But Sergeant Embler didn't accept that. He knelt beside Nelson, placing his hand on the lieutenant's face. Shaking his head, he got to his feet and went to the fire where the coffeepot sat on the coals. With a tin cup of coffee, he sat down on a wagon tongue, his eyes on the men and women his outfit held captive. His emotions were mixed. This woman the lieutenant favored had gone out of her way to see that there was whiskey to treat the seriously ill Nelson, and had personally administered that treatment. Had he, Embler, been wrong about her? Then reality set in, and he had to admit neither he nor they had any inkling of what might be wrong with Nelson. The man still might die, but in fairness to the woman, she had gone to great lengths to try the one remedy that might save Nelson's life. The last rays of the evening sun shone on her red hair, and Embler was more aware than ever of the emptiness in his own life. The woman must feel something for Nelson, and Embler felt pangs of envy, for he had never had a woman he hadn't bought and paid for.

"No home, no woman, no nothin'," he gritted under his breath. "A damned miserable way for a man to go."

Trinity and her three companions spent the night near the snoring, drunken Lieutenant Nelson. Not that they were needed, but under the watchful eyes of Sergeant Embler, they were protected from the bawdy, shameful spectacle they had feared and expected. Whatever the rest of the soldiers might have had in mind, they seemed unwilling to risk the ire of Sergeant Embler. An hour before dawn, Trinity felt Nelson's forehead and found it moist.

"He's sweating," Trinity announced.

Bleary-eyed, Sergeant Embler came to see for himself. He felt Nelson's sweating face, got to his feet, and for a moment he said nothing. Finally, when his eyes met Trinity's, he spoke.

"You done it. By God, you done it. He's a lucky man."

Without another word he walked away.

"I believe it's safe for us to get some sleep now," said Hattie.

"You all do exactly that," Port Guthrie said. "When he finally comes to, he'll want to take himself a bath, I reckon."

Trinity nodded. Lieutenant Nelson stank, and it wasn't all sweat. Sergeant Embler had stretched out under one of the wagons, and Trinity hurried to Mac and his three companions.

"You handled that just right," said Mac. "We're still neck-deep in trouble, but you've bought us some time, and just maybe Nelson will keep that bunch of dogs off all of you until we can break loose."

"If I haven't won his confidence after this," Trinity said, "I don't know how I can. I'm counting on Sergeant Embler to tell him about going after the whiskey."

Trinity, Hattie, Rachel, and Elizabeth were allowed to rest unmolested, and when they awoke, the sun was noon-high. Lieutenant Nelson was obviously awake, and Sergeant Embler was kneeling beside him.

"God," said Nelson, "I stink. How long have I been out?"

"Two nights and a day," Embler replied. "The damn troops had drunk all the whiskey, and I had to ride to Austin for more."

"You *what*?" Nelson roared.

"I rode to Austin for more whiskey. It's all that saved you. That redheaded woman practically run me off. The four of 'em was up with you all night, feedin' you whiskey."

"I gave a direct order, Sergeant," said Nelson. "Towns were to be avoided."

"Yes, sir," Embler replied. "I remember. But there was nobody else to take charge, sir, and a decision had to be made."

"And you made the right one, Sergeant. Was there any trouble in town?"

"No, sir," Embler lied. "I rode out to the north and then to the south, keepin' my hoss in a creek for maybe six miles. Watchin' my backtrail, I rode straight back."

"We'll move out in the morning at dawn, Sergeant."

Sergeant Embler nodded and turned away.

"One thing more, Sergeant."

"What's that, sir?"

"The key," Lieutenant Nelson replied.

Without a word, Embler handed him the key to the irons the men wore.

South Texas. December 8, 1873.

While Nelson needed another day and a night to recover his strength, time dragged for everybody else. The soldiers, uncertain as to the mood of the lieutenant, avoided any further contact with the women.

"You made a good decision," said Red, when he next

spoke to Trinity. "With Nelson alive, we have a chance."

"He seems changed, somehow," Trinity said, "and I don't know if that's good or bad. Tonight, after another day, perhaps he'll settle down. I'll try to spend some time with him and see if I've gained any favor."

Red had said nothing about Mac, and Trinity wondered how he was feeling about her late-night meetings with Lieutenant Nelson. But what she had begun, she would see to its conclusion. She wanted only to be free of these captors, to deliver these wagons and their troublesome cargo to Austin, and to begin a new life.

After they left the Colorado River, it became necessary to seek water, a task assigned to Sergeant Embler. As the wagons again took the trail, Lieutenant Nelson sent Embler ahead.

"I hope he knows this territory better than I think he does," Buck said. "We had it made, just followin' the Colorado right into Austin."

"I'm gettin' the feeling we'll never see Austin," said Haze. "We got to come up with a plan to bust loose. These damn leg irons are workin' their way to the bone."

"There's more of a plan than you know," Mac said. "We must get the key to these irons and free ourselves before we go for the guns."

"I believe I know what that plan is," said Port Guthrie. "That damn lieutenant's got the key to these irons, and before we can get our hands on that key, somebody's got to win his confidence."

"So *that's* what Trinity's up to!" Haze said.

"Quiet, damn it," said Mac. "This is costing the hell out of her. Don't spoil it."

They had been resting the teams, and it was again time to move on. Nobody said anything more, but every man realized the sacrifice that might be required of Trinity on their behalf. The teamsters mounted their wagon boxes while Mac, Red, Buck, and Haze mounted their horses. Trinity and her three companions had already ridden out ahead of Port Guthrie's lead wagon.

"Looks like the lieutenant ain't as bright-eyed and bushy-tailed as he reckoned he was," Red observed.

Private Haynes had taken over the wagon while Sergeant Embler had gone in search of water, and on the wagon box beside Haynes sat Lieutenant Nelson. His horse followed the wagon on a lead rope.

"All the better for Trinity if the varmint's off his feed for two or three more days," said Mac.

Red understood. While Mac had resigned himself to Trinity doing what she must to get the key and free them from their chains, he still hoped she might be able to avoid having the renegade soldier take her, body and soul.

The creek Sergeant Embler had reached was decent enough, but the Texans were quick to notice something that Embler had either overlooked or ignored.

"Cat tracks," Buck said. "Godawful big cougar, and he likely waters here regular."

"We ought to say somethin' to Nelson," said Haze. "This varmint could gut a mule with one swipe of a paw."

"To hell with him," Red growled. "He's took over all the watches. I aim to keep a lead rope on my horse, but that's all."

"First chance you get, suggest that to Trinity," said Mac. "He may not actually come close, but he won't have to. If he sings out during the night, the mules and horses could light out and not stop runnin' till they reach the Gulf of Mexico."

During supper, Lieutenant Nelson made it a point to speak to Trinity.

"I will see you late tonight," he said.

But as it turned out, Lieutenant Nelson had other things to keep him busy. At the start of the second watch, Sergeant Embler approached.

"Sir," Embler said, "we have a problem with four of the men scheduled for the second and third watches. Privates Haynes, McCarty, Stearn, and Willis are dead drunk."

"How in thunder could that have happened, Sergeant?"

"They got into the whiskey I brought back from Austin," said Embler. "It was put into the wagon with the medicine chest. When you sent me to look for water, you had Private Haynes take over the wagon."

"Then use the remaining men to finish the night's watch in whatever manner you see fit," Nelson replied, "and in the morning, before breakfast, I'll see Haynes and his friends."

They were well into the second watch when the cougar made his presence known. The first screech was some distance away, carried on the wind, but when the animal squalled a second time, it was near enough to spook the horses and mules.

"See to your horses!" Mac shouted.

Every man had his horse picketed, and despite their shackles and chains, they were able to get to their horses. Hattie had taken Mac's advice, and the women had secured their mounts. Only the mules and extra horses were free.

"Every man in the saddle!" Lieutenant Nelson bawled.

But the spooked, braying mules had already started to run, taking with them all the horses that hadn't been picketed. A third time the cougar screeched, sounding like it was in their very midst, but Mac's outfit—besides being shackled hand and foot—was without arms. They stood helpless, unable to mount their horses. Somewhere in the night, one of the soldiers had cut loose with a Winchester, firing as rapidly as possible.

"Damn it," Lieutenant Nelson shouted, "hold your fire!"

Sudden silence prevailed. Even the wind ceased. Sergeant Embler had lighted a lantern, and set it on a wagon tongue. One by one, the soldiers straggled in, until there were five.

"Where's Gerdes?" Sergeant Embler asked.

"Dunno," said several of the others.

"Sergeant," Lieutenant Nelson said, "take the lantern and look for him. Irvin, you and Odell go with him."

The trio was gone only a few minutes. When they returned, Irvin and Odell carried a limp and battered Private Gerdes.

"Some of you get a fire started and some water boiling," Lieutenant Nelson ordered.

Trinity and Hattie were well ahead of the order, and a fire was soon blazing. Trinity put the water on to boil, and without being asked, knelt at the side of the injured Gerdes. First she felt for a pulse and then tried the big artery in the neck. She got to her feet, and even in the pale light from the lantern, they could see blood dripping from her left hand. The back of Gerdes's head had been crushed.

"The damn mules got him," Odell mumbled.

"The mules wasn't at fault," said Port Guthrie, "not with a big cat squallin' out there in the night. Any segundo with the savvy God give a prairie dog would of had more men on watch."

"We'd of had more men," Corporal Irvin said bitterly, "if Haynes, McCarty, Stearn, and Willis wasn't roostered."*

"Corporal," said Lieutenant Nelson, "you will keep your opinions to yourself. Private Odell, you and Corporal Irvin will wrap Private Gerdes in a blanket. We'll bury him at dawn. Then the lot of you will go looking for those horses and mules. Sergeant, I want to speak to you in private."

Sergeant Embler had an idea what was coming, and once they were alone, Lieutenant Nelson didn't disappoint him.

"Sergeant," Nelson said, "I want those four irresponsible, drunken privates sober, and I want them sober *quickly*. Use any method you see fit, as long as you don't break their bones."

"Yes, sir," said Embler.

He took a wooden bucket, and with a tin cup began dipping water from one of the kegs secured to the side of the wagon box. Despite their being captives, Mac and the

*Dead drunk.

rest of the shackled men looked on with some amusement, for they had learned of the four drunken privates.

"If this bunch don't round up mules any better than they do other things, I reckon we'll be here a while," Port Guthrie said. "If we hadn't been bound up in these irons, we could of held them mules."

"I'm startin' to feel some shame, us havin' been hog-tied by this bunch," said Red. "I'm beginnin' to think they'd have trouble outfoxin' a pack of digger Indians."

"They could have fooled anybody," Mac said. "They saved our hides, but God knows, we've repaid them a dozen times over."

Privates Haynes, McCarty, Stearn, and Willis—all looking hungover and sick—had to dig a grave for Private Gerdes, who was buried without ceremony. After a hurried breakfast, Lieutenant Nelson sent nine men in search of the stampeded horses and mules, leaving only himself and Sergeant Embler with the wagons.

"Nice of the varmint to just take our horses without even asking," said Red. "Horses that would have stampeded with the others, if it hadn't been for us."

"He's still holding all the high cards," Mac said. "Besides, when we take back these wagons, we'll need the mules, too."

Hattie managed to get Trinity alone, and for the first time since the stampede, they were able to talk.

"I wanted to talk to you last night," said Hattie, "but I believe he was watching you."

"I wouldn't be surprised," Trinity replied. "Last night at supper, he said he'd talk to me late last night. Of course, the stampede and Gerdes being killed changed all that. But I expect him to see me tonight."

"I hate to mention this," said Hattie, "since it's you sacrificing yourself to him, but suppose he's impressed enough with you that he decides to become a gentleman? Suppose he saves you until this thievery of the wagons is all behind him? How will you ever get him distracted enough to take the key to those irons?"

"I don't know," Trinity said, "but I'll do it if I have to grab his gun and bash in his head with it."

"There's one part of your plan that needs changing," said Hattie, "and Mac shouldn't be told."

"He's not going to like that," Trinity said.

"He will when it's all over," said Hattie, "and he won't know until then. When you go to Nelson, think of some way to get him to your wagon, and see that he sends the others away. Then when you make your move, the way will be clear to the wagon where all our guns are."

"That makes sense," Trinity said. "Mac won't object to that."

"He will to the rest of it," said Hattie. "Once you have the key to those irons, you'll start releasing the men. Rachel, Elizabeth, and me will take Winchesters from the wagon and kill any one of them that may discover you. As you release the men, they'll get to the wagon as quickly as they can, for their guns."

"My God," Trinity said, "the three of you will be targets for all of them."

"Better us than the men who are without weapons," said Hattie. "Red says if any of these soldiers can shoot worth a damn, we'll all be killed, for they'll be shooting at our muzzle flashes."

"He's right," Trinity said. "Mac will never stand for it."

"That's why Mac won't be told," said Hattie. "We're gambling that you can reach the men and free them without being discovered. If you are discovered, there'll be three of us, and we can shoot back. Mac's just one man, and should they discover him before he can reach the wagon, they'll kill him. Even if he gets his hands on a gun, he'll still be drawing all their fire. Even if they catch on to what we're doing, we'll keep their attention from the wagon until the men have armed themselves."

"It's a nervy thing to do," Trinity said. "Have Rachel and Elizabeth agreed?"

"Yes," said Hattie, "and none of us will be talked out of it."

"I'll admit our chances are better if all the men are armed," Trinity said, "but I'd not be able to forgive myself, if one of you died in the fight."

"We have no intention of doing that," said Hattie. "As soon as we can get our hands on Winchesters, we'll get as far from that wagon as possible. Red's already pointed out a place where we can belly-down and draw attention from the wagon, with small chance of any of us being hit."

"Perhaps it will work like you've planned," Trinity said. "I can't believe Red would let you do this if there was the slightest chance you'd be hit."

"We're not risking nearly as much as you," said Hattie. "Suppose this man just won't settle for anything less, and you have to . . . give yourself to him?"

"I'm prepared to," Trinity said, "if that's what it takes. It's Mac's advice, although he didn't have this in mind. He says you don't bluff, that you must be prepared to go all the way, if you're going to win. I can stand a few minutes of unpleasantness, if there's no other way."

"As soon as you know when you're going to . . . be with him," said Hattie, "get word to one of us. We must be ready to move when you do."

"You'll know," Trinity said. "We mustn't fail."

CHAPTER 18

❧

*L*ieutenant Nelson's soldiers wasted most of a day rounding up the stampeded horses and mules. The animals were gathered in twos and threes. Nelson was ominously quiet, and the soldiers equally so.

"He's finally laid some discipline on the varmints," Port Guthrie said.

"That may not be good for our cause," said Mac. "They're likely to be harder on us, making our escape more difficult."

Trinity and her companions had their misgivings about the apparent change.

"They look like children who have had their toys taken away from them," Rachel said. "I wonder if that means he's told them to leave us alone?"

"I wouldn't be surprised," said Hattie. "There's not much else he can do, when it comes to discipline."

Trinity laughed. "He can't court-martial them, can he?"

"If he makes the rest of the men leave us alone," said Elizabeth, "It will only be fair if he leaves you alone. At least until he's done with these wagons."

"There goes your plan, Trinity," Hattie said.

"Perhaps not," said Trinity. "He said he wants to talk to me, and even if that's all he has in mind, I'll try to lure him to our wagon."

But it seemed that while Lieutenant Nelson had declared

the women off limits to his men, he had applied the same rules to his own conduct. He spoke not a word to Trinity and seemed to go out of his way to avoid her. The soldiers seemed more watchful than ever. Testing their vigilance, Trinity got up far in the night and immediately found herself facing the muzzle of a Winchester. Finally Trinity got up enough nerve to approach Nelson with a question.

"You said we would be talking some more. When?"

"There'll be time enough for that when we've reached the end of this mission," Nelson replied. "You won't be disappointed with my decision."

"There goes our best chance," said Trinity, after she had been joined by Hattie, Elizabeth, and Rachel.

"Mac won't be disappointed," Hattie said, "and neither am I. There must be another way."

"Then some of you come up with it," said Trinity tiredly.

"I'll have to tell Mac," Hattie said. "He told me to tell him if there was any change in the situation, and this is change enough."

Mac listened as Hattie told him of the latest development.

"I'm glad it didn't work out like Trinity planned," said Mac. "However this turns out, I wouldn't feel like much of a man, allowing her to prostitute herself to save me."

"I'll tell her that," Hattie said. "Is there anything else we can do?"

"No," said Mac. "Just tell her that we'll come up with a plan of our own."

Mac waited until he could talk to Red, Buck, Haze, and the teamsters. Port Guthrie and the teamsters hadn't been told of Trinity's plan, so Mac went over it, before telling them it had been abandoned.

"That was mighty self-sacrificin' of the lady to even try such a thing," Guthrie said, "but there must be another way."

"There is," said Mac. "I have to get to that wagon, get my Winchester, and gun down as many of these varmints as I can. But I need a diversion, something to get them all as far from that wagon as possible.''

"You'll still have irons on your wrists and ankles,'' Red pointed out.

"No help for that,'' said Mac. "We won't get our hands on that key until we take it from Nelson's dead body.''

"We can stampede the mules,'' Port Guthrie said. "That's a pretty good diversion.''

"Yes,'' said Mac, "but we'll have to do it in such a way that we can't be held responsible. If we fail this time, we may have to rely on the stampede again.''

"A good dose of skunk would do it,'' Buck said. "There's one been doin' his thing not too far from here.''

"Yeah,'' said Haze. "He's upwind from us.''

"You want skunk,'' Gourd Snively said, "leave a big hunk of meat where he can smell it, and he'll show up.''

"There's still some of that deer Sergeant Embler shot,'' said Port Guthrie. "By now, it likely ain't fit for nothin' but skunk bait.''

"I'll see that Hattie gets us the bait tomorrow night at supper,'' Red said. "I just wish there was some other way of creating a diversion, without stampeding the mules. Sooner or later, this bunch of short-horns will lose some of them for good.''

"There ain't a mule alive that I wouldn't sacrifice to save my hide,'' said Port Guthrie.

"That's about the way I feel,'' Mac agreed. "We'll do what we must.''

It was after dark the next evening when Hattie produced the piece of deer meat.

"Oh, I hope this works,'' she said. "Trinity's a bundle of nerves.''

"I reckon it'll lure the skunk,'' said Mac. "From there, we'll have to wait and see.''

Mac managed to drop the deer meat near where the mules and horses were grazing. He then spread his blankets as near Trinity's wagon as he felt he could, without arousing suspicion. He waited for what he believed was three hours without result. There wasn't a sound from any of his comrades, but he knew they were awake, ready to follow him if his desperate act proved successful. The moon had risen, and while Mac could see the shapes of the grazing horses and mules, he could see little else. He must depend on the skunk making his presence known. The first sign of his coming was the nervous nicker of one of the horses. A mule stomped his feet, braying, and then there was a chorus of them.

"All you men on your feet," Lieutenant Nelson bawled. "Something's disturbing the horses and mules."

Nine men, half-dressed, seized their Winchesters and went on the run. The incident might have passed, but the shouting of the soldiers convinced the skunk he was in danger and he acted accordingly.

"Skunk!" shouted Private Puckett, who was leading the charge.

The soldiers fell over one another attempting to retreat, and all of them received a dose of the skunk's venom. It was more than enough to stampede the horses and mules, and they lit out along the backtrail.

"Head them," Lieutenant Nelson shouted.

But the unfortunate soldiers stood there rubbing their eyes, scarcely able to see. Mac made his way toward the wagon containing the guns, restrained by the leg irons, forced to take short steps when he desperately needed to run. His heart sank when a man stepped away from the shadow of the wagon, a Winchester at the ready.

"It had to be you, didn't it, Tunstall?" said Sergeant Embler. "Now you just go right back the way you come. The lieutenant will want to make an example of you."

It seemed Lieutenant Nelson had forgotten about the stampede. He spoke to Sergeant Embler in an almost casual tone.

"March him to that tree, Sergeant."

The tree forked about head-high, and Mac soon understood what was coming. Nelson unlocked one of the manacles securing his wrist and passed the loose end of the chain through the fork in the tree. He then replaced and locked the manacle on the loose wrist, and Mac was secured, facing the tree, his arms over his head.

"Pass me your weapon, Sergeant," Lieutenant Nelson said, "and fetch a rope."

Sergeant Embler returned with a lariat, and seemed to know exactly what to do with it. He doubled and tripled it until it had the weight of a club. The rest of Mac's outfit had gathered, and it was to them that Nelson spoke.

"Discipline is about to be administered to Mr. Tunstall. If the rest of you are wise, you will learn from it. Proceed, Sergeant, until I tell you to stop."

"No," Trinity sobbed.

Her protest was ignored, and Hattie held her back. There was nothing any of them could do, for besides the Winchester Lieutenant Nelson held, most of the other soldiers had cocked their weapons. Despite himself, Mac groaned as Sergeant Embler administered the beating. His friends wept for him, as he took one blow after another, until finally he felt them no longer. Unconscious, he hung from the chain that secured his wrists between the fork of the tree.

"That's enough, Sergeant," Lieutenant Nelson said. "I trust that will be sufficient to discourage Mr. Tunstall's friends who might be considering something equally foolish."

Nelson unlocked one of the irons securing Mac's wrists, and allowed him to slump to the ground. He then locked the loose manacle back in place and spoke.

"If you wish to see to Tunstall's hurts, Sergeant Embler will get the medicine chest from the wagon."

"Get it," Hattie said, through gritted teeth.

Lieutenant Nelson waited until Embler returned with the medicine chest. He then spoke to them all.

"This is just a sample. If Tunstall—or any of you—try this again, the punishment will be doubled."

He then walked away, Sergeant Embler and the rest of

the soldiers following. Red and Buck turned Mac belly-down and began picking the shreds of his shirt from the bloody welts on his back.

"Let me help," Trinity begged.

"Get a fire going," said Red. "We need hot water, and lots of it."

Trinity and Hattie started the fire and put on water to boil.

"My God," Hattie said, "the man's a beast."

"He's somewhere below that," said Trinity. "I'm going to kill him."

"I think that's something Mac Tunstall will want to take care of himself," Hattie said.

Mac had been brought near the fire so that there would be enough light to tend his wounds.

"How bad is it?" Trinity asked anxiously.

"Plenty bad enough," said Buck. "I've never seen a man beaten like this who lived to talk about it."

"He won't have to worry about ridin' for a while," Port Guthrie said. "This bunch of poor excuses for soldiers has got to round up all them mules and horses."

After Mac's wounds had been cleansed with hot water, it was apparent they were even more severe than they had at first seemed.

"Dear God," said Trinity, "there's less than a bottle of whiskey left. Suppose it's not enough?"

"It'll have to be," Red replied. "We can't count on this bunch of varmints for anything but more of the same."

"There's another bottle with disinfectant," said Hattie. "We'll use that to disinfect his wounds and save the whiskey for infection."

"There's still plenty of laudanum," Rachel said. "He'll need that to see him through the pain for a while."

"Oh, Lord," said Elizabeth, "what are we going to do now?"

"We're going to keep Mac alive," Haze said, "if we can. When we've done that, we'll find a way to take care of Nelson and the rest of those bastards."

Mac's outfit was up the rest of the night, nobody willing to leave him until they knew whether or not he would survive.

"His pulse is stronger," Trinity announced, along toward dawn.

None of the soldiers, including Lieutenant Nelson, seemed to care if Mac Tunstall lived or died. At first light they prepared to search for the missing horses and mules. It would be no easy task, for they all were afoot.

Red laughed. "It's just like Mac planned it. We could have saved our horses, but these varmints would have taken them to search for the others and the mules. Now, by God, they'll be hoofin' it. They'll be lucky if they find 'em all in two or three days."

"I hope you're right," Trinity said. "If Mac heals at all, he'll need time."

Heavily dosed with laudanum, Mac slept all night and most of the next day. Even then his fever still raged. When he opened his eyes, he found Trinity beside him.

"Water," he croaked.

Once, twice, three times, Trinity filled a tin cup with water. Mac then closed his eyes and was asleep again.

"The boys ain't havin' much luck on their horse and mule hunt," said Port Guthrie.

At the end of the day they had managed to recover only half a dozen mules, and none of the missing horses. Twenty-four hours after Mac's beating, his fever broke and there was hope that he would recover. Before dawn, he was awake, wanting to know what had taken place while he slept.

"That was a good idea, lettin' all the horses stampede with the mules," said Red. "This bunch of short-horn soldiers just ain't havin' much luck afoot."

"I hate to lose the horses," Mac said, "but this will buy us a little time. Whatever we have to do to free ourselves must be done before we reach the coast. Once they get us aboard a sailing ship, we're lost."

"We know Trinity was right about one thing," said

Red. "We have to get loose from these irons, at least one or two of us, and get our hands on some weapons."

"Yes," Mac agreed, "and creating a diversion and rushing the wagon won't work. They were prepared for that. Embler had been told, regardless of what happened, to guard the wagon with the weapons. As soldiers go, this bunch leaves a lot to be desired, but I'll have to admit they have us in a bad situation. Have Port Guthrie come talk to me."

Guthrie wasted no time.

"Port," Mac said, "at least one or two of us must be free of these irons and have our hands on some Winchesters, if we're to free ourselves from this bunch. We're goin' to try something else, and we'll need your help."

Mac talked rapidly and Guthrie listened, speaking only when Mac had finished.

"Yeah, I can handle my end of it. Tell me when."

"It must be while we're still near Austin," said Mac. "If Nelson has a rendezvous with a sailing ship, there may be even more men for us to contend with. I think the third day after we leave here, we'll make our move. I'll talk to you again before then, and you're not to speak of this to anyone else."

"*Bueno*," Guthrie said. "I understand."

The second day, Lieutenant Nelson's soldiers were more successful, gathering another four mules and six horses.

"Another day," said Haze, "and they may find the rest of 'em."

"That won't mean nothin' to us," Buck said, "if it brings doomsday a little closer."

Port Guthrie was as good as his word, saying nothing about what he and Mac had discussed. It was more difficult for Mac, for he was faced daily with the stricken looks of the women.

"There's one thing we're going to change," said Lieutenant Nelson, when at last the mules and horses had been recovered. "Until this mission has been completed, three of you will remain with the livestock from dusk until dawn. You are authorized to shoot anything or anybody coming near. If there are any more untimely stampedes, punishment of those responsible will be severe.''

"But sir," Private Puckett said, "there was a skunk—"

"You heard me, Private," said Lieutenant Nelson. "Punishment will be severe."

The third day following the stampede, Lieutenant Nelson's men managed to round up the rest of the missing horses and mules. True to his word, Nelson assigned three men to stand watch near the animals from dusk to dawn.

"Well, there's nothing more we can do, where the horses and mules are concerned," Haze said. "I think Nelson suspects we had something to do with that last stampede."

"Let him suspect all he wants," said Mac. "He can't prove a thing."

"He's got Sergeant Embler and Corporal Irvin eating and sleeping at Trinity's wagon, where our weapons are," Red said. "Now *that* bothers me."

"It bothers us in a different way," said Trinity. "They won't let us in the wagon even to get a change of clothes. Embler told me to wash what I'm wearing, put them on and let them dry."

"I feel so dirty, I can barely stand myself," Elizabeth said. "Before we leave here in the morning, I'm going to get some of my clothes out of that wagon."

"No," said Haze, "you stay away from that wagon. Nelson's been rough on them, and they'd like nothing better than to take it out on some of us."

But Elizabeth didn't heed the warning. After supper, her companions missed her when they heard her agonized scream. Because of their leg irons, the men were slow reaching her. When Mac and Haze were within sight of Trinity's wagon, Sergeant Embler and Corporal Irvin had Trinity, Hattie, and Rachel covered with Winchesters. Elizabeth lay on the ground sobbing.

"Get away from her," Hattie snarled.

"She was told to stay away from this wagon," said Embler, "and she didn't. One of you come forward and take her away, and let this be a warning to you all. Next time—if there is a next time—somebody *really* gets hurt."

Hattie helped Elizabeth to her feet and led her away. Blood dripped from her smashed nose, and her left arm hung useless.

"Her arm's broken, I think," Hattie said.

"I've set plenty of busted bones," said Port Guthrie. "I'll have a look at it. Why don't you give her a big dose of laudanum first? It'll not be so hard on her, if she can sleep through it."

The arm was broken, and Guthrie set it. As he was binding the splints in place, Lieutenant Nelson approached. Aware of their anger and disgust, he spoke.

"There is always a penalty for disobeying orders. My men did as they were told. If you wish to blame someone, then you are welcome to blame me."

"We are blaming you," said Mac through clenched teeth.

Nelson turned away without responding.

"I never wanted much," Haze growled, "but I want that bastard graveyard dead."

Elizabeth slept through the night, and when the wagons were again ready to take the trail, she had to be helped into her saddle. She eyed Lieutenant Nelson with undisguised hatred. With the exception of Mac Tunstall and Port Guthrie, they were all disappointed, angry, and frustrated. Mac and Port eyed one another, but said nothing. This day and one more. Then on the third day they would make what well might be their final move to free themselves and reclaim their wagons . . .

Austin, Texas. December 15, 1873.

Captain Vance, the officer at the ordnance depot, had just received a puzzling answer to a telegram he had sent to the ordnance depot at Fort Leavenworth, Kansas. Lieutenant Schorp, his second in command, had brought him the wire, and waited while he read it.

Arms shipment in question should not have gone by way of Fort Griffin.

"According to the telegram we received from Captain Stockton at Fort Griffin," said Lieutenant Schorp, "the wagons left there heading south on November 21. That's twenty-four days ago, sir."

"I know, Lieutenant," Captain Vance replied. "If they followed the Colorado, they've had more than enough time to get here. There are entirely too many unanswered questions to suit me. Why did these teamsters and their outriders elect to come by way of Fort Griffin, when it was considerably out of their way? When they eventually left there, why did Captain Stockton, the post commander, take it upon himself to telegraph us? Probably the most important question, however, is where are those wagons now?"

"We can rule out the Comanches," said Lieutenant Schorp. "We've had no reports on Quanah Parker and the Comanches since they crossed the Red into Indian Territory. There are outlaws and renegades, of course."

"If there was going to be trouble from outlaws and renegades," Captain Vance replied, "I'd have looked for that before they ever crossed the Red into Texas. Hijacking wagons with a shipment of this magnitude wouldn't make sense unless the arms were to be taken out of the country. That would involve a sailing ship, and getting the wagons secretly to some point along the coast."

"Perhaps that's where they're headed," said Lieutenant Schorp. "Frankly, I'm surprised that ordnance at Fort Leavenworth didn't question the fact that those wagons obviously had not reached Austin. If they had, why would you have inquired about them having gone by way of Fort Griffin?"

"I don't know what they're thinking at Leavenworth, or if they're thinking at all," Captain Vance said. "What I am thinking is that if our suspicions are valid, and those arms have fallen into enemy hands, we should be attempting to locate and recover those very important wagons.''

''But sir,'' said Lieutenant Schorp, ''of all the military involved, we're the least able to make such a move. There's only a sergeant, a corporal, two privates, you, and myself.''

''I am aware of that, Lieutenant,'' Captain Vance replied, ''and if the army were to even consider such a maneuver, a patrol would be sent from Fort Griffin. If what we suspect is true, the men from Fort Griffin would never reach the wagons in time. If we're to attempt to save that arms shipment, we'll have to call on some friends who are not bound by red tape so common to the military.''

''And who are those friends, sir?''

''The Texas Rangers,'' said Captain Vance. ''There's a Ranger outpost at Houston. If I can convince the Rangers here that enemies of the United States may be about to steal six wagonloads of advanced weapons . . .''

''Rangers from the Houston outpost can be alerted by telegraph, heading off the arms and the thieves.''

''Perhaps,'' Captain Vance said, ''but more important, I want the Rangers to ride the coast from Galveston to Corpus Christi Bay, looking for a ship at anchor offshore. Such a vessel close in won't be immune to search and seizure. Better yet, if there is such a ship lying in wait for those stolen arms, it'll be reason enough to arrange a welcoming committee on shore for those arriving wagons.''

Ranger Bodie West got to his feet when Captain Vance entered the small office.

''Howdy, Cap,'' said West. ''I ain't seen you in a while.''

''It's been a while since I had to ask for help.''

West laughed.

''I'm sorry,'' Captain Vance said. ''I didn't mean that exactly like it sounded.''

''It's all right,'' said West. ''We understand one another. I'm just glad the Union sent some gents to Texas that didn't want to fight the war all over again. Tell me what's diggin' the gut hooks* in you, and I'll help if I can.''

Without even bothering to sit down, Captain Vance told West the little that he knew for certain and of the considerable he suspected regarding the long-overdue arms shipment.

''I believe you have cause for concern,'' West said, after a moment's consideration. ''I realize that in Washington the thinking is that this country and Mexico are at peace, and that's probably true if you don't go beyond the bureaucrats in Mexico City. But there are criminal elements in Mexico who would gladly enter into a conspiracy to steal a shipment of arms such as you describe. These are outlaws who are at odds with the Mexican government, so it's entirely possible they would be forced to move so massive a quantity of stolen goods by sea. Now what do you want me individually, or the Rangers collectively, to do?''

''It'll make fools of us both, if I'm wrong,'' said Captain Vance, ''but I'd like Rangers from the outpost in Houston to ride from Galveston Bay to Corpus Christi Bay, looking for a suspicious craft anchored offshore. Finding one would vindicate my suspicions and perhaps generate enough credibility to stop this thievery.''

''It could also get you reprimanded for exceeding your authority,'' West replied. ''Do you not think that by now the army has begun its own investigation, trying to determine what's become of those six wagons and their invaluable cargo?''

''Yes,'' said Captain Vance, ''I am certain they have. I became involved in this because I received a telegram from Captain Stockton, at Fort Griffin, telling me the wagons had just left there, heading south. I have no idea why Stockton relayed this information to me, unless he was aware that the freight line in Kansas City hadn't intended for the wagons to pass through Fort Griffin. I telegraphed the ordnance people at Fort Leavenworth, expecting them

*Spurs.

to authorize me to investigate from this end, and all they told me was that those wagons weren't supposed to travel through Fort Griffin.''

"Without comin' right out and sayin' it,'' West replied, ''you were told to back off.''

"A by-the-book soldier would have taken it that way,'' said Captain Vance.

Bodie West laughed. "But you didn't.''

"No, I didn't,'' Captain Vance replied, ''because I believe if we're going to save those arms, we don't have much time. Needless to say, I'd appreciate this being kept confidential. If I'm dead wrong, maybe I can back off short of being busted down to buck private, or cashiered out of the service entirely.''

"I'll keep the lid on for you, Cap, where the Rangers are concerned,'' said West. "If it turns out you're right, where do you aim to go from there?''

"I'm going to exceed the hell out of my authority,'' Captain Vance said, ''and establish a force of men to greet the thieves who have stolen those arms.''

"I reckon I can help you there,'' said West. "The worst the army can do is tell me to mind my own damn business in the future.''

"Like hell they will,'' Captain Vance said. "If we pull this off and you help me save these Winchester wagons, I'll see that you're commended by the president of these United States.''

CHAPTER 19

❧

*T*exas Ranger Bodie West didn't hesitate after Captain Vance left the office. West took a pencil and a tablet and composed a telegram to the Ranger outpost at Houston. Unsatisfied with his first effort, he ripped out the sheet and started over. While some Rangers were unsympathetic to the trials of Union soldiers in Texas, Bodie West had learned that most of them—like Captain Vance—were decent men, performing difficult duties under trying circumstances. When West had the telegram composed to his satisfaction, he had it sent to one of the Rangers he knew at Houston. But something troubled him. While Captain Vance was attempting to head off the thieves he believed had taken the six wagons and their government cargo, what would become of the men who had undertaken the hazardous journey with the wagons? West rode to a boarding house where two other Rangers—Wells and Marks—shared a room.

"Oh, God," Marks said, when he opened the door, "it's West, and he wants something more than our company."

"Yeah," Wells agreed, "he never tracks us down where we live unless he's looking for a few days off. How long this time, Bodie?"

"Muy bueno amigos," said West humbly, "you misjudge me."

"Like hell," Marks scoffed. "Where are you goin'?

How long you aim to be gone? Is this Ranger business, or do you have the hots for some *señorita* in Laredo?"

"It's not really Ranger business," said West, "but it's not quite personal, either. I aim to ride up the Rio Colorado a ways on an errand for Captain Vance."

"By God," Wells said, "when you cash in, instead of lettin' you into heaven, Saint Pete will deck you out in Union blue and shuffle you off to Washington."

Marks laughed, enjoying the fun. "Can't you just see that monument, old Bodie twelve feet high, in solid marble?"

"Damn it," said West, becoming irritated, "are you goin' to cover for me or not?"

"Don't we always?" Wells said. "What in tarnation ever give you the idea we wasn't?"

The next morning at first light, Bodie West rode northwest, following the Colorado. He was virtually certain that if the wagons had traveled south, it was for the purpose of reaching the river. The river flowed directly through Austin and was a reliable source of water. While West considered Captain Vance's suspicion regarding a sailing ship a possible means of taking the stolen weapons out of the country, it wasn't the only consideration. It was entirely possible that the thieves had connections in Mexico, and would simply take the wagons across the border at the most convenient point. Suppose the wagons, instead of being taken toward the distant coast and a sailing ship, had crossed the Rio Colorado and had continued south, toward the border?

"Hoss," said West, "it'll take us a mite longer, followin' the river, but we got to find what direction those wagons took after reachin' the Rio Colorado."

South Texas. December 13, 1873.

Supper was over, and Mac's outfit had distanced itself from Lieutenant Nelson and his men. There was little conversation, each of them occupied by the same grim thoughts. Port Guthrie finally spoke.

"Three months since we left Kansas City. I'm wonderin' why the army ain't started a search for us. I can't see 'em takin' a loss such as this, without at least tryin' to recover it."

"Neither can I," Mac admitted, "but the army's godawful slow in starting any kind of investigation. If they've made any moves, I reckon they started in Kansas City."

"All cut, dried, and boiled down," said Buck, "that means by the time they get to the truth of things, they won't be in time to be of any help to us."

"That's it," Mac admitted. "Their common sense never catches up to their good intentions."

"Well, I don't aim to go on like this," said Haze. "Hell, we're still in irons without a plan of escape. I'd as soon be dead. I'm goin' over yonder and punch Nelson in the mouth and let him shoot me."

"No," Red said, "you're goin' to ride this out another couple of days. The rest of us don't give up until Mac does, and I don't believe he has."

"No," said Mac, "and I don't intend to give up. Something's got to happen. We'll get a fighting chance. That's all I can tell you."

Port Guthrie was careful not to look at Mac. He was only too well aware that much of Mac's plan depended upon him. He had never been called upon to break an axle before, and he pondered a means of accomplishing it that would seem accidental.

"Two more days," Lafe Beard said, "and we'll be three months out of Kansas City."

"Stop remindin' us," said Gourd Snively. "Hell, I druv a wagon all the way from Kansas City to the Yellowstone, an' it didn't take this long. We was held up three times on the Bozeman, fightin' the Sioux."

Smokey Foster laughed. "I remember that, Gourd. That's when you and three other hombres circled your wagons and kilt every Sioux in the war party except Crazy Horse. He had to ride for his life, with the four of you chasin' him like hell wouldn't have it.''

"That was the easy part, gettin' rid of Crazy Horse and the Sioux," Port Guthrie said, a twinkle in his eyes. "It's a heap harder than you'd imagine, circlin' four wagons.''

They all laughed, Gourd Snively along with them. They desperately needed something to lift their sagging spirits. With nothing better to do, they retired to their blankets. With no moon, they could move quietly within a pre-scribed area without drawing the attention of the sentries. Trinity dragged her blankets near Mac's, so they might talk.

"I can't sleep," Trinity said. "I'll never sleep again until we free ourselves and go on to Austin.''

"Keep it soft," Mac cautioned. "They're downwind from us. The last thing I want them thinking is that we're planning something.''

"But we're not planning anything, are we?''

"Yes," said Mac, "I have a plan, and I don't want you to so much as breathe a word to any of the others. I mean to *nobody*. Understand?''

"I understand," Trinity said, "but why not tell the others? They need something to lift their spirits.''

"That's the last damn thing we need," said Mac. "I want everybody looking as down and as hopeless as pos-sible. The minute we stop looking worried and scared, that's when Nelson and his bunch begin keeping a closer watch on us, and our last hope of escape goes up in smoke. Do you understand?''

"Of course I do," Trinity said.

"Good," said Mac. "Now can you go on looking as beaten and as forlorn as everybody else?''

"I'll try," Trinity said. "This is not something that's going to get one of you shot or beaten half to death, is it?''

"No," said Mac, "and that's all I can tell you.''

"Thank you for telling me that much.''

*   *   *

Privates Puckett, Haynes, and McCarty were on sentry
duty watching the mules and horses. Their conversation
dealt with what they had just learned from Sergeant Embler.

"That's what the sarge said," Puckett insisted. "Once
we get these wagons off our hands, we can all have a go
at these women."

"I'll believe that when it happens," said Haynes. "Embler's just tellin' us that so's we'll keep our noses to the
grindstone."

"I heard the same thing," McCarty said. "We're gettin'
two or three days' use of them females, and that includes
the high-toned redhead that thinks she's too good for us."

"She won't be good for nobody, when we're done with
her," Haynes said. "Hell, we could of been havin' 'em
ever since we took over these wagons, if Nelson had just
let us gun down the men."

"Maybe he knows what he's doin'," said Puckett.
"Why shoot a man, when you can get paid for sellin' him
into the mines? I'd like to see this highfalutin bunch bustin' their backs diggin' silver for the Mexes."

"Not me," McCarty said. "I never want to see 'em
again. I aim to take my share of the money and go to
California."

"Some of the others—Irvin and Collins—are talkin'
about us all sticking together, even after ridding ourselves
of the wagons," said Puckett.

"Let Irvin and Collins stick together, then," McCarty
said. "It'll be that much easier for the army to track 'em
down as deserters."

"Damn it," Embler shouted, "them of you there among
the horses and mules are too noisy. Hold it down."

"Aw, stuff it," said Puckett, but not loud enough for
Embler to hear.

Mac and his outfit spent a restless night. They arose at first
light, and as usual, the women started the fires and pre-

pared breakfast. The horses and mules had all been led in close enough for all the sentries to eat without having to watch the animals. The trouble started when the quick-tempered Sergeant Embler almost dropped his tin cup, just as Hattie was filling it with coffee. Fumbling for the cup, Embler struck the coffeepot in such a way that Hattie spilled its scalding contents down the front of Embler's trousers. Shouting in pain and fury, Embler drew his Colt and was about to slug Hattie with it, when Rachel swung a heavy skillet. It slammed into the back of Embler's head, and as he fell, the Colt roared. The slug burned a furrow along the flank of one of the mules, and the animal screamed in pain. It then lit out in a dead run toward the south, taking with it all its companions and the frightened horses.

"Head those mules!" Lieutenant Nelson shouted.

"Head 'em, hell," said Private Puckett. "They're gone."

And so they were. Lieutenant Nelson looked first at the fallen Sergeant Embler and then at Hattie, who still held the offending coffeepot. Rachel stood beside her, defiantly holding the heavy iron skillet.

"If it isn't too much trouble," Nelson snarled, "some of you tell me how this began."

"I'll tell you," said Hattie. "That idiot, Sergeant Embler, struck the pot as I was trying to pour his coffee. Most of the hot coffee spilled down his front."

"The skunk was about to hit Hattie with his pistol," Rachel said, "but I just happened to have this skillet, and I hit him first. He fired the shot that struck one of the mules."

The furious Lieutenant Nelson looked from one of his men to the other, each of them trying mightily not to laugh. Suddenly Nelson drew his Colt, cocked it, and shoved it under Private Stearn's chin.

"Now, Private," Nelson gritted, "why don't you tell me how this all began?"

"I—I . . . she . . . told it straight, sir," Stearn mumbled.

"You're telling me all this is Sergeant Embler's fault?" Nelson bellowed.

"Y-yes, sir," said Stearn.

For a terrifying moment, it seemed that Lieutenant Nelson was going to blow off the unfortunate private's head. Finally Nelson eased down the hammer, holstered the weapon, and went after Sergeant Embler. Rubbing the back of his head, Embler sat up, regarding the Colt in his right hand with some confusion.

"Get up, Sergeant," Lieutenant Nelson snapped.

"I ain't sure I can," said Embler. "I think my skull's busted."

Holstering the Colt, he got to his knees. A hand up would have been helpful, but nobody offered one. Embler stood there weaving like a tall tree in a hard wind, his eyes on the soaked front of his trousers. One of the women laughed. Then they all did. Embler's face went red and his hand dropped to the butt of his Colt.

"Sergeant," said Lieutenant Nelson coldly, "don't even think about it. Now move, you bungling fool. It seems you're responsible for the stampeding of the horses and mules, and you don't have three days to round them up. Take all the men with you except Corporal Irvin. He will remain here with me."

Sergeant Embler stumbled off, apparently uncertain as to the direction the stampede had taken. The privates followed, having heard the order shouted by Lieutenant Nelson.

"Well," Hattie said, "I don't know if I accomplished anything else, but I enjoyed that."

"No more than I did," said Rachel. "I've never put a skillet to better use."

"Hattie," Mac said, "did you plan that?"

"Of course not," said Hattie. "If I had, I'd have poured it all on him, not just half of it."

"Well," Rachel said, "aren't you going to ask me if I planned to slug him with an iron skillet? The truth is, I'd have hit him with anything. I was just lucky, having this beautiful skillet in my hand.''

The laughter began with Buck and spread among the others like a prairie fire. Much to the unfortunate Sergeant Embler's relief, the stampeded mules and horses hadn't run very far. Embler and the men quickly caught some of the horses and were thus able to go after the missing mules. Before sundown, they had accomplished the impossible. All the stampeded animals had been recovered. Port Guthrie had a chance to speak to Mac before they turned in for the night.

"We lost a day," said Guthrie. "Are we gonna make our move the day after tomorrow or delay it an extra day?"

"We'll go ahead as planned," Mac said.

There was little conversation among Mac's outfit, and that was the way he wanted it. Time after time, he considered and discarded possible plans, always returning to the first one he and Guthrie had discussed. As the time drew nearer, he couldn't help having some misgivings, but there seemed no better way.

Houston, Texas. December 16, 1873.

Texas Rangers Dan McDaniel and Arlo Camden were being briefed by the commander of the outpost, Captain Dillard.

"This is strictly a surveillance mission," said Captain Dillard. "The information is of a confidential nature, and is needed by the army. You are to ride the coastline from here to Corpus Christi, using binoculars to observe the gulf. The possible vessel under investigation probably won't be near an established port, but in some out-of-the-way cove with an easy access to shore. It likely won't show any markings or a flag. If you reach Corpus Christi Bay without a sighting, stay the night and return, repeating the procedure."

"Clear enough," McDaniel said. "Should we spot such a ship, what are we to do?"

"Study it for markings," said Captain Dillard. "Anything that might identify it or the country from which it came. Take careful note as to its location, and then get that information to me pronto. *Comprender*?"

"*Sí*," the rangers replied in a single voice.

McDaniel and Camden rode out, following the shoreline from Houston, bound for Corpus Christi Bay.

"We do an almighty lot to help the army, after the shabby treatment we got from them durin' the war," McDaniel said.

"I've noticed that," said Camden. "Durin' the war and Reconstruction, they always had enough troops to stomp our suspenders down around our boot tops. Now they never have enough soldiers in one place to fight off an attack by Comanche squaws."

"I hear they're needin' all the soldiers on the high plains," McDaniel replied. "They let the Indian situation go to hell while they whupped us. Now they got some catchin' up to do, I reckon. Maybe they got Quanah Parker and the Comanches on the run, but old Red Cloud, Crazy Horse, and them Sioux ain't goin' nowhere."

"I'm kinda wonderin' why they're expectin' a sailing ship to be anchored somewhere between here and Corpus Christi," said Camden. "Sounds like some varmints from outside the United States aims to bring somethin' in or take somethin' out. In either case, wonder what it could be?"

"White slavery, maybe," McDaniel said. "I hear there's a pile of money bein' made by sellin' women from this country into Mexican whorehouses."

"What a stinkin', lowdown thing for men to do," said Camden. "I could hold a stick of dynamite in my teeth, swim out there after dark, and sink their damn ship."

McDaniel laughed. "Whoa. Pull in your horns. We don't know anything about this ship, or even if there is one. All we got to do is find out if there is or if there ain't, and report back to Captain Dillard.''

"It ain't quite two hundred miles to Corpus Christi,'' Camden said. "A two-day ride.''

"Maybe longer,'' said McDaniel, "because we got to stop every few miles and sweep that water with the binoculars. If there's a ship at anchor, the sails will be furled, and we won't have an easy time findin' it.''

They rode on, stopping at regular intervals to study the seemingly endless blue water of the Gulf of Mexico. Finally, a few minutes before sundown, they reached a freshwater stream that flowed into the gulf.

"Good place to bed down for the night,'' McDaniel said. "We've covered near seventy miles, I figure.''

"At this pace, we'll be three days gettin' to Corpus Christi,'' said Camden. "I thought Captain Dillard seemed a mite anxious for us to investigate this and get back to him.''

"He is anxious,'' McDaniel agreed, "but lookin' across miles of nothin' but water is a lot like lookin' across a desert. Your eyes get to seein' things that ain't there, or maybe overlookin' things that *are* there.''

South Texas. December 16, 1873.

Ranger Bodie West reined up, unsaddled his horse, and picketed the animal on the north bank of the Rio Colorado. As the westering sun hid its face from the approaching darkness, West stretched out, his head on his saddle. He had removed only his hat, and close at hand was his Winchester. Wary of lighting a fire, he did without coffee, drinking water from his canteen. As so often was a Ranger's lot, a handful of jerked beef became his supper. Finishing that, he followed it with the rest of the water in the canteen. Tilting his hat over his eyes, he dozed, depending on his horse to warn him of any danger. As he thought of Captain Vance and his suspicions, he weighed them against his own. West had allowed himself two days to reach the point on the Rio Colorado where he believed the six wagons would have approached the river. If they crossed it and continued south, they had to be headed for the Mexican border, which meant they would already be lost to Captain Vance. However, if Vance was right—if there was a sailing ship waiting to receive the stolen arms—the wagons would have followed the Rio Colorado for at least three or four days. It would have been a convenient source of water until it became necessary for the caravan to travel to the south of Austin, on its way to the coast. Tomorrow, West would know, one way or the other. Unless he found evidence the wagons had traveled eastward along the river, eventually veering away toward the south, his ride would have been all for nothing.

Victoria, Texas, overlooking Matagorda Bay.
December 16, 1873.

Rangers Dan McDaniel and Arlo Camden had reined up a few minutes before sundown. The never-ending waters of the gulf looked bloodred as purple shadows crept across the face of the earth. By the time the crimson waters of the gulf faded to black, the first distant stars would be winking sleepily. Having unsaddled their horses, Dan and Arlo waited for the animals to roll.

"If you'll picket them," Arlo said, "I'll take the binoculars and have a look at the big pond. Won't be nothin' there, but we'll have to tell Captain Dillard we looked."

"Yeah," said Dan. "Go ahead."

Dan had picketed the horses and was gathering wood for a small fire, when there was an excited shout from Arlo.

"By God, there's somethin' out there!"

"Tarnation," Dan said, "let me have the binoculars."

"I aim to," said Arlo. "I saw somethin' kind of dancin'

around, and then it was gone. Here, aim these binoculars in the direction I'm pointin' my finger.''

Dan took the binoculars but could see nothing. The gray curtain of night had met the blackness of the far-reaching waters of the gulf.

"We'll have to wait until tomorrow," Dan said. "If they're the kind of pilgrims Captain Dillard seems to think they are, this would be a more logical place than Corpus Christi."

"Damn right," said Arlo. "Corpus Christi's a government port. It's the last place a bunch of smugglers would drop anchor. I just hope we can get the word back to Captain Dillard before they load their cargo and escape."

"We can ride back in half the time," Dan said. "We won't have to stop and search the gulf with those binoculars."

South Central Texas. December 16, 1873.

"Damn it, get those wagons moving!" Lieutenant Nelson shouted.

"We're restin' the teams," said Port Guthrie. "We rest 'em every hour, and you know that."

"The policy has just been changed," Lieutenant Nelson said. "You'll rest them once every two hours, starting today."

Guthrie said nothing. Mounting his wagon box, he led out. The other wagons rumbled along behind, followed by Mac Tunstall and his captive outfit. Behind them rode all the soldiers except Lieutenant Nelson and Sergeant Embler. Nelson rode ahead of Guthrie's lead wagon, while Embler still drove Trinity's wagon, the seventh in the caravan. Mac had seen Nelson double back and speak to Port Guthrie almost immediately after the teamster had halted the wagons to rest the mules. Nobody doubted what Nelson's order had been.

"The lieutenant don't know any more about handlin'

mules than he does men,'' Red observed. ''Overwork the teams, and these wagons will all end up stalled.''

''Would that be so bad?'' Hattie asked.

''It would be for us,'' said Mac. ''That would scuttle Nelson's plan to sell all of us into Mexico, and he'd have no reason for keeping us alive.''

In the lead wagon, Port Guthrie fumed, his eyes on Lieutenant Nelson's back. Under his breath he spoke.

''One more day, you bastard. Just one more day.''

Mac Tunstall had similar thoughts, and when Trinity's eyes met his, he knew the same ominous clock was ticking in her mind. Late that night, when the camp had settled down, Red took a chance reaching Mac.

''You have somethin' in mind,'' said Red. ''When do you aim to tell the rest of us?''

''I've kept it quiet,'' Mac said, ''because I didn't want Nelson suspecting anything. Now I reckon it's time all of you know what's coming. If it works out, you and me will each have a loaded Winchester in our hands. We'll have to raise enough hell for the others to arm themselves from Trinity's wagon. There'll be no time for indecision. Now here's what I've planned for late tomorrow afternoon . . .''

Mac spoke quietly, and not until he had finished did Red speak.

''Risky, *amigo,* but I can't improve on it. You want me to tell the others?''

''Yes,'' Mac said, ''but do it quietly and impress upon them all the importance of this being kept quiet. Tomorrow, I don't want Nelson or any of his men to see any difference in any of us. This is our only chance.''

''I'll pass the word,'' said Red, ''and I'll play my part.''

''Speak to Port Guthrie,'' Mac said, ''and have him alert the rest of the teamsters. It's best that I not be seen talking to any of you.''

Red slipped away into the night, and Mac sighed. It seemed they'd been captives for months. They were more than three months out of Kansas City, and just nine days away from Christmas, he thought dismally. Would they be celebrating the most joyous Christmas any of them had ever experienced, or would they all lie dead in these lonely wilds of south Texas?

Victoria, Texas, overlooking Matagorda Bay.
December 17, 1873.

The day dawned clear, and as soon as it became light enough to see, Rangers Camden and McDaniel had their binoculars trained on the distant Gulf of Mexico.

"Now I don't see a damned thing but water," Arlo said. "I wonder if what I saw last night was kind of like a mirage, somethin' that I wanted to see?"

"Maybe not," said Dan. "We'll wait a while, until the sun's up. Let's have some coffee and breakfast. Then we'll try again."

An hour later, Arlo again got out the binoculars. "Here," he said. "You first."

Dan scanned the distant horizon but saw nothing. Again he tried, and froze.

"There it is!" he shouted. "There it is!"

Arlo grabbed the binoculars. "You're right," he yelled. "I see it, too."

They waited for the vessel to come closer, and slowly but surely it did.

"We'd better get off this rise," said Dan. "They may have a man on deck, watching the shore through binoculars."

They led their horses over a rise and took a position where they were unlikely to be seen from the approaching vessel.

"She's without a flag," Dan said. "That means they don't want to be recognized."

"That means there won't be any markings on the ship itself, then," said Arlo. "There's no reason for us to kill another day waitin' for it to come close enough to see the hull."

"You're right," said Dan. "We can better use the time gettin' back to Captain Dillard with this information. Let's ride."

**South Texas, along the Rio Colorado.
December 17, 1873.**

Ranger Bodie West was nearing the end of his second day, without having found any sign of the elusive wagons along the Rio Colorado.

"Well, hoss," said West, "if sundown finds us with no more sign than we got right now, it's back to Austin and goodbye, Winchester wagons."

The sun was less than an hour high when West reined up at the shallows where the wagons had crossed to the south bank of the Rio Colorado. He rode across, satisfying himself that the wagons, while leaving the river, had continued eastward. They had not gone south, toward the Mexican border! He studied the tracks of the horses and learned there had been at least twenty mounted riders.

"Hoss," said West, "I got me an idea all them riders ain't outlaws. I reckon we'll just ease up on 'em tomorrow about sundown, and offer our services to them that's in need."

CHAPTER 20

Houston, Texas. December 18, 1873.

*R*angers Dan McDaniel and Arlo Camden reported to Captain Dillard as ordered, and Dillard listened while they told him what they had seen. Only then did he speak.

"I'll telegraph this information to the Ranger station at Austin. What they do with it is up to them."

"But Captain," McDaniel said, "if this bunch on the ship is up to no good, it'll be a shame to allow them to escape."

"I fully agree with you, Dan," said Captain Dillard, "but we have no charges against anybody. There's nothing illegal about anchoring a ship off Matagorda Bay. I think it's a situation where the army's not sure which way to turn, and what we've done, probably, is provide them with an alternative. If anything more is asked of us in regard to this, or if I eventually learn what it's all about, I'll satisfy your curiosity."

"Damn it," Arlo grumbled, "they let you get just deep enough to get interested, and then you have to back off without knowin' what happened."

South Texas. December 18, 1873.

Despite Mac's admonition to the contrary, he could feel an underlying excitement that had become all too obvious among his outfit. He only hoped their captors didn't pick up on it before his plan even saw the light of day. Only Port Guthrie showed no emotion, and Mac was thankful for the resourceful teamster. The day was unseasonably warm, and by the time the sun was noon-high, the teams were heaving, their hides dark with sweat. Mac approached Lieutenant Nelson with a request he fully expected to be denied.

"Nelson, the mules are about ready to drop in their tracks. They should be rested at least once an hour, and you—or somebody—should be riding ahead, looking for water. We don't have enough in the kegs aboard the wagons for another dry camp."

"Tunstall," said Nelson, "when I want your advice, I'll ask for it."

Nelson kicked his horse into a lope and rode on. Mac said nothing, his eyes on the sun. He studied the rugged terrain with approval, and found many stone-littered ridges and drop-offs where a wagon might be disabled. Mac slowed his mount, allowing the lead wagon to come alongside him. For just a moment, Port Guthrie caught his eye, and quickly the teamster held up three fingers. In three hours—the sun a little more than an hour away from its daily rendezvous with the western horizon—they would make their desperate bid for freedom. Mac dropped back until he rode behind the seventh wagon. Sergeant Embler was on the box, while Privates Willis, Odell, and Konda trailed well behind. There was simply no way Mac or his friends could reach the weapons within Trinity's wagon, until Embler and the outriders were eliminated. One thing bothered him. As long as the wagons were moving, the positions of the soldiers were predictable, but when Mac and Red made their desperate move, the wagons would be standing. If the soldiers gathered around Trinity's wagon, some of Mac's comrades would die attempting to reach their weapons. He rode on, troubled, unsure as to what he could do to forestall such a tragedy.

The Rio Colorado. December 18, 1873.

Ranger Bodie West had unsaddled his horse and spent the night on the Colorado, for it was near sundown when he had learned where the elusive wagons had gone. Again he had eaten jerked beef and drunk river water, for the wind was out of the northwest, and he didn't wish to reveal his presence with a fire. He ate breakfast under the same circumstances. He then saddled his horse and took the trail of the wagons, confident that he could overtake them before sundown.

The left rear wheel of Port Guthrie's wagon lurched over a stone and then slid off to one side, throwing the massive weight of the load on an axle that had been purposely and surreptitiously weakened. The axle snapped, and Guthrie reined in the teams. The rest of the wagons ground to a halt behind him. Lieutenant Nelson, who had been riding ahead, wheeled his horse and came galloping back. Mac and Red made it a point to be there, for everything depended on Nelson's response to the situation. Port Guthrie did his part convincingly, speaking before Nelson could get past his anger.

"It ain't more than an hour till sundown. We might as well wait till mornin' to start on this. Somebody will have to fashion a new axle."

"We are not waiting until morning," Nelson said stiffly. "We will begin immediately, working by firelight, if necessary. This wagon will be ready to move out at dawn. Tunstall, you and McLean secured a tree for previous repairs, and you are ordered to repeat your performance. Privates Puckett and Haynes, you will accompany them. Do not hesitate to shoot either or both, if circumstances warrant it. Now move out."

"Cut your own damn tree," said Mac. "I'm through taking your orders."

"That goes for me, as well," Red said.

It was a calculated risk. The temperamental Nelson

could simply shoot them both, ending their bid for freedom and dooming their comrades. But the man's need for the axle overcame his temper.

"Tunstall," said Nelson, in a more conciliatory manner, "you and McLean found and cut a perfect tree before, and I am asking you to do it again."

"Last time," Mac said, "I wasn't shackled."

"Me, neither," said Red.

"Very well," Nelson said. "I will remove the manacles. Just bear in mind that should you attempt to escape, I will personally shoot two of your friends. Privates Puckett and Haynes, you are responsible for seeing that these men locate the necessary wood and are returned here as quickly as possible."

Careful not to come between the captives and his men with Winchesters, Lieutenant Nelson removed the manacles from Mac and Red, freeing their arms and hands. There was a light of victory in Port Guthrie's eyes, but the rest of Mac's outfit showed no outward emotion. The main trial—recovering their weapons—was yet to come. Mac and Red each took an axe from one of the wagons. Mounting their horses, they rode out, while Privates Puckett and Haynes followed, their Winchesters cocked. Unable to communicate, Mac and Red rode close enough for eye contact, and the grim look in Red's eyes said that he would follow Mac's lead. A problem that hadn't been resolved required the taking of the weapons of their guards without Puckett or Haynes firing a shot. The bark of a Winchester could be heard for miles, proof enough that Privates Puckett and Haynes were in trouble. There was a light wind out of the west, and with that in mind, Mac rode north. Red rode alongside him, while Puckett and Haynes followed. They passed up many suitable trees, and Red spoke not a word. If there were shots, the farther they were from the stranded wagons, the less likely were those shots to be heard. They had ridden almost ten miles, when Mac reined up. He spoke loud enough for Puckett and Haynes to hear.

"That one's the right size. Let's go with it."

The oak was on the crest of a ridge, with a sudden drop-off to a dry arroyo, and it was with this in mind that Mac began his cut. After a few minutes, he paused in his work, speaking to Red.

"Finish it, and I'll do the trimming and topping."

Predictably, when the tree came down, it was along the ridge, parallel to the steep drop-off. Mac began lopping off limbs, and in so doing, stumbled. With a yell, he tumbled over the drop-off. It was a controlled fall, and he seized one of the tree's limbs.

"Hey!" Puckett shouted.

He ran toward the place where he had last seen Mac, and it was as much a break as Mac could have asked for. He seized the startled Puckett by one leg and sent him plunging over the rim. Puckett screamed, and for just a moment, Private Haynes forgot about Red McLean. Red moved like a vindictive cat, seizing the Winchester. He wrenched the weapon free and slammed the butt of it into Haynes's face. Haynes dropped without a sound, and Red quickly cocked the Winchester. But there was no danger. Mac had hauled himself up and was looking into the arroyo.

"Haynes is out of it," said Red. "What about Puckett?"

"He went over headfirst, into some rocks," Mac said. "He's dead as he'll ever be. I'll go down there and recover the Winchester."

Red finished trimming and topping the tree. They would still need a new axle. When Mac returned with the Winchester, he examined the silent, unmoving Haynes. Red looked at him questioningly.

"Remind me never to get on the bad side of you while you have a Winchester in your hands," Mac said. "You busted his jaw, but that won't make a hell of a lot of difference. His neck's broken, too."

"Him and Puckett's learned what the rest of those varmints are about to learn," said Red grimly. "When you stack the deck, never allow your opponent to get his hands on the cards. I think we just filled an inside straight, *amigo*. My Winchester's fully loaded.''

''So is this one,'' Mac replied. ''It'll be plenty dark enough, by the time we reach the wagons. Let's ride.''

Red had looped his lariat around the butt of the newly trimmed tree and had dallied the other end around his saddle horn. He and Mac had slipped the Winchesters into the saddle boots and were about to mount, when a voice stopped them cold.

''You hombres back away from your horses with your hands up. You're covered.''

Numb with shock, Mac and Red obeyed the command.

''Now,'' said the voice, ''I reckon you have some good reasons for the killing of those bluecoats.''

''Damn right we do,'' Red replied. ''They're part of a pack of deserters who stole our wagons and have kept us in irons for longer than I care to remember. We were let loose only because one of the wagons broke an axle. We aimed to take these Winchesters and free the rest of our outfit, or die trying. Since you got us by the short hairs, just who the hell are you?''

''The name's West. Bodie West.''

He stepped out of the brush, looking for the world like a Texas cowboy. But there was a Colt tied low on his right hip, and pinned to his vest was the famed star-in-a-circle shield of the Texas Rangers. Mac laughed and Red was speechless.

''Starting with your names, I reckon you'd better tell me the rest of it,'' said West. ''From the time you and your outfit were taken captive, until now.''

''I'm Mac Tunstall,'' Mac said, ''and this is Red McLean.''

Mac started the story and Red finished it.

''Before we go any farther,'' said West, ''you should know that the military—at least, the ordnance officer in Austin—didn't forsake you. I didn't come this way by accident. You and your outfit owe a mighty big debt to Captain Vance. He believed—and the two of you have proven him correct—that these arms were to be smuggled out of the country by sailing ship. Rangers from the Houston outpost are riding the coast, looking for that ship.''

"After our experience with this Lieutenant Nelson and his deserters, I was about to drop the army into a hole so deep it would never have crawled out,'' Mac said. "I reckon I'll have to revise that opinion and just call it even. Of course, we still have to free the rest of our outfit.''

"I believe we can do that," said West, "but only if we do it my way.''

"We're listenin','' Mac said.

"I'll challenge this Lieutenant Nelson," said West. "Who's next in command?''

"Sergeant Embler," Mac said. "He's always closest to the wagon where our weapons are, and may be more of a problem than Nelson.''

"When I challenge Nelson," said West, "the two of you will be in a position to call on the sergeant to surrender his weapons. How much a threat are the rest of the soldiers?''

"With Nelson and Embler out of it," Mac said, "the rest will fold like a bunch of empty feed sacks.''

"I'll go along with that," said Red, "but these varmints are just renegades decked out in army blue. Why risk our necks with a challenge, when we can just gun them down?''

West laughed. "Spoken like a true son of Texas. I'd have to agree with you, if these men were just common outlaws, but despite what they have done, they're still soldiers, and subject to military discipline. I must demand they surrender in the name of the State of Texas. If they refuse, then we are justified in using whatever force may be necessary.''

"We'll do it your way," Mac said, "as long as Red and me can cover you.''

"I'm counting on that," said West. "Just forget about Nelson, and concentrate on this Sergeant Embler and the others that I won't be able to watch.''

"You got it," Mac said. "Red, leave that damn tree here, and let's ride."

"Damn it," Buck said, "I don't like the way Nelson stalks around with that Winchester under his arm."

"Nor do I," said Haze. "It's like the varmint's just waitin' for some reason to shoot some of us. I wonder what's takin' Mac and Red so long?"

"It's a good sign," Port Guthrie said. "You may be surprised."

And so they were. There was the sound of a horse approaching, and Nelson cocked his Winchester. But the horse came on, and when it was close enough for the moonlight to reveal a rider, there was none.

"Who are you? Where are you?" Lieutenant Nelson shouted.

"I'm here," said West, off to Nelson's right. "I am Texas Ranger Bodie West, and I demand, in the name of the State of Texas, that you surrender."

Nelson began firing at the voice as rapidly as he could lever in the shells, but West had issued his challenge from a belly-down position, and the slugs went over his head. He cocked his Colt and fired three times. Once at the muzzle flash, a second time to the right of it, and a third time to the left of it. Nelson stumbled backward and fell.

"Nelson's down," West shouted. "The rest of you lay down your arms and surrender, in the name of the State of Texas."

"Damn you and the State of Texas," Embler bawled. "Men, this is Sergeant Embler, and I am in command. Kill him!"

"Embler," Mac shouted, "this is Tunstall and McLean. We're armed and we're within range. If you don't surrender, we'll cut you down, along with any man obeying your command."

"Don't shoot," half a dozen frantic voices cried. "We surrender."

"Shoot, damn you," Embler cried.

From beneath Trinity's wagon, he cut loose with a Winchester. While Bodie West was unable to see him, and he was beyond the range of the Ranger's Colt, Mac and Red faced no such limitations. They began firing, and after the first volley, there were no more shots from beneath the wagon. The next voice they heard was Port Guthrie's.

"Embler's done for, and the rest have surrendered."

Someone had thrown more wood on the fire. The corporal and six privates had their hands up, and looked terrified. Bodie West had recovered his horse, and stood beside the animal. Mac's outfit stared at the Ranger as though they couldn't believe he was real, and it was Trinity who recovered first. With a glad cry, she ran to Mac, and then everybody began laughing and shouting. When the uproar finally subsided, Mac spoke.

"Red and me haven't had supper, and Mr. West don't look well fed, either."

"Nothing but jerked beef for three days," West admitted.

"After we eat," Mac said, "we'll make plans for going on to Austin."

Supper was a joyous meal, and afterward, savoring the hot coffee, they listened while West told them what had been done on their behalf in Austin, and how he had come upon Mac and Red as they had freed themselves from Puckett and Haynes.

"I believe this pair of Texans would have freed the rest of you without any help from me," West said, "but I can truthfully tell the military that these two dead men were given every opportunity to surrender."

"The others will be turned over to the military at Austin, I reckon," said Mac.

"Yes," West replied, "and since it's no more than a day's ride, I'll take them with me when I ride out tomorrow."

"There's seven of them," said Buck. "Can you handle that many?"

"Please," West said, trying to look offended, "I'm a Ranger."

After the laughter had subsided, Corporal Irvin spoke.

"We won't cause no trouble. All we're wantin' is to get back to our outfit. We been lied to and misled."

"Sure," said West, without sympathy, "save it for the court-martial."

"For the sake of water," Mac said, "should we return to the Colorado and follow it on to Austin?"

"You can," said West, "but you'll be taking the long way home. Traveling almost due north from here, you're not more than forty miles from Austin. You'll find springs, maybe a creek or two, and you'll still get there in time for Christmas."

Bodie West rode north the following day, and so intimidated were his seven captives, he hadn't bothered roping their hands.

"I reckon it's time for Red and me to ride back for that tree that's to become Port's new axle," Mac said. "Red, get a couple of shovels. We'll bury Puckett and Haynes while we're there."

"While you're gone," said Guthrie, "the rest of us will jack up the wagon. I reckon, for the first time in my life, I'm goin' to enjoy replacin' a busted axle."

"Well," Haze said, "I reckon Buck and me can bury Nelson and Embler."

"Yeah," said Buck, "elsewise, all the buzzards and coyotes in south Texas would end up sick or dead."

When Mac and Red returned with the trimmed tree, Port Guthrie cut what he needed for the new axle and set to work on it with an axe. Still it was near noon before the job was done and the wagon ready for the trail.

"I know it's the middle of the day," Mac said, "but if nobody objects, I'd like to head north, toward Austin."

Their shouts and cheers told him they agreed, and with Port Guthrie's wagon leading, they moved out. The men again carried Colts, and their Winchesters rode in saddle boots. Trinity was on the box of her wagon, while Hattie, Rachel, and Elizabeth rode horses.

Austin, Texas. December 19, 1873.

Captain Vance and Lieutenant Schorp were speechless when Bodie West delivered his seven captives. The officers spoke not a word until West had told them the story of the missing wagons and announced they would soon be arriving in Austin.

"I suppose there's no point in reporting the sailing ship that's anchored in Matagorda Bay," Vance said.

"No," said West. "We know why it's there, and we know it's waiting in vain, but we have no proof of what was about to happen. The important thing is the wagons and their cargo haven't been lost, and the persons responsible for taking them have been captured. So I reckon all's well that ends well."

Captain Vance sighed. "I suppose I should be more satisfied, but I'm saddled with the realization that the military gets not a shred of credit. It all goes to one Texas Ranger."

"I don't want any credit," said West. "When you file your report, tell them *you* rode out, captured the deserters, and saved the wagons. It could win you that promotion you may otherwise never get."

Captain Vance laughed. "I'd be promoted one day and busted the next, for exceeding my authority. I suppose I'll have to content myself with the safe arrival of the arms."

Austin, Texas. December 23, 1873.

"Yonder she is!" Mac shouted, when at last they could see the distant town that was the end of a long, hazardous trail. "Thank God we can finally rid ourselves of these damn wagons and enjoy some peace."

But there was no peace, for the Sunday edition of the

town's newspaper had published the story of the missing
wagons, their mysterious cargo, and the fight to save them.
There was a brass band waiting, and the mules were terrified of the unfamiliar sounds. Captain Vance was called
upon to speak, and when he did, he gave special credit for
the saving of the wagons to Texas Ranger Bodie West,
without detracting from the sacrifices Mac and his outfit
had made. When there was no escaping it, Bodie West
spoke to the crowd, and he told of the desperate plan in-
volving Port Guthrie's wagon, of the killing of Puckett and
Haynes, and the taking of their weapons. Finally, Mac
Tunstall was forced to speak on behalf of himself and his
outfit. He said little about himself or his people, but
thanked Bodie West and Captain Vance for their concern.
The event lasted an entire day, and nobody was able to
escape until dark.

"Red," said Mac, "I haven't seen Trinity, Hattie, Elizabeth, or Rachel since we rolled in. What happened to
them?"

"They were practically in rags," Red replied, "and the
women of the town took them in. They've been put up at
the Capitol Hotel, and there's rooms for us, too. Let's get
over there and see about some town grub."

"As I recall," said Mac, "the Capitol Hotel is a fancy
diggings with tablecloths, real china, plush carpets, and the
cost for one night is more than you'd spend in a boarding
house in a week."

Red laughed. "It's all of that, *amigo,* but we ain't paying. It seems Austin regards us a hell of a lot higher than
I've ever been regarded before, and I ain't about to deny
them that privilege."

Mac had no answer for that, and when they reached the
hotel, there was an even greater surprise awaiting them.
The four women they had once rescued naked from an
outlaw camp were waiting in the lobby, dressed in the
height of fashion. Haze and Buck were already there, staring in awe.

"My God," said Buck, "somebody's took Rachel and left me a fancy, high-steppin' filly I've never seen before."

Mac just stood there and stared. Rachel *had* changed, but no more so than the others. The arrival of Port Guthrie and the other teamsters created a stir, and Guthrie took Mac by the arm.

"By God," said Port, "what do you reckon's just happened?"

"Somebody stole our women and left some strangers here," Mac said.

"What's happened, Port?" Red asked, having recovered from the initial shock.

"Me and the boys has been offered our own freight outfit, freightin' as far west as El Paso, east to New Orleans, and—"

"You're stayin' in Texas, then," said Red.

"Damn right," Guthrie said. "We got money behind us. We're buyin' them teams of mules and the Winchester wagons, to start."

The rest of the evening was a whirlwind of activity. After supper, the local newspaper interviewed Mac, Red, Buck, and Haze individually. The mid-week edition spoke of their ambition to raise cattle, to own ranches of their own, and suddenly there were prosperous men ready to back them with money, land, and cows.

"I never believed in Santa Claus before," Haze said, "but I'm startin' to."

Austin, Texas. December 25, 1873.

The dust finally settled. Mac had an opportunity to spend some time with Trinity in all her finery, getting used to her all over again. Her room was next to his in the hotel, and that was getting next to him.

"I don't know how Red, Buck, and Haze aims to handle this," Mac said, "but I'm of a mind to stand you before a preacher and have him read from the Book."

"For what purpose?" Trinity asked innocently.

"You know, damn it," said Mac. "I had a look in the candy store near three months ago, and now I'm ready for a feed."

Trinity laughed. "Perhaps you should have just taken it, when you had the chance."

"Maybe I should have," Mac said, "but I was interested in more than just a roll in the hay. I still am. Now will you stand with me for a reading from the Book, or do I have to build a ranch and wrassle the damn cows by myself?"

"I'm interested," said Trinity. "In fact, Hattie and the others are thinking we might all jump into this at the same time, with one preacher. How does New Year's Day suit you?"

"A month ago," Mac said, "I'd have agreed to it, but this is Christmas. You mean I got to wait another week before the candy store opens for real?"

"I said we'll stand before the preacher on New Year's Day," said Trinity. "The candy store will be ready when you are. Damn it, do I have to draw you a map?"

Mac laughed. He found Red, Buck, and Haze in the hotel lobby, and the four of them walked down the street, past the building that would house the freighting operation to be started by Port Guthrie and his friends. There already was a corral, and the mules nibbled at hay. In the wagon yard were the six wagons that had made the hazardous journey from Fort Leavenworth to south Texas.

"I'm glad for Port and his *amigos*," Buck said. "It bothered me some, thinkin' that we might never see them again, once we got to Austin."

"I'll never forget those old freight wagons, either," said Red. "The Winchester Wagons kind of grow on you."

"We ain't bucked the tiger yet," Haze said. "Hell, we got the promise of everything we need. Why don't we take the money we got, find us a saloon, and jump neck-deep in a poker game?"

"The rest of you go ahead," said Mac. "This is Christmas, and the candy store opens tonight."

The three of them regarded him as though he was playing shy a full deck, but Mac Tunstall only grinned.

In 1889, Bill Tilghman joined the historic land rush that transformed a raw frontier into Oklahoma Territory. A lawman by trade, he set aside his badge to make his fortune in the boom-towns. Yet Tilghman was called into service once more, on a bold, relentless journey that would make his name a legend for all time—in an epic confrontation with outlaw Bill Doolin.

OUTLAW KINGDOM
MATT BRAUN

OUTLAW KINGDOM
Matt Braun
_____ 95618-5 $5.99 U.S./$7.99 CAN.

TERRY C. JOHNSTON
THE PLAINSMEN

THE BOLD WESTERN SERIES FROM
ST. MARTIN'S PAPERBACKS

COLLECT THE ENTIRE SERIES!

SIOUX DAWN (Book 1)
92732-0 _____\$5.99 U.S. _____\$7.99 CAN.

RED CLOUD'S REVENGE (Book 2)
92733-9 _____\$5.99 U.S. _____\$6.99 CAN.

THE STALKERS (Book 3)
92963-3 _____\$5.99 U.S. _____\$7.99 CAN.

BLACK SUN (Book 4)
92465-8 _____\$5.99 U.S. _____\$6.99 CAN.

DEVIL'S BACKBONE (Book 5)
92574-3 _____\$5.99 U.S. _____\$6.99 CAN.

SHADOW RIDERS (Book 6)
92597-2 _____\$5.99 U.S. _____\$6.99 CAN.

DYING THUNDER (Book 7)
92834-3 _____\$5.99 U.S. _____\$6.99 CAN.

BLOOD SONG (Book 8)
92921-8 _____\$5.99 U.S. _____\$6.99 CAN.

Publishers Book and Audio Mailing Service
P.O. Box 070059, Staten Island, NY 10307
Please send me the book(s) I have checked above. I am enclosing $_____ (please add
$1.50 for the first book, and $.50 for each additional book to cover postage and handling.
Send check or money order only—no CODs) or charge my VISA, MASTERCARD,
DISCOVER or AMERICAN EXPRESS card.

Card Number_____

Expiration date_____Signature_____

Name_____

Address_____

City_____State/Zip _____
Please allow six weeks for delivery. Prices subject to change without notice. Payment in
U.S. funds only. New York residents add applicable sales tax.

THE TRAIL DRIVE SERIES
by Ralph Compton
From St. Martin's Paperbacks

The only riches Texas had left after the Civil War were five million maverick longhorns and the brains, brawn and boldness to drive them north to where the money was. Now, Ralph Compton brings this violent and magnificent time to life in an extraordinary epic series based on the history-blazing trail drives.

THE GOODNIGHT TRAIL (BOOK 1)
_____ 92815-7 $5.99 U.S./$7.99 Can.
THE WESTERN TRAIL (BOOK 2)
_____ 92901-3 $5.99 U.S./$7.99 Can.
THE CHISOLM TRAIL (BOOK 3)
_____ 92953-6 $5.99 U.S./$7.99 Can.
THE BANDERA TRAIL (BOOK 4)
_____ 95143-4 $5.50 U.S./$6.50 Can.
THE CALIFORNIA TRAIL (BOOK 5)
_____ 95169-8 $5.99 U.S./$7.99 Can.
THE SHAWNEE TRAIL (BOOK 6)
_____ 95241-4 $5.99 U.S./$7.99 Can.
THE VIRGINIA CITY TRAIL (BOOK 7)
_____ 95306-2 $5.50 U.S./$6.50 Can.
THE DODGE CITY TRAIL (BOOK 8)
_____ 95380-1 $5.99 U.S./$7.99 Can.
THE OREGON TRAIL (BOOK 9)
_____ 95547-2 $5.99 U.S./$7.99 Can.
THE SANTA FE TRAIL (BOOK 10)
_____ 96296-7 $5.99 U.S./$7.99 Can.